# I'll Think About That Tomorrow

# Evelyn Keyes

# I'll Think About That Tomorrow

A DUTTON BOOK

DUTTON
Published by the Penguin Group
Penguin Books USA Inc., 375 Hudson Street, New York, New York 10014, U.S.A.
Penguin Books Ltd, 27 Wrights Lane, London W8 5TZ, England
Penguin Books Australia Ltd, Ringwood, Victoria, Australia
Penguin Books Canada Ltd, 2801 John Street, Markham, Ontario, Canada L3R 1B4
Penguin Books (N.Z.) Ltd, 182–190 Wairau Road, Auckland 10, New Zealand

Penguin Books Ltd, Registered Offices:
Harmondsworth, Middlesex, England

First published by Dutton, an imprint of New American Library, a division of
Penguin Books USA Inc. Distributed in Canada by McClelland & Stewart Inc.

First Printing, April, 1991
10  9  8  7  6  5  4  3  2  1

REGISTERED TRADEMARK—MARCA REGISTRADA

LIBRARY OF CONGRESS CATALOGING-IN-PUBLICATION DATA:

Keyes, Evelyn, 1917–
    I'll think about that tomorrow / Evelyn Keyes.
      p.    cm.
    ISBN 0-525-24969-9
    1. Keyes, Evelyn, 1917– . 2. Motion picture actors and actresses—United
States—Biography.   I. Title
  PN2287.K655A3    1991
791.43′028′092—dc20
[B]                                                                90–49235
                                                                    CIP

PRINTED IN THE UNITED STATES OF AMERICA
Set in Garamond Book
Designed by Leonard Telesca

My happy thanks to sister Julia and brother Sam for
remaining such a faithful cheering section.

And at the Fifi Oscard Agency, Ivy Fisher Stone,
who is not able to do, or say, one single thing wrong.

To Rosemary Ahern, for her gentle patience
and to Joyce Engelson for
uttering those most magic of all words, "Yes, I will."

# Contents

# I'll
# Think About That
# Tomorrow

# PART ONE

# *Starting Over Again—Again*

# One

I took a limo to the airport. A stretch one at that. There's something terribly comforting about first-class accommodations when the rest of your life is in shambles.

I may not have learned a hell of a lot of things I should have learned during my first forty-something years, but one thing I *did* learn extremely well was how to get out of town when the time came. How to get to the next thing, the next circumstance, even the next country if need be. Hadn't I left the family hearth at a tender age to seek my fortune in Hollywood? Discarded my southern accent, my Dixieland attitudes, changed husbands and living abodes any number of times? (Hadn't I moved into *their* houses, thereby making it easier—and swifter—to move *out* as soon as the grand finale was over?)

No, I was no stranger to rushing off into the night to catch a plane for somewhere. Acapulco . . . Paris . . . Rome . . . most any place besides where I was.

It was just that with the last one, with Artie, what with building our house together the way we did (doing everything together the way we did), I had thought, really, truly felt in my heart, that all the running around, seeking, ever seeking, was over. That I had finally found whatever it was I was supposed to be looking for.

It had seemed so right, too, from the instant we met—not where you might expect to meet an Artie Shaw (clarinetist, bandleader, writer, multimarried, all-round complex fellow and Peck's bad boy of the musical set), say in some yesteryear

Stardust Ballroom with the revolving globe of colored mirrors hanging overhead, oh my no, nothing so plebeian as *that!*

Paris. That's where we met. Paris. On the Île St. Louis, in the middle of the River Seine, where I had taken up residence near Marie Antoinette's old digs. Naturally it was love at first sight (or some reasonable facsimile). How not, for crissake, in such a splendiferous setting. Just like a movie-meeting, wouldn't you say? Bandleader meets movie star in apartment where the river flows past on both sides.

Looking back I'm not sure I made any distinction at all between on-screen and off. The same things were happening to me, weren't they, in both places? Girl meeting boy, and running the gamut of boy/girl trials and tribulations? The falling for/laughing with, the winning/the losing, the crying over, the loving, and all variations thereof? Repeating the scenario off-screen almost as often as I did on?

The script with Artie was especially good. It had a castle in Spain to do the "living happily ever after" in. That's right. Exotic, mystical *España*. The land of the matador and Don Quixote and the olive. And that's not all. I would do Cinderella one better. I and *my* Prince would build our castle together!

Sounds so good, doesn't it? Well, I can tell you, *I* certainly thought so. I didn't realize then, you see, that the old story never gave us an inkling about what went on in the castle in the years after the right foot for the slipper had been found. I mean, what did those two *do* up there on the hill, what did he, the royal heir, and she, the scullion, have in common? My movie scripts had always ended when boy got girl—or vice versa.

Two minutes after we'd met, without any second thought whatsoever, off we went, driving down through the vineyards of southern France, across the border and into castanet country, there to put our plans into motion posthaste.

We settled in, on a mountain top (where else), overlooking the Mediterranean (Homer was dead right, it *is* wine-dark!), and believed . . . well, I did, anyway, that I finally had it made.

It was the perfect "happy ending" that I'd been taught to believe was my inalienable right (pretty little thing that I was).

And the truth is, I *did* have it made—oh, for maybe a good five years. That was about how long "ever after" lasted for *that* particular episode of my life. If you ask me, we'd do well to rid our vocabulary of words like "ever after" and "always." They give us too false a sense a security.

Then restlessness got the better of my prince. I can't say it was Don Quixote's spirit rubbing off on him or anything like that. Restlessness was the permanent state of the man—if I had had the wisdom to recognize it. Wasn't he the guy who dropped his baton and clarinet at the height of his success and disappeared into the wilds of Mexico, leaving a string of broken contracts worth millions strewn across America? I mean, shouldn't that have given me some sort of clue to the future, right there?

But what did I know. I even admired (when I heard of it) the bold and unfearful manner in which he thumbed his nose at the establishment. It never crossed my mind that one day the same behavior might come home to roost at my own doorstep.

I was to learn, during my Bobbsey Twin time with Artie, what a big taker-upper of things he was. He would get turned on by something and fling himself into the pursuit of said thing with all the passion of a besotted lover. Worry over it like a dog with its bone, study it, read every single thing about it, practice it as if it were Carnegie Hall tonight. Absorb it like a sponge, ingest it with such thoroughness that nothing would be left except maybe a few shells or a couple of rinds.

And then move on.

Take that Spanish "castle" of ours, and the gusto with which we threw ourselves into its formation. We selected each stone ourselves, each tile and brick and nail and screw. We chose each piece of furniture, each light fixture, doorknob, pot, pan, and lock. We supervised the landscaping, the digging of the swimming pool, the laying out of the greenhouse, the cote for the pigeons. We scoured the countryside for just the right flowerpots and the greenery to go in them, we picked the old woods that would go into the mosaic of the hand-carved front door.

No house *ever* had more loving attention than that one.

And then one day when it was about finished, Artie said he had been thinking. He said that he wanted to return to the land of his birth.

Ah . . . Well. There you are. Who could deny him that. Certainly not I, in the throes of playing follow-the-leader to the hilt as I was. Besides, the dream I had in mind at the time didn't have the mountain-top castle being lived in by just the girl. (And I do mean *girl* in more ways than one, immature notions fluttering around in my head like bats in their belfry.)

So next Artie picked a twenty-five-room house (already built, in 1905). It was on a lake up in the foothills of the Berkshires in northern Connecticut and it had ten fireplaces and nine bathrooms. It turned out that it reminded Artie of some doctor's house he had known and/or admired when he was a kid.

But no sooner had we moved in than he wanted to (and did) purchase a motor home, a thirty-six-foot-long land yacht. Off we went, squeezed into this oversized pea-pod contraption—along with two dogs, now, in tow—with its stamp-sized toilet/shower arrangement, to roam this land of Artie's birth (and mine, too, incidentally) for the next three months, while twenty-five roomy rooms and nine bathrooms stood waiting back in Connecticut.

You may be wondering why I went along so readily (nay, eagerly) with these twists and turns of Artie's, these abrupt changes in life's big plans. Well, I've been doing some wondering about that myself. Of late, that is. I confess I never gave it much thought at the time. But the mosaic that we are, this composition of endless bits and pieces of living experiences and feelings and reactions, all repeated over and over and over again, maybe six hundred million times, causing new layers of bits and pieces to form over the *old* layers of bits and pieces, with entirely new contours and color and tone, makes it really tough to locate the bits and pieces that might have got me started on the business of going whither Artie wentest.

I do know I was uprooted early in life, around the age of a year and a half, to be hauled away from everything I had ever known up until then, never, ever, to return again.

I know I never had a room of my own—until I got to Hollywood—so that I'd never much got into the habit of making my own nest.

I know I was taught to read when I was not much more than two, in order, I've been told, to "give me something to do." And so at quite a tender age, I'd begun to read about distant and glamorous lands, where lovely females in stressful situations got rescued (fairly consistently) by brave and dashing males, who then swept them up and away to gorgeous places where they proceeded to do all that "living happily ever after" stuff.

With those sorts of fantasies as my expectations, little wonder I picked the men I did, up to and including the leader of the band, himself. And I evidently hadn't done so to have him abdicate his leader's duties immediately thereafter. And I have to give Artie full credit. He never, ever failed me in that respect.

Upon our return to Connecticut, a New York City apartment was added (the leader's idea, of course) to the number of places the Shaws were able to lay down their heads. So that then, glory be, we could spend two hours each way—with the two dogs—driving back and forth along the Saw Mill River Parkway between the two establishments.

Which was how it became so easy for the Shaws to start being in different places come nightfall.

And that led to the inevitable.

Artie found himself another woman.

A younger one, most naturally.

This sort of put a crimp into the "happy-ever-after" business for Artie-and-Evelyn. Our dreams of happy endings, it would seem, his and mine, didn't quite match. In his the "girl" had to remain just that. A girl. Remain the same tender age, evidently, as she who had turned him on in the first place, when he himself had been a sweet young thing, too.

The thing was, however, that all the bobbing about from place to place, interesting though it had been, had taken time. Years, in fact. Years that had been added, perforce, to my age. Artie's, too, of course, but even back then, I had the distinct feeling it was *my* advancing years that bothered him most when he began to make such remarks as, "Isn't that dress a little too young for you?" Or, "I feel like going out tonight, I'm sure you'd much rather go to bed."

And so there I was, the big 4-0 come and long gone, the half-century mark coming up, and me back to Square One.

Guilt threatened to overwhelm me for a while. Artie had always said that marriage was strictly a woman's racket and therefore up to her to make it work. If ours was tottering as my others had—he was number four (not counting live-ins)—clearly I was the culprit. So I went about suffering for quite a bit on account of my lack of marriage-making abilities.

Until the real reason for my guilt dawned upon me.

My main feeling for the cracking apart wasn't sorrow. It was . . . relief, of all things. A marvelous sense of *freedom* had swept over me when I realized I wouldn't have to do those wifely, holding-together-the-marriage chores anymore! None of that running-a-house stuff—seeing to meals, shopping for food, making sure the laundry got done, the grass cut, the button box filled—under whose weights I seemed to have disappeared. "Didn't you used to be Evelyn Keyes?" more than one person said to me up there in Connecticut.

Well, hey, now I could go back to being her again and Artie could look after his own goddamn meals. Though I supposed he would indoctrinate the new young woman, and *she* would see to his meals. I mean, isn't that what you get a young woman *for,* to teach her your old ways—new ears for your how-to-treat-a-man lessons, your stories, your life's philosophy, etcetera? (That is, after the "old" wife has heard it all a few thousand times and has said so in no uncertain terms.) A comedian I knew once summed it up rather neatly. "Never change the jokes!" he said. "Change the people!"

Except . . . how could I go back to being Evelyn Keyes? I wasn't that person anymore. At least not the one I caught on my TV screen occasionally (if I stayed up late enough). She wasn't bad looking at all. And so young. Like Artie's new friend. She always got her man, too. I could still see the resemblance between us, though. The shape of the face, the eyes, the nose, the figure. Except . . . if I were to go back to doing what Evelyn Keyes used to do, I mean that acting business, I would now have to play her . . . mother, wouldn't I . . .

It was a sobering thought. If I were to go back into the marketplace, things wouldn't be the way they once had been at all, would they. Not the same at all . . .

A little ruffle of apprehension scooted along my frame. So I quickly grabbed the phone and began to dial a former agent of mine. Fear wouldn't do. Fear could stop you in your tracks if you let it get hold, so you had to move fast.

His burst of enthusiasm upon hearing my voice after such a long time was gratifying. It only began to wane when I told him *why* I was calling. When I said I was thinking of going back to acting again. Ah, but he was a nice enough guy, and he made a stab at making good noises instead of telling me I was out of my cotton-pickin' mind. "Swe-e-etheart!" he immediately cried, with as much sincerity as he could muster on such short notice, "Too bad you're not in London, right now! I hear they're getting ready to cast a TV series over there with an American lady in it who is . . . who is . . . uh . . ." He paused, searching for the *mots justes.*

I helped him find them. "Over the hill?"

"You said it, I didn't!" he whooped raucously. As if what I'd said weren't true at all. He didn't fool either of us, though.

I didn't know if what he said about the casting of a TV series was on the up and up or not. It could have been something already cast, for all I knew. It could have been nothing more than an idea in somebody's head that was destined never to get to first base. He was that kind of guy. He liked upbeat conversations and dealt in positive thinking, even if he had to make things up to do it. I knew that and I didn't care. I chose to believe him. What he said would give me the impetus to get out of town. To leave my burst bubble behind. Well, it *is* the thing to do, isn't it, when your bubble goes ker-plooey? Get the hell out?

After I had lined up the limo, I booked first-class passage on the plane as well, not really caring whether I could afford it or not. The way I was feeling, I figured I couldn't afford *not* to . . .

# *Two*

**I**'ve always loved those night flights, especially across an ocean. The deep, steady drone of the motors is such a soothing sound as you sit there high up in the sky, with the womb-like darkness all around, suspended in time, safely out of reach—for a while, anyway—from all those earthly entanglements that have a habit of wrapping themselves around you like that pesky kudzu vine does to trees down in Georgia.

I had some salad, lobster newburg, drank some not-all-that-first-class champagne, then snuggled down under a blanket, and with eyes closed, half asleep, let my thoughts wander wherever they wanted to go for the rest of the trip.

How many times had I been right here, just like this . . . Ah, too many times to count . . . or to remember the reasons for the journeys. Though they would, by necessity, have to have been either for getting away *from* something, or going *to* something, wouldn't they? And so, which one was it this time, I asked myself, drowsily . . .

Both, this time, wasn't it? Yeah. That was it. Both.

My heart stirred. This was a biggie. This wasn't just the end of one job, the beginning of another. The finish of one more romance/marriage/love affair, call it what you will. This was more. Much more. This was probably the end of—actually the end of an era. The end of life-as-I-had-known-it-up-to-now.

It had to be, didn't it, since the very things I appeared to have based my entire existence on—without even being *aware* that I was—were disappearing on me.

I guess I'd simply always taken youth, and looks, for granted. Well, we do, don't we, while we still have them. Until they begin to slip away . . .

I eased myself upright to gaze out into the darkness.

Appearance, though, wasn't the only thing that had changed. Things inside my head, hadn't they changed, too? I wasn't the same person who had run off to marry John Huston three weeks after I met him. Not the same person who had gone off to do the "happy living" with Artie a week after I had met *him*. Not even the same person who had got on the train to go out to Hollywood. Those dreams I'd been after, of getting into the flicks, of finding my prince. They'd been done. Been accomplished. Several times over.

With a little shiver I lay back down again. So what was next, then? I didn't expect to be dying any time soon, since I had inherited these perfectly splendid genes that would probably last me for another fifty years. The only trouble was I hadn't prepared for anything, didn't have a single dream whatsoever to carry me through my later span.

But then, when had I *ever* prepared *anything* very far ahead. "I won't think about that now," sister Scarlett had said, "I'll think about that tomorrow." *I seemed to have picked up her ways very early in life.*

Except . . . *Tomorrow was here.* A tomorrow that never in my wildest imaginings had I ever visualized; an older woman, on her own, on her way to an uncertain . . .

I chopped off that thought fast. This was surely the worst moment ever to change a lifetime habit and start planning ahead. I'd better at least wait until I got where I was going, sniff around a little, see how things went first, slowly feel my way before I began to make any big (or even little) decisions.

I closed my eyes and cleared my head as best I could.

One of those unmistakable high-riding London taxis that can turn on a sixpence, complete with cockney driver, took me to Belgravia and a small hotel I knew. I was somewhat acquainted with London. Artie and I had often driven up from Spain. I had even shot a movie there (by the name of *Shoot First*) in the early fifties. Back then, the place had still been hurting from the war. There had still been all kinds of shortages. Clothes were as somber as the Brit weather in those days, dusty charcoal, dark blue and black under bowlers and brollies of the same shades, with that slightly frayed look that comes from washing and rewashing and ironing and reironing an infinite number of times.

But since then I knew things had changed considerably (just as I had). The Beatles had happened and been heard around the world, changing the thrust of popular music forever, not to mention men's hairstyles. A new breed of British clothes designers was making its mark everywhere, too. In fact the staid old city at this moment in time was being called "Swinging London." And I was rather looking forward to taking in the scene.

But not yet. Not on my first day of arrival. I knew well that a flight east, and losing five or six hours, can be murder on your system if you don't take time to adjust. So I'd made it a point to arrive on Friday, in order to give my body the weekend to figure out what the hell I was doing to it.

After checking in, though, I did make some phone calls. First my agent's London connection. They were expecting me (which was nice). They said welcome to the British Isles in their posh accents, and that the first of next week would be lovely, indeed, to have a get-together and discuss plans.

It sounded good to me. If I could get work instantly, it would be simply wonderful. Acting was such a handy occupation for taking your mind off yourself. Because what you had to do right away, the minute you got the job, was to forget who you were all day and pretend to be somebody else. Immediately rid yourself of your own thoughts and words and fill your head with the dialogue and thoughts of the person you had to become. You had to do it thoroughly, too; it would show if you didn't. Right there in your eyes. You couldn't fool the camera.

And I could certainly use a respite, I thought wearily. I had been driving myself bonkers lately with thoughts of myself, and what I should do, and how I should go about it. And getting nowhere. Yes, a bit of acting would be a great help.

I called the Kubricks, too. Stanley and Christiane. Artie and I had known them back in New York, where we all used to play chess together and exchange science fiction literature. But they lived outside of London now. Stanley preferred England, evidently, for his picture-making. He had made *Dr. Strangelove* there, and was in the middle of something called *2001: A Space Odyssey.* So he wasn't home. But Christiane was, in her studio. She had been an actress, once, but she painted now, gorgeous, enormous canvases of growing things. She said welcome in her catchy German/British accent and said they were having a gathering tomorrow night, Saturday, and that I had to come.

This was music to my ears. It was perfect. An instant party to go to, and just the right distance away. By tomorrow night I would have adjusted to the new time zone, surely, and I couldn't, shouldn't, *mustn't* come all this way and do my recluse bit. Which I seemed to be preferring more and more the older I became. I had to get out and around in London if I was to readjust my life, which was, after all, the reason I had come.

I didn't make any more calls, though. One definite date was enough. I didn't like having them lined up, all my time filled. I felt trapped when I did. Besides, I wasn't going anywhere,

I could call other people I knew here later, I wasn't leaving town for quite a while. Who knew, maybe this was where I'd live forever . . .

Ah, but that was what I was always thinking, wasn't it, every place I went. "Forever," indeed. Hah!

By then it was close to five in the afternoon, a little early to retire, but since I had been sitting for most of the day, I decided a bit of a walk, and a stretch, might not be a bad idea. And maybe see a thing or two at the same time.

And did I ever.

I put on some flats and headed up Sloane Street toward Knightsbridge. It was the going-home hour, and thousands of Londoners seemed to be bent on doing just that. The streets and the sidewalks were jammed, and the change in the place was instantly noticeable.

Color was what did it. Oh, certainly one could still find the straitlaced Englishman who had obviously been a member of the Cavalry with a back like a ramrod and shoes so polished you could see yourself in their toes, and ladies wearing little hats and pearls around their necks. But bright splashes of color were everywhere, people in reds and oranges and yellows and blues all over the place. And the things I saw in the windows completed the story. They were advertising brocade (brocade!) jackets for men as well as ruffled shirts of pinks and mauves and flared-at-the-bottom trousers, sometimes in emerald velvet or sapphire satin.

Actually the male clothing was rather interesting, relating, as it did, to an earlier epoch when men did wear frills and colors and shining materials instead of relentless wool and gabardine and flannel day in and day out.

But what had happened to the female attire was another matter entirely. Skirts had risen. I mean, up . . . to . . . *here.* Bare legs were flashing along all over the place, racing past me, getting into taxis, waiting for buses, young women dressed in clothes only little girls—no, worse, only baby dolls, the kind that say "ma-ma" when you tilt them—had worn before.

What in the world was going on here? Here I was, about to go over the hill, and London females seemed determined not even to arrive at puberty!

Why, I wondered? Weren't Europeans supposed to have an admiration for older women?

Hah, I decided, walking along, I bet the truth was that older had never been all that much "older." Probably thirty had been older. Thirty-five at most.

But what was most disconcerting, I thought, walking on, observing the phenomenon, was that these young women didn't seem to even want to become teenagers, for crissake. They seemed to be determined to keep hanging on to childhood itself.

But why? Had the image of growing up become so awful? What in the world had happened in this place that had so scared all these young British women. They seemed more frivolous than we Americans, and I had always thought of them as so solid, such a down-to-earth people. Was this any place for me to come to, when I had my own problems to deal with?

Shit. What kind of thoughts were these to be entering into a new London life with, making snap judgments before I had even unpacked. Not now, I said to me, don't start trying to figure anything out, today. Tomorrow will be soon enough. Tomorrow, remember? Is another day?

I turned around and headed back toward the hotel, my new home-away-from-home. Once there I ordered tea and crumpets—well, I *was* in England—and looked at the telly for a while. *Rose Marie* with Jeanette MacDonald and Nelson Eddy was on. After a bit I climbed into my latest slumbering place, and crashed . . .

The Kubricks sent a car to pick me up, and a good thing, too. I would never have found their place. It was out in the country—at least it seemed like the country—the driver went across London and out the other side. Then down first one tree-lined lane, then another and another until we came to the

Kubricks' gate, through which we swept, and onto several acres of that lush, green vegetation England is famous for.

Besides a big, rambling house there were several other edifices. I would learn that Stanley kept his offices on the premises, filled with all kinds of equipment—models of sets, designs, and whatever else was his grand passion of the moment. Christiane's studio was in a separate building, and she had had built several very large greenhouses filled with the green growing things that she was always painting.

There were big hugs after such a long time. Christiane was so good to look at, she had a mop of dark hair, cut short with heavy bangs, and a laugh that was a tonic for the ears. Stanley sported a beard and a navy blue ski jacket that he would wear (or others just like it) for the entire time I was in London. There were children, too, and as in New York their things were everywhere. And I do mean *everywhere*. On the stairs, in the middle of the hall, the bathrooms, under the dining room table. Stanley and Christiane ran a loose establishment; no one concerned themselves with needless tidiness, figuring it would all straighten itself out at some time or other.

There was a mixed bag of guests that evening, as there usually was around the Kubricks, from actors (of course) to politicians to journalists to lawyers—or should I say barristers? And that was what this fellow I met there that night turned out to be.

I would have bet anything in the world that what I got into after that night would never have happened to me as long as I lived. And it probably wouldn't have if I hadn't gone to Harrod's a couple of days later.

I've always been attracted by the sound of the speaking voice, and the way words are spoken. Of course a few other things must *follow,* like what is *said* with the words, plus a bit of humor in the mix. And this man sounded really great. I mean, even in a gathering of delicious-sounding accents, his caught my ear.

We guests had been invited out to help Christiane and Stanley celebrate Guy Fawkes Day. (Though, actually, I haven't the foggiest notion why. I looked the gent up later in my trusty dictionary and it described Fawkes as "English conspirator; executed. 1570–1606.") The first time I saw this barrister fellow was in the flickering light of a huge bonfire down at the bottom of the Kubrick gardens (again I haven't the faintest idea why a bonfire was used to celebrate this English conspirator). We guests (per instructions) were doing our part in the proceedings, running around in the dark, hurling stuff (which had been furnished by the Kubricks) into the flames to keep the blaze going, when I heard the man speak. "This ought to do it," I believe were the sterling words he uttered as he tossed an empty crate into Mr. Fawkes's celebratory conflagration.

It was enough to cause me to turn around to find out who belonged to such delectable sounds.

Our eyes met. And so I smiled. Well, who wouldn't. Isn't it the polite thing to do? And he smiled back. Two civilized members of the human species acting out a tribal custom. And that would have been the end of it except for the follow-up encounter at Harrod's.

Now, you can't go to London (can't even *live* in London) and not go to Harrod's every so often. It's just not done, not going to Harrod's. You don't have to *buy* anything, you just have to walk through. Halls, they call them. Food Halls, Banking Halls, anything-you-want Halls. An elephant? A toothbrush? Rack-of-lamb? Yacht? Whatever you're looking for, you'll find it at Harrod's.

And so this man with the delectable tones that I had smiled at in the flickering light of the Kubricks' bonfire was at Harrod's the day I went there myself. He was looking at things at the bon-bon counter. "Well, hel-lo!" he exclaimed as I came into view, as if he were pleased as punch. "How very lovely to see you again!"

God. He did sound so absolutely terrific. A richness of quality. Pear-shaped syllables that wouldn't quit. He had blue eyes, too. I mean *blue,* no halfway measures. I've never known many blue-eyed men, for some reason. A couple of early husbands, that's about it. And impeccably dressed. With everyone else in those bright colors and ruffles, he was the picture of conservatism (well, he *was* a barrister), as if he had just stepped out of Savile Row, in a perfectly tailored gray suit with the narrowest and faintest of maroon pinstripes and tie to match, shoes polished within an inch of their lives, and plain white shirt, the kind that rides high on the neck. A good look, I've always thought.

"I'm purchasing a gift," he said to me, bringing me into his circle. "Do you think this would do?"

I didn't see how he could go wrong, no matter whom it was for. He was looking over a box of bon-bons of milk chocolate in the shape of champagne bottles with some kind of liqueur inside, and almost as expensive as the elephant upstairs.

"For me?" I cried jokingly. "You shouldn't have!"

"Two of them," he said to the person behind the counter, and after they were gift-wrapped and paid for as we stood chatting about the Kubrick party, he presented one to me.

Rather stylish, I thought. For a barrister.

We strolled through the Food Halls, admiring melons from Israel, salami from Hungary, enjoying our talk. "Care for a spot of lunch?" he soon said. We were having too good a time to break off quite yet.

"A *smashing* idea," I responded instantly. (It's catching, that Brit talk. I never have been able to resist joining in when I'm around it.)

We wound up at a fish house, a place that looked as if it had been there since Guy Fawkes's time. Tiny, square floors stacked on top of each other, a few tables on each level. We had to walk up a number of flights to get to ours, holding our gaily wrapped packages of bon-bons.

I had a perfect meal there. I remember it in detail to this day, though very little of the conversation.

Memories. Aren't they selective. For reasons I wonder does anybody understand. Like sieves, our brains seem to be, some things slipping through and lost forever. Others carefully culled and left behind. I had sole, cut in thin strips and sautéed until crunchily crisp, though not dry. The parsley, too, chopped fine, was done the same way. With a mixed green salad tossed in a mustard dressing. Really good.

The theater was mentioned, I know that. My new gentleman friend said that *Oedipus Rex* was being put on at the Old Vic with John Gielgud, a very interesting production, he understood, and would I care to see it. And I believe I said oh-my-yes I would, that I preferred the British theater to any other, that no one *but* British actors should ever be *allowed* on the stage.

But almost immediately afterward I grew rather rattled.

First the rain, which had been threatening as we came out of Harrod's, had begun to pour down, and the windowpane alongside us had darkened considerably, becoming all shiny and wet.

"Uh . . . oh!" I'd said cheerily (not really caring). "There goes my hair!"

"Not to worry," he'd reassured with a smile, "there is a taxi stand just outside."

Then I looked out the window.

God knows why. Perhaps to peer out for a look at the taxi stand below. Something. But what I saw was my own reflection looking back at me from the shiny, wet windowpane.

And it was unnerving. What I saw wasn't the vision I had of myself in my head at all.

Evidently, if you are in a quaintly charming old fish house on a rainy day in London Town—surely a setup for a romantic interlude if there ever was one—sitting across from a posh-sounding fellow, blue of eye, slim of build, with the most graceful of hands and just the right amount of gray at the temple, a man quite as old, if not older, than you, even so you automatically, without question, *without thought,* give him, as a female companion, your younger self. She was the one, after all, that Artie, and John, and Mike, and the rest of them had first gone for. The one to be having romantic interludes in quaint fish houses on rainy days.

The older version looking back at me from the wet windowpane quite threw me. She spoiled the mood. Mine, any-way. I said then I'd best be getting back to my hotel.

We splashed out through the downpour to the taxi stand, leaning over to protect the brightly wrapped packages, to hell with my hair, what did I care if it got soaked through (and it did). I thanked him for the present, the lunch, and he inquired if he might ring me up about the theater. I said, ah . . . uh . . . why don't you give me your card and I'll ring *you,* as I expect to be moving somewhere else any day now.

That part was true. I did intend to find a flat for myself, if I could find a short-term lease. I didn't know if I would call him or not. Well, yes, I probably would, why not. I would need friends, wouldn't I? After I got over this identity crisis. God. Did they keep coming throughout one's entire life, these puzzling crossroads? This one seemed quite as confusing as the one from childhood into puberty when, for a while, you didn't know whether you were child or woman. Maybe that's what all the young women in London were going through, come to think of it.

My problem now, though, was that I could still fool myself most of the time. Could avoid, and forget about, that woman in the windowpane. Because out of years of habit, whenever I looked in a mirror, I always quickly lifted my chin and turned my head just so, in order that the available light would fall in the most flattering way possible across the planes of my face, and keep me looking (to myself) like the retouched glossy that I was accustomed to seeing. And I didn't get caught short any too often, either.

I had a dream that night. I was out looking for Artie's dog. His, not mine. I don't know why. I was on a farm, with many fields and buildings, barns and such. And I found the dog in one of the barns. A little dog. Furry. And almost dead. He wagged, glad to see me. I picked him up, cradled him in my arms. He was so feeble he couldn't walk. I walked and walked with him, holding him, looking for some warm milk. Looking for Artie, too. I asked strangers on the road where he was. They were indifferent. They didn't know. Or care. The little dog was dying in my arms. His head lolled about, though his body was still warm. But then he shat on my white pants, so I knew for sure he had died, even though his little body was still warm . . .

I woke with a fierce headache, wondering what the dream was all about. Wondering if the little dog was . . . me . . .

## *Three*

The London Agent Connection came through almost immediately with an acting job, damned if they didn't. Not the one I'd come over to see about, which had been postponed for some reason or other, and what did I care, anything would do. This one was a TV play, and I was delighted. Of course I promptly dropped everything else to go off and do it. (It was, I'm afraid, a habit of mine to do just that: drop everything and everybody when I went off to do something new. And the reason, I suppose, looking back, that my life has always been so disjointed. And it certainly has been that.)

They were a stylish lot, the London Connection. I had gone to see them in their offices near Marble Arch, and if the desks and chairs and rugs that made up the decor I saw there weren't the most fabulous antiques in all of Great Britain I didn't want to know about it.

I was so pleased. *Pleased.* I hadn't done any acting for ages. And it can be a joy, sometimes. Sheer joy. And I was quite ready for a bit of *that.* And what better place to be beginning again than in London, England, in person.

Not wanting to come back to a hotel every night, wanting now to settle in if only for a little while, I quickly found myself a place to live before I started to work. It was the two top floors of an old Georgian house in Markham Square off King's Road, in the heart of Chelsea. I had discovered that along King's Road was where a lot of the action was taking place in "Swinging London." The shops of the new designers, Mary Quant and Jean Muir and such, all filled with their enchanting wares, could be found up and down the Road, and it turned out that every Saturday was parading day for the very young, who would come from far and wide to walk up and down dressed in the wildest of outfits they could muster together.

Oh yes. Little doubt that I had come across a very diverting spot. It was great fun to watch. When there was time.

We rehearsed the TV play, *A Matter of Diamonds,* for an entire month, as if it were a stage play. And then we shot it, in large chunks, as if it were live. It was, indeed, one of the joy times. The cast and crew, except for me, were all Brits, naturally. So there I was, the only American surrounded by a passel of dishy accents.

I simply reveled in it. My costar, Cliff Richard, was a gorgeous young man who was one of Britain's hottest rock stars, now trying out his acting talents in a dramatic role. The two of us were playing a couple of jewel thieves, I, in my role, pretending to be Cliff's aunt, when, in fact, I was masterminding the heist. And when Cliff, in his role, falls in love with the would-be victim (a young girl, natch), I (as aunt) am highly annoyed.

It was during the rehearsal of the scene in which I discover the young lady in my nephew/Cliff's arms that I became aware that for the first time in my long career I was not the one who was playing the "love interest." "Veteran Evelyn Keyes," they called me in a newspaper about this time. "Reckon she'll see Cliff Richard through," it went on to say.

They weren't going to go away, were they, these reminders of the passage of time. Not only had I been put in this venerable position of "veteran," now I had been given responsibility along with it. That of "seeing Cliff through."

Well, I hoped they were right. That I'd learned a thing or two by now. It *was* the purpose of growing older, wasn't it? Yes, it looked as if I were going to have to join the grownups' circle whether I liked it or not.

And so when the play was finished with, I called up the barrister. I would take *him* to the theater, to dinner. Wasn't that how grown-ups behaved? The man had presented me with a nifty gift. Sprung for a splendid lunch. I would reciprocate. Gone were the days of waiting for the man to call, waiting to be invited. Especially if simple friendship was what you had in mind. The constant and rigid playing of the mating game every time a male and female got together surely had gone by the boards.

I did ask him to make reservations, though, assuming he had an efficient secretary and that he knew the city better than I did. I even had him come to fetch me, saying jokingly that if he ever got to northwestern Connecticut, I would be happy to do the same for him!

The Old Vic wasn't in its present digs, that mass of cement alongside the River Thames. Back then it was still a nice, crumbly old building you had to cross Waterloo Bridge to get to, and I wish it had stayed there. The whole world is turning into one big complex of mortar and brick and you might as well go down the street to your own local mall instead of spending the money to go halfway around the world only to see the same thing you can see right where you started from.

I remember the evening for a couple of reasons, and John Gielgud was one of them, for something he did in the play.

Gielgud is one of those consummate actors who come into the world, seemingly, to act and do nothing else, who make the rest of us who try it look like imposters. They use their craft perfectly each time out, do something that will grab your attention and make you remember them forever and ever. As John Gielgud did that night.

What he did was the damndest thing, for a man over sixty,

that is (and maybe for somebody even a lot younger). In mid-scene, while delivering dialogue, he would begin to bend his knees, as slowly and smoothly as a well-oiled machine, until his bottom rested atop of his heels, speaking all the while. And then, somewhere along, and just as easily, he would proceed to straighten his legs, until once again he had gained his full height, still delivering lines as only John Gielgud can deliver lines. And if you don't think that's a mean feat, you just try it, sometime, whatever your age.

But actually that was nothing compared to what was done at the end of the production, just before the final curtain.

Up until then, the play had been presented in a fairly orthodox manner (except for Mr. Gielgud's deep-knee bends). But then the Old Vic flipped out. They put on a spectacle the likes of which I had never seen in my entire days and doubt if I'll ever witness again.

For their smash finish they didn't mince around. They didn't chicken out. They didn't play the least bit coy. What they did was go straight to the heart of what *Oedipus Rex* was about.

Should I refresh your memory as to what an Oedipus complex is? The dictionary describes it as "the unresolved desire of a child for sexual gratification through the parent of the opposite sex, especially the desire of a son for his mother."

Here was how the Old Vic interpreted it, that night, over there across Waterloo Bridge.

As the last curtain descended, from somewhere in the back of the theater a band started up. A modern, up-to-date band it was, too, with brass sections and drums and such, and it was very loud, blaring, in fact, as the musicians began to march down the aisles toward the stage, blasting out, of all things, "When the Saints Go Marching In." The actors from the production had sneaked around to the front, and they, too, came cavorting down the aisles with the instrument players. Meantime something had been pushed on stage, and when the curtain opened again, there it was, looking for all the world like a very tall Maypole, maybe twelve feet high or so, only a great cloth was draped over it so that all that was showing was its outline. The approaching musicians and players behaved as if it were indeed a Maypole, rushing up on stage and beginning to circle it, dancing and cavorting and blowing on their instruments as they went.

Then one of them picked up a corner of the covering cloth and gave a little tug. Another followed suit. Then another. Slowly, slowly, the cloth was pulled, in a grand striptease fashion, away from what it was hiding, while the circlers emitted little squeals and giggles and yips.

Then all at once the cloth slid away and dropped to the floor.

The audience was stunned. It took a few seconds for the brain to comprehend what the eyes were seeing. A penis. A male organ of copulation. In full detail including the balls. Jutting into the air in full erection, to the distance of about twelve feet. And colored gold. Bright and shining and gold as could be.

I heard a small gasp in back of me. And from the corner of my eye I saw it came from a young girl, probably fifteen, her eyes riveted to the stage. I was tempted to whisper, dear child, you'll never come across one of that size in your life, or a gold one either. But I kept quiet, feeling it best, perhaps, to deal with life's little disappointments each in our own way.

The audience left the theater in a lighthearted mood, all of us feeling we had got our money's worth. My friend had chosen a restaurant in the Covent Garden district called Inigo Jones. He said it was named for an English architect who dated back to the early seventeenth century. (One of the great things about going around London, you drag lengthy lines of history along after you.) The markets were still functioning, then, and we had to work our way through crates of all kinds of produce to get into the restaurant. Cabbages and pears and sacks of potatoes.

It was a classy place, though; there was little doubt of that when I saw that Rex Harrison was seated at the table next to us. The decor was warm, the lighting very flattering. You can feel it when it is—the kind of thing that puts you immediately at ease, and this time there were no stray mirrors (or wet panes) to glimpse myself in.

We were in a lovely frame of mind, the fun at the theater having put us there. And we both knew the choreography of such evenings. How to order the right things. The right wine to go with the meal, the proper approach to the waiter. The way to keep the conversation flowing. The barrister even made interesting remarks about the theater for somebody who was, as Mike Todd used to call non-show-biz types, a "civilian."

We were still enjoying our companionableness so much that when we arrived at King's Road later, we decided to get out of the taxi on the Road and stroll through the square in which I lived. At the center of the square was a neatly laid-out, grassy-green garden filled with trees and flowering bushes, discreetly lit so that one could half-see it even on a misty night, which this was.

At my door I offered a nightcap. Well, you do, don't you. We were still in the middle of a heated conversation, he saying that my country was a frightfully unruly place, Martin Luther King having been shot down earlier that year, as well as Bobby Kennedy, like his brother before him, and that even as we spoke, British television was filled with pictures of policemen bashing young people over the head out in the city of Chicago at the Democratic Party's convention. He said I was well out of such madness.

I'll say one thing for the United States of America. It doesn't bore people to death out there in the world. If it isn't doing one thing to get them exercised, it's doing another.

I wasn't about to get into an earnest conversation about American politics with a Brit on a misty night in London Town. "You're just jealous," I teased instead, "because you're not one of us."

That brought a guffaw. I had thought it might. And since the British are everything in spades, he then said to me, "Your uppishness about yourselves knows absolutely no bounds!"

"And you, old chap," I replied in my best British, "ought to know."

I know it doesn't sound much like the kind of thing that might lead to something more. But we were having fun with it, and it got us upstairs. Of course if getting-it-on is what you have in mind, most anything will get you upstairs. Even the three floors it was necessary to climb to get up to my place.

But it was worth it when you got there (for whatever reason), with its terraces and windows on both sides, one facing the handsome square below, the other looking out over the rooftops of London. (My thirty-ninth abode, I think. But who was counting. My first away from Artie in eleven years. But who was thinking of *that.)*

Oh yes, by then getting-it-on was in the computer. Anybody who has ever been there before could tell *that.* The mood of the evening had gone into that gear somewhere along the line, the course set.

Each of us, he and I, for different reasons, right? Men's and women's always *are* different, right?

I won't—can't—speak for the gentleman. Me? Why was I entering into such a game? Damned if I knew why. I suppose I was simply following yesterday's old script. The one I knew like the back of my hand. And there I was, where I'd been so many times before. In a new town. A new place. Ready to make a new life. And here was a man who had (enough of) the things I liked. After all, more than once, after just such an evening, my life had swerved off into some pretty wonderful interludes—which I have never regretted, either. (It's what we *don't* do that we regret, right?)

Or maybe . . . Maybe it was just the necessity of wiping the old slate clean, and getting on with tomorrow.

I'll probably never know. Thought, at the time, wasn't what was carrying things along. Lack of it was.

It went smoothly enough. We both knew the routine. I handed him his glass. His hand closed over mine. I smiled into his blue eyes. He closed in. Lips met, etcetera, etcetera . . . Who doesn't know the routine. Since television even the smallest of kids knows the routine.

He smelled good. Had a nice skin. Was a good enough lover. I mean, I couldn't *fault* him. Bells don't *always* have to ring, do they? Rockets go off? And there *was* this terribly déjà vu feeling about it all, too. At least he didn't stay on for the entire night. I realized, after he had gone, that I'd been glad to see him go. And I wondered why. And decided, or so it seemed to me, that sleeping, and I do mean actually *sleeping,* with another person, sharing your most private time of day, when all guards are down and you are most vulnerable, might be, oddly enough, a far more intimate act than a brief copulatory encounter. That sleeping together through the night was more of a commitment and should not be done lightly.

There was little doubt that things were certainly changing— maybe already *had* changed—irrevocably, for me.

If I only knew exactly in what way . . .

# Four

We went around some, the barrister and I. Not exclusively, nothing foolish like that. We both kept our distance, he not wanting further involvement any more than I. In passing he mentioned an ex-wife, grown children, so he had been around the track himself. We had some meals together, repeated the theater, a concert or two, went to pubs called things like Dagger and Crown, or Hare and Vulture. I liked the space between us—it was a nice and relaxing pace after Artie and the heated discussions over every little thing. He had his barrister life (whatever the hell that was), and I had got in touch with others I knew around town. Like the Bob Parrishes—he had directed that picture I had made in London, and he had taken up residence there afterward. I caught up with the Eric Amblers. Eric had written the script of the said picture, and she had been a producer for Alfred Hitchcock. They were both Brits, which gave *them* a good reason for settling down in London.

Since I'm not a gregarious person—actually I'd adored the isolation of Spain—I made myself keep going around. Reminding myself it's what I had come for, to make some new kind of life for myself. And how would I know what kind to make if I didn't get out there and *see* what choices there might be.

So any time I was asked anywhere, I went (within reason). Sometimes I would take my barrister along, too. And on more than one occasion I would find myself in a corner somewhere with someone (more often than not a female, though not always) whispering to me, "Oh, he's absolutely *perfect* for you!"

Perfect for what? I would ask myself.

They figured, I supposed, that I was looking for another mate to pair up with, since that's how the world seems bent on traveling. At least that's how those around me, those whispering to me, traveled. I guessed they couldn't imagine it any other way.

So I didn't say anything about how I wasn't all that anxious to climb back into the mating pigeonhole I had just crawled out of. Wasn't at all sure I would *ever* again want to squeeze back into some tight little space with another person. Where I'd have to be thinking all the time of that other person before I could make a single move. Before I could even decide what I would have for dinner that evening, for crissake.

Surely there was some other way to go through life, wasn't there? *Wasn't there?*

So I kept going around. Sometimes with, sometimes without, the barrister. Here and there. Hither and yon. Looking for *it*. The other way. Looking to see if there *was* another way. For me, that is, older person that I was.

And before long growing older began to be a rather interesting experience. (A better way to look at it, surely, than going around moaning and groaning.) Because a day seldom passed when the fact that I *was* older wasn't pointed out to me in one way or another (just in case I didn't know it myself).

After a while I began to understand the reason, too. Realized it was probably bound to happen since I'd been out of the mainstream for so long, living some other life. And all these years had zoomed by while I was doing it. And now I was running into people I hadn't seen—nor they, me—in donkey's years. So it was probably only natural, I decided, that the sight of me would bring yesteryear to mind.

Only . . .

It was the *manner* in which they remembered that I sometimes found a little unnerving. Because, almost without exception, their reactions were . . . well, *fraught.* I don't know of any other word for it.

I had once read somewhere (or been told, probably by my walking encyclopedia, Artie) of certain categories that triggered instant twittering in the human psyche (à la Pavlov's little doggie). Love is one. Sex another (natch). Religion, food. Money is a very big one. But . . . *growing older?* I didn't believe that one had been mentioned at all. But to my mind it certainly should have been.

Because there were some people who, at the mention of a happening back in earlier Hollywood days, say a movie being shot, a party attended, a tennis game, would actually shudder and groan or squeal as if in pain. "Oh!" They would cry out, "Don't *remind* me! That was . . ." And a hand would wipe across the mouth so that the number of years gone by would be garbled and (they hoped) lost.

Then there were their opposite numbers. The ones who gathered yesterday around themselves like a protective cloak and refused to acknowledge there had *been* a passage of time. They spoke of earlier events as if they were occurring at the moment.

Nor was there any escape around the very young, either.

Like the day Christiane Kubrick and I were entertaining ourselves walking through Carnaby Street where the furthest-out gear (as clothes were then being called) could be found. "Take a look here," Christiane said, and guided me into a kiddy-clothes shop filled with these teeny tiny garments made for teeny tiny tots, maybe a year or two old; studded pants, studded skirts, shirts, shoes and belts, all of them flaming orange or deep purple or gold and silver lamé, all about the size of a postage stamp. Pink and blue wouldn't be caught dead in the neighborhood.

It was hilarious. Christiane made a purchase for a child of hers, and we were on our way out when she ran into some woman she knew who had a kid in tow, a boy of maybe ten or eleven.

Introductions were made, and when the woman heard my name, her eyebrows shot up. "Oh!" cried she, "you were on the telly last night!" And she turned to her young son. "Remember the film we watched after dinner, darling? This is the lady who was in it!"

And the young son said, as he looked up at me, "Well, you look a lot older, now."

I thought his mother was going to hit him.

*"William!"* she hissed, *"what a . . . terrible thing to say!"*

"Not at all!" I quickly interceded, seeing the confusion on the boy's face, "He's—" I stopped and turned to address the boy. "You're *absolutely right!* I *am* a *lot* older! Thank you for noticing! That movie was made, oh, a long time before you were even *born*—oh what a good eye you have!"

But neither of them was listening to me. The mother had grown deaf and dumb with her embarrassment. The kid was melting like a wax candle under the humiliation of having done some terrible deed. But what that crime was thoroughly baffled him since all he'd done was tell the truth, which was what he'd always been told a good boy *should* do.

The mother slunk away with her offspring as soon as she could, in order, no doubt, to kill him. Surely she had already severely maimed him for life. They do it to us so very early on, don't they? Start us thinking as children, already, that aging is a fate worse than death.

What had I got myself into, I wondered, by living on and on. It was somewhat like continually walking across land that had been heavily mined.

The image brought to mind a story that John Huston had once told me. It was during the war and he was in Italy making a documentary called *San Pietro* for the army. Needing to relieve himself (actually he had said "take a leak"), he walked some distance from his crew. Having finished his chore and about to rejoin his men, he was stopped in his tracks by hysterical yells from the road.

It seemed he had wandered into a stretch of land the departing Italians had left treacherously mined.

Well.

There was no way anybody could come to John's rescue. Nobody had the faintest idea where the mines might be located. So John was on his own, and had to work his way out of the fix he had got himself into.

Getting older was turning out to be something like that. You were constantly having to pick your way through other people's agitations and fears, hoping they wouldn't explode while you were in range, and if they did, that the fallout wouldn't spatter all over you.

Fear.

Damned if it isn't always sitting there. *All the time.* Night and day. Just waiting for an opening so that it can leap right in.

But you can't just sit out there in the middle of a field for the rest of your life, can you. Scared to move in any direction. You have to get up and go . . . *somewhere,* don't you?

John obviously had. And he did get out. And had one hell of a life afterward. And if he was afraid on occasion, he kept it to himself. Or maybe ignored it, the way he must have had to ignore the land mines that day out in that field.

So I would do well to follow his example (as I already had many a time), I told myself. Just keep on walking through the mined fields, baby, I said to me, until you get to the other side. Until you get to . . .

Well, I wouldn't know where, if I didn't go and see, would I.

Wherever it was, though, I wouldn't be going with my barrister friend. Not because Artie arrived in London or anything like that. Long before Artie arrived the barrister and I had simply drifted in different directions. I'd hardly noticed I wasn't seeing him anymore until long after I wasn't seeing him anymore. Too many things had gotten in the way of a closer relationship, including that woman in the wet window pane whose image insisted on lingering on, smack in the middle of my memory bank.

It had been several months since I'd seen Artie and, lo, it turned out that I had actually missed the guy! I hadn't even suspected it until he arrived. Almost at once I discovered, with something of a shock, how well our . . . what shall I call them—our *basics*—matched, Artie's and mine. I mean, those things that are the *essence* of us. Those deep down, gut reactions to . . . well, most everything, I suppose. Why we like this person, and not that. Want this one for our President, would loathe having the other. Find this joke funny, the other one childish. Speaking the same language doesn't mean we speak the same language at all, does it. Apparently, we all communicate with some hidden, unexplainable antennae. And on that level, I swear, Artie was almost like my alter ego. I had known that, once upon a time, but things had gone so wrong for so long, I had forgotten all about it.

Artie had business in London, some record deal talks, I believe, some damn thing, but he stayed with me. Where else. I had one bedroom, one double bed. And that's where we slept. (And I do mean sleep.) Without thinking twice about it. Hadn't we done just that for years? The arrangement seemed as natural and right with Artie as it had not with the barrister. Artie, I decided happily, was obviously my family from here on in. My mother, my brother, a permanent fixture in my life, and that was that. My name was still Shaw, we hadn't divorced, the subject hadn't even come up, a divorce seeming to be more trouble than it was worth.

Before we retired, though, we had stayed up half the night talking ourselves silly, almost hungrily, until Artie finally said, "Jeezus, we do wear each other out, don't we, I gotta get some sleep . . ."

The familial euphoria lasted until morning. When Artie woke up and asked me to bring him some morning coffee.

The thing was, I had been reading the abundant new literature on the lot of women and it had pointed out to me the absurdities of the divisions of labor among males and females. Especially when it came to someone like me who had always been a wage earner herself, and who, without a second thought, had dumped all her worldly goods into the mutual marriage pot (believing it to be a permanent union). So why was it that I and I alone had been assigned to the make-and-bring coffee detail when I'd never so much as previously boiled an egg? (Not, mind you, that I looked back with regret, having learned a thing or two in the process I had never known before.)

Not only could I now boil an egg, I could decipher most any recipe at all, in three languages, too, even up to and including bread. I can make, if I set my mind to it, an herb-seeded loaf that is positively delicious! And any gained knowledge about most anything puts you that much more ahead of the game, does it not?

And by that particular morning Artie was there I had learned a thing or two further. Learned exactly why I'd been the one assigned to the kitchen detail.

It was because of my particular set of genitals.

Only those weren't what I used to spoon up coffee crystals (or boil water) with. I used my hands, the way all members of my species do, regardless of their sex. And Artie, player of the clarinet, had, God knows, a very workable set of hands.

But evidently, that morning, he still hadn't come to realize that it was now turn-about-is-fair-play time. He was still coming on as if our old arrangement was carved on Mount Rushmore, to be repeated every instant we came across each other to the end of time. The new attitudes afoot in our society about female-male relationships seemed (in spite of all his reading) to have passed him by.

So I decided it would be terribly wise of me to head this new relationship of ours in the proper direction right from its inception. Therefore what I said to Artie that lovely morning in London was, "There's a jar of instant on the kitchen counter. Why don't you help yourself?"

Artie frowned. He blinked, as if he hadn't heard quite right (and I expect he hadn't). "W-what . . . ?" he sort of burbled.

I spoke louder. (And dumber.) "All the stuff is right there on the—"

"Can't *you* do it?" He interrupted.

"I gotta go take a shower," I quickly ad-libbed, determined to make my point, and started for the door.

I could have, *should* have, simply minded my manners and got my guest (that's all in the world he was at the moment, a guest) his coffee.

The trouble was, you couldn't just give Artie a cup of coffee. He would hover, he would direct the entire procedure to the number of sugar grains to be added, how the water must boil, the intensity of the bubbles, when and how it was poured into the cup, to the last drop, so that it would wind up a certain distance from the rim, no more, no less, to a fraction of a millimeter. And if toast should follow, it, too, would have to be done to just the right (*Artie's* right) shade, and buttered right up to the crust, no ifs-ands-or-buts about it, not missing a single minute surface anywhere on the piece of bread.

*Every*thing you did for Artie went like that, and so the memory of all my straitjacketed years in his company was flickering at my nerve-ends, causing me to launch the foolhardy course I was on.

Of course I didn't make it through the door.

*"Can't . . . your . . . show . . . er, wait!?"* He snapped ir-

ritably, his voice beginning to rise. "Jeezus! You *know* I'm not all there first thing in the morning!"

My lesson was going down the tube. But did that stop me? "It doesn't take a genius, Artie," I told him, then, "to boil water and spoon instant into it."

He looked at me with absolute disgust. A neat, unadulterated version. And the stream of words began, flowing like lava from his mouth, like a force of nature. "I don't know why I bother, you are not reachable, I think we can be friends and then you . . ."

I hadn't the faintest idea what he said from then on. When his anger went into that gear (and it had, oh, maybe two zillion times) my ears simply closed up tight, and what it was all about flew straight out of my head, I was so overcome with humiliation that the neighbors might be hearing the ruckus, had probably stopped whatever they were doing to put their ears to the walls and listen to the uncouth Americans in their midst.

And because Artie was so loud, I did the most irritating thing I could do. I lowered my own voice. "Look," I whispered, "never mind, this is silly, I'll go make the coffee, okay? Okay? Okay?"

Too little, and too late, of course. Trying to turn off Artie after his dander was up was like trying to stop a stampeding rhinoceros with a slingshot.

He heaved himself to his feet and plunged into the kitchen. I stood where I was, listening to the racket that ensued, the clattering of kettle and cups, the bangs of cabinet and fridge doors, the crashes of heavy objects to the floor, the curses rending the air.

It didn't take too long for him to reappear at the door, ragged and panting as if he had run an obstacle course filled with barbed wire. "I can't do it," he puffed, and dropped like a rock into a chair. "How can you do this to me?" he started again. "It's no use trying, you are unable to . . ."

But I was already on my way to the kitchen, to make the goddamn coffee after all.

Which was what I should have done in the first place. There was no way I could become teacher. It hadn't been set up that way between us. My fault he got mad? (Which was what he'd been trying to tell me, as he always *had* told me it was.)

Fine. Right. My fault. So be it. As my friend (well, a little more than that) Mike Todd used to say, if ten people tell you you're drunk, go home and lie down, even if you haven't had a drink. I didn't care *whose* fault it was. It was jerky. It was a bloody *bore.* And we weren't even *living* together. So now it looked as if we shouldn't even *see* each other.

Enough of this sentimental nonsense. We were a lost cause. Like magnets that, when you touch them backward, leap in the opposite direction.

It was a relief when he left town.

And not a minute too soon, as it turned out. I wouldn't have wanted Artie there the night I came home and found an intruder hiding behind the kitchen door. He and his macho ways might very well have got us both killed.

Fortunately I did have *some*one with me . . .

# *Five*

I had met George Baxt at some gathering or other, and he had told me about a science fiction movie script he'd written with a part in it he'd like me to do (probably somebody's aunt from outer space was my guess), and would I be interested?

You bet I'd be interested, I told him, and he'd come around to bring the script to me. I read it, and it was pretty good, too, and in the course of our discussions about it, how he planned to get it off the ground (find the money, the cast, the distribution), we became friends.

George was plump and witty and gay (as in sexual preference), and therefore much more restful to be with than my latest companions, and I could certainly use some of that for a while.

This evening we had been to the theater (you do that a lot in London), and George wanted to come in with me and get me caught up with his latest wheelings and dealings for the would-be flick.

It wasn't very late when we started up the stairs toward my digs—theater started early in those days, around seven or so— and as we turned into the last flight of our upward journey, I saw that the door to my flat was ajar.

"Oh *George!*" I cried. "Look at that! You didn't pull the door shut after us!" In time-honored fashion, I had gone out first, and George had brought up the rear.

"Of course I did!" he answered indignantly, puffing from the enforced exercise of walking up so many steps. Since he was overweight and out of shape with reflexes to match, I didn't believe him for one minute.

With the living room on the top floor, poor George had quite a haul before he made it to the overstuffed chair across from the sofa. As he sank into it I continued on into the kitchen to get us nightcaps.

"All my friends live at the top of stairs," he was gasping as I was arriving at the threshold of my destination, "it's revenge, I know it is, you're all trying to do me in . . ."

I have tried to trace my actions from this point on. But I've been unable to do so. They don't make the least bit of sense, whatsoever.

The door to the kitchen swung inward, see, and was always open, always kept flat against the wall. And somewhere in my brain, this night, it did register that the door was *not* flat against the wall as it normally was. And that an odd shadow, not usually there, could be seen through the crack between the hinges.

But what did I do, then?

I stepped *inside* to see what it was. Nor was that all. When I saw it was a man crouching there I had never seen before in my life, I jumped backward and further *into* the kitchen. Thereby placing the intruder between me and the only way out.

I did start screaming my head off. I did do that. Something somewhere in my brain told me that was a good thing to do.

Plump George appeared in the doorway. "What in the *world* are you—"

He saw what, gasped, and clutched his chest.

So there we were, on the top floor of an old Georgian house in the heart of London, I trapped in the kitchen, George Baxt in the doorway, the intruder sandwiched between us.

Then came the most ridiculous dialogue ever heard. If read in a book or seen in a movie (other than a film by Woody Allen), no one would believe it.

"Please don't do that," the intruder said in the thickest cockney I have ever heard, referring to my screaming. "I'm more frightened than you are."

He was a little weasel of a man, in pitifully shabby clothing, suitably dark for robbing, and grimy.

He must have heard the thumping of my heart, it was rattling the chinaware in the cupboards. I stopped screaming. "W-what are you d-doing here?" I demanded foolishly, breathing hard.

"My mates," the weasel said, "were chasing me. I didn't have anyplace else to go."

That's what he said, this wretched creature. I stared at him, and under my fear I flushed with anger. Why, the miserable bastard was lying to me! He had come here to *rob* me and now he had the audacity to *lie* to me about it! How *dare* he!

But none of these thoughts would form on my tongue. *"You've . . . got . . . gloves on!"* was what I finally spat out in my rage.

And he had. Filthy, dirty-white kid ones. In order, I thought furiously, to keep his nasty little fingerprints all to himself!

But none of that would come forth, either. All I did was

keep repeating, maybe ten times, "You've got gloves on! You've got gloves on-you've-got-gloves-on-you've-got-gloves-on . . ."

I might still be standing there repeating my phrase if George hadn't at last come to the rescue. "Evelyn," he said from his stand at the door, "let him go."

I stared at George. I stared at the weasel. "I'm not holding him," I said finally.

George, too, eventually had the presence of mind to stop blocking the way. But he did it like a crab edging sideways, with infinite slowness.

It sort of set the pace. The intruder, as well, moved in slow motion, like glue out of a bottle, keeping his eyes fixed on the two of us as he crept through the living room. It wasn't until he was halfway down the stairs that he finally took off with the speed of a bullet. We could hear him crashing down through the house stairs and into the night, while George hurried down, me trailing after, to slam the front door shut and firmly lock it.

Then he turned to me. "I was afraid," he said sotto voce, "he might grab up that bread knife you have on the counter."

I remembered and grew chilled. Yes, there it had been all the while. A twelve-inch blade lying on a carving board. Ready for bread-slicing. Or anything else a person might have in mind.

Mostly George wrote mysteries for a living. I've often thought his penchant for plotting murders could very well have saved our lives that night. He understood the danger we were in. Had Artie been there, he'd have probably tried to talk the guy out of his life of crime, given him a lecture on the merits of good citizenship, and the fellow would have picked up the knife and cut our throats just to shut Artie up. (I know such thoughts have crossed *my* mind.)

Later George's breezy humor turned the whole thing into a hilarious event, he saying what a pity it was he had let the young man loose, their being such a shortage of available studs in London.

What with knowing George, then meeting this one and that, it wasn't long before I found I had begun going about town with quite a goodly number of gay men.

I don't know when I became aware that there were sexual arrangements in the world other than the boy/girl one. Certainly not while growing up. Where would I have learned? Any literature I read, any movie I saw, were all boy/meets/girl (or vice versa) stories. Any visible home life was strictly mom/pop. Even my introduction to porn, by way of a comic book handed around study class at Girls' High, was a specific and unequivocal display of heterosexual togetherness.

There was Popeye, the sailor-man, with this gross male organ that looked somewhat like a baseball bat, sticking out the front of his sailor suit, which he was poking into one female after the other, page after page. A girl in every port, as it were. (There was a subliminal message, of course, in the ratio of [one] boy to [multiple] girls—not that I understood *that* at the time.)

Nor did my own eagerness for firsthand information on these sexual mysteries lead me to any boy who might be more interested in teaming up with Popeye, himself. I was never turned on, somehow, by a gay male. (Nor did I, them, obviously.) In the early fifties I made a picture with Rock Hudson, called *The Iron Man,* one of his first, I think. He played the brother of Jeff Chandler, and I thought, this guy will never make it, he has no sex appeal. (Which goes to show how little I know.)

So my limited knowledge on sexual variations stayed pretty limited until I began to take up with hetero males, and they, yes it was the heteros who told me what was what. And in the most appalling ways—though I didn't recognize *that* little fact until a number of years later. (God, how very easy it is to instill prejudice in ignorant ears.) They spoke of these boys who preferred boys in the most contemptuous ways. As figures of fun. The butt of cruel and insulting jokes, to be tittered at, and scorned as being "less than men." People who would never *dream* of using derogatory words like "nigger" or "gook" or "kike" would say "fag" or "queer" without thinking twice. (And still do.) And I confess I didn't think too much about it one way or the other, either, at the time.

Small wonder the majority of gay men (lesbians, too) stayed in the closet for so many years. Who would want to face such a hostile world, to be ostracized and discriminated against, simply for being who and what you are. For the way the cookie crumbled for you.

The trouble was, though, that all the secrecy brought about by closet life created a pretty absurd game for us all, homo and hetero alike.

It went something like this:

Whenever homos stepped out of the closet and into the hetero world, they'd have to pretend (for their own protection) to be hetero, too. And though they never really fooled much of anybody except maybe a maiden aunt or two (George Cukor never fooled Clark Gable for one minute, which was why George wasn't allowed to direct *Gone With the Wind*), most heteros would go along with the charade—at least as long as the gay person was around.

This sort of thing, though, had a tendency to keep relationships between the two orientations from becoming much more than casual acquaintanceships. Heteros in this country have a greater fear of being thought of as gay than they do of being labelled Communist. (Though the two run fairly neck and neck.)

But I think it was the secretiveness of it all that rather put me off. I mean, it's hard to become buddy-buddy with anybody you feel is kind of hiding from you, holding out on you. (And, of course, it never even once *occurred* to me that anything *I* was doing might be a contributing factor!) And I was surrounded by homosexuals a great deal of the time; they did my hair, my makeup; they designed my clothes, my dance steps; sometimes directed me, often wrote the scripts I acted in. And it was, God knows, pleasant enough. Easy, and often great fun to be in their presence.

But on the whole, gay men seemed to remain on the periphery of my life. They were certainly not at the core. How could they be? Hetero men were the ones who ran my world. (The whole world, actually.) They, in fact, *ran my life.* All of it. The (as they say) entire ball of wax.

Not only did hetero males run my country for me—Franklin, Harry, Ike, Jack, staunch heteros all—they also ran the movie studios, those bastions of culture I was determined to scale or die in the attempt. So they, the hetero males, were the ones whose attention I had to grab, if I were to ever have a shot at the brass ring.

And sure enough, those who heeded, and gave me the shot—Cecil B., David O., Harry C.—were, one and all, your ultra, classic, vintage, hetero male, not to be taken for anything else. They orchestrated my career. They were in a position to break it off, too, if they so chose. A pretty powerful spot, wouldn't you say?

And that wasn't all. That was only half the power these heterosexual males had over me. Only half, do you hear? And maybe the *lesser* half, at that.

Because it was they, these heteros, who'd first set my budding pubescent buttons aspinning with carnal rustlings. They to whom, from then on, up and through Artie, I turned as the source of life's goodies: romance, marriage, and the everlasting happiness factor. And I actually believed, with all my heart, that they could furnish it, too.

Oh yes. They'd had me, coming and going, the hetero males. No matter which direction I'd been looking, no matter which thing I might have been looking for, it was one of their kind who had done the string-pulling.

When would I have had time to notice any variations on the theme?

I wouldn't have, is the answer, and didn't—until there I was, in London, on my own for the umpteenth time.

With this difference, however.

I wasn't looking in any of the former directions, anymore, being thoroughly weary from all the years of trying to make the girlie dreams come true. And beginning to understand at long last that it was—and I guess always had been—a hopeless cause. At least for me. And so for the first time in my entire grown-up life, I expect, I wasn't going about with an eye to meeting the *right* (finally!) Mr. Right. And for that reason could look around me, and really *see,* for a change, through untinted glasses.

And what I happily discovered was, how so very much *easier* it was, how so much less complicated, indeed quite relaxing, to be around somebody like George.

There were none of those silly divisions, for starters, about who did what. George not only handled intruders with aplomb, later turning the event into laughter, he could cook like a dream, sew on a button if need be, as did many other of his fellow "club members" (as he called them) that I came to know.

And me? I was learning to open doors for other people, pick up checks, and call to make dates! Nor was there "girl talk" or "boy talk" among us, either, as if we were a different species. There was simply similar-species-type talk.

And the only sexual pass that I had to fend off was instigated by a young lady . . .

# Six

Such a thing happened only once before in my life. I have never been aware of which women preferred other women as their sexual partners. Though, surely, they'd been about. It's just that, in that respect, my antennae worked only for men. For the simple reason, I imagine, that men were the yang to my yin. I doubt that I gave out the right signal, either, to anyone of the sapphic inclination. In any event, the two, some twenty-odd years apart, came as total surprises both times.

The first invitation to join their ranks occurred back in the late forties. I was married to John (Huston) at the time, though he wasn't at the party that particular night—off shooting something or other, I suppose. It was a lively gathering down at director Anatole Litvak's place in Malibu, a big, three-story house perched right on the edge of the sandy beach, so that, at high tide, breakers from the Pacific Ocean could roll up and splash smack against the lower windows.

People (good-looking, all) were milling through the various rooms, sometimes spilling outside and onto the terrace, chatting animatedly, eating, drinking, enjoying themselves. Movie folk at play. I happened to be sitting and talking to David Niven when the first of the lesbian encounters came about.

If David was at a party you didn't need anybody else to have a good time. He was marvelous fun, witty, caring, and generous with himself, a pleasure to be with. We were sitting on a couch, slumped on it, I should say, it was one of those deep, bedlike kind with big, soft pillows that sort of swallowed you up. David had just pushed himself upright to go and fetch us some more champagne.

As he walked away, suddenly, on the other side of me, a body dropped down and sank in alongside. It was a French actress, actually quite a big star in her own country, who had come to Hollywood to make a name for herself on this side of the ocean as well. I scarcely knew the woman, having come across her only once before in my entire life, and that was a time when I happened to be in New York City with John. John had gone there to direct a Broadway play and I had gone along with him, simply for the fun of watching the man in action, only I'd gotten a bigger dose of excitement than I'd bargained for when one of his female leads came down with the flu during the last week of rehearsals and John had said, maybe you could do it, and I'd spent a frantic few days there hastily learning the ailing actress's role in case I was needed to go on in her place opening night! And so I might not have remembered the first encounter with this French lady at all if she hadn't plopped down beside me later at Tola's house.

The time in New York was an evening when everybody connected with John's company had been invited to the apartment of Oliver Smith, the set designer, and I, as John's wife, went along, too. And for some reason I happened to be near the front door when the *vedette française* swept in, in a great rush, as if she were just passing through on her way to the next place, and in a hurry to get there. That evening she whirled in my direction as she entered the room. "Oh!" she cried, in her very accented English. "Eet ees so *hot,* tonight!"

And with that she flipped up her dress, up and up until it swung around her neck and head.

She had absolutely nothing on underneath. The woman was as naked as a jaybird. I remember a flash of breasts and a very large thatch of pubic hair before the dress came down again.

At the time I hadn't as yet been to this French star's country. So what did I know. Maybe that was the way French women acted on hot nights. I'd been told they had a certain freedom we Americans didn't have. I made no other connection at all. Not until the night at Tola's.

"Ever do eet with a woman, *cherie?*" was what I thought she said, close to my ear.

Because she spoke with an accent I thought maybe I hadn't understood properly. But her smile, secretive, knowing, gave me my first clue.

I think I shook my head as I stared at her, startled at this turn of events.

"*La pauvre bébé,*" she tsked-tsked seductively, "she has not yet lived. I must feex this for her—"

She was up and away as David returned with the champagne, her pattern for the night; in and out, here and there.

She must have been on the lookout, because the minute David's attention went somewhere else, she was back.

"You do not know what you are missing, *mon ange,*"

she whispered, "a woman knows what to do for anozzer woman . . ."

And then, ". . . no need to worry about pregnancy . . ."

And, ". . . not necessary to sneak about, since no one will suspect anything if they see women togezzer . . ."

That last told me more about her than anything else. I was never much of a sneaker-around-er. Why would you want to stay with someone if you wanted to be with someone else? I've always wondered.

I had begun to be aware that another woman seemed always to be lurking nearby. And once or twice I found her looking my way with a not-too-friendly glare. Were she and Frenchie there "togezzer"? This one was rich-rich-rich. Her name placed her in one of those American families that we all know about because of their wealth. That we've grown up knowing. Was she jealous, or something? Or was this supposed to be a three-way thing?

It was getting very uncomfortable for me. I was out of my bailiwick. I was trying not to say an outright no and risk hurting *la femme*'s feelings, but I seemed to be getting in deeper and I didn't know exactly what to do about it.

When I thought she wasn't looking, I jumped up and hurried to the powder room, maybe to collect my thoughts there (or at least my wits).

I was wrong. She had been looking. I was no sooner inside than she burst through the door, yanked me around, flung her arms out, pulled me close to her, and planted this big, long, passionate and juicy kiss square upon my mouth.

Actually, I'd done a goodly amount of kissing in my life by that time. Aside from all the various loves-of-my-life I'd indulged with, there was all the screen osculating you get called upon to do if your job is movie acting. Sooner or later, in just about every film I'd ever done, a kissing scene had found its way into the script. But on all counts, off-screen and on, the kissers had been male.

Until that night in the powder room at Anatole Litvak's house.

Well.

There is one thing I can say for sure about it. It was certainly different from all the others. Squishy, for one thing. My breasts, instead of pressing against a nice, hard, flat chest, pressed against another pair of breasts. It felt really peculiar. The arms around me were soft, and hairless. Even the texture of the mutual clothes was odd. Instead of soft material against firm tweed or gabardine or flannel, both participants were in chiffon and silk and such, all mushing together. And both mouths had lipstick on them, so that made the lips all gooey and slippery.

Fortunately a click at the door signalled the arrival of someone else, which caused my French would-be friend (if that was the word) to dart away again while I, myself, made a dash into the cubicle, there to try and tidy up my messy and blurred mouth with wads of toilet paper.

I decided there was only one thing for me to do. Get the hell out of there. Which was what I did.

I never had occasion to see the woman again. So that the memory of that evening had faded and dimmed and was pretty much forgotten until there, in London, these twenty years later, a second member of my own sex made a similar move. Similar in that they were both females. But otherwise not the same at all.

Age, of all things, made the difference. With the first, I'd been the younger one. And as I have often seen men do with women they are on the make for, she had taken the aggressive approach, playing the role of teacher, guru, the one to initiate the newcomer into certain rites she may not have heretofore experienced.

But this time the woman was the younger, and she attempted to seduce me in soft, helpless, flirty Marilyn Monroe ways. The way I have often observed girls coming on with men.

I had been to a Sunday gathering that day, a kind of barbecue affair out in St. John's Wood, a suburban-ish part of London. Both the conversation and the food were good, and I wasn't particularly aware that I might have been the only straight person there, I was so used to that happening by then. When it was time to leave, a young lady asked if she could catch a lift into town with me and the guy (gay, of course) who had driven me out. But when we arrived at Markham Square, she got out with me, saying she would take a taxi from there. Then she asked if she could come in to make a phone call.

And she was inside. As easy as that.

She was a beauty, this young creature. Early twenties was my guess. Willowy and graceful in brightly colored, loosely layered garments, pale British skin, and big dark eyes, thickly fringed. Long, straight hair, hanging in strips about her shoulders, with a big, purple, fuzzy-brimmed hat on her head. A knockout.

Back in my Paris days, I'd visited, on occasion, a well-known lesbian nightclub where women sat and danced together—in a rather defiant way, actually—and wore mannish clothes, suits, ties, shirts, and sported close-cropped hair, which was the going style for men, then. I suppose somewhere in my head that was the image of lesbianism that I carried.

Wrong.

This girlish *girl,* about as feminine as it is physically possible to be, didn't repair to the phone once we were inside, didn't so much as ask where it was. Instead she came up to me, wound slender arms around my neck, and gazed, doelike, into my eyes. "I like you best of anybody I've met in ages," she whispered in a husky purr that was evidently supposed to send quivers down my spine.

Oh shit, I thought, what the hell had I got into? "Uh . . . thank you very much," I told her politely, minding my manners as I unfurled her arms from my person. I pointed to my desk. "There's the phone," I added, gesturing in its direction. "I believe you want to use it."

But she didn't move. Didn't look anywhere else but at me

so that I would be sure to see the big doe eyes filled with hurt. "Don't *you* like *me?*" she whispered in tones of pain.

She was full of tricks, this young lady.

"You're very nice indeed, my dear," I told her, rather prissily, really; I was trying not to be harsh, or anything. I saw no reason to be unkind to her. All I wanted was her *out* of there. "But you see . . ." I smiled to let her know I meant her no harm, "I don't . . . don't go that way. So you'd better make your call and be on your way, okay?"

She did turn away then. But only to sink into the nearest chair. "I'm so lonely," she murmured, sort of into her lap. The picture of rejection. And there seemed to be a glistening of tears.

It was a pretty hokey performance. If acting was her bag, I found myself thinking, she had better go back to RADA (Royal Academy of Dramatic Arts) for further instruction. "Yeah?" I muttered, to say something, vamping until I could get her out the door, "Well . . . uh, who isn't, these days, so listen, you'd better . . ."

"I've just broken up with my lover," she then whispered.

"Ahh . . . well, these things do happen," said I lamely. Man or woman I remembered wondering, and then found out almost immediately.

"Would you like to see her picture?" she said, and didn't wait for an answer. Quick as a wink, she took a snapshot from her bag, jumped to her feet and, moving next to me again, extended the photo in my direction.

I saw an older woman (hah!) with short, tight curls bleached to a platinum shade, in white, tight satin, seated at a piano, playing it, evidently, and singing, too. In a nightclub somewhere.

"That's in Marbella," she told me.

"Ah yes." The south of Spain.

"I spent seven months there, and I loved every minute of it."

"It's quite a place . . ."

"But she's gone to South America, now . . ."

"I see . . ." She was beginning to tell me more than I cared to know.

"You . . ." She was looking at me with her doe eyes soft and shining, and full of invitation. I hadn't realized how close she had come. I'd been looking at the snapshot. Her hair was brushing my shoulder. "You remind me so of her . . ."

In her rather sneaky way, this young woman was every bit as determined as her French counterpart had been twenty years earlier.

But the thing was, the husband before John, one Charles Vidor, who was Hungarian by birth and possessed the wisdom of two continents, of the old world as well as the new, had taught me many worthwhile and useful things. One of them being that I could, of course, sleep with anyone I wished (after him, *bien sûr!*), but that it should always be *my choice.* That I should never allow anyone to talk me into anything I didn't want to do.

The young thing was pressing her body against me by then, letting my body feel hers. "I can stay with you, tonight, if you wish," she was whispering huskily.

Charles had meant men, of course. But I didn't see any reason to stray from his philosophy simply because it was a woman who was trying to have her way with me.

So I walked away from her, and then turned back.

It was time to make things perfectly clear. "Your tricks won't work," I told her, and this time I was harsh. I had had it. "I just am not of your faith, and that's all there is to it. So if you're not going to use the phone, then I suggest you run along now."

The soft doe expression was wiped from her eyes as if an eraser had been run across them, and one of pure hatred took its place. And she, too, as the would-be burglar had done, turned and ran, pell-mell, down the stairs, down and out with a house-shaking bang of the street door, into the outside world and out of my life.

But not, quite so quickly, out of my thoughts. After all, it wasn't every day that a gorgeous young wench tried her wiles on me. And then, too, as I reviewed it, it struck me as being, brief encounter though it was, a perfect little script. Rather like one of those TV commercials that tell an entire story in a matter of seconds.

Setting: Party in St. John's Wood.

Enter Stage Right: The Young, Gorgeous One.

Enter Stage Left: The . . . ahem . . . Mature One (no slouch, either, in the Looks Department, though Time has passed by and left his mark), a Visitor who hails from, oh thrills, oh chills, the most glamorous place in all the world, the one, the only, Holl-y-wood!

The Young One, whose dream it has been to get to Hollywood someday, now sees her chance. (I remembered, at the gathering, how she had confessed, in breathless tones, that this was her dream.) She will charm The Older One and get her to take her there one day soon.

Enter Sexual Titillation. The Young One brings out her big guns. Aims her most powerful assets, her Youth and her Beauty (and they *are* a form of power, you better believe it!) at The Mature One.

Then comes the smash finish. The Rejection Scene. (Always Emmy Award material.) Which will tug at our hearts, since who, among us, has not experienced Rejection. *(I certainly have, on-screen and off.)*

Except.

The script was all upside down, this time out. (For me, anyway.) Topsy-turvy. (For me, anyway.) Like walking through Alice's Looking Glass.

Because I was cast in roles somebody else had always played before. Not only was *I* The Mature One, this time out, I was also The Prince. The very gentleman *I* had been chasing all these many years.

Or maybe Sugar Daddy was more like it—or should I say, Sugar *Momma*?

A perfect set of bookends, it seemed to me. My older, female "admirer" back then, interested in my Youth-and-Beauty. And twenty years later, a purple-hatted charmer in London wants *me* to be interested in *her* Youth-and-Beauty.

So. They had got me again. Those who would remind me

of my advancing years. From left field maybe, this time, and with a different flavor, but the message was the same, in case I had forgotten it for a couple of minutes.

Who needed reminding, though. *Couldn't I see it for myself, for godsake?*

I walked up to the big framed-in-mahogany mirror that hung over the back of the couch and looked straight at the person reflected there. A good, hard look. I didn't tilt my head to try for a more flattering angle, but simply let the strong afternoon crosslight do what it would.

There was still, well, yes there were, remnants of youth. Remnants. No ungainly bulges, no unsightly sags. Not too bad a face, as faces went. I'd earned a living with it, after all. Taken care of it.

But there *were* things there that *hadn't* been there before. Yes there were. Things that spoke of passing years. Lines around the eyes. Furrows alongside the mouth, stretching from the nose to the chin. And the texture of the skin was no longer that smooth, tight, glowing sleekness of the very young. The way it had once been . . .

These things, then—lines, furrows, textures—these *surface things,* were what people were reacting to. My looks. My present-day looks.

Well, I said to my image, what's so all-fired surprising about that? Aren't looks always what people react to? Always had? Had not DeMille reacted to the face I'd had when I first walked into his office? Wasn't the contract he gave me a response to *my looks?* Weren't my looks what prompted Charles Vidor, when I walked into *his* office at Columbia, to put me in the picture he was directing, thereby launching my career at that studio? And to marry me later? Neither he—nor John—nor Artie (nor Tom nor Dick nor Harry) would have given me the time of day if they hadn't liked the way I looked. Nor I them, for that matter.

I leaned in closer to the mirror and ran my fingers along my cheek.

These then, these signs of receding youth, these were what

were causing people to keep trying to thrust roles upon me I wasn't prepared for, hadn't chosen, hadn't sought, hadn't even *considered,* one way or the other.

Ah so, said I to myself that bonny Sunday afternoon, suddenly straightening up and aiming imaginary six-shooters at the mirror's image (sometimes I am a card when I am alone). Just stand back, all you would-be casting directors! All you smart-asses who would restage my life without my consent before I've had a chance to figure out for myself just how I want to play this upper-echelon part. I am not necessarily going to play it the way *you* have decided I should play it, see? I might very well play it the way *I* decide to play it— decide *all by myself*—without anybody's direction *at all.* It's called growing up. And if I don't do it now, when the fuck *will* I ever do it! Surely that *is* what growing older is all about? Growing up? At last?

As I came down off my high, my cockiness ebbed away as quickly as water off the sleek back of a seal. It was one thing to have grandiose thoughts. Another to put them in motion.

The truth was, I didn't know all that much about growing up. Never had . . .

## Seven

I'd been the baby of my family. "Evelyn is the family baby." That's what my mother wrote in a book about such matters.

I'd been the baby around the DeMille office after he put me under contract. That's what the staff called me. The baby.

Husbands (and lovers) had to play Daddy, like it or not.

(God knows what they wanted from me. Artie might have wanted Mommie, in which case no wonder we were at odds so often.) I wouldn't even play with dolls when I was a kid. Whenever anybody would give me one, I'd always find a way to see that it got broken. This baby wouldn't even *pretend* another baby was anywhere in sight.

So the course of my life, the role I was to play in it, was set from Day One. And the career I chose did nothing to dispel the set-up. The old Hollywood studios cuddled and coddled their contract players, offering better protection than the Mafia ever dreamed of, while their heads played Big Daddy to the hilt (much to my satisfaction).

Not the greatest preparation for learning how to stumble your way through this obstacle course known as adulthood, was it.

Well, I did know about readjusting, though, didn't I. I mean, I'd done a hell of a lot of *that* kind of stuff, God knows. I mean, you readjusted, didn't you, every time you changed a spouse, or a city, or a country? Maybe even when you changed abodes. So why didn't I look at this being "The Older" as one more place I'd never been before. Wouldn't that do the trick? Think of it as some kind of adventure?

Adventure.

That word. Boy. It has never failed to turn me on, carrying, as it does, all the mysteries of the unknown, the plaintive cry of the passing train's whistle, the lonely call of a coyote somewhere out there in the desert, the winking lights of a passenger liner far out in the vast expanse of darkness that is the sea . . .

Yeah. That had to be the way of looking at this being "The Older" business, right? As an adventure?

While I was in the throes of my own personal *perestroika,* I got a call from some friends to come to dinner, a couple I had met at a cocktail party. I had already been to their place a few times, and I loved being there. It was such a handsome house, done in soft leathers and thick carpets, all in tones of rust and beige. They collected things, too, and knew what to do with them—to-die-for paintings hung on the walls, exquisite vases and sculptures graced corners, pieces of antique furniture all placed exactly where they should be.

Although more married than anybody I knew, this couple were not man and wife. They were man and man. Nice-looking guys, too, both of them in their late fifties or thereabouts, and they had been together since their youth. They had not let their figures spread, one's hair was going, the other had plenty that had turned white, one was a writer with a book always in progress, the other did something or other in the production end at the London office of a Hollywood company. And for the first time (I'm ashamed to say), I looked at them, that night, as a couple living-together-the-same-as-we-hetero couples do.

Ah, no. Let me correct that. Not as we heteros do (not as *this* hetero did, anyway), but rather the way—to my mind—it *should* be done if you are bound and determined *to* do it, no matter the odds.

It was during dinner that I began to take notice of my hosts' smooth and easy togetherness. We were six at table, the other three guests being two men and a woman, of various ages, a late twenties (one of the men), a mid-thirties (the woman), and a lower forties (I thought, though who can tell ages, anymore). The woman was a literary agent, and the two men were actors, I gathered, at least they talked of some West End thing they were involved in.

The dining room, too, was a cozy affair, off a small garden where a nude male (what else) statue knelt in the center, with roses everywhere, some of them cut and arranged in the middle of the table, which sported a lace tablecloth the color of old ivory. *Lace.* Can you imagine? Probably picked up for a song in a flea market on Portobello Road, where bargains were if you knew how to spot them, and these guys most assuredly did.

They also knew how to get a meal on and off the table without anybody being aware it was being done. (The kind of stuff Artie had always insisted was the little woman's job.) They served several courses, too, a soup (something like Potage Saint-Germain), a chicken dish (something like Poularde Flambée), salad, of course, plus cheeses and fruit for dessert, and besides all that they had to get the wine (the best) and coffee and mints, things like that, to the table. One of them would slide away to do a chore, choosing a moment when it wouldn't be noticed, while the other kept the conversation afloat. Then when he was back, the other would do his turn. Another work of art, their teamwork was.

When I thought of the rigid sexual divisions of the past, I wanted to cry. When I thought of all the grief they had caused (and worse, trained us all to be such fakes!), the young girl broken-hearted at not having a boy-date for the prom, for instance, when all the while she had a close and dear girlfriend she could have gone with—and probably even have enjoyed it more. The necessity of having a male "escort" in order to dine in fancy restaurants or go to nightclubs or a premiere. And a dinner party at someone's house? Though you'd driven yourself all day, opened your own goddamn doors, by nightfall you had to come down with a case of sudden helplessness, in order to be picked up by your male and wait for him to open the doors before you dared to make a move. And if the "hims" and "hers" didn't come out even at the table, lightning would strike the hostess (not the host) dead.

And married couples had the strictest rules of all. The women could do things together, and the men could do things together. But you couldn't cross over. You were *supposed* to be friends with them *both,* but you could only see *her* alone, do things with *her* alone, never, *ever,* with him alone. Even if you called to make a future date with them, and got him by chance, he passed you on to *her* to make the date he was to be in on.

The old system seemed downright archaic after being around these London people. Because these two like-married fellows were, well, friends was what they were first and foremost. Even-Steven friends. And they had friends, *of both sexes.* And went around with them separately, too. And nobody screwed around (oh yes, that was the fear if apartheid rules were not kept) a whit more than they had screwed around before. Maybe less. Because it ceased to be such a big deal.

It was while I was in the middle of this overflowing admiration for the way these gents handled their togetherness—the way they managed to keep their even-Steven arrangement going—that I met the art dealer at one of their gatherings and fell into . . . I don't rightly know what to call what I fell into, except maybe an attempt at having, I suppose, what the two fellows had.

Their exemplary example of how-to-do-togetherness was so very winning, so charming and easy, that it obviously had its effect on me. And too, the art dealer was so unlike any of the other men I had ever been involved with. So unlike them that I thought maybe my tastes had changed. And for the better. (For me, that is.)

The other men in my life, I mean in a big way, had all been bold, bigger-than-life figures. Used to the spotlight, themselves, to being the center of attention, themselves. Used to being in command, and having their way, at all times.

And besides that, they were all taller than I was, too.

This one, for starters, was not. This one was just my height. (Five feet five.) Eye contact, therefore, was on an even keel. A fine way, if you ask me, of setting the tone, the spirit of even-Steven-ness right off the bat. Artie used to say, in moments of tenderness, when he was feeling affection for me, seeing me walk by, enter a room, something like that, he would say in soft tones, "You're so . . . *little!*"

And I would feel so pleased, so *flattered,* and bask in the stream of his warmth, feeling it was his way of saying that he loved me.

It took years to catch on that this was the same sentiment he felt toward puppies, kittens, and small children—all creatures it would never cross his mind to consider as equals.

The new guy had a boyish look, although I don't think he

was younger than I (though he might have been). I think he looked that way because he was small boned and slim, and his brown hair, though it did have some gray running through it, was on the curly side and tended to be unruly. He wore enormous horn-rimmed specs, behind which his face almost disappeared. And though I had met him at my even-Steven couple's house, I didn't believe him to be gay, himself. He had become acquainted with them when they had acquired some things at his gallery in New York, which was where he was, most of the time, coming to London only on occasion, as well as other European ports-of-call, to sell and/or buy, or whatever it is you do in the art-dealing business.

He had an engaging manner, this man did, bouncy and bright spirited. And he had a marvelous way of listening, almost like a bird dog on point, making it seem like part of the conversation. At a dinner table or over cocktails, with everybody chattering, you'd hardly realize he hadn't said anything at all.

He was most pleasant to be around, so that, after I had run into him two or three times, when he asked if I would like to go to an art exhibition with him, I was pleased to do so.

We had a good time, too, not because of the pictures we saw, they were rather absurd, I thought, immense things, eight feet by maybe twelve, and looked as if somebody had taken buckets of random colors and flung them, in any old order, at the canvases. "What in God's name are those things meant to be," I muttered, speaking rhetorically, not expecting an answer.

But my friend answered, anyway, and turned the occasion into a game. He tucked an arm through mine, snuggled in close, and whispered, pointing. "That's three men jumping off a cliff, eating cabbage . . ."

And again (pointing) ". . . an elephant sleeping in a corn bin in the rain . . ."

He had a bent toward game-playing, I was to discover, whether it be the spur-of-the-moment things, as at the art exhibition, or card games, any old variety. He liked board games, too, or it could just be walking down the street and seeing who could guess the right number of cracks in the sidewalk to the corner.

It made for some light and companionable interludes when he came to town. A nice change from the spitting and spewing Artie and I had reduced our relationship to. I certainly wasn't thinking of him as a possible lover, nothing like that—hadn't I (with my advancing years) said good-by to all that?

Besides, my loves had never started out in this calm, easy-going fashion. They had, one and all, always begun with a huge bang (in more ways than one), and worked their way backward to calm. (When they were over.) I didn't know any other system.

Besides, too many other interesting things were happening in London Town to be thinking much about a fellow I might have seen a couple of times, but who now was out of sight and far away. Like John (Huston) coming to town . . .

# Eight

When I was a kid, contrary to the way things are today, I looked up to older people. Everybody around me was older than I was, and therefore in a position to run my life—tell me what I could or could not do, say or not say. They were my teachers and I listened to them. It didn't occur to me not to. Or that they might not know what they were talking about.

Respect. That's what I had for older people. Even admiration.

When I got to Hollywood, the chief filmmakers at the time were all plenty older, too. And most assuredly in the position to tell me what to do or not do. And I listened to them, too. Boy, did I ever listen to them! I even sought their company, when I could, finding their talk so much more interesting than that of my peers. Wittier (I thought). More profound (I thought). They had *lived.* They had learned a thing or two (I thought).

Actually I was often a bit jealous of those who had known each other for a lengthy period of time, and who had memories of long ago to share. They seemed to have such a special way of looking at each other when they hadn't met for a long spell. Their eyes would fill with some secret and private understanding and a lovely kind of warmth seemed to reach out and wrap itself around them.

When Charles Vidor (the then husband, he in his forties, me in my twenties) would sit around and schmooze with his older friends—whom he had known back in Budapest, a place I had never been—about things that had happened before I was even born, I would feel so left out, so envious of their apparent pleasure in remembering—in having things *to* remember that they got such enjoyment out of—that I longed to be there, myself, one day.

Which was why I was looking forward to seeing John again. If you didn't have memories to share with an ex-husband (or lover), who in the world *would* you have them with! Even *trying* to live together took a fair chunk from your life. A time when you'd gone all out with another person. Shared dreams, houses, beds, sunsets, books, animals and any number of . . . well, adventures. Things that would surely be most pleasurable to reminisce about.

(Of late I had begun to secretly feel that maybe I was kind of lucky, after all, that the Cindy myth *hadn't* worked out for me. Wasn't it plain more *fun,* this way, more interesting than if I'd been stuck with just one guy for an entire lifetime? More edifying than if I had had only one kind of living experience throughout all of my days?)

John and I had a veritable cornucopia of goodies we could look back on. For instance, that particular Academy Award night when John won not one but two Oscars. It had seemed so unreal when his name was called out, and off he'd gone, bounding up the aisle and onto the stage, and then there he was, holding up the golden statuette he'd been handed and saying he wished it were empty so he could drink to his producer. Then he was back beside me in the dark, holding his bright and shining Award with both hands, both of us as rigid as statues, ourselves.

And all at once John's name was called again. But before he leaped to his feet to rush stageward for the second time, he shoved the gold fellow he was holding into my lap.

So there I had been. In the dark. At the Pantages Theatre, in the heart of Hollywood, on Academy Award night, my peers all around me, sitting alone clutching an Oscar in my own hot little hands.

It was nice. Very, very nice.

There had been trips to Cuba, and sailing out into the Bay of Havana on Papa Hemingway's boat. Trips to Mexico. To racetracks when our own horses were running. Too many things to toss away and forget. You wouldn't want to, would you. It was all part of us, there to bring out and enjoy again; to reshare any time we felt so inclined.

John was staying at the Dorchester, so instead of going to some restaurant I went over to his suite to have a bite with him. It had been his suggestion, and when I saw him I understood why.

He had the sniffles. And when that happened, because of his lungs, he had to take it easy. John's lungs were not in the best of condition. Hadn't been, for some time.

A couple of years earlier I had visited John over in Ireland, in County Galway, where he had taken up residence (as well as citizenship). And even then it was plain to see (if one were looking) that time was taking its toll on him faster than it should.

When I first met John, in July of 1946, or thereabouts, he would, even then, develop a bit of a cough when he smoked and/or drank and partied too much. As would be his practice from time to time.

I confess I thought nothing of it, back then. I smoked, too, back then. Everybody I knew smoked back then—like chimneys—and thought nothing of it. It was sophisticated. It was chic. (Sometimes I would get a sore throat in those days, to be sure, but my doctor never once said, "It's because you smoke." The doctor, himself, smoked, the asshole, dropping ashes all over the place as he examined you, even offering you a cig if you weren't lit up, yourself. Needless to say he didn't live too many years longer.)

And with my ignorance still intact, I had arrived at John's County Galway place. Even though I soon saw how bad his cough had become, so deep and hacking that it doubled him over; saw how he struggled to pull air into his lungs and struggled to push it out again, I still hadn't put two and two together. I would sit right there, in the room with him, puffing along with the rest of the smokers present.

His cough hadn't kept him off his precious horses, however. (Not then, anyway.) Off they would go, the Galway Blazers (the local hunt club), several times during my stay, the people astride their mounts, the baying hounds leading the way over hill and dale and stone wall, John steady in their midst, after some poor little bastard of a fox. (Fortunately they never caught one while I was there.)

After one such outing, with all the participants (plus the trailer-after-ers, like me) sitting around John's great and handsome dining room table—with the light of fifty-odd candles all around the room (lit by somebody or other every blessed night) flickering across our faces, and everyone animatedly discussing the afternoon's romp—John had had one of his strangling cough fits.

After he'd got through it, and was able to speak again (if only barely), he turned to me. "Tell them, honey," he said with effort, "how it came about that I have this wretched cough."

I'd known exactly what he meant. He had had me tell this

story before. It couldn't have been a more perfect tale to relate to these Irish neighbors of his, whose very *raisons d'être* were The Hunt and The Jumping Horse you did it with.

So I proceeded to tell the bunch of them how, shortly after John and I were married, John, who hadn't been on a horse during all of World War Two, got himself an animal he'd never seen before in his life and entered a jumping contest down at the Will Rogers Polo Field. But the horse was quite wild (evidently not having jumped for the duration, either), and not only didn't care for the jumps, didn't even want to stay inside the field, and tried instead to take off into the parking lot, managing, somehow, to straddle the half fence that separated the two. So, of course, down went horsey, fence, man, and all.

But it was the man who came up spitting blood. A broken rib had scraped a lung.

No doubt about it. A horse escapade was a far more interesting reason for troubled lungs than smoking too many cigarettes. John surely *wanted* to believe it to be true. And maybe he actually did believe it. I know I did, then. I had never even heard of this thing called em-phy-sema.

But by the time I was visiting John at the Dorchester, word was out. Smoking was not the smart thing to do. And John, sitting across from me on the sofa in his hotel suite, was undeniable proof. He looked very tired. He looked pale. And when he turned on the telly, I understood why. The effort to speak to me, to hold a conversation with anyone for any length of time, was apparently too much for him. It was easier to sit quietly and silently and look at something on the boob tube.

As luck would have it, a flick of mine happened to be on. One that John obviously had never seen, called *Ladies in Retirement,* and absolutely perfect for London viewing since its setting was on the marshes of the Thames estuary, with me playing a cockney maid, yet. And furthermore it was directed by the husband-before-John, Charles (Vidor).

So that's how we spent the evening. One ex-husband and I

watching another ex-husband's movie. Just, I amused myself thinking on the way home, one of your typical Hollywood family gatherings. Too bad I couldn't tell Charles about it, but that was out of the question, since he was quite dead. Had been since I was still back in Spain, not even making it to sixty, his heart evidently unable to take the onslaught of nicotine he had kept blowing at it. John had made it past sixty, but he'd better watch out, it seemed to me.

Oh well, I thought, after I got out of there. Never mind. There'll be other times, other places.

But damn it all. I'd been very let down by the evening. It wasn't what I had hoped for at all. I had seen the movie, more than once. And I'd never expected ever to be *bored* around John. It's something *he* would never have put up with for two seconds—being bored. I hadn't even learned what he was up to, what he was doing in London, much less had a chance to delve into any remembrances of things past . . .

However, the evening was not a total loss.

As soon as I got back to my own pad, the minute I had climbed all the stairs, opened the door and walked into my flat, I headed straight for the cupboard where my cigarettes were kept. In I reached, took out the carton I had bought only the day before, and began ripping the contents therein to shreds.

Each and every pack.

Each and every cigarette.

It was time to stop the smoking nonsense. That was crystal-clear. And if I were ever tempted to pick up one of the filthy little things again, all I had to do was to remember this night at the Dorchester Hotel, in London, and visualize the hunched over, thin-cheeked, coughing fellow, sunk down in a corner of a low, brown couch, and then think back to the honey-voiced man who had bounded with such vigor and spirit up to the Pantages Theatre stage, in Hollywood.

As if to make up for this depressing evening with John, Sam Spiegel, movie producer nonpareil, came to town a short while later.

Did I have memories of Sam . . . not as husband or lover, but as dear friend whom I had known for as long as I had known John. The two of them had been partners when I came into the picture, and they had made a couple of movies together. I, too, had made one with Sam (my best, I expect, something called *The Prowler,* directed by Joe Losey), and we had remained friends through the years.

Sam used to be kind of a figure of fun, with his protruding belly and spindly legs and Polish accent (of course he spoke about a dozen or so languages, including Sanskrit, so the laugh was on us), but after his big successes with *On the Waterfront, The Bridge on the River Kwai, Lawrence of Arabia,* and all the prizes that came with them, including money, he had become a very solid citizen.

Maybe too solid, as it turned out.

These "older friends" get-togethers didn't seem to be going the way I had envisioned them, somehow. Because, God knows, I'd never expected to be bored around Sam Spiegel, either. I had always enjoyed Sam's company enormously. Besides his entertaining accent, he knew just about everything there was to know, and he was famous for his parties, whether for two or for a thousand. So when he said come to lunch, you bet I went.

But of all things, he had invited one other person—just one more—who turned out to be a Rothschild. One of those people with all that money. Just the three of us, that was it. Sam, me, and a Mr. Rothschild—in this round booth in the Connaught Hotel's elegant dining room. (Elegant enough for a Rothschild, even!)

But here was the thing.

Usually on such an occasion as this, Sam would have had one or two twenty-year-old blonde-brunette-redheads with breathtaking good looks to decorate his table. But for some reason that escapes me to this day, there was just little ol' me (and I do mean "old") filling in, sex-object-wise. I knew Sam's hearing was fading. That day I wondered if his sight was going, too.

If Mr. Rothschild was disappointed by the arrangement, he hid it very well. He, in fact, hid everything very well. Including his charm. But then, maybe it was just my own reaction. I've never been very taken with the extremely rich—those, that is, who have been left their loot, and never had to do anything to earn it. (Those who made it, themselves, ah, that's another thing altogether.) The inheritors never seemed to have learned—never had to, I suppose—to be very giving of themselves in social situations. At least this Mr. Rothschild certainly hadn't.

Though maybe I was simply becoming jaded, since Mr. Rothschild was already my *second* rich-rich person inside a month's time. I mean, you couldn't call J. Paul Getty exactly a piker in the rich-rich department. And I had been sitting just as near to him as I was to the Rothschild chap.

I hadn't had the slightest suspicion who Getty might be, though. How could you think some ancient, bent-over, wizened little guy with skin so tightly pulled back over his cheekbones that he looked like a death's head (from too many face-lifts was my guess) could be one of the wealthiest human beings on our planet.

We had been seated at a longish dinner table with eight or ten people along its sides, and this little man was in the place next to me. So minding my manners, I began to make some small talk until some subject or other was located to engage in with this stranger at my side. "Are you . . . British, or . . . ?" I began, wanting to know, first, if he even spoke English. (There was an assortment of nationalities around the table, conversing in various languages, so he could have been from anywhere.)

The man paused in the battle he was having with a piece of tandoori chicken (we were in an Indian restaurant), and without looking up he murmured, "No, I am American." With that said, the little man returned to his tussle with the fowl. And that was that. My conversation *in toto* with one J. Paul Getty. (I didn't even learn who he was until the dinner was over.)

The talk in the booth at the Connaught, that day, wasn't much more scintillating. Sam and his guest chatted on about gold prices. Which wasn't all that surprising, come to think of it. I mean, what the hell else *would* you talk about to a Rothschild. Whether gold prices would go up or not, obviously.

You've got to be pretty dumb, too, not to listen to a conversation like that. But I was. Just that dumb. I let my mind wander off as the two men talked, wondering if it was time to move on. That maybe London had served its purpose at this point. The *purpose,* in coming here, having been to break the strong thread that bound Artie and me together. To disentangle myself so that I could go on to something else. So that I could, at least, *think* clearly enough to be *able* to think of something else. Some *thing* else. And just what that would be, and where, was not yet clear.

Though it did cross my mind, as I sat there between the two men discussing financial matters, that there were times when I sorely missed Artie's lively, in-depth, passionate conversations about some new discovery, a book he had come across . . .

I should have been listening to Sam and that Rothschild person that day, though, with as much attention as I had once paid to Artie. Because gold prices did go up soon after. Sky-high.

When I got home a fat letter was waiting in the mailbox from the art dealer . . .

# *Nine*

The art dealer. Tom, I'll call him. He had been sending postcards from time to time, with chirpy little notes. Greetings from Hamburg, or Amsterdam, and once, San Francisco. He traveled a lot, evidently, in search of titillating—and salable, no doubt—objets d'art.

But this was the first full-fledged letter, written in longhand, too, sprawling across the page in a racing-along manner, as if his thoughts were ahead of his pen.

He wrote that it was raining "cats and dogs" in New York. (He was always very big on weather.) That he had been to see *Hair* and something called *Oh, Calcutta!* Taking off your clothes, he wrote, was the big thing in the New York theater at the moment. A little behind the times, weren't they? After all, he wrote, the art world had been doing nudity for centuries. He also informed me he wouldn't be getting back to London for another whole month.

But then he added something that rather surprised me. He wrote that it wouldn't be all that bad, not seeing me for a month, as I had begun to appear in his dreams. And what did I think of that?

It was far more personal than anything that had come before, was what I thought of that, and I wondered what it meant. Was it an opening of some kind? Was he testing the waters from afar to find out whether it was safe to jump in or not?

Oh God. He wasn't going to start rocking the boat, was he? I hoped not, since I so liked things exactly the way they were.

Friendship. We had a once-in-a-while-coming-to-town kind, and that's all in the world I wanted. A platonic, even-Steven friendship, absolutely nothing more.

And maybe, just maybe, come to think of it, not even that.

I had been thinking, again (well, I did a lot of that), and kind of deciding that maybe a relationship, I mean, *any* kind of relationship with a male of the species, wasn't a good idea, after all. A relationship with a man would take time and energy and require a great deal of attention on occasion. I wasn't at all sure whether or not I wanted to use what I had left of those things—particularly after flinging them around with such abandon during the Artie years—on another relationship, no matter *what* form or shape it might take.

And anyway, wouldn't it be nothing more than a repeat of some kind? Because, surely, I had already *done* whatever it was this relationship would turn out to be, had I not? Really, truly done them *all*?

So it seemed to me that if I had good sense (which was questionable, of course), it would behoove me to try something I had never *done before,* instead of spinning and spinning around on the same damn wheel like some idiot hamster for the rest of my days. There ought to be *some* other direction I could take in this second half of my life, this other-side-of-the-hill part.

What about going all out for a *thing,* for instance, instead of for a person? Some *thing* I had the hots for, say. Use my energies in *that* direction, for a change.

My heart began to doodle around in there at the thought. Because lately I had become aware of just how many *things* I had started throughout my life, with great gusto, too, and never finished. Hadn't really ever hung in there all the way through with a single damn one of them. I had never become that concert pianist I'd been so determined to be when I was eight and nine and ten years old. My dancing was half-assed, so was my French, even after I'd gone so far as to make a bloody *film* in the language. (And in Spanish the subjunctive eludes me to this day, dammit.) Nor did I ever play center (or any other) court at Wimbledon.

And my acting career. Poor thing. It just fizzled away, as things are apt to do if you don't give them sufficient tender, loving care.

But now here I was, once again, on my own. And I *knew* history, and therefore was *not* doomed to relive it. So why didn't I, this go-round, just use the time to go ahead and, well, *do* it. Buckle down and fine-tune my focus. Abandon my grasshopper ways, and hang on to one thing all the way through.

*Before it was too late.*

All at once I flopped down into a chair and began to laugh. It had just crossed my mind that this glorious space I had, this valuable time in which to finally get off my ass and do something, to get it together just once, *just once,* before I bowed out, had been given me by the man himself, Artie baby.

God! I should be thanking the fellow for the precious gift he had presented me with, duty-free, too, not a string attached, instead of being half-pissed off at the guy most of the time, since it was he who had guided me to this spectacular spot and then so graciously cleared out and left me to my own resources.

And I would. I would certainly do just that. Thank him profusely the next time I saw him!

But in the meantime what, exactly, was this great *thing* I was going to launch myself into? What was it that I would like to spend these precious, dwindling-down years engaged in doing?

If some miracle occurred, and the acting career dropped into place again, I wouldn't mind. I certainly enjoyed acting when I got around to it. I knew how. And the money was nice. It was just that acting, too, would be a repeat. A comfortable old friend.

But was *comfort* what I wanted, I wondered. But if not, what was it I *did* want? Ah, there was the rub . . .

I wasn't sure if I rightly knew what I wanted, actually. Something . . . challenging, that was for certain. Something that was, perhaps, a little *beyond* me, I decided. Something I would have to *reach* for, stretch to get. So that I'd never be quite sure whether I was ever going to make it or not. Something that would keep me on my toes . . .

My, my, what a cascade of thought Tom's letter had brought on!

Well, why not, I told myself. What was wrong with just going ahead right this very minute and trying to figure out what to do with the rest of my life. It was hardly as if I were pushing the idea along too swiftly, for crissake. In fact I could hardly postpone the figuring out any too much longer, if the truth be faced.

Only, I didn't even know if I was capable of doing such a thing, never having had a hell of a lot of practice, to speak of, before. But I could at least try, could I not? Give it a whirl?

And there actually *was* a little something that interested me. A little *thing* that might have possibilities, if I hung in there with it long enough. I hadn't mentioned it to too many people, though. Once I had said something, in passing, to this friend.

"You're . . . *writing*?" she had said back to me in this profoundly bored way. "Yeah, well, isn't that nice." Then she'd yawned, and changed the subject.

Once upon a time Artie had given me a little traveling Olivetti typewriter that he wasn't using anymore. (He had bought a much bigger and grander one.) So I got myself a do-it-yourself typing book and started fiddling around. Before long I was able in a half-assed fashion (my usual style!) to make my way around the Olivetti keyboard, improving considerably when I discovered how much easier it was to write letters on a machine. (I wrote considerable numbers of letters in those days, having moved around so much I'd left trails of connections all over the place.)

And then one day a story idea jumped into my head. And I thought, hey, why don't you see if you can turn this into something. And so I'd begun sitting down to my little machine every day, every single day, until doing so became an integral part of my daily routine.

Nor had I left it behind when I came to London. The keyboard had Spanish letters on it, and for that reason I was sentimentally attached. And here in London, too, I had continued to sit down to it every day, as I had in Connecticut. So that by now, the typewriter had pretty much turned into my anchor-of-the-moment.

As a matter of fact, I've always found it rather a good idea, when your life is upended, to have something to do every day. Something to rise and shine for on a daily basis. Something you do as regularly and conscientiously as brushing your teeth. That way you'll be thinking of *it* when you wake up instead of some stupid bullshit that's over and done with and that you can't possibly do anything about anymore, even if you wanted to.

So after receiving Tom's letter, and after thinking over its contents, I proceeded to sit down to my trusty machine and write a small answer back to him.

First I simmered down and decided I was making far too much of the guy mentioning some silly little dream of his. That he'd only meant to be amusing and that any sexual inference was probably the furthest thing from his mind.

*Really,* thought I to myself with a soupçon of disgust, is it never going to sink into your dimwitted brain that you are no longer the pulchritudinous young nymph you once upon a time *were* that men fell all over themselves for, that you're not anywhere *near* it, anymore!

You are an *old broad,* now, sweetheart, and nobody's panting on your doorstep. Nor is anybody likely to do so, and you ought to be counting your blessings that this is so instead of falling back into some outdated, antediluvian response of yours every time some member of the other sex says hello.

God. The man was simply trying to be amusing, to be friendly, and I ought to be pleased as punch. I couldn't do without friends! I needed friends. Everybody needed friends. It was silly to come all the way to London and not make some friends, whatever their sex might be.

So I wrote and told Tom how super terrific his timing was.

That I was about to go to work on a TV thing, but that I would be finished with it before he arrived.

It was true, too. My agents had called up about another acting job. An aunt, again. I believe it was a pilot for a TV sitcom, though I don't know for whom or what. I never saw it anywhere. I enjoyed doing it, though. I played somebody dowdy, who was then transformed à la the ugly duckling by smashing clothes and an up-to-date hairdo into a snazzy, with-it woman. It was the old story, done in "auntie" terms this time. I even got to perform a sprightly dance, and you can't ask for much more than that, can you—when you're an old broad!

I did finish shooting, too, several days before Tom arrived. But the very morning of the day he was arriving, I got a call about another acting job. Only this one was about doing a play. News that promptly caused my nerve-ends to sputter like frayed wire.

A . . . *play*? On the *stage*? Right here in London? In front of a lot of British people used to seeing all those fab *British* actors act? I started having opening-night jitters right there on the phone listening to the agent at the other end tell me about it.

I could think of little else from then on, and it wasn't the warmest greeting in the world that I gave Tom, who had come straight from the airport to my flat. Oh I did manage to say, "Welcome! It's good to see you again! How was the trip?" A few noises like that, though my heart wasn't in it. I even restrained myself until we were walking along the Chelsea Embankment on our way to an Italian restaurant we'd been to before, a family affair kind in one of the little side streets off King's Road, with red-checked tablecloths, pasta al dente, and good Chianti in fat, straw-encased bottles.

Finally I couldn't keep my news to myself any longer. I did start out in a positive way, though. "You know something?" I told Tom gaily. "It looks as if you are going to turn out to be a good-luck charm for me!"

He then tucked his arm through mine and snuggled in close, as he often did. It was practically his trademark, this gesture of his. And not a bad one. It was nice, it was warm. "Of course I'm your good-luck charm!'' he chuckled. "I'm glad you found it out so soon!''

I told him of the call about the play.

His response was not what I expected. He stopped smiling. "Does that mean,'' he said worriedly, "you can't go to Paris with me on Thursday?''

*"Paris!"* I was nonplussed. What the hell did Paris have to do with what I was telling the man!

"Don't you like Paris?'' He looked distraught.

"Of course I like Paris!'' I said quite crossly, "I *lived* there once for a couple of years!''

"Did you now!'' He gazed at me as if astounded. "My goodness, I have absolutely got to learn *everything* about you! Tell me more!'' And he snuggled in even closer.

This man jumped from subject to subject like some demented kangeroo. I gave up on my play news. He evidently couldn't care less about my play news. "What,'' I asked him instead, "are you going to Paris for, pray?''

"To see a couple of painters,'' he told me. "I thought you might enjoy doing that, their work is most interesting.''

"Ah . . .'' Yes, that's what art dealers would do, wasn't it. Go see painters. "Yes, well, that would be fun, but I couldn't possibly . . .''

"It's only for the day.''

"Oh! The *day!*'' That was different. I was thinking he had something more elaborate in mind.

I did love my Paris years. Classes at the Sorbonne. Trying to absorb all things French, shooting the film (the one in the local language called *'C'est Arrivé à Paris)* all over the city. Falling in love (or thinking I had)—and what better place to make a run at it. It would be lovely, indeed, to see one of my hometowns again, if only for a day.

"Ah well, I could do that, I don't have to see the play people until next week . . .'' The invitation really was irresistible.

I was glad it was. The day turned out to be one that I would never forget.

We wound up in a part of the city I had never seen before.

Everything old and crumbly, something out of another era. I swear you half-expected van Gogh to come tearing along, catch sight of Gauguin having his *coup de vin* at the corner café before toddling off to the South Seas.

Place Pigalle was the last thing I saw that was in the least familiar. After going around it, the cab twisted and turned through all manner of crooked little streets, the driver himself getting lost every so often and having to back up and turn around and start over.

We finally did find both painters, in their separate ateliers, surrounded by stacks of canvases and painting paraphernalia. Neither of them spoke a word of English and none of us was all that great in French (mine having thinned out into the Spanish that followed it), but that was the language we tried to reach each other in. It was a good thing we all had hands and fingers to gesture and point.

One of the artists was so pale his skin had a green tone, with light red hair to top it, as well as pale blue eyes. He was the most emaciated person I've ever seen outside a concentration camp victim. He was from Reykjavik (I think), at least Iceland was the direction he pointed. And he seemed to be following in Léger's footsteps where work was concerned; his pictures were all of pipes and factories and assembly lines.

The other fellow was like a negative of the first. He had dark skin, dark hair, and dark eyes. Tunisian (I think). And he painted feet. Nothing but feet. Feet walking, on sand, on pavement, on grass. Feet coming out of the womb, diving into water, in bed making love. Feet at war, cut and bleeding. Feet dead and feet dancing. He had painted everything feet can do. It was quite astonishing how much this painter could express with just feet.

They both had jugs of wine waiting for us. The pale one popcorn and nuts in shells to go with it. The dark one some kind of paté I had the feeling he had made himself. It was mashed sesame seeds, I believe, with a pita-type bread to spread it on. It was delicious.

Tom and I nibbled and drank our way through both places,

looking at paintings, Tom picking out the ones he wanted shipped. And finally, very unhungry, we made our way back to the airport, having visited a city famous for its cuisine, not having eaten a single proper meal. There's such a sense of abandonment, too, when you can get on and off a plane without any luggage.

It was altogether a splendid day.

And the next night we had dinner with our mutual friends, the gay couple. The two of us regaled those present with anecdotes of our trip the day before, laughing, remembering things. Exactly like every other couple does the world over.

I should have realized how it must have appeared when one of the guys whispered so excitedly as we were leaving, "Oh, I just *knew* you two would take to each other!"

But I wasn't paying that much attention. I had other fish to fry. Monday I was going to see the play people. And by that time, Tom had left town . . .

# *Ten*

As it turned out, I hadn't been paying sufficient attention, either, to the fact that the play people were having me meet them at a theater. See, I thought these people merely wanted to look me over. I thought that and that alone was the purpose of the meeting. Which I understood. People do change as they add on years, some becoming the size of the Goodyear blimp, others turning into prunes.

But these people wanted more than a look. They had hardly said how do you do before handing me some pages of a script and indicating I should step up on the stage and read it for them.

I was pitifully ignorant about this sort of thing. In the beginning I had simply walked into people's offices and they signed me on. That's what Cecil B. did. That's what Harry Cohn did. And the few auditions I *had* done were so stunningly high class that I'd never even classified them as that.

Like the time I ran into George Axelrod at a party in New York. At the time George was the hottest playwright on Broadway, having just had several hits, including *The Seven Year Itch.*

George looked me over. (When you've been in the movies that's what people do a lot, they look you over.) He cocked his head. He said, "Hey, you know something? I am going to *discover you!"*

Well, now, *that* certainly perked things up at a rather dull party. I did so love being discovered, hoping always that *this* time might be the big push to the top.

"They've never done right by you out there in Hollywood," George went on, "you've never had the right part or the right presentation. I'm going to change all that. I'm going to do it right. How would you like to be in a show of mine?"

I am not altogether crazy. I said yes as fast as was humanly possible before George could change his mind.

I got pretty excited. I said wow, I said whatever it is, I'm yours, I'm yours!

"First," he continued, taking right over, "I'm going to change your hair. Bright red, I think, and plenty of it, down to the shoulders."

"Absolutely!" I cried. "Anything you say, George dear!"

Jule Styne joined us. (The composer of *Gentlemen Prefer Blondes, Gypsy,* and later, *Funny Girl.)* It turned out that he and George were in this thing together, plotting a show around the old Rodgers and Hart songs. (Like "Bewitched," "My Funny Valentine," "Where or When," and a few dozen other such mellow oldies.) "How," Jule said to me, "is your singing voice?"

My heart fell to the bottom of the well. My Broadway debut was over before it began. "I d-don't have a . . . a *trained* voice," I told him sadly, "but I do stay in key." You have to be *ready* when you get discovered (or rediscovered). I knew that, and I was failing.

"But we don't want a trained singing voice," I thought George said.

And when I got over my shock I found out that's exactly what he did say, amazing as it was. Rex Harrison had, a few years earlier, been a smash hit as an actor-who-sang-spoke-the-words of the songs in *My Fair Lady,* and that's what George and Jule had in mind for me to do.

Except there was one teeny-tiny obstacle, they said. Richard Rodgers, himself. (The only living member of the famous songwriting team.) It seemed that Mr. Rodgers liked formally *trained* voices to sing his songs, and evidently wasn't all that thrilled with George-and-Jule's idea of using some actress to perform his (and Hart's) lovely compositions whose singing voice, even if she did stay in key, couldn't come anywhere near, in the furthest stretch of imagination, a bel canto.

"What we'll have to do," Jule said brightly, "is *show* him, Evelyn!"

Ah . . . right. That was the ticket! We would show Dick Rodgers, we would, what a nonsinger could do with his songs!

And so Jule proceeded to work with me. And I can tell you it was pretty exciting. Jule Styne, himself, the great composer, working with me on a Rodgers-and-Hart song, showing me phrasing and tempo and style. And when he thought I was ready, off we went to do it for Mr. Rodgers.

The scene was exactly the way we've all seen it done those infinite numbers of times. In the Judy and Mickey films. With Alice and Don and Ruby and Dick. The darkened theater. The dim stage with only the one harsh work light. An upright piano to one side. And one small cane chair in the center, there to lean on should I begin to tremble too much.

But in this case the only person out in the audience was one Richard Rodgers, the super composer, in person. All alone.

An audience of one. There to listen to me, Evelyn Keyes, non-trained-type singer, sing his song.

Jule was at the upright. He was accompanying me. I mean, you can't be more stylish than that for an audition, can you? And Jule had said there was no need to be nervous, you do the song very well, he'd said, Dick will be pleased.

So now Jule gave me a sweet smile and a kind of encouraging wink, and off we went. "My . . . fun . . . ny Val . . . entine . . ."

Sometimes I hung onto the back of the chair, sometimes I circled it. I even sat down on it. I remembered everything Jule told me to do. And to tell you the truth, it felt pretty good. I thought I had done remarkably well when it was over. I, in fact, was rather pleased with myself.

I went home elated. Broadway was mine! No doubt about that. Move over, Ethel, move over, Mary, here comes . . . Evelyn!

But then.

Several days passed, and no word. Then a few more. Until it dawned on me I wasn't *going* to hear from them. Not at all. And I didn't, either. And that wasn't all. They even junked the whole project and went on to other things.

It *was* a bit unnerving, I do confess. I mean, I honestly hadn't thought I was *that* bad!

So now, here I was, umpteen years later, being asked to get up there again and demonstrate my wares. Be *judged* again. (Because that's what it is, every damn time—Judgment Day.) Only this time there were several more down there in the darkened theater. A couple of producers, a director, other odds and ends.

I had the most terrible urge to say, "Up yours, people. Take your play and shove it. Who needs this shit!"

But I didn't do that. Instead, a kind of cockiness suddenly swept over me. A burst of pride, as it were. I'd show *them,* dammit, that's what I'd do! Show them what a pro I was! I'd read their bloody scene *ice* cold, and I'd do it . . . do it better than . . . than *anybody*! Who were *they,* after all, these would-be entrepreneurs, next to that renowned composer of ballads, Richard Rodgers!

I would soon learn who they were. People in a position to do to me exactly what the composer of renown had done to me, that's who they were. My spurt of arrogance had got me nowhere. History, as it is wont to do, simply repeated itself— this time with manners. Being British, they minded theirs, and did drop me a note saying, in essence, thanks but no thanks.

I knew rejection, however, when I saw/heard/read it, manners or no manners. (As Mike used to say to whomever he was turning down, "Do you want a short no or a long one?") Although the experience may not have got me on the London stage, it did help remind me of a few home truths—such as the fact that rejection, in whatever form, *is* the chronic condition of show biz. The minute you put your foot inside the door, you've set yourself up for it as neatly as one of those tenpins down at the bottom of the bowling alley, waiting to be whacked at on almost a daily basis. Somebody else is *always* getting that part you covet. Nor does gaining stardom change a thing. Bette Davis, Katharine Hepburn, Tallulah Bankhead, Paulette Goddard, Susan Hayward, all did *not* get to play Scarlett O'Hara. Nor did Gary Cooper get to play Rhett Butler. (Gary Cooper!)

Was this, then, I asked myself, the kind of *tsimmes* I wanted to let myself in for, again? Did I really want to run around to perfect strangers saying please, oh *please* put me in your play (film, show)? Wouldn't I be *perfect* for the part? Just watch me act (dance, sing)! Am I not wonderful?

No . . . ? Ah . . . well . . . then next time, perhaps . . .

Isn't it one thing to do that sort of stuff when you're a kid? Another when you're *not* a kid and everybody's busily reminding you you're not?

For instance, when I had first arrived at the theater that day and been introduced all around, one of the women—one of the "judges"—said to me with her swanky accent, "Such a delight to meet you, Miss Keyes, I've been enjoying your films since I was a little girl."

Zap! Get into your proper time slot, you old movie star, you!

The fact was, though, after I got the note, I stewed for quite a while. Paced the floor. Stayed awake all hours trying to locate exactly what it was that was troubling me. Because something was . . .

Of course the action back there at the theater, 1 finally told myself, wasn't exclusively *kid* stuff. It was anybody-who-wanted-to-*do*-it stuff . . .

But that was the thing. You had to *want* to do it. Not as a lark, but with all your heart and soul. And nothing else would do. That was the way it had to be if you were to handle all the constant repudiation, the fierce competition. The way you had to feel about it in order to be good enough *to be successful at it.*

And that was the thing that was making me uneasy. When the note had come turning me down, I didn't seem to care all that much, one way or the other. Oh, a *little.* Rejection is never a bundle of laughs. But this one wasn't any big deal at all. I amused myself thinking I had been rejected, in my time, by the very best; so maybe that was the reason this one was painless!

But something was up. Something different. It felt as if some kind of switch-over had come to pass. That the center of me had moved on.

Holding that thought, my mind began to do a pan the way a thoughtful camera does. It moved from me up to the stage, being watched by some strangers down there in the dark. Then it eased on over to look in on my mornings . . . at me, getting up at the crack of dawn . . . exercising . . . cooking rolled oats . . . eating a bowl of them, drinking a nice hot cup of English tea, the camera then following me as I cross the room and take my place in front of my writing machine . . .

I had even gotten over being afraid of the empty page. Finally got it through my head that no one was reading over my shoulder as I typed along. That nobody could *ever* read *anything* I put down on my pages, *if I didn't want them to.* I could tear my pages up and throw them away, *if I wanted to.* I was in charge. Nobody else. Just me.

It was a heady feeling.

Had I ever been in charge of me before? I wasn't at all sure I ever had. I may have *thought* I'd been, but I wasn't at all certain of that, anymore, there in London. Hadn't I always been looking somewhere else for my fulfillment—whatever that might have been at the moment? Looking to some*one,* to give me *the* part? To a man to fill the prince role, and help create the happy ending? Hadn't I always thought the perfect place to *live* would maybe do the trick? Wasn't I here in London, thinking that very same thing, *again* . . . ?

In the middle of one of my mulling-over-life sessions— something I was doing on an almost daily basis of late—along came another fat letter from Tom. This one was ten pages long, written longhand on legal-size paper, words scrawled pell-mell across the sheets without periods or commas or paragraphs. You could almost see him bent over, scribbling feverishly, afraid to lift the pencil (yes, pencil) from the paper for fear of losing the thread of his thought.

What he was writing about was our day trip to Paris. Except I hardly recognized it. His version was pure *Rashomon,* the way it was in the Japanese movie in which each character tells the story from his/her point of view.

It had been one terrific day, no doubt about that. I had loved every minute of it from start to finish. From the French stewardesses on the plane to the earthy cab drivers and rides through the streets of Paris, all of it made doubly memorable by the glimpses into the two artists' lives.

But Tom had seen and heard and felt, according to his letter, more than I had. Much more than I had. For him, he wrote, it was the day something called "us" had been born. The day he and I, Tom and Evelyn, ceased to be separate entities and had become a couple. A twosome. A pair.

I was completely taken aback. God knows I'd been an "us" enough times to know when it happened. I'd always done my share to make sure it *did* happen.

But this time I hadn't done anything but go along to Paris with the man for the fun of seeing Paris again. But Tom wrote of shared tastes, of laughter-at-the-same-things, of exchanges of meaningful glances and understandings. His assumption that I felt the same way was the most alarming thing of all.

What in the world had I done to cause the man to respond this way? One of Artie's recent complaints had been how charming I could be to perfect strangers, to people I *didn't* live with, and then drop it all when we were home alone. His contention was that it should be the other way around. And then I'd say that goes both ways, and why didn't he practice what he preached, and off we'd go on another of our snapping-and-spitting matches. Wasn't this an example of what Artie had meant? I certainly *had* been on my good behavior in Paris. After all, I was the man's guest, and he had been showing this "girlie" a very good time.

Tom wrote of the future. Of how we were going to have to find a way to be together. I suppose, I told myself, I should be pleased that someone would still feel this way about me. Maybe even flattered. How many more times, *if at all,* would something like this come my way again? I had been spoiled in these matters, I knew that, nature having dealt me not too bad a hand.

But things were bound to begin slipping—oh for crissake, they *were* slipping—couldn't Tom see that? See I was way past the girl/boy monkeying around business? And if he couldn't, there were certainly plenty of people around to give him a nudge. I didn't have too many secrets, after all, most everything had been in print at some time or other, including birthdates.

And there was this other little thing that had come along, too, something I had to give some thought to. Something brand new. (This was my life's one consistency, that something new would come into it sooner or later.)

My periods had begun to slow down to every other month. The doctor I consulted to find out why set me straight pronto. It was the beginning, I was told, of menopause.

Well. Here was a milestone, if there ever was one. Middle

age was upon me in no uncertain terms. I couldn't pretend otherwise, anymore, even if I wanted to. The choice of having children, too, was finally out of my hands.

It sure as hell *was* pause-for-thought time. I didn't rightly know whether to be relieved that I didn't have to worry about pregnancy anymore, or to be sorry . . .

Another type of sorting out was going to have to be done. Another bout of thinking. These things, apparently, were never going to stop showing up as you went your way, these signposts along the road that brought you up short and set you to mulling again.

What, I wondered, would a man's reaction be if he knew? I was thinking of Tom, of course. Hey Tom, guess what, my menses are pausing, what do you think of that?

Is that what I would do, nitwit that I am? Tell the man?

God, the man writes me a nice letter, and already I am deciding to share my bodily functions with him!

What the hell did my pausing menses have to do with Tom, the art dealer! Or anybody else, for that matter, besides me. I sure wouldn't tell Artie, I knew that. I wouldn't want to hear what *that* man might have to say about it. It was *my* business, and mine alone, and that's all there was to it, no big deal. Look at the positive side of it all, I told myself. You won't have to cart all those goddamn boxes of Tampax around with you anymore.

That image, combined with a memory of Artie, made me laugh.

When I had left Paris and gone off with Artie down to Spain, I was so afraid that I wouldn't be able to find tampons to my liking in the obscure little Spanish village we were headed for that I took several months' supply along with me, filling up all the odd spaces in the car with them. And Artie had teased me about it for quite a while after.

"You expected to stay for a long time, did you?" He would say, amused.

"Oh yes," I would answer smugly, "I knew I was going to stay forever and ever."

He liked that, I think. Then. Now I wasn't sure if he'd be all that pleased to be reminded of the passage of time.

Tom's letters kept flowing in, so full of things he wanted us to do, places to visit, that they read like travelogues: a park in Berlin, a restaurant in Geneva, a river in Florence, the Opera House in Vienna. He was too late on the last one, I had already been there. With Artie, of course. A fantastic evening it was, too. What better place to catch *The Marriage of Figaro* than the place it originated?

I had come out imitating the soprano as we walked across the parking area to our car, singing way up there, as high as I could, making up the tune as I went along, not altogether remembering how the music of the opera actually went. And Artie joined in, an octave lower, naturally, not knowing where I was going (since I didn't), but in perfect harmony, and staying there, no matter where I went. The man wasn't a jazz musician for nothing.

I had had some good times with Artie. Delicious times. Memorable times I would never forget. That made me feel good just to remember . . .

But that was *then,* wasn't it, it wasn't *now,* I reminded myself. So remember the choice moments if you must, and get on with your life, I said to me. (I also reminded myself not to forget the lousy times with him, too, just to keep things in balance.)

So what was I going to do about Tom and his letters? I wasn't sure I wanted him to get lost altogether. It didn't look as if the two-by-two Noah's Ark arrangement for gatherings was going to fall out of vogue anytime soon.

But would he settle for plain friendship? The even-Steven kind? Tom was no spring chicken, either, for crissake. Why was he rocking the boat, making those "us" noises? Why couldn't he just go his way and I go mine? He had his art dealing, and I had—would have—my thing (whatever it turned out to be). I certainly wasn't *ever* going to drop everything and string off with some man; I had learned my lesson(s) in *that* department.

Though I had to admit that the places he wrote about did

sound awfully intriguing. And maybe with Tom it wouldn't be *quite* like spinning around on the same old wheel. Wouldn't be *exactly* a repeat performance, because, unlike all the others, this man wasn't in show-biz . . .

It was a startling thought when it dawned on me that I had never been out of my own enclave. That every man I'd ever gotten tied up with—most of my women friends, too, for that matter—had been a part of my own business.

How limited could I be? Wasn't it time I broadened my horizons a bit, for heaven's sake? Spread my wings, learned another thing or two in this glorious big world of ours while I was still in it?

Ah . . . there I went again. Giving myself the same old spiel I always did every time I was thinking of soaring (again) into the wild blue yonder.

Boy. It really boggled the mind how good I had always been at giving myself such excellent reasons for doing whatever it was I was going to do in any event . . .

Well, sweetheart, I said to me, I would advise you to get it together this time around, and remember just *which side of the hill you are on.* You no longer have the *time* for side excursions, baby, unless you want to wind up once again, even older, *farther* on up the road, still without your own focus, because when you and the man (which*ever* one) you had been living with separated, he had departed and taken his life with him, and rightly so, *since it had been his all the while.* You had merely joined him for a spell and lived his life with him. And that would be what you would do again, if you didn't get your act together. Now. *Now!*

Yes. I had to stop the nonsense. It was truly now or never. No use paying attention to people telling me how young I looked. Cary Grant said it. When people started telling him how young he looked, he knew he was getting older.

It simply had to be played my way this time. Or I'd better withdraw from the game . . .

# *Eleven*

After all my stewing and wondering what in the world should I do and say to Tom when he came to town, it turned out I didn't have to do or say anything I hadn't done (or said) the last time he came to town, since we followed the same routine we had gone through on his previous visit.

Upon arrival he rushed from the airport straight to my place. Picked me up and off we went to the same Italian trattoria, and once there, damned if we didn't talk about the same things we had before. Shows he saw in New York. The weather (naturally). How traveling takes a lot out of you, and blah blah blah. We even ordered the same things. Lasagne al forno, salad, and the straw-encased Chianti.

Later, with a peck on the cheek, he dropped me off and went on to wherever he was staying, to collapse (he said) and recoup after his tedious journey. It was as if the letters had never been written.

I was so terribly relieved. I'd expected a very difficult hour or so (maybe more) with him, going through one of those little life-drama scenes; explaining, cajoling, philosophizing, you know the kind of thing. How *he* felt, how *I* felt, and all that falderal trying to work toward some comfortable arrangement (and seldom managing). I thought I had escaped, and that maybe everything would remain gracefully status quo. That he had gotten the message from me without any words.

But then. *Then,* the phone rang shortly after I got upstairs. Tom.

We chatted for a while, warmly, laughing at this and that,

enjoying. Until . . . Tom began to sound like his letters. Saying it was so good to be here. To be with me. That he missed me. That it was going to be so wonderful to be doing things together again . . .

By the time we hung up, I was uneasy again. Why, I wondered, hadn't he said these things at dinner? When he was with me? I was glad, of course, that he *hadn't*. Except I had the feeling I was missing a clue, somewhere. Had I, thinking back, detected a nervousness I didn't understand the reason for?

Unless . . . *Could he be gay?* And I hadn't caught it? Oh, but wouldn't it be *perfect* if he were! We could have our cake and eat it, too. We did have a good time together. It would solve absolutely everything if he were.

Should I tell him how I felt about it, I wondered. Or, was he one of those who thought he was "passing," and would hate knowing his cover was blown?

Ah, why don't you just relax, I told myself, and stop trying to figure everything out ahead of time. Just let it play itself out, and see.

I would simply stick to my usual routine, exercising, eating my oats, having a go at my typewriter, and wait and see.

He'd said also that he had to pop over to Brussels in the morning, but would be back by evening, and could I possibly meet him at our friends' house, as we were expected for dinner. That since he'd probably be running late, he would go straight there from the airport, if that was all right with me.

I had told him I would be happy to do that, and I was. I looked forward to the evening, too, their house was still one of my favorite places to go.

Until that night, that is . . .

It was a somewhat bigger gathering than usual, maybe twenty people, none of whom I knew, with dinner served buffet-style on the dining room table.

Everybody was quite young, I noticed. I recognized Laurence Harvey in a corner, but that was about it. A noisy bunch, too, the decibel level in the upper range of the scale. Frightfully un-British, I thought, but what did I know.

Tom, too, was so keyed-up he seemed to be spinning like a top. Dashing here and there, guzzling down wine as if he were desert-thirsty, urging me to drink, too.

Peals of laughter exploded around the room every so often, like BB shot. When I saw a joint being passed along I understood why. Whoever was sucking in smoke would turn away from me, as if to hide the fact. They thought they had invented it, I supposed; the Beatles were theirs, after all. Music, too, was blasting through the loud speaker, drowning out even the thought of conversation.

It was my usually sedate hosts' night to be "hip," I gathered. Unfortunately I had been to one too many of these empty affairs. So I was glad when Tom whispered, over yet another glass of wine, "Would you like to leave?"

Outside we had to hail a cab, and when one appeared down at the cross street, Tom made a run for it. He looked like a teenager, the way he ran, all loose and lanky, like a galloping young colt. It was quite endearing, and I hugged him when he came back and told him so. (Evidently I had had more wine than I thought.)

He hugged me back and said, "Want to see where I'm staying?"

Yes, I said.

And just like that, we slipped into another stance.

In the taxi he did his snuggling bit, our lips lightly brushing once in a while. Somehow his teenageyness made me feel teenagey, too. And I simply shoved dignity out into the night and turned to look at this man I was with as giddily as he was looking at me.

God, it was fun. I hadn't had this kind of fun since . . . since I didn't even *know* when. I hadn't known I could even *have* this kind of fun anymore.

The place was in Mount Street, around the corner from the Connaught Hotel, where I had had lunch with Sam Spiegel and his super-loaded pal.

"Will your friend mind someone coming in like this?" I asked Tom.

"No one's home," he whispered, "they're out of town." He squeezed my hand.

The flat was gorgeous. Old, and rich, and solid. Paintings-of-ancestors-type decor. Furniture handed down through many wealthy generations. Old silver that you never saw, anymore, except in museums. And everything just so. I always wonder what people who live in such places do with their . . . *stuff*. I mean, anywhere I'd ever lived, including the twenty-five-room house, there were things lying about. Books that were being read. Magazines. Notepads. Stray pieces of jotted-on paper. Tennis rackets or fishing equipment, chess boards and their pieces. *Things.* Lying about.

People like these, I decided, must have a secret room behind some elegant panel to stash their clutter. I wondered if Tom would explore with me, and we could find out.

He had gone to get us some more wine. (They would have that, of course, and only the finest.) Sure enough he came back with a Romanée-Conti.

"I actually don't know if I should drink any more," I murmured.

"Just a drop," he said, pouring anyway, and quickly gulping his own down. He didn't seem to know about the merits of sipping noble wine. "Let's turn on," he said then, "I've got a joint."

"Oh! Do you?" That was a surprise, he didn't seem the type. But then, exactly what was the type, come to think of it?

Out of Tom's pocket came a neat, well-rolled, professional job. "Where did you get it?" I asked him.

"Never mind," he said, winking.

"Did you fly with it?"

"Who are you? The FBI?" he mocked.

"No," I teased, "Scotland Yard."

He lit the joint, took a deep drag, and held it out to me.

Here goes nothing, I thought as I took the hand-made cigarette. Don't be a prig. When in Rome. I'd had grass, here and there. Musicians coming around to see Artie when we visited from Spain would pass it around. It was pleasant enough.

Soon we were giggling, the way they had been doing at the party. The way I had seen John and his father, Walter, do it down in Mexico lo those many years ago when the two of them had boldly tried the local weed, their first time (probably last, too), and the first time I had ever been around it. It *is* a lovely feeling. Which is why people indulge, of course. Tom put on some music, something unraucous to match the decor. We nuzzled, touched, let ourselves move to the rhythmic sound filling the room as we drifted into the foggy dream world of the pot smoker.

Entangled by then, arms interwoven, our legs seemingly unable to support us further, we slowly, slowly slid down to the carpet like melted butter, there to continue our dance in a prone position.

I lost track of time—one does, alas, when turning on—it could have been minutes, it could have been hours before I was aware that a subtle change had occurred. That the nice euphoria was slipping away and some unpleasant thing was taking its place.

Tom had grown tense. His body alongside mine had become as rigid as a plank. It had heated up, too, I could feel it even through all the clothing, and he was trembling as well. It was as if a motor were running inside him somewhere.

It was very disconcerting. "Tom . . ." I started to say, when all at once he jerked upright to a sitting position, his spectacles falling off as he did, and began to cry.

*"Tom!"* It scared me. *"What's the matter?"* By then I was on my knees in front of him.

"L-life," he blubbered through his sobs, ". . . is . . . so . . . sad . . ."

"Are you . . . ? Have you . . . ?" I didn't know what to ask, what to do. I had never seen anybody, grown-up or child, cry the way this man was crying. It was beyond tears. A veritable *river* was flowing out of his eyes. The amount of water was incredible. I had never seen him without his glasses, either, and it looked as if his eyes had shrunk to little slits, out of which water was falling, dripping down his jacket, big drops splashing on his hands, which were clasped in his lap. He didn't try to stop his crying, either, or wipe the water away. Or show signs of trying to pull himself together in any way. He simply sat, his head bent forward, shedding copious tears.

When it went on and on I began to have a funny feeling that something wasn't quite . . . kosher. That this wasn't sorrow. This was some kind of performance. A repeat one at that. That the man did this for some kind of result . . .

I rose from the floor, then, and took a chair. If I was supposed to respond in some way—feel pity, play Mommy, or some such thing—he had picked the wrong partner. I didn't care for this game at all. I was, in fact, repulsed.

Finally the tears tapered off. He got out a handkerchief, blew his nose, and wiped his eyes. "I'm sorry," he murmured at last beneath the piece of cloth.

That gave me the opening I had been waiting for. "I expect you'd like to be alone, wouldn't you," I said to him, getting to my feet, "so I'd best just run along now, I think."

He scrambled to his feet, too. "I don't know what came over me."

"I'll bet you are tired as all get out, I'm sure that's it," I said, "from New York yesterday, and Brussels, today, you've just overtaxed yourself, that's all there is to it." I gave him every excuse I could think of. "So I'm going to get out of here so you can take it easy now and get yourself some rest."

"I'll see you home . . ."

"No no, you'll do no such thing, I'll just get a taxi . . ."

He went out into the street with me, waiting with me until one came along. We stood for a while, both uncomfortable.

Then he said, "Feels like rain." (Always a handy subject.)

"Yes, it does," said I to him.

It was like a bad movie you think will never end.

Even after I was home I had a hard time getting my mind

off the scene on the floor. Or getting over my antipathy to it. It wasn't the tears, surely. Artie could be moved at the sight of Canadian *geese* swooping over our house in their neat formation to make a perfect landing on the lake. And John. I thought of the night after his father's death—we were divorced by then—but he came by to talk about Walter. To reminisce. And his tears flowed freely. His *and* mine.

I got into bed. And I got out again.

And after a while I believed I understood what was bothering me. Not the man's tears—they were *his* problem—he was going to have to figure *those* out for himself. No. What was troubling me was . . . *me.*

God, the picture of myself smoking pot made me shudder. When I didn't even *smoke* anymore, for crissake. Down there on the *floor* in some strange Mayfair flat, fooling around with some art dealer I *hardly* knew from Adam. *Me.* Of the pausing menses. *Me,* who didn't even know how to do an *audition* right. Who didn't have even the vaguest concept of how an aging movie star should gracefully grow older.

I was pretty ridiculous, wasn't I. I was a *joke* . . . So why wasn't I laughing, I asked myself as I crawled back into bed, instead of feeling like crying? Just the way Tom had. Which was what I finally did. I woke up, of course, with a perfectly wretched hangover, and raw, aching lungs. And it served me right. I didn't remember ever being more thoroughly ashamed of myself.

Next morning, having groped my way around the kitchen to brew my tea, then walking around the flat with it, trying to stretch the weariness out of my body, I chanced to glimpse a man through the front window who appeared to be pacing up and down in the square below.

It startled me at first, since he was about Tom's height and build, and I never, ever, wanted to see the art dealer again as long as I lived.

But when the man turned around and I saw it wasn't Tom,

I proceeded to forget all about him as I went about pulling myself together, doing my exercises, sitting down to the typewriter for a session . . .

It was around three in the afternoon when I got hungry again, and, remembering there wasn't a damn thing in the fridge, I threw on some outdoor clothes and headed for the market.

I was already outside the front entrance before I saw that the same man I had observed in the morning was still there.

And walking straight toward me.

Had he been here the *entire day?*

My heart skipped a frightened beat. He was smiling in my direction. "Miss Keyes?" he said. And that frightened me even more. He knew who I was. And not a soul in sight.

"Y-yes . . ."

"I was hoping I would see you, Miss Keyes," the man then said. "I have seen *The Jolson Story* twenty-four times, and I have been an ardent fan of yours ever since. I was so hoping that you would do me the honor of giving me your autograph."

I stared at the man. *You . . . silly . . . twit,* I thought, *you have been waiting here all the live-long day? For an autograph of mine? Me, of the pausing menses? Me of the faulty audition technique? On account of because I was in a movie over twenty years ago? You, sir, are out of your cotton pickin' mind!*

I didn't say it, though. I didn't. I smiled, instead. And tried my best to muster some charm. "I'll be delighted to give you an autograph," is what I managed to say to the gentleman, "and thank you for asking." Spoken (I hoped) like the movie queen he wanted me to be.

What confusing lives we lead, we old (and young) movie stars, I thought, as I headed on down the street toward the supermarket . . .

\* \* \*

Artie couldn't have chosen a better time to check in. Never mind it was because he wanted me to do something—like get on back to Connecticut.

Hadn't I been in London long enough, he said on the phone? Our finances were beginning to stretch too thin (I *knew* I should have listened to that Rothschild fellow!), what with a flat in London, a New York apartment, and a house in Connecticut that was just going to be sitting there empty. He had to go to the West Coast to see about a lawsuit and winter was coming and he was worried that the pipes in the Connecticut house would burst and the ice would back up and cause the roof to leak, so why didn't I come back and go up there, wouldn't I be better off with all that space than in some lousy little flat in London, what was I doing there all this time, anyway?

He had a point. What was I doing here? Nothing that I wanted to go on with, that was for sure.

Except one thing. *The* thing. My morning routine. It had become the part of the day that I cherished the most. The time I spent with my writing machine. Alone at last, just the two of us, playing around, inventing our playmates, telling them what to do, wear, say. To *think*. I wouldn't want to leave them behind. They had become rather dear to me. A kind of immediate family, you might say.

But then. I wouldn't *have* to leave them behind, would I. I could take them anywhere I went, couldn't I.

I smiled at the phone. "Sure," I told Artie, "I'll be happy to go on back to Connecticut . . ."

# *Twelve*

**B**efore I'd left for London, Artie and I had sold the big house and acquired a more modest one with a mere ten rooms. And this was the one I went back to.

It was on a mountain top again, as the one in Spain had been, all by itself, no other houses for miles around. Here, however, instead of the Mediterranean to gaze out over, there was now a sweeping valley below with a rolling mountain range beyond.

I arrived in mid-October, and if there is anything more beautiful than a New England autumn, I don't know what it is. The entire landscape was ablaze with color. Down through the valley and up the slopes of the mountains on the far side, the trees were outdoing themselves, splashing their golds and oranges and bronzes and scarlets in every direction in the most brilliant display I have ever seen. It was truly something.

First I filled the fridge, the fruit and nut bowls. Then I went down to the village to pick up seed for the bird feeders, logs for the fireplaces, and a salt lick for the deer. I liked to encourage them to come around—they had been known to stroll right across the front lawn—as well as the other wild creatures, rabbits and raccoons, foxes and chipmunks, and even skunks. It was their territory, after all. Even the returning geese got into the act, sailing by overhead in their orderly flying arrangement, calling out with their ever-stirring cry.

I was having trouble settling in, though, and I didn't know why. Unless it was awareness that the swinging sixties had just gone by with the speed of a whirling wind, and that the next decade was already pushing its head up over the horizon. These sudden flashes of clarity as to how swiftly time passes can sometimes be a wee bit unnerving. Especially when you don't have all that much time to play around with.

I kept roaming about. Going down to the village on errands that didn't need to be done. Stepping outside the house to wander through the trees, enjoying the crunch of the leaves underfoot, the delicious smells that rose around me, that weren't to be had anywhere near a city. Sometimes I'd do nothing more than sit in front of the glass doors and watch the slanting sun as it caught and lit the bright leaves below, making them look like little single spotlights.

But there was an edginess that wouldn't go away. Here I was, in these picture-postcard surroundings, not quite at peace. It didn't make sense.

I was eating one of the ripe, juicy apples-right-off-the-tree I had bought from a neighboring farm a couple of days earlier when I got an inkling as to what might be poking at me. That all the while I was going about looking and marveling at this beautiful spot I found myself in, I seemed to be constantly asking myself, is this it? Up here on this mountain top? For the rest of my life? Is *this* the thing to do? I mean, what I *really* want? The place to settle down in, forever and *ever?*

Me. Of all people. Asking such dumb questions. Me, who knew very *well* there was no "it." No "forever." How many times did that have to be shown to me, for crissake.

I sighed, and took another bite of apple, enjoying the crisp crunching sound. Probably on my deathbed I'd still be asking myself, is this "it"?

I smiled.

And *that* would be the *first* time I'd ever have been able to come up with the right answer!

Relax, sweetie pie, and just enjoy, I told myself as I chomped on my apple and gazed out over the sea of color that stretched before me, and slowly, slowly, took in a deep breath.

With that the nicest, most peaceful feeling began to float in and all around me. It felt like warm honey.

There might not be an "it." But there certainly was a "now." And look where it was. Not exactly chopped liver, was it. And there couldn't be, furthermore a more ideal place to go on with the thing I had begun in London. What more could you possibly *want,* my dear?

I smiled again. I couldn't help it. Not another blessed thing did I want. For the moment, anyway. "Thanks, Artie," I said aloud, "wherever the hell you are." Artie most assuredly was the one who had made this possible, was he not. Give the devil his due, was the way the old saying went, if I remembered correctly. And hadn't I promised to do just that?

I raised my apple to him . . .

This was the third house I'd shared with Artie (not counting the New York apartment), and the first thing he always attended to upon moving into new quarters was to set up his study. Desk, chair, bookshelves, filing cabinets, you-name-it, it was instantly arranged. In Spain he had built a whole wing for this purpose, practically an apartment with a room on two levels, a fireplace, a bathroom, his own balcony (overlooking the sea, naturally). In this house I had returned to, we'd had to build on an extra room for this study of Artie's, and I was now most pleased that we had. It was big and roomy, and carpeted with Artie's favorite red rug. All this plus a view that stretched to infinity.

I unpacked my typewriter and settled in contentedly. To continue what I had begun in London. A novel was what it was, oh yes, I had just plunged right in when I'd begun, I hadn't wanted to start anything I could finish in a hurry and then be at a loss as to what to do next. I'd wanted something that would keep me hanging in there until I arrived at an understanding of what I might be up against. Until I found out if I actually *could* string words and sentences together on a page and make them add up to anything, see if I would be able to even find the *right* words and sentences to tell the story I had in mind. (As Artie had always said, talent didn't count for beans, it was what you did with it that counted. That first you had to work your little backside off—on whatever it was you chose to do—and only after a few million hours of practice-practice-practice would you find out just how much of the thing called talent you might possess.) He'd also added that even if you didn't have any outstanding ability to speak of you'd still wind up being pretty damn good at it.

Soon the rest of the world slipped away almost as if it had never been. In no time at all the leaves fluttered down from their trees, and the snows came, transforming the scene before me into a wondrous winterland. Most of the animals disappeared into their burrows (as I had in mine). The birds, though, kept coming around, the little chickadees even so bold as to take seed right from my hand. A fire at the hearth became a daily occurrence, particularly when the snowflakes were swirling around outside.

The hours I spent in Artie's former study with my invented people sometimes reminded me of those earlier years, which seemed such eons ago, when I was left all day in the care of a grandmother who evidently wasn't all that elated to be burdened with a tiny tot to watch over, and therefore paid as little attention to me as possible.

So I did the only sensible thing a solitary kid could do with all that time on her hands. I invented my own world. Gave myself a playmate (a little girl like myself). A big shaggy dog who loved me and understood every word I said. I gave us a house of our own, too, alongside the chicken coop, where I spent the day making up conversation and games for the three of us—sometimes including the chickens. (True, from time to time, Mother came home and wrung the neck of one of my feathered friends so we could have it for dinner that night. As good a lesson as any other to prepare your daughter for the cruel world that was no doubt awaiting her without.)

Things weren't all that different these many years later as I pursued my latest endeavor. I did keep my reclusive tendencies at a minimum, however. I went out, had people in. That is, on days it didn't snow, and the snowplow person had been around to clear and sand the way up. You couldn't make it up that hill without it being done, not even on foot. I had a regular bridge game going. There was poker once in a while. And tennis all the time. A big, indoor place had been built nearby. I think I liked it better, playing inside in the dead of winter with the snow piled up all around, than out in the sun and the heat of summer.

Artie returned from the West Coast, and he started driving up for weekends once in a while. He had his own quarters and we tried not to fight. Sometimes we succeeded. Sometimes we didn't.

A spring came and went, a summer, too, as well as another winter, and by that time, by George, I had done it. I had finished my book. Me. All by myself, a whole, entire, honest-to-God *book!* The writer Robert Ruark, who used to live in the next village to ours in Spain—we could see his house down the coast from our terrace—had a study that was filled with (he being the poor man's Hemingway) heads of animals he had shot, and on his desk there would always be a stack of pages that Ruark never failed to point at when you came in, and say with pride in his voice, "There're my keepin' pages for today."

At last I understood him. (Not the animals' heads, I will never, ever understand *those*.) Now I, too, had a stack of "keepin' " pages. Not that I showed mine to anybody. But I must say, to see them there on Artie's former desk gave me a very satisfying sense of accomplishment, a kind of tranquil, coming-home feeling that made me even wonder if maybe things might very well be going to be all right from here on in.

I would then remind myself just how often I had had *these* sentiments before. I did have this tendency to keep looking for silver linings.

Ah, and why not, I would then say to me, you never knew, did you? Weren't there people who *did* win the lottery, in *spite* of the odds? *Somebody* wins almost every time. Or often enough to keep feeding the thing we call hope, anyway, no?

It turned out to be Artie baby himself, damned if it didn't, who, prowling around *my* studio one weekend to see what he might have left behind, a book he might die without, a decorative box to put his paper clips in, espied my stack of "keepers," and said, "How's it going?"

He had been supportive. I mean, he'd said if that's what I wanted to do, why then by all means go ahead and do it.

"I . . ." It was hard to say for some reason. "I guess I've finished it."

"Congratulations. Want me to take a look at it?"

It was heart-attack time. *Look* at it!? Was that to be interpreted as . . . *read?* "Uh . . ." Well, somebody had to sometime, right? Wasn't that the idea? "Yeah, sure, would you like to?" Fortunately he was too busy poking around among the bookshelves to notice I was on the verge of fainting dead away.

"I'll take it back to town with me," he said. "Got a title?"

"Oh! Oh, yes. *I Am A Billboard* I thought I'd call it."

"Mmm." Artie nodded. "Interesting . . ."

He gathered up my pages, tucked them into his overnight bag, and off he went. *Taking my firstborn with him.* I had a funny sort of hollow feeling inside. And wondered if it was akin to what new mothers went through.

I played a lot of tennis the next two days. Played a lot of cards, read fiendishly, until he called. "Yeah," is what he said. "it's okay, I know a publisher, he's a little *meshugge,* but if you like I'll give it to him and see what he says."

I played a lot of tennis the next few days. Played a lot of cards, fiendishly read. At the end of the week it was the publisher himself who called. He said he was going to publish my book.

Just like that. Just like all the big things in my life had come about. How my motion picture career began. Marriages, love affairs, all burst into flame at first glance. So I don't know why I was taken aback at the quickness of my first novel's acceptance, but I was. I think because this phase of my life, this last half (fourth? eighth?) was supposed to be something apart, with a different set of rules and values and regulations. The publisher even invited me to his house in Jamaica—which was near Noel Coward's and Ian Fleming's place (he of James Bond fame)—to do the editing, so that was just like old times, too, going off to glamorous places to get the work done. From the plane on the way back I even saw a fiery rocket go whipping past and into the heavens, something one just doesn't see on a daily basis. All in all I was quite taken with my new profession. And while the edited pages were being turned into galleys, I went back to my hilltop and started another book, having quickly discovered I didn't much like *not* having one going. That I definitely wanted some unfinished pages *there,* waiting for me at all times. They seemed to give me this lovely impression of being *focused.* Of being nicely *anchored* to a solid and secure place. True or not, it was the way it *felt.* And that was good enough for me.

By the time the call came from the theatrical agent, many months later, the galleys my pages had been turned into had themselves been turned into a book. I mean a real, bona fide *published* book. The kind you see in the Doubleday bookstore's window on Fifth Avenue. I know because *I saw mine there.* It was like . . . what can I tell you, something so private, so wonderfully . . . mine. I remember the first time I ever saw my name in lights on Radio City Music Hall's marquee (in *The Jolson Story*), and it was quite exciting, all right, I can't deny that. I paused when it came into view and stopped breathing to gaze upward while my heart jumped into high gear as if I had been running the New York Marathon. The letters in my name winked and flashed up there as I realized I had just made it to the Big Time. But the sight of my book in a window on Fifth Avenue was so beautifully peaceful and quiet. And I felt as I stood there in front of the Doubleday window as if I had finally achieved whole-person status.

The agent had called about a performing job. And what a job. It was another "aunt" role, to be sure, but what an aunt.

This one kicked up her heels in a couple of smashing dance numbers in the big hit musical, *No No Nannette,* and now they were about to send out a road company to tour the country, and had turned to me because of my Al Jolson connection. Ruby Keeler, who had played the "aunt" role on Broadway, had been Jolson's real-life wife, and I'd played her in the movie. (The one for which my name had been up in lights.) It was such an exciting possibility, but what a time for it to come along. Just as I was pretty much deciding the thing to do was to settle contentedly down with my new love, the writing machine, and live happily ever after.

But I had never, ever toured in any show before, much less a musical! So how in the world could I say no knowing, as I did, that missed things were the heartbreak, not the other way around. To tour in a *big, smash-hit musical,* at this late date in my life! When would such an opportunity ever come again to go do knock-out dance numbers all across the United States and Canada, too? It *wouldn't* ever come again, and so what could I do, I had to grab the brass ring and climb on board, that's all there was to it. I had been a performer too long to throw such a moment away.

Besides, hadn't writers come to visit us every so often in Spain, dragging their writing paraphernalia behind them, setting up shop in one of our guest rooms to continue with their work during their stay? In the big house, too? Didn't one continually run into them everywhere you went? That was the *advantage* of being a writer; you could travel anywhere you liked, and sit down to do your work any place you chose.

I could simply take my typewriter right along with me on tour, wherever we went! That's all there was to it . . .

After a month of intense rehearsing and getting into dancing shape and costume fittings and hairstyling in New York's last gasp of fierce summer heat, our company hied ourselves onto a plane, and headed down to Dallas, where, on October 6, 1972, we opened in a theater not much smaller than the Lone Star State itself, called, appropriately enough, The Magnificent

New Music Hall of the State Fair of Texas, since it had been newly, and sumptuously, refurbished in time for our overture—to the tune of five and one half million dollars. Nor had *No No Nanette*'s producer, Cyma Rubin, been chintzy, either, with the restaging, costuming, and choreographing of her show's road company version.

Not only that, she had hired a couple of stars from "The Golden Era" (as it was beginning to be called) of Hollywood, one Don Ameche—he of telephone fame—and . . . uh, well, yours truly, to add a dollop of nostalgia to the whole undertaking. Which, after all, was what the show was all about. Nostalgia, I mean. *Nanette* was a simulated trip back to yesteryear, the original having first been put on in 1925.

And it worked. They said Yes! Yes! to *Nanette* down there in Dallas, and rose to their feet in a standing ovation, something the audiences would keep doing—and that we came to *expect*—as we moved on up and down and all around this country of ours (and Canada, too). NANETTE NICE NOSTAL-GIA headlines would say. NANETTE'S CHARM IS ITS NOS-TALGIA.

And it was fun. Plain *fun*. It really was. I was so glad I had done it. To get out there on a stage every night with a handsome gang of boys and girls behind me and do an explosive tap number was an absolute *ball*. Although the fact that I was twice their age was duly noted in one way or the other in almost every one of our weekly reviews.

". . . the *non-youngster* . . . comes through in marvelous style . . . as one hoped she would." (As if the reviewer thought there was a good chance I might break my neck, evidently.)

". . . dances nimbly and with zest sometimes *not seen in girls half her age* . . ."

". . . the years have treated her kindly . . ."

". . . *returns from a zillion old movies* . . . to bring down the house . . ."

Well, listen, the reviewers meant well, and I certainly *had* been around for a long time, a fact hard to hide with evidence of it everywhere in the form of those "zillion old movies" sure to be on display somewhere in the world.

And we *do* change physically as we move on up the road. No getting around it, no matter what we do to try and circumvent it. And if you put yourself on public display, it *will* be noted. A public person, I expect, becomes the yardstick by which one of her/his generation can judge themselves. If she/he still looks okay up there, maybe I do, too?

As the critics had observed, I actually was in superb physical shape (inside and out), having believed all my life (unlike Shirley MacLaine) that this was the *only* body *I* was ever gonna come by, and that I had bloody well better take care of it. Which was what I had always done (except for the smoking period, halted when I learned the horrible truth). I was heeding the remark Adolph Zukor, former head of Paramount Pictures, made on his hundredth birthday. "If I had known I was going to live this long," said Mr. Zukor, "I would have taken better care of myself."

Don Ameche, too, was in good condition. Some of our most profound conversations, held backstage pre-curtain, would be an exchange of what we had had for lunch that day, and the calories involved.

It was splendid to have Don as a role model on this, my first time out on tour. He was the consummate professional. Never late, never forgot his lines. And for the entire year, he never stopped improving his role.

And Hamlet it wasn't. It was a bit of highly stylized fluff. But that didn't change what was obviously a long habit. Every night Don would make some subtle adjustment—a gesture of a hand, a movement of a foot, a slight pause, an inflection. When he was on, and I wasn't, I would stand in the wings and watch with fascination. Because it is that sort of minutiae in a performance that grabs us and moves us and we don't know why (as in John Gielgud's deep-knee bends).

I felt, watching Don, that I was learning some new and important tricks of the trade. And that couldn't hurt, could it?

To learn a couple of new things? I mean, it's never too late to do that, is it?

Don was a gourmet, too. He spoke of writing a cookbook one day. Probably for that reason he was acquainted with a string of top-notch restaurants in various cities along the way, to which, on occasion, some of us would repair after the show, and have us a fine time. Once Don even cooked himself, on a day off when he happened to have a kitchen in his suite—a pasta and a marinara sauce that should make his cookbook a hit all by itself.

Ours was a nice company, without friction (we prided ourselves on that), and it made it easy—for me, anyway—to slip into the never-never land that I found life to be on the road. I felt suspended in time. In a place where reality became the show itself—the hours we spent on stage the real world.

Oh, things *happened* elsewhere. Nixon got reelected. Truman died, and then Johnson did, too, soon after. (As if they couldn't take one more term of Republicans in the lead.) The Vietnam War was winding down; the Watergate business got underway. But it all seemed to reach me from a great distance, as if there was a veil of gauze between these events and me. As if it were all some other play being performed at another theater. (The evening news can give you that impression, wouldn't you say?)

And people showed up here and there. Friends, family, acquaintances, as well as those I had never heard of. A guy in Houston called to say he had looked up his family tree, and that I was his thirty-second cousin. Some people came around in Indianapolis who said they were related to my father. A cousin I did know appeared in Denver. (She told me she had visited us when we were both around eight years old, and that my mother had tucked us in for the night in the same bed. *My* bed. And that when my mother left the room, I said to this cousin, "Get out of my bed." When mother came back in to check on us, found the cousin on the floor, and wanted to know what happened, I quickly spoke up. "She fell out of bed," I told my mother. Mother tsked-tsked, helped the cousin up, tucked her back in alongside me, and exited once more. As soon as she was gone, I turned to my cousin. "Get out of my bed," I told her. And I'd always thought of myself as this soft, sweet little girl.)

Two sisters and an uncle caught the show in Atlanta. The dance teacher, too, who had started it all. Down in Dade County in the state of Florida, a man, formerly with a New York moving-and-storage firm who had so often packed and repacked my delicate pre-Columbian statues and vases for me back when I was constantly on the move, came around to say hello, obviously having retired to Florida. He had carted my things around so many times in those bygone days I expect he thought *he* was related to me. A sweet woman named Ruth, evidently retired, too, who had taken care of the wardrobe on a million of my pictures at Columbia in California showed up, too, and she *was* family.

Senator Muskie paid a backstage call in Washington. And I had lunch with the noted pundit Eric Sevareid. He told me that the great surge of society's discontent, which caused so much crime to ensue, came about when we began to leave objects worth thousands of dollars sitting in the streets in plain sight, ready to be snatched. (He meant our automobiles, and I believed him. Well, he *was* a pundit.)

Even Artie came to see me do my stuff in New Haven.

"Hey!" exclaimed he afterward. "I didn't know you could do anything like that!"

Which went to show as much as we talked, and talked and talked through the years, we hadn't said everything. (I hadn't, anyway. Maybe you never do. Maybe you can't.)

Yes, everything went swimmingly—until I broke my arm. Yes, arm. The right one at that. And in just the absurd way these mishaps usually occur.

No, not dancing. Not on stage. Not even in a theater. At a fish place alongside the harbor in Boston, that's where.

I had taken some of the kids to lunch, and afterward, since it was February and cold and snowy, I said wait inside and I'll get us a taxi. As I rose and started out, I saw one pulling away from the curb through the front door, took a flying leap off the step outside onto the sidewalk, and found myself skidding full speed ahead across a patch of ice.

My fall would have done Charlie Chaplin proud. But even as I was going, a voice somewhere in my brain screeched, *Don't break a leg, you're doing a show!* So I flipped them, I don't know how, out of the way, and used my arm instead to make a crash landing.

I had never broken a bone, before. But this one was easily recognizable. My lower arm was kind of bent in the middle with the hand hanging limply at the end of it.

My first reaction was fury. How could this dumb, *stupid* thing be happening to me!

Three men, who evidently had come out of the restaurant behind me, rushed over to help up the nice, klutzy lady who had taken such an all-out tumble. But what they heard as they reached down towards her was the nice lady saying, "Oh . . . *shit!* Oh . . . *fuck! Goddamn . . . son of a . . . bitch!*" So they recoiled and stepped back, evidently never having heard such language from "nice ladies."

"Help me up!" I yelled at them. I was in such a rage.

Finally, I think it was one of the men, somebody with a car took me (and the kids) to Massachusetts General Hospital, a good place to go if you must break your arm. There they put me in a cast from shoulder to fingers (it was quite a break), and back at the hotel, lying on my bed of pain, my first call from those in charge was from Buster Davis, the musical director. He didn't say, how are you, what a pity, does it hurt, nothing like that. He said, "Here's the new line when you make your entrance to explain the cast on your arm. Lucille [one of the characters in the show] will say, 'Oh Sue! [me] What happened?' And you will say, 'I was helping Jimmy crank the Hupmobile, and it backfired.' "

As everyone knows, the show must go on. In no time at all, the costumes were adjusted, dancers and actors learned to compensate for the rigidity of my unbending elbow (though my shoulder moved quite easily), and for six weeks, that's the way I did the show.

Soon the place back in Connecticut began to recede and dim. As London had. And Spain before that. (And Hollywood before *that*.) I don't think I was aware it was happening, occupied as I was, learning to do things with one arm, one hand. Like brushing teeth, dressing-undressing, keeping the cast from getting wet in the shower (forget going to the toilet, I just gave *that* up for six weeks!).

The first inkling that I had removed myself from yesterday came when the first year of the tour was about to end, and the company would be changing over to what is called Bus-and-Truck. Meaning that instead of playing in one place for a week or more, the company would now do mostly one-night stands, occasionally two-ers, once in a while three. We all had the option of continuing if we wanted to, or calling it quits.

Well, the thing was . . . I was so very *content,* the way things were. Felt I had it made. My cake and the eating of it, too. Had both my things rolled up into one. The scribbling by day and the flashy dancing by night. Wouldn't it, I asked myself, be a crying shame to rock such a nice boat as that?

I quickly signed up to continue before I could change my mind . . .

## *Thirteen*

I hadn't made a mistake.

Bus-and-Truck turned out to be even more satisfying than when we were flying from place to place, dragging ourselves and our luggage to and from airports, a feat that usually took longer than the trip itself.

Now the crew went ahead in their great big trucks with the sets, the costumes, and the props. And we, the cast, would follow in our buses, two Greyhound-size jobs that would roll right up to the front door of the hotel/motels in perfect limo style.

I had the first couple of seats right behind the driver, where I'd settle in for the ride, my things all around me—books, fruit, pillows, and a big yellow pad with lots of pencils, doing my thing as the handsome scenery of North America rolled past my window.

It was, I fantasized, like the old vaudeville days, when performers came to town, put their show together, presented it, and then moved on. Once—I think it was Erie, Pennsylvania, up there on the lake—we arrived late, quite a bit past curtain time (the weather had been trying), and people, all dressed in their finery, were drifting out of the theater, having given up, as our buses rolled in, snow everywhere.

Our manager leaped out and told them that if they'd wait for a half hour more, until we could get into makeup and costumes, the show would go on. And they did—they waited. They went back in, all of them, some two thousand or so, and it turned out to be one of the better performances that we gave.

Meanwhile, as the days went by, the number of my "keepin' " pages kept growing and growing. So that when the tour finally came to an end—and end it did, as everything must— after some eighty-odd cities, I had collected a goodly number of them.

And then, one day, after what seemed like no passage of time whatsoever, there I was, back on the mountain top, from whence I had set out, the entire experience seeming rather like an interesting excursion, with nothing more to show for it (besides the pages) than a well-worn pair of tap shoes, and a bunch of newspaper clippings.

As I stuck the clippings into the boxes already filled with similar stuff accumulated through the years, it occurred to me that that's what life wound up being. Boxes of old, faded clippings, shoved in the back of some closet.

Artie wasn't around at all, anymore. He had moved on (again). With somebody new, somebody I didn't know—but I would have guaranteed that she was young, I would have bet my bottom dollar on that—evidently to try tandem living (again). "Never say die" appeared to be his motto. Out to California he'd gone, this time.

Ah well. Wherever. All the business with him—the ups and downs, the turmoils—seemed far away, too, and the memory of it all had to fight its way to me through layers and layers of Salomé's veils.

It reminded me of a cartoon I had seen once. A funeral, evidently, a guy lying in a coffin, mourners standing all around it, weeping, and the caption read (as if it were the dead person's thoughts), "I wonder what that was all about."

After checking in with the locals, with the bridge and poker and tennis players, and making a few dates to pursue some of these pleasures, I gathered up the "keepin' " pages of my latest literary endeavor and sent them on to the publisher, Lyle Stuart by name, the one who had put *I Am A Billboard* out there into the world. No use stalling. I might as well know the worst and get on with it. I had heard all those stories about rejection slips. Sometimes lots of them before anything happened. Twenty, thirty. Hundreds of them, even. Just because it hadn't happened to me the first time out didn't mean diddley-doo, it most assuredly could now. Was I not thoroughly versed in all the knockabout antics that could come after the greatest of beginnings?

Ah, yes, I was prepared for most anything. If I didn't know about rejection by *now,* what the hell *did* I know about? If I was turned down, I would just take my pages elsewhere, that's all. Or do them over again. As many times as I had to. It wouldn't be the end, to be turned down, it would be the beginning. Right? (I tried to believe it.)

While I was waiting to hear, a ferocious storm blew in, tumbling and swirling in a sort of whiplash effect as it sped across the mountain. The snow became so thick it looked like a wall of milk, while the wind howled like banshees around this sole house on the hill and lashed at the trees so hard they danced and swung every which way as the limbs went flying, the noise loud and shrieking.

Of course the phone went out, and the electricity went off. So there went the heating system and the means to cook, with the temperature outside at nineteen degrees.

Fortunately there was plenty of firewood inside.

So I built a fire in my bedroom, put on thermal underwear, several pairs of socks, three sweaters, found a candle along with a match, and by its playful light groped my way downstairs to the kitchen, found some cheese, some bread, some celery sticks, an open bottle half-filled with wine. I found a flashlight, too, and took it all back upstairs with me. I gathered up the book I was in the middle of reading, wrapped a blanket around me, and settled down in the big chair beside the flickering fire, ate the cheese, drank the wine, read my book with the aid of the flashlight, cozy as a cricket while the world stormed and raged outside.

It was a fantastic happening. For some mysterious reason, as alone as I was, and in the midst of a whirling maelstrom, completely cut off from the rest of humanity, I felt so extraordinarily safe and secure. So exquisitely tranquil.

Later I would marvel at my reaction—it never even crossed my mind to be frightened—and wonder what it had been all about . . .

Simple respite from . . . *every*thing. There had been nothing to figure out, since there was nothing *to* figure out. Nothing to do. Nowhere to go. It was heaven not to have to make any decisions about anything whatsoever, even if only for a short while. Temporary surcease from the *judgments* we are constantly being bombarded with.

I had just come off a tour where I had been judged (make that reviewed) just about every single day. Now back home, I had just sent my pages off into the publishing world, to be set up for judgment.

That night, then, was a lovely interlude, a stopover at the oasis, so that the caravan could catch its breath and then get on with the journey . . .

By morning the storm had passed, a feeble sun spread its pallid light over a landscape washed white and littered with twisted and broken tree limbs. By afternoon the power was back on, and the snowplow had worked its way up the hill and to my door.

The telephone, though, took a little longer, and when the call came, a couple of days later, it wasn't in the least what I expected. Neither the polite thanks-but-no-thanks, nor an enthusiastic yes.

"Listen here," the voice of Lyle Stuart said in my ear without preamble, "why don't you stop screwing around and simply write your autobiography?"

"W-what? What?" cried a startled me. "Auto-biog-raphy? You mean . . . w-write about . . . *my own life?*"

"It's what you're doing, anyway, with those cockamamy novels you keep shoving at me, you're in all of them—very thinly disguised, too, I might add . . ."

"I am *not!*" I cried hotly. I thought I had disguised it exceedingly well. Wasn't that what you were *supposed* to do? Use your own experiences?

"Start using real names," the voice said in my ear, "instead of fakes and we can make ourselves some real money . . ."

"Oh, no. No. No no no, I couldn't *possibly* do that, people are right here, alive, living, they'd . . . they'd . . ." Had I heard him right? "*Real* money, you said?"

"That's what sells, the inside dope on Hollywood. The behind-the-scene life of the Stars. The Rich. The Famous. That's the kind of thing people line up for."

Money.

Money made it sound so . . . so professional, didn't it. Not amateur night anymore, fiddling around in the privacy of your room. Like acting isn't acting done alone in front of your mirror. You have to have an audience to make it the real McCoy. The exchange of money, and readers, would do that for a book, would it not.

I realized my heart had begun to pound. *I Am A Billboard* had done . . . well, okay, but not what you could call *real* money.

"Uh..just..how much *real* money are you talking about?"

He got into percentages and numbers, then, and I stopped listening, the same as I did when Sam Spiegel was chatting with the Rothschild about the gold back there in London. I dunno. I guess I had always thought my husbands would be good at the money business—you know, big strong man takes care of little weak woman kind of thing? Hah. They hadn't known much more about financial matters than I did. And now that I knew very well it was up to me and nobody else to handle these things, I still couldn't hack it. I just couldn't seem to get myself to *care* enough.

But I *did* care about my relationship with my writing machine. And I wanted to be a pro at it. But I didn't know if I could write the kind of book the publisher was talking about. Inside Hollywood stuff . . .

It was what I knew, of course. What I *was.* How many times had Artie said to me, "You're a Hollywood *product,* don't you *know that?*" He wasn't being particularly complimentary when he said it. But he surely did know what he was talking about, having had a go with Lana and Ava and Betty and God knows who else from that part of the world. (So we must have been doing *something* right, we products, since he kept coming back for more, so many times!) And yes, it was dead true, no doubt about it, you couldn't be the property of a movie studio for years and years while they reshaped and reformed you to make you into their image, teaching you all the while their upside-down values, and not come out at the other end as their kind of handiwork.

Only.

Could I translate it to paper? Did I even remember what it was like, anymore? "But . . ." I began.

"But *what?*" Mr. Publisher wanted to know.

"It's been such a long time since I've lived out there. I hardly know the place, anymore."

It was true, too. I had scarcely recognized anything when we were back there in *No No Nanette.* Freeways had taken over the entire city, the Fox back lot was a mass of highrises called Century City, and Columbia had left Hollywood altogether and gone to Burbank in the San Fernando Valley.

"So go out," Mr. Publisher then said, "stay a while and get reacquainted."

"Ah . . ."

I hadn't thought of that possibility. But go stringing off again? When I had just got back?

Of course, this would be for a very definite purpose, wouldn't it? My own cause. My own work. Not trailing off *after* somebody, like most of the other times.

But. It seemed to be turning out that those times were quite okay! Great, in fact. They were experiences, weren't they, *usable* experiences? *That I could write about!*

God. Wasn't it all simply marvelous!

"But . . ."

"What now?" He was beginning to be the slightest bit irritated. I could hear it in his tone.

"What about my house, I've got this house, I can't leave it sitting here alone, and Artie's gone . . ."

"I'll rent it from you while you're gone," the man said. "For a year. How's that? I could use a country place for the weekends."

"No kidding!"

Just like that. It was Westward Ho, once again.

# PART TWO

# Tinseltown
# Revisited

# *Fourteen*

"Hollywood isn't what it used to be," a couple of million people must have said to me when they heard I was going out. Over and *over* they said it. It didn't help to tell them nothing was like it used to be. That I wasn't, either. They would go right on as if I were Rip Van Winkle, down from the mountain after a hundred years. "It's all changed since your day [*your* day!], you won't know it at all."

Of *course* the place had changed. Changed completely. You didn't have to live there to know that. The big studios no longer held sway. Television was king. People who had been young no longer were (me). It was going to be interesting to go see firsthand these changes everybody was talking about. See how the place had dealt with the onrush of new and newer techniques. See how those who had grown older and were still living in the land of Eternal Youth had survived the passage of time.

Not that I'd ever thought before about going back, removed as I had been from Hollywood for so long. But, as Artie had said, there *was* no removing yourself. So here I was, after all these years, about to head in that direction.

Wasn't that something. I wasn't even sure how I felt about it. Certainly not the way I had the first time . . .

Fresh out of high school I'd been, the idea being to go out to Hollywood and become a big movie star while attending classes at UCLA on the side.

I had gone by train, the old, long-gone kind that belched smoke and steam and made choo-choo noises and clickity-

clickity-clacked along the rails. The seats were covered with green plush that scratched the back of my legs, I remember that. I remember sighting my first palm tree after we entered the state of California. My first orange grove. Pre-air-conditioning, the windows of the train had been open, and the delicious fragrance of orange blossoms that floated in was overwhelming.

And for the entire trip, I had been reading a fantastically entertaining book, the number one bestseller of the moment, something called *Gone With the Wind*.

This time around, I decided to drive out. Why not. I had the time. I enjoyed driving and liked the privacy a car furnished.

Besides. Since all the touring my country had shrunk on me. A trip from Connecticut to California didn't seem much farther than a quick run down the mountain to the local grocery store. The network of all the interstates that cross and crisscross this land of ours was sitting right there in front of my eyes like a finished jigsaw puzzle, we in our buses had traveled them so often.

So I threw things into some bags again, revved up the white Subaru Artie had left behind, took the George Washington Bridge across the Hudson River, hooked up with Interstate 80 on the other side, and was on my way.

Through the rolling hills of Pennsylvania I went, on across Ohio, on through Indiana and Illinois and Iowa. I would get up at daybreak, drive the live-long day, stop at nightfall to find food and shelter until dawn, happy as a lark through it all.

I remember a particular day when I had Nebraska, for instance, all to myself. I did, I swear I did. There was not a car on the road except mine. The sun was slanting softly through the trees, casting lacy shadows on the black-and-white cows who were munching in their pasture. Just them and me. In the whole world.

It was truly a moment worth the entire trip.

From North Platte, I turned south—still on 80—dropping

down into Colorado until I reached Denver, where I was picking up a passenger.

When *Nanette* had played there the year before, I'd become friends with the impresario of the theater in which we performed, Bob Garner by name. In talking to him on the phone the week before, I happened to mention I was about to drive to L.A. And he said he had to go to the Coast on business, would I like a companion part of the way.

It seemed like a splendid idea. Bob was a most pleasant fellow, very easy to be around.

And so it was because of him that I found myself in Las Vegas. I would never, ever, have stopped there on my own, it not being one of my favorite watering places in spite of my various and sundry ties to it.

Once upon a time I'd spent the six weeks there that are necessary for getting a Nevada divorce. Overnight, another time, for getting married. (It should be the other way round, if you ask me; overnight for divorce, six weeks before getting married!) And I had lost count of the number of times I went there with Mike Todd, so that *he* could gamble. Gambling has never been anything that interested me. After those days, I had in fact concluded that if I ever even had to *watch* another dice or roulette or chemin-de-fer game, I might choose to kill myself, instead.

I said as much to Bob. And he said, I'm with you. What he'd thought we might do was to take in one of the shows on The Strip.

Now that was all right, and that's what we did. And it turned out to be Debbie Reynolds whom we saw.

Boy. Did seeing Debbie start a regular avalanche of memories rolling in. Which was precisely what I'd hoped would happen if I came West.

I hadn't come across Debbie since her Eddie Fisher days—and my Mike ones. Mike and Eddie had been buddies, and for that reason the four of us had been together on many occasions. I remembered being down in Palm Beach when Eddie and his ever-present retinue showed up, hiding out from Debbie, trying to weasel out of the coming marriage. But Debbie wasn't having it, and hung right in there. I remembered seeing—and hearing—them sometime later, singing together before a great crowd at The Palladium in Hollywood, as if they meant it, "Love and mar-riage, love and mar-riage, go to-gether like a horse and car-riage."

Since then, of course, a lot of shifts had taken place, often involving Elizabeth Taylor. Both of our men—Mike and Eddie—had their day in the sun with her.

And now. There was Debbie. Still looking good. Better than ever, actually. Up on the stage in Las Vegas, strutting her stuff, evidently earning pots of money doing it, too. And deservedly so. She was really good.

A damned good beginning, I thought, for my research into yesterday.

From Vegas I took Route 15, up, up, and over the San Bernardino Mountains and down to Interstate 10, which takes you straight into Los Angeles (even all the way to Santa Monica-by-the-Pacific-Ocean, if that's where you should want to go).

Once in the big city, Bob went on his way, and I checked in at a Holiday Inn out on Wilshire Boulevard in West L.A., the side of town I knew best, unpacked the bare necessities, and instantly set out to find an apartment I could settle down in for the year to come.

It was wonderfully exhilarating, driving around, getting my bearings once again, reacquainting myself with streets and landmarks—those that were still where they belonged, that is.

I had forgotten how lushly green Beverly Hills was. As if it were a part of the Emerald Isle—where rainfall is a natural happening. Southern California, however, is a natural *desert,* and the waters that make it green have to come from some place else.

Nobody, as far as I could see, though, appeared to be too concerned about it. Busy sprinkler systems were merrily splashing everywhere I went, as they always had.

The apartment complex in which I came to roost was lushly

green and wet, too. Among the trees and bushes and vines in its center was a sparkling swimming pool, constantly refilled by a tumbling waterfall. And if this weren't enough, the halls encircling the junglelike patio were open, with lots of wood paneling everywhere.

It was only later that I learned the handsome-looking siding was synthetic. Nor was that all. The stones around the fireplace in the apartment that I rented turned out to be synthetic, too. And even the massive coffee table gracing the center of the living room, which looked like a butcher's block on short legs, was made of ersatz wood. As was the countertop of the wet bar.

I loved it. After all, I *was* in the land of make-believe, was I not? What did I expect?

Soon I got busy on the phone to old friends. To find out if any were still around, and, well, dying to see me.

I began with the William Wylers, for a couple of excellent reasons. One, they still lived in the same house they had when I was living here, and therefore were easy to locate. The other was that I went back with Talli Wyler further than anybody else in this part of the world. Margaret Tallichet, she had been, and under contract to David Selznick, himself, back in the *GWTW* days.

Talli was supposed to have played something or other in that splendid flick. But she met Willy about then, they got themselves married two weeks later, and Talli got herself instantly pregnant, which pretty much loused up her being able to fit into those tiny-waisted hoop-skirted styles of the pre–Civil War period.

I had sometimes run into them in Europe, Willy being European, himself. This super-director's work took him there on occasion. For instance, when he was directing *Ben Hur* (the Charlton Heston version), he and Talli had lived in Rome for more than a year.

But even though they *were* the sort of people who did these traveling kinds of things, they had had the good sense to hold on to the same house through the years in order for me to be able to find them again when I needed them.

Because, boy. The Wylers knew enormous chunks of my yesteryears.

Except they weren't home, when I called.

Whoever answered the phone said they were expected back, though, in about a month.

Ah well. I had given up expecting to win them all long ago.

Next I checked in at the Beverly Hills Tennis Club. My former home-away-from-home back in my gung-ho tennis days. And found that it, too, was right where I had left it. Oh sure, they had perked up the clubhouse quite a bit (though I preferred the informality of the former). But the general layout—the courts, the pool, the tables and chairs and umbrellas alongside—was the same as it had always been.

Not only that, some of the people at the tables, under the umbrellas, hadn't changed all that much, either.

There was Gilbert Roland, sitting right there, the same as he had been in the olden days. Amigo, we called him, as he called all of us. He had made a picture with John while I was with John, and shortly after it was finished, we had all gone off together on a hunting trip, one of John's macho ideas, up in the mountains of Idaho.

Was Amigo older? I suppose so. Except he looked pretty much the way he always had. Slim, flat of stomach, graceful of movement. Amigo had always had his jackets lined with colorful material, and then turned their cuffs back so that the color showed at the wrists.

And he was still doing it. It made one's heart sing with pleasure. That and his warm hug of greeting.

And there was Joe Cohn. J.J. Former production head of Metro-Goldwyn-Mayer Studio. It was J.J. who had made that studio run. Older? Who could tell. J.J. had always had his white hair (what there was of it) and his wrinkles. He had always walked, too, with a slight stoop so that he appeared to be a miniature Atlas carrying the weight of the sky on his shoulders.

J.J. said he still played tennis, only his eyes weren't so good, anymore. He said he saw two balls instead of one. "But," he added, with a twinkle, "it helps, in a way. I'm bound to hit at least one of them."

Milton Holmes, who had produced a picture of mine at Columbia, called *Johnny O'Clock,* came over to say hello. Older? Sure. Like the rest of us. In shape, too. He was the tennis pro at the club, now. There was a sadness about Milton, though. A certain tone in his voice. As if he missed his picture-producing days.

A former agent of mine was there, too. He had dyed his hair. It hadn't helped. He *had* aged. And his memory was floating around.

Ah, but then, whose wasn't. Yesterdays began swirling about like wind-blown clouds in everybody's minds, brought on, no doubt, by my appearance; this familiar (though older) face out of their past. "Remember," first one would say, and then another, "the time when he . . . when she . . . did this . . . did that?"

Names were brought up who'd been around in those days of yore, and sometimes I would learn that not each and every single one had made it this far up the road.

I, too, got caught up in this flood of fond memories, as I pointed to Center Court, smiling as I did. "Remember," I began to say, "that Sunday morning when—"

I got no further. Because everybody burst into laughter. "How could we forget!" they exclaimed, one and all, grins on their faces.

"And how *is* Charlie?" I asked them, then.

They shook their heads sadly. "Gone, too," they said.

Charlie Lederer, we were talking about, the screenwriter responsible for, among other things, *His Girl Friday,* with Rosalind Russell, and *Kiss of Death,* the picture in which Richard Widmark pushed the little old lady down the stairs and became a star for his trouble. That was the kind of thing Charlie was known for writing.

But he was even better known about town for the outrageous pranks he played. A sort of master of shenanigans, Charlie was, and in a place, too, that was famous for such things. (Wasn't Peter Lorre said to have slipped John Barrymore's quite dead body out of the funeral home for one night, and propped it up in a chair in Errol Flynn's house, to greet him when he came home from work? Hadn't Carole Lombard knitted this dear little sweater for her then-husband, Clark Gable, in the shape of, well, of his . . . "private parts," while he was working on *Gone With the Wind,* and sent it over to him with the following note attached, "This is to keep you warm until you come home to me."?)

Charlie was the nephew of Marion Davies and appeared to have spent a large part of his childhood up north at the famous San Simeon estate with auntie and her good friend, William Randolph Hearst. Which could account for his rather bizarre way of looking at things.

The particular caper of his that had set us all to smiling had been witnessed by just about the entire club membership, including me.

As it was a Sunday, most everybody was around that day— on the courts, in the pool, having a bite of something to eat. But when Charlie's prank got underway, everything came to a grinding halt as everyone gathered to watch. Some even quickly ran home to grab their cameras, their spouses, their children, so that they, too, could come and watch what promised to be jolly good fun.

Charlie, as everyone at the club knew, had a running bet as to who would win his weekly matches with the then tennis pro, Jack Cushingham.

Now, Jack's game, of course, was light years ahead of Charlie's. Jack had gone to USC with several-times U.S. and Wimbledon champion Jack Kramer, and had at one time been Kramer's tennis partner. Jack's service was a bullet, as were his ground strokes, and you couldn't get past him at the net. He was a wiry six-foot-three blond who moved like lightning. To make his and Charlie's games even, Jack would give Charlie any odds Charlie wanted.

For instance, Jack would have to hit only into the singles court, while Charlie had only to *touch* the ball with his racket. Or Jack, who was right-handed, had to play left-handed. Or with no racket at all. Just catch the ball with his bare hands. Things like that.

But this Sunday was a brand-new one. Jack, it seemed, had promised to play tied to any animal Charlie showed up with.

Well, it certainly sounded like great fun, and so we all sat around eagerly waiting for the beast to arrive.

That is, everybody except Jack. He was pacing up and down somewhat nervously. Charlie, apparently, hadn't disclosed what the animal was to be he was bringing along.

Suddenly Jack slumped down into a chair next to me. "I'll bet it's an ostrich," he muttered under his breath, "those goddamn things, they fly up and claw at you with their feet. I've seen them do it. Or peck your eyes out. I'm gonna be blind, oh, Jesus, oh, Christ, oh, *shit,* how did I get into this *stupid* fix?"

"It's here!" someone cried out excitedly.

And indeed it was. We could see through the gate that a very large truck had pulled up in front. The kind with high sides and open on top that carries herds of cows or crates of chickens to some place or other, or maybe enough bales of hay to last a horse for five years.

We held our breaths as the ramp in back of the big vehicle was lowered—and gasped as down strolled . . . a baby elephant.

Maybe baby is the wrong word. The creature was not exactly newborn. It was probably several months old, weighing, oh, maybe a couple of thousand pounds, I imagine, but still a long way from its final size. And we spectators all thought it was absolutely adorable with its big ears and curled-up trunk and waddling walk.

Shouts of laughter rose from one and all—with the exception of Jack. He alone looked at the cute beast rather warily. And understandably so. After all, it was about to be *his* tennis partner.

The gate to the center court turned out not to be wide enough for the creature to pass through. So a piece of fence had to be removed in order for it to be able to take its place alongside Jack at the baseline. There, the two of them were properly tied together with a thick, heavy rope—one end around Jack's waist, the other around the elephant's neck.

Charlie took his place on the other side of the net, and with cameras clicking and children squealing excitedly from all around, the game began.

Charlie had won first serve with the spin of a racket. Nor did it take him long to win the first game as well. All he had to do was serve the ball straight at the young pachyderm. Which prevented Jack from getting his racket on it. Or serve at such an angle that the ball caught the outer line. And Jack, tied to this all too solid mountain of flesh, couldn't make a move in the ball's direction.

Then it was Jack's turn to serve.

He won the first point with his usual swiftness. Ball tossed high into the air, knees bending slightly, the body swaying back as the racket dipped behind his back, to come curving up and over the ball in mid-air and with a pop and a whooshing sound smash it over the net and past Charlie, faster than the speed of light.

But then.

To get over to the other side of the court, in order to serve his second point, Jack had to work his way out and around this partner of his, who was stationed dead center of the proceedings, not budging one way or the other.

Though it wasn't easy moving around all that bulk he was tied to, Jack somehow managed, and once again sent a bullet over the net and past Charlie to win point number two as well.

It was the last point Jack would win that day.

As he would soon learn, all this activity around the immature elephant—first the whizzing of Charlie's balls past it on both sides, and now this fierce swish of racket right next to its ears, and these round, fuzzy objects flying up into the air alongside its head—were most unsettling. Nothing like this went on back at the compound.

After Jack's first serve his hefty companion had begun to make a kind of low, grunting noise. After the second it began to sway uneasily back and forth, swinging its trunk from side to side. And as Jack circled it once more to get into position for his third serve, the trunk reached out and sort of tapped Jack on the shoulder.

It should have been a warning.

But then, neither Jack nor anybody else around the Club had had all that much experience with elephants as tennis partners.

When Jack began to serve the third go-round, tossing his ball into the air, up went the elephant's trunk, rising into the air right after it. Try to hit a tennis ball with an elephant's trunk between it and your racket. Not even Jack Cushingham could manage to do that. While the rest of us shrieked with laughter, Jack was standing there muttering something to his partner, no doubt trying to explain the rules of the game.

A bet was a bet, though, and so Jack valiantly tried again and again, with similar results. Once the elephant even wrapped its trunk around the racket.

By then, the din from us spectators had reached epic proportions. Which may have helped to bring on what happened next.

Jack, I think (though I am only guessing), may have had in mind to try and serve underhand. Or perhaps he was simply swinging his racket back and forth as it hung down from his hand in pure frustration. Whatever it was, it was one thing too many for our member of the animal kingdom, who then proceeded to squat, elephant-style. That is to say, kind of bent all four legs until its entire body was lowered somewhat, and let go. I mean, emptied itself. I mean, of *everything.*

Perhaps only those of us who were there that day (or circus people) can vouch for how much excrement can come out of an elephant—and a youthful one at that. The tennis court soon turned into a pool you could swim in if you had a mind to. And the number of turds, piled so high, made you wonder if this was the way the Rocky Mountains might have been formed.

And Jack. Poor Jack. There he stood, in the center of it all. Tightly tied to the creator of it all, the matter swirling and rising slowly but surely around and over his feet. He stood there, head bowed as if in prayer, looking somewhat like Joan of Arc at the stake. He said later that the stench had threatened to overpower him, and what he'd been trying to do was not throw up.

But he had lost the match, fair and square, no doubt about that. He gave Charlie a silver cup with the following inscription on it: "Charles Lederer, Winner. Elephant crapped out."

As we sat, reminiscing, enjoying ourselves, it came to me that I was doing it, at last. Doing the thing I'd been so envious of all those many years ago; the sitting around and *schmoozing* with old friends. Remembering other times together, earlier times, the way Charles Vidor used to do with his friends from Budapest. As I had expected it to happen when I got together with John. And with Sam Spiegel. And, alas, hadn't.

But today, here at my old Tennis Club, it *was* happening, by jingo. And it was every bit as nice as I'd always thought it would be . . .

I left the Club feeling the nicest glow. And on the way out ran into yet another member coming in. Matty Malneck, his name was. Matty had been a band leader, I believe, back in the thirties. He'd written a hit song, too, I knew that for sure, with Johnny Mercer, called "Goody Goody."

"Matty!" I cried. "How in the world are you?"

Matty grinned broadly. "Still got my teeth!" he exclaimed lightheartedly. And with that he clicked them at me several times so that I could see for a fact that he did still have his teeth.

Getting older, I kept learning, took many forms.

Little did I know, however, that I had only *begun* to scratch the surface.

Take that letter that was waiting in my mail box for me when I got home . . .

# *Fifteen*

It was almost the first mail that arrived at my new digs, and though it was posted from Los Angeles, it had traveled the most circuitous route imaginable. The letter was addressed to me in care of the Screen Actors' Guild, who sent it to the William Morris Agency's New York office. They, in turn, had forwarded it to Connecticut, and my dear publisher then sent it on out to the new address I had just given him.

This much-traveled letter was from a former producer at Columbia Pictures, of all things, who had been there during my tenure, and who had no idea that I was back in town. (It would turn out that he didn't even know I had ever *left*.) His reason for communicating with me at this late date was to let me know he had just seen *The Jolson Story* blown up to 70 millimeter, and that it was even better in the bigger size.

Well, wasn't it adorable of him to write and tell me such delicious news, when actually, I didn't know him all that well. He had made what they used to call B pictures, meaning small-budget quickies, and our paths hadn't crossed much back in the old Hollywood days.

But the man would certainly know the Columbia lot backward and forward. And what with most everybody I had known there having gone to their rewards—Harry Cohn, Larry Parks, Jolson himself—here was somebody who could help jog my memory of those days in a big way.

There was an address on the letterhead. Somewhere on the edge of Beverly Hills, it was. Not any studio I'd ever heard of. But of course things had changed radically (as I knew, and had been thoroughly informed of). There was a phone number, too, so I called it.

A female voice answered in a secretarylike manner. When she asked who was calling, I told her. Then waited while she evidently announced me.

The man seemed to still be in business. I wondered if it could still be film. Wouldn't that be something if it were!

*"Well . . . well!"* he said into my ear. "Ev-e-lyn Keye-sh! Ni-sh to hear . . . from you."

His voice sounded, well, *slurred.*

*Drinking?* I thought, at three in the afternoon?

On the other hand, it could be his natural way of speaking, couldn't it, what did I know. I didn't remember his voice at all.

He wanted to know if I had received his letter. And I told him I had and that was why I was calling.

"Good . . . girl!" he said into the phone.

I wasn't sure why he called me "girl." Maybe he thought I still was one? There was this thing, when you didn't see people for a long time, you expect them to look the same as the last time you did. (There are those who call even elderly women "girls." There are even elderly women who call *themselves* "girls," oy vay.)

He then wanted to know if I could come around to his office to see him. Which was what I had hoped he would say. I told him I would be most happy to do so, and we decided on a time.

I arrived to find, if not a studio, a rather elaborate suite of rooms. A receptionist was in the first one, who buzzed me through to the second one, where a secretary greeted me—as well as a nurse in a white uniform.

Yes. A nurse.

I must say I was rather taken aback. In fact it was she, the nurse, who ushered me into the producer's presence.

He was in a very very *very* large—and carpeted—room, with a six-feet-across desk at the farthest end, behind which this former Columbia-producer of B-pictures was ensconced. Just like the olden days when you had to walk a few miles to get to Harry Cohn's desk.

Except this producer was in a wheelchair.

"Ex-cu-sh me if I don't get up," said he with the same slur I had heard on the phone, "but I had a stroke." (Pronounced sh-troke.) "See?" he then said, "This . . . leg won' . . . work." And with that, the man clutched one of his legs and hoisted it, limp and lifeless, into the air for a brief second before letting it plop down on his wheelchair again. "See?" (pronounced sh-ee) he repeated.

I nodded yes. I certainly did see. I could hardly have missed it.

We did the amenities. Nice to see you again, nice to see *you,* all that stuff.

"Where . . . you livin' now?" he inquired.

I told him about taking the place in Westwood.

Then he asked if I had ever gotten married. Which was really most odd, since I had married both Charles and John while I was still at Columbia—not to mention the joining up with Artie later—all facts rather noisily publicized in their day.

"Wha' . . . about . . . now?" He wanted to know after I had filled him in.

"Yes—uh, no, not really, I live by myself, now," I told him. I wasn't going to try to explain Artie and me to him. (I didn't understand Artie and me, myself.)

From that point on, the conversation seemed to take a kind of nutty turn. Somewhat like an old joke I'd once been told back in London. About two Brits, both hard of hearing, who were riding along in a parlor car. Said one to the other, "I say, old chap, does this train stop at Wembley?"

"No," said the second gentleman, not quite hearing, "it's Thursday."

"Ah," said the first fellow, "so am I! Let's both have a drink!"

Because the next thing the producer asked me was if I needed money. But I had no idea that he actually meant it, *literally.* Thinking it over later, I figured it must have been my outfit. I was being "with it," wearing worn and well-faded jeans with vest to match along with Nike running shoes, and maybe the man didn't know these things were the fashion-of-the-day. But at the time I'd thought, when he mentioned money, that he had turned to business. That, having seen me, he had decided I was perfect for some movie he was about to make, and was asking me if I was going to insist on my money up front, or would I be willing to defer.

And so I answered the man with what I thought was a logical (and safely noncommittal) question. "What," I inquired, "do you have in mind?"

I was quite puzzled when a leer appeared on his face.

Well, *sort* of a leer. His cheek didn't move much better than his leg had. (Though I am able to report that a lopsided facial expression can be quite effective in relaying lascivious intent.) "The . . . nex' time . . . I'll come . . . an' see you," he whispered in his slurring way, "only . . . somebody'll . . . have to . . . help me on . . . an' . . . help me off . . ."

I got out of there as soon as I was able. And didn't laugh until I was in my car. I know I shouldn't have, even then. It wasn't *nice* to laugh at the poor shell of a man.

Except, well, he *was* pretty ridiculous. Still trying to hold on to his macho past in spite of insurmountable handicaps. Still trying to play it the way he (evidently) and the majority of men had played it back there in the "good ol' days." Maybe I should have even admired his effort. Never say die. A là Artie.

He had sure started my memories twirling. I had to say that for him. Which was, after all, the reason I had gone to see him. Reminding me just how it had been for us members of his opposite sex, back there in those earlier times . . .

That men made sexual overtures to females was considered quite acceptable behavior back in those practically prehistoric days of the big studio. Par for the course. The phrase "sexual harassment" hadn't been invented. People still said that if a woman was raped "she must have asked for it."

Actually, females, particularly actresses, were supposed to

be *pleased* to be the object of such gambits. It meant you had turned some man on. And turning some man on was what got you the job you sought, since it was men and men alone who held all the hiring positions, from head-of-studio to producer to director. And their thinking was that if *they* found you fuckable, so would the audience out there.

Therefore, it was your *duty* (if you wanted to make it), your obligation to be/look as alluring as possible. It meant, in fact, your very *livelihood.*

Except here was the rub.

At the same time you were busy turning would-be employers *on,* you had to find a way to keep them at *bay.* Because they wouldn't give you the job if they thought you slept around. *That* they didn't approve of, at *all.*

It was a kind of lingering, turn-of-the-century good girl versus bad girl mentality. All of which caused some pretty messy emotional confusion in us young and eager damsels.

First there was the heady power one felt at the ability to knock over a man just by walking into the room. Only, there was this other part that went with it. The premium that it put on the physical aspects of you. Your looks, your shape, your flesh, all had to be arranged in the right proportions—even the muscle tone beneath had to be shipshape—and without all that, no amount of brains could help you any too much.

The butcher in the village near my house in Connecticut made it perfectly clear. On the wall of his shop behind the meat counter hung a chart of a naked Marilyn Monroe, her body marked off in sections the way they do steers, to demonstrate the various cuts of meat. Chops here. Flank there. Brisket exactly where brisket usually is.

Yeah, I reflected, as I pulled into my space in the underground garage at my apartment complex, that was pretty much how we got accustomed to thinking of ourselves. As Marilyn Monroe charts. While the men, no doubt, got used to thinking of themselves as livestock judges at the State Fair competition, deciding which filly to give the blue ribbon to. Like the producer back there. He had never gotten over it.

Out by the pool what sight should greet my eyes but acres and acres of tits and ass—smooth skin and streamlined bodies everywhere I looked. Absolutely the most gorgeous creatures of both sexes were draped all over the place, in slivers of bikinis, taking as much sun as possible. The news of the sun's rays causing cancer (and early aging) evidently hadn't reached their tender ears yet.

Yeah. I was back, all right. In Hollywood. Where else would you come across that sleek, long-legged look in such numbers except in a show-biz town. Where else would you run across a guy in a wheelchair still trying to play a latter-day Lothario.

My town. Where—as Artie had said—I'd been shaped. I had *been* one of those sleek sunbathers. I had learned to handle fellows like the one back there when they still had two *good* legs.

As I passed by the rampant display of youthful flesh, I had the most terrific urge to stop and tell the lolling beauties to stop frying their pretty skins *instantly,* as they were going to need every single asset they could possibly hang on to in order to cope with what was waiting for them on up the road. That preparing for their older years couldn't start soon enough.

Fortunately I kept my counsel, and went on quietly by, the invisible (to the young) older woman . . .

## Sixteen

It is the damndest thing. If you've become *any* kind of name in this world, grandiose or minuscule, you can be found, even if you drop out of sight for years on end the way I had.

An advertising agency called me up. At least, that's where the woman said she was from, anyway. She said they were thinking of doing a commercial for some kind of soap or other, and had remembered that I had been in a bubble bath in my role as a genie in a picture called *A Thousand and One Nights*. (These people who call usually know things about you that you don't even remember yourself.) She asked whether I'd be interested in doing their commercial if they did, in fact, *do* their commercial. That they wanted to connect the "then" and the "now."

My my. A commercial. I knew they had become the thing to do since I was here last. You saw actors all over the place doing them—and getting paid for them, too. We—I—used to have to do them for nothing. Did them because the studio told us to do it for publicity—usually in connection with some picture release. I've photos of myself advertising Lux soap, Max Factor makeup, a dozen kinds of things. All done *for nothing*.

I didn't know how to go about this. "Well . . . sure . . ." I began, trying to play it cool, in the middle, not too enthusiastic, but interested nonetheless. Nobody had ever asked me to do anything like this before, and it was rather exciting. The woman on the phone said she would get back to me.

When we'd hung up, I quickly rang my friend Talli, (the Wylers having returned from wherever they had been,) and told her about the call. "Hey, that's great!" Talli said. "Everybody's doing them, these days, I understand you'll make a fortune."

Wow. I had absolutely nothing against making a fortune.

"You'd better get yourself a commercial agent to handle it, though," Talli went on, "since there are probably contracts and *contracts.*"

"Ah. You mean regular agents don't handle commercials?"

Talli chuckled at the other end. "You don't know much of anything, anymore, do you . . ."

That was a little disconcerting to find out, and me in my second childhood. I asked her if she knew of a commercial agent. She said no, but she would ask around and see if she could locate one for me.

It truly was terribly exciting. A whole new world was opening up. I hadn't been thinking about going to work in the acting business, anymore, having decided that the *Nanette* tour had been my grand finale, and that I was going to stick strictly to my writing machine from here on in.

But, on the other hand, why not do something if the opportunity to act came along. After all, here I was in the seat of the action. Especially if it was something done in front of a camera.

The truth was—though I was aware it was supposed to be a sacrilege to even *think* it—that I preferred camera acting to stage acting. Preferred the intimateness of it. The subtleties of it, instead of having to reach that bloody back row each and every performance. So to do something once in a while in front of a camera, even a commercial, would be very nice. Especially something that involved a *fortune*! It wouldn't interfere any too much with my new thing, any more than touring had.

So when Talli gave me the name and number of a commercial agent I called immediately. When a man answered I told him who I was, and we made an appointment for the following day. It was a Beverly Hills address, so that seemed like a good beginning.

What to wear to a commercial agent's office? I hadn't the foggiest. What did it matter, I decided. If I was going to do a bubble bath commercial, I wouldn't be having much of anything on, would I? So I just wore my usual—the jeans, the shirt, the vest, the running shoes.

Once I was inside, the office was a little disappointing. I wasn't sure I was even in the right place, being accustomed to the more spacious offices of the former MCA agency, as well as the London outfit, with their fabulous antique furniture everywhere and sleekly decorated interiors. This agent even seemed to be sharing his space with someone else. His little cubbyhole appeared to be in front of somebody else's little cubbyhole.

But what did I know. Maybe commercial agents didn't waste money on fronts. He was small, the agent person was, and talked fast. As we exchanged the opening small talk, his eyes seemed distant and hidden. How I was didn't interest him in the least, and he didn't bother to pretend that it did. He got right down to business.

"Ever do a commercial before?" he asked in his fast way.

"No," I told him. I knew he wasn't referring to those posed-photo jobs I had once done.

"There's a knack to it," he informed me rather sternly. Now that he was talking about the only subject that evidently counted around *this* office, he began to look me straight in the eye as if challenging me to dispute what he was saying.

"I imagine so," I agreed. Yes, I supposed there was. I had never thought about it. I was not that big a TV watcher. News, a sports event, a Big Happening. That was about it. When the commercials came on, I usually rushed away to do some chore. Or went back to the book on my lap.

"People think they can do them off the top of their heads," he told me rather sharply.

I didn't know I had come here for a lesson in how-to-do-commercials. But what the hell. It was all stuff I should probably know if I were going to start doing them. "Yes . . . well . . ." I murmured, "I wouldn't think that . . ."

"You have to *believe* what you're saying!" The man seemed quite put out by people who didn't understand that.

So I hastened to assure him that I, for one, certainly *did* understand that. "Like doing a scene, you mean, a regular scene? Is that what you mean?"

It was the strangest thing. There was kind of a gap in the proceedings. As if I had missed a beat. Or the tape had skipped forward. Because the next thing the man said to me didn't seem to follow the course of our previous conversation. "Do you wear dentures?" was what it sounded as if the man had said.

"I beg your pardon?"

I had to be mistaken. He couldn't have said that, could he.

"Do . . . you . . . wear . . . dentures?" He repeated, loudly and slowly, obviously believing me deaf as well as toothless.

And I had thought that I looked—well, maybe not exactly a teenager in the mirror before I left—but like a pretty well-preserved middle-aged woman, at least. "No, I don't wear dentures," I told him. "Why do you ask?" I started to add, facetiously, do you do dentistry on the side?

But his eyes had turned sly, and he was giving me this kind of little sideways grin. "Ah," said he in a most knowing way, "you can tell me the truth."

I was taken aback. The man wasn't kidding. For some reason he seemed to believe that I wore dentures.

"But I *am* telling you the truth!" I cried.

I said it too forcefully. I knew it the minute the words came out of my mouth. You do that when somebody thinks you're not telling the truth. You behave as if you weren't.

The man smirked with amusement. "Are you sure?"

I then behaved the same way Matty Melnick had behaved on the front steps of the Beverly Hills Tennis Club. I clicked my teeth at the person before me. For the benefit of this perfectly strange man I had never seen before in my life until a few minutes earlier, I found myself curling back my lips and tapping vigorously on my front teeth with my fingernails. "I've spent a great deal of money hanging onto these, sir!" I snapped. "They are all mine! I don't even have caps!"

"What about a bridge, then?"

"Not . . ."

"Surely you've got a bridge or two?"

*"Not . . . even . . . a bridge . . . or one!"* I hissed, coming to my senses. What kind of mad conversation was this I was having with some so-called commercial agent in a cubby hole somewhere in Beverly Hills. "What the hell business is it of yours, anyway?" I asked him angrily.

"I have a denture cream account," the man said, "and they demand authenticity. You gotta have at least one falsie."

I nodded, staring at the fellow in utter amazement, trying to understand this bizarre new world of product-selling. "I see," I murmured.

"Say . . ." As I watched, the man suddenly snapped his fingers as an idea apparently struck him. "Maybe you'd be willing to pull one out?"

Needless to say that relationship was nipped in the bud before it began. Maybe there was a commercial agent for me somewhere in the world, but this one wasn't it.

Had I just run into the "real" Hollywood, or what? Certainly the "youth-oriented" aspect of it, anyway, that was for sure. A woman walks in who may not have looked like an angel of Charlie's, but nevertheless with all her teeth (and maybe marbles), her hair color holding its own, figure too, no extra pounds anywhere in sight, and all the man could think of for her was denture cream.

I stopped off at Talli's to tell her what happened and we had a good laugh. I told her about the earlier visit to the producer's office, too. "You," Talli advised me, "better stay away from offices, if you ask me!"

I stayed for a glass of wine, a salad, and some cold chicken—Willy was playing cards somewhere, The Friar's Club, I think—and then I went home thinking how much I enjoyed Talli's company. We had good discussions, laughed at the same things. I could even trust her taste in movies. I mean, if Talli said something was worth seeing, I could believe her. Did I have anybody like that in Connecticut, I wondered?

Connecticut. Mmm. It was beginning to fade away, too, just the way all my other places had.

And only last year I had been so *sure*. So positive it was there that I wanted to live out the rest of my years.

But now . . . It had begun to seem awfully farfetched, to hole up on a mountaintop, miles away from everything, and everybody.

I was going to have to do quite a bit more thinking, after all, wasn't I . . .

# Seventeen

Something Artie used to say floated to the surface, back when he was trying to explain why he wanted to pack up and leave our Spanish establishment. And I was fighting it hard. "I have the need," he would cry passionately, "to *enchufar* into the world again!" *Enchufar* is a Spanish word, meaning "to plug in."

In great heat he would say that being so far away from everything he had ever known meant he was throwing away a big chunk of himself. "I want to be around *my own language!*" he'd say with feeling. *"It's who I am, what* I am, and I can't even *use* it half the time!" Couldn't use its subtleties, he said, its nuances. He longed for social exchange. Where new ideas, and thoughts, could be expounded *in English.* Where libraries and lectures and concerts were available. He said it was like certain muscles never being used. (He didn't say he missed being with people who knew music the way he knew music, but I wouldn't be surprised if that was almost the main thing he missed. After all, music is a language, too, is it not?)

I only half understood him, then, because I didn't want to understand. Didn't want to leave where we were. I was having too much pleasure in learning everything in a brand-new language; learning *its* subtleties, *its* nuances. So I kept dragging my heels, closing my ears, for as long as I could.

But now, here I was, beginning to catch on to what he meant at last. Connecticut, if I thought about it, was about as far from anything I had ever known before as Spain had been.

The language about as different. I was up there, anyhow, because of Artie. Living out some old dreams of *his,* when *he* had already gone on to the next thing.

Honestly. I had without a doubt better get my *own* act together before . . .

The little ripple danced along my shoulder blades. But I made myself finish the thought, anyway. *Before time ran out on me,* that's what. It really was coming through loud and clear, these days—this realization of time's limitation. That it actually could . . . would . . . *was* . . . running out on me, like it or not. Like sand through an hourglass, and there was no way to turn the damn thing upside down and run it through again.

I think I'd finally gotten the message because of all the unrelenting prodding at me about getting older. As the dear commercial agent had just finished doing, along with the multitude of similar reminders before him. Including birthdays that kept on marching right along. Fifty had long come and gone and sixty was rushing up like Secretariat at the finish line, and so it would behoove me to act accordingly.

Whatever that meant.

Figure out carefully, that's what it meant, I decided, where I wanted to spend the rest of my *time.* That's what I'd better damn well do. Not *plunge,* the way I'd always done before. Or just fall in because it was *there.* Zap, off the high dive without even looking. Better think it over, this time out. Plan ahead. *Look* at things. Think them *through* . . . and through . . . and *through* . . .

All those solid, careful things were most assuredly what I should do. Or at least give it a shot, I told myself. (A couple hundred times.)

So where to begin. I could, for instance, make lists, couldn't I. Of the pros and cons of each of the places. Of the East one, and the West one, and see how they measured up. Yes, I could do something sensible like that.

Mmm, let's see. For starters, most of my old friends, old acquaintances, people I had worked with, been associated with in some capacity or another, were in and around L.A., were they not? Or if they weren't, they'd be sure to show up there sooner or later. It was a lot of fun to run into, say, Glenn Ford, with whom I had made six pictures, just walking along Rodeo Drive. Or Ann Rutherford, my *GWTW* sister, whom I bumped into at a Thrifty drugstore around Christmas time; and Lloyd Bridges, the pilot of the plane in *Here Comes Mr. Jordan,* in Robinson's department store. I would never, ever, have run into any of them on Main Street, Connecticut, in a million years.

Yes, Hollywood was chock-full of old friends and acquaintances. There was J. J. Cohn and his schmoozing cronies over at the Tennis Club, where I could drop in every once in a while.

And lo, even as I was making my lists, who should arrive in town from London but dear Sam Spiegel (without his Rothschild, this time). Maybe he had timed it this way, I wouldn't put it past him, because he had shown up in the Yuletide season, and Sam's New Year's Eve party had always been the one to go to, the one none of us would ever-be-caught-dead-*not*-going-to.

So, most naturally, he took time out, rented a sizable house, and threw one once again, as gloriously splashy as ever. Everybody dressed to the nines, as always, a big orchestra going full blast, as always. All the old faces were there, of course, mixed up with some up-to-date ones (of course—Sam was never, *ever,* behind the times!). DeNiro, Farrah and friend Ryan. And Audrey Wilder (Billy's spouse) sang a number or two, the way she always had. The air reeked with sentiment, it was kiss-kiss, hug-hug, all over the place—people I hadn't seen in donkey's years, some I'd never met before except on the screen, but it made no difference, we all *knew* each other.

I put the happening down on my list, too, as something that could never possibly come to pass on a mountaintop in the far Northeast.

And there was another thing in favor of California, too, that wasn't anywhere else. Maybe the most important thing of all.

A brother. Mine. I mean, a real one, not a make-believe. The *only* brother I had, actually. Sam was his name.

Odd as it may seem, I had never known brother Sam all that well. He had fled the family compound when I was still knee-high to a flea. I imagine until then I had been nothing more than this little pain-in-the-ass, this baby sister trying as best she could to follow big brother everywhere he went (probably trying to turn him into the Daddy who had vanished on her). But how could a young boy about to turn into a man want some little thing—a female at that—trailing him around. I remember (vividly, I might add) a time when I tried to climb up after him onto a horse-pulled wagon that was standing in front of our grandmother's house. The road wasn't paved then, and it had been raining, so the bare foot of my brother's that he shoved down into my face to stop my upward progress was squishily muddy. (I think I cried. I'm pretty sure I did.)

But with all the Christmas presents that came my way, I being the only child around, and star of the occasion, one of my brother Sam's is the only gift of my young years I can remember receiving.

I can see it to this day, clear as can be. Perched, the way it was, up in the branches of the fragrant Christmas tree taken out of the woods, chopped down with an axe and brought in, and decorated with hand-strung popcorn and cranberries, and real lighted candles.

It was a red kite. The diamond necklace Mike Todd once gave me many years later in Palm Springs one sunny Christmas morning wasn't anywhere near as thrilling as that red kite had been.

I remembered when brother Sam flew the coop, too. I was devastated. I sobbed for days, and couldn't stop. It was as if the world had come to an end.

But all that was a number of centuries ago. Wars had been fought. Careers followed. Traveling done. A lot of growing up, too. And I was finding out at this late date just what a splendid fellow brother Sam was. A successful businessman, too. He was an hour's drive south down in Orange County, where successful businessmen abound. Not only did he wear shoes, these days, they were of the Gucci genre, and his suits, also, were gorgeously impeccable. I suspected he had made it, not only with know-how, but with charm and warmth and a bit of wit, too. Getting to know my brother was like finding a treasure I didn't know I had.

A definite plus for the California side.

I put UCLA on the list, too. Mainly because I liked the look of it there.

Fortunately I was going to *have* to go back to Connecticut fairly soon, anyway. The year's arrangement with the publisher was about to come to an end and the house would again be all by its lonesome up on its hill. I figured that being on the premises once more, experiencing again what living up on the mountain was like after this spell in California, would help me to judge whether moving on at this late date would indeed be the right thing to do. The *wise* thing to do.

And sure enough, in the wink of an eye it was spring and time to hit the road again. So I packed up, again, leaving stuff behind at brother Sam's—not unusual, I had left a trail of baggage scattered over two continents—said a fond farewell to various and sundry, got back into the Subaru, which now sported California license plates, and took to the freeways, happy as ever in my bubble.

I took the southern route, this time, Interstate 10—the one that begins at Santa Monica—and stayed right on it all the way to Mobile, Alabama. What a great time of year it was to be traveling along, with all the growing things beginning to pop. Mississippi was particularly eye-filling with its long stretch of divided highway paved, I swear, with crushed pink marble. It gave the effect of two pink ribbons rolling out ahead through the lush new green of spring, the sun spattering gold over the gently dancing leaves.

And that's where I was, driving along that lovely corridor. I had traveled thousands of miles before I got around to remembering that the bubble-bath commercial woman had never called back. Nor had I left a message anywhere telling how I could be found.

My guilt about it didn't last any too long. Somehow, all that faded into the sunset, too. Anyway, the woman had found my whereabouts one time. If she really wanted to, which was highly unlikely, she could find me again, right? Television and the soap-selling business could muddle on without me, that much was for sure.

Getting lost in Georgia soon had more than a passing claim on my attention, anyway. At Mobile I had taken Route 65 north, then 85 out of Montgomery to get into Tara-land, but there had been some road work going on on the main highway, and some posted signs about a detour ahead. I don't know exactly what happened, except that all at once the main artery disappeared, and I found myself on a dirt road the color of red brick, deep in the Georgia piney woods, with no other cars, no buildings whatsoever, only twittering birds and trees. Wild wisteria dripped from their branches, in full bloom, too, their clusters of pale lavender everywhere.

It fairly took my breath away. I swear my wrong turns through life have always been spectacular. (Which was another ponderable thing for the list.)

The entire trip was like that, all the way north, and up the hill, where I found my very own lilacs and forsythia bushes— ones that I had planted my very own self—also in rampaging bloom.

Spring had outdone itself, that year, nationwide. Was it trying to tell me something? (I was leaving no stone unturned for any possible sign of guidance!)

I quickly settled in. It was easy to do since everything was pretty much as I left it. And nature's spectacular display continued. As if it were showing off. As if it were daring me to leave it behind. The very next morning a huge buck crossed my front lawn at the break of day. He had antlers the size of the Empire State Building and moved so sedately and with such grace. The bucks never came down this far, staying high,

high up in the top of the mountains. A young doe was dithering around him, flirting, and then prancing off again.

Would I, I asked myself, see anything like this in the Hills of Beverly?

The woodchucks nibbled at the newly budding clover, the raccoon mom and kiddies came around to say hello. A fawn, spots and all, Bambi in person, bounced stiff-legged right up to the sliding glass doors, stared in with his Disney eyes, and bounced off again. The geese flew over, right on schedule.

The air, too, was so fresh and scented, so clear I could see the mountains all the way to Massachusetts on a sunny day.

So why was I even considering abandoning this absolute Garden of Eden to go to a city whose air you could slice with a knife? Where commercial agents looked at an older person as a walking ad for denture cream . . .

Greta Garbo, one of the all-time great faces up there on the movie screens of the world, had taken herself out of view years and years and *years* ago. Still in her prime, too, when she did it. Marlene Dietrich, as well, had vanished into a Paris apartment, and out of sight. There were others, lots of them, who never appeared anywhere, were never heard of at all, evidently having decided to do their aging in private.

Was that what I should do, too? Get out of sight while the getting was good? I had a strong suspicion that I tended to think I looked a lot better than I actually did.

Maybe if I played my cards right, stayed up here on the hill, stayed away from mirrors and cameras and Artie—who seemed to think it was his duty to keep me straight about my appearance—I need never know what was happening to the way I looked as the days and years and decades rolled by.

Or. Yes, there was another choice. There *was* something else that a lot of people did out there, in La La Land. That maybe I could do, too. Maybe *should* do if I went back. One woman I'd come across out there had referred to it as having some "little tucks" done. I guess that was supposed to sound better than "face-lift." More like a minor alteration, a little unimportant nothing—like getting your skirt shortened, or maybe a manicure.

The thing was, though, you always seemed to *know* who had had these "little tucks" done. Knew it was somebody older doing what she—or he—could not to look it. Except you knew that they *were* older, because the face isn't the only thing that *gets* older. Hands do. Legs do. The look *in* the eyes changes. One has seen more as the years go by, and it shows. It just does. The way the body *moves* changes. It just does.

Even so, people didn't want to have wrinkled faces, anymore, did they? They just weren't used to *seeing* wrinkled faces, anymore, anywhere. Not on television, not in movies, not on their friends (at least their Hollywood ones). So that when they saw wrinkles appearing in their own mirrors, on their own faces, they hied themselves to the "little tuck" person as quickly as possible, evidently. I had seen people out there crippled with arthritis, walking with canes, but their face skins had been smooth as could be. When I thought back to that former Columbia producer I had gone to see, the one who'd had the stroke, I seemed to recall that he hadn't had any wrinkles, either. Had he, too, had some "little tucks" done, so it wouldn't be a total waste of time as long as he was in the hospital, anyway, recovering from a sh-troke?

If I went back was that what I should do? Go get some "tucks," too? Why fight City Hall, I asked myself.

But then I remembered Miriam Hopkins. And an absolutely unforgettable evening at her apartment in New York City back in the mid-sixties . . .

Miriam Hopkins was an actress from the early thirties. I believe she made her debut in movies the year after talking pictures made *their* debut in 1929. So by the time the mid-sixties came around, Ms. Hopkins was a bona-fide, no-doubt-about-it senior citizen.

It was during the summer that this particular evening took place, and therefore quite warm, as New York can be that time of year, and so the doors of her apartment were wide open and the gathering was spilling out onto the terrace as well.

There was a spectacular view of the city out there. And also a bulbous, overgrown tub filled with water plopped in the middle of everything, which apparently served as a swimming pool of sorts. A ladder on one side of it was how you got up to the top rim, from which you could ease yourself down into the water. Actually you couldn't really *swim,* but you could get wet on a hot summer evening.

Which turned out to be what our hostess decided to do.

Or so I discovered when Miriam went inside, somewhere, reappeared in a swimsuit, a regular one-piece affair, and proceeded to mount the stairs alongside the giant tub.

I had never—nor have I to this day—seen anything like it.

This senior citizen had a network of wrinkles from her toes to her head. Her skin looked like crepe paper that had been tightly squeezed up into a ball, and then stretched out. Her stomach bulged, too. All those things people concern themselves with and try to, if not fix, at least camouflage somehow.

But not Miriam Hopkins. She flaunted hers before guests as well as the entire city of New York, if anybody out there cared to take a gander. She went up the ladder with as much presence and panache as if she had been Miss America herself.

I've never forgotten her. Have never lost my admiration, either. That woman had been a big, big star. And wrinkled or not, fat stomach or not, she didn't seem to have any doubt about who she was or who she had been, and had no intention of pretending otherwise. She seemed to be thumbing her nose at those ads that keep trying to scare the wits out of us all the time, shrieking, "Use me!" from the billboards and magazines and TV screens, "And you'll stay smooth and wrinkle-free and FOREVER YOUNG! YOUNG! YOUNG!"

Miriam's was the way to go, I was convinced of that, that evening on her terrace. Be *whatever you are,* all the way to the end. Other people don't like it? That was their problem, not yours. Beauty, I was sure Miriam was saying, is in the eye of . . . *yourself.*

The Spanish "castle" on the Mediterranean.

"Hear no evil"—
clowning with Artie
at Robert Ruark's villa.

*En famille* in Bagur, Spain (Artie is to my right, a young Joan Juliet Buck facing the camera, her mother, Joyce, behind her.)

My London flat (The traveling Olivetti, left uncharacteristically neglected, is in the background.)

Plotting a heist with pop star Cliff Richards in the BBC production of *A Matter of Diamonds*.

A triumphant return to Atlanta for a *Gone With the Wind* reunion in the 60s.

Suellen, Melanie, Tara's overseer, Careen, and the woman who perfected our Southern drawls.

Opposite page: Another "aunt" role—the ugly duckling becomes a swan.

Slapped by Scarlett in 1939 . . .

. . . feted on the 50th anniversary of *Gone With the Wind*.

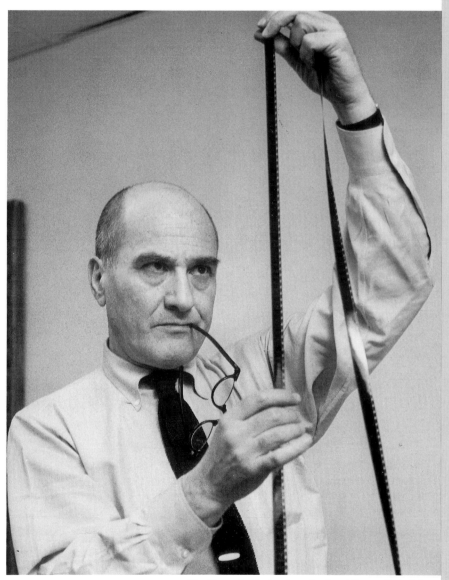

Restless Artie trades clarinet for celluloid.

"Trying a new point of view"—Evelyn Keyes the writer (Photo taken around time of publication of *Scarlett O'Hara's Younger Sister.*)

I sighed, remembering . . .

Admiring somebody and following in the same footsteps were two entirely different things.

However.

Any further pondering about such weighty (for me, at any rate) matters was going to have to go on hold for the time being, since the first and foremost item on my agenda at the moment was finishing book number two; the one my publisher said would rake in all that deliciously exciting "real" loot. So now that I was back on the hill and absolutely up to my eyeballs in "remembrances of things past" following my California interlude, I had damn well better get on with it. Better hole up in my study (and it was *mine* now, make no mistake!), put on blinders, and spend all my days type-type-typing my little heart out. I doubted there would to be too many hours in which to give much of anything else any too much thought any time soon . . .

# *Eighteen*

As it turned out, I spent not only the spring but the summer as well, along with the following fall and winter, creating that which my publisher had requested, an unabridged rendition of The Life And Times of One Evelyn Keyes. And when at last I turned the manuscript in, Mr. Publisher insisted on naming it, too. "Let's call it *Scarlett O'Hara's Younger Sister,*" was what he said.

"But it isn't about *Gone With the Wind*!" I cried, dismayed, "it's about me, as you wanted!"

"Everybody knows who Scarlett O'Hara is," was his reply, "and nobody remembers you."

Lucky me, right? If it wasn't Artie around to keep me in my place when I started getting too big for my britches, I now had a publisher to do the honors.

I kept trying, anyhow. "But wouldn't *A Good Man Is Hard to Find*—from the song—fit my theme better?" I asked him.

But he told me that title had been used by an ex-hooker who'd turned it around to a *Hard* Man is *Good* To Find, and people might confuse me with her.

They did, anyway. I mean, I was often treated like some former madam when I went out on tour with my book.

Yep. I went on tour again. The kind, this time, that the studio used to send us out on in the olden days in order to advertise their product for them. Sure, you were in the movie, but the studio kept the profits your appearance helped the picture engender, and paid you the same old salary your contract called for. And those tours were *work*. You got on trains and planes, you got off planes and trains. You got into limos, you got out of them. You posed waving hello, posed waving good-by. You stood alongside mayors and firemen and policemen and local congressmen and dog catchers and had your photograph taken. You received keys to cities, you made speeches on city hall steps, in state senates, at the theater where your picture was showing. And you did it for months. Over and over and over again. For the studio. Without so much as even a bonus.

At least, I thought happily in the beginning of my book tour, I would now be selling my very own product!

Except it wasn't too long before I began to notice something too peculiar for words. Something I didn't comprehend at all.

Back in those earlier days, when I had been simply a young girl, an actress-who-was-in-the-movies, who wasn't asked to do much more than smile and look pretty as I visited their cities, I was given a respect that bordered on downright awe. Simply because I was from that magic place called Hollywood.

But now. Older, with two books under my belt, not "as-told-to's" but written myself, it was as if I had done something a little shameful. Interviewers sometimes carried on as if I'd written pornography fit only for adult bookstores.

Like the young lady on *Good Morning, America* whispering to me with a pained expression, "Did you have to be so . . . *explicit?*" She said "explicit" as if *it* were a pornographic word.

Since "explicit" means "plain in language, clearly stated," I think (I confess I was rattled), I told her that yes, I did have to, how else would I have written it.

Then some smart-ass guy on another TV program, one of those morning things, had had huge poster-sized photos blown up of every man I had mentioned—even in passing—and put them on a chart in back of me, and proceeded to treat me, complete with leer, as if I had been the call girl of the century who had done quite a big business, indeed.

Some British columnist in London wrote how sad it was that these men "who loved me so" had been written about by me in such a "naughty" way. That surely they were "terribly hurt." If the man believes *that,* I thought when I read his column, maybe I can sell the fellow the London Bridge.

Finally, in Canada, I lost my cool. A woman interviewer went too far. (Or maybe I simply ran out of patience.)

Said this one, suggestively, and in front of an audience, too. "I hear your book is very raunchy."

Now, "raunchy" is not an attractive word. It means "dirty and slovenly, obscene or smutty" in my dictionary (and I daresay all the others). And the woman had not even read the book she was talking about. That is to say, *mine.*

I had had it. I broke. "Now look here!" I snapped. "My book is about a female, *me,* who went to Hollywood in a day when men ran the place! *Men,* alone, in the catbird seats! *Men* put me under contract, *men* produced the pictures, directed the pictures, wrote the scripts, made the still photographs, did the makeup, the clothes, the lighting, the sound, the props, were the cinema photographer and his crew; name it, men did it! And not only *that,* since I am heterosexual, I *married* them, *lived* with them, *slept* with them, went to parties with them, drove in their cars, had meals with them. Is it so surprising that it is *men* that I have written about?''

My outburst let off a bit of pent-up steam. After that my cool returned, and in future, similar enounters, I simply laughed, because by then all of it had begun to seem pretty ridiculous, anyway. And besides, the book was doing so very well, what did I have to complain about? Maybe they had all done me a big favor, after all. My book was even selected as a Literary Guild alternate, and I was invited to their fiftieth anniversary gala in New York City.

I wanted very much to go, too. There would be writers galore there, and I had been writer-struck since I was a kid and learned who had been responsible for those things with pages that you turned, one after the other, to be transported on their magic carpets of words to thrilling and exciting other worlds. I had never met a writer, though, until I arrived in Hollywood. And then I hit the jackpot. I met Thomas Mann, for instance. There as an escapee from Hitler's Europe.

Mann wasn't much to look at, though. Plain. Proper. A teller in a bank. A teacher in a junior high school. But I gave him an aura, anyway. (Or maybe he really did have one all on his own.) There was John Steinbeck, too. And Evelyn Waugh. John Collier and Aldous Huxley and Norman Mailer and Eric Ambler. I always listened carefully in case any Pearls of Wisdom dropped from their lips. (Not that I remember any, though. I expect *they* listened, and saved what they heard for their books.)

Alas, I didn't hear any Pearls at the Guild party, either, even though it was certainly jam-packed with writers everywhere I looked. Gore Vidal over there. Erica Jong on the dance floor (evidently thinking she knew how to dance as well as she knew how to write, the way she was flinging herself about with such awkward abandon). Shirley MacLaine was there as well (and in her own body). I was proud to be there, too, to be counted as one of them. And the next day I was being interviewed by *The New York Times. As a writer.*

Oh yes. I was in their league, now, no doubt about *that.* I fairly beamed with delight the entire evening.

The date with *The Times* reporter was set up for lunch in the dining room of the Sherry-Netherland Hotel on Fifth Avenue. I've always found lunch a quite pleasant way to do an interview, the business of ordering and eating, buttering bread, sipping tea breaking up the monotony of questions and answers being bandied about. We ordered something or other, the reporter and I, and as I began to answer the gentleman's questions about my two careers, first the acting, now the writing, I happened to look over and see Irwin Shaw sitting at the bar across the room.

Now, I had known Irwin practically since The Flood. Not only in Hollywood, playing tennis at the Beverly Hills Tennis Club, but skiing in Klosters in Switzerland, the time I went there. He was living in Paris, too, when I was living there. And now, here he was, in New York City, over at the bar, and I was over here at a table being interviewed by *The New York Times* as a writer, a *writer,* the same as Irwin was!

Why, we were in the same business, now, Irwin Shaw and I. Fellow travelers. Birds of a feather. We would have an understanding we had never had, before, Irwin and I! Wouldn't that be simply *scrumptious*!

I smiled and waved, and when he started out, he stopped by our table to say hello. He shook hands with the reporter (whom he evidently knew) and leaned down to kiss me on the cheek. We all ran through the faithful old standbys, the how-the-hell-are-you's and great-to-see-you's and then, not to interrupt our lunch any longer, Irwin turned to go.

But just before he did, he grinned down at the *New York Times* man. A sort of buddy-to-buddy man-type grin. "Too bad," Irwin Shaw, writer, said to the reporter, but nodding in my direction, "You never saw this girl in tennis shorts. She had the cutest little ass on the courts, bar none."

So much for equality. Macho-ism was alive and well and at the Sherry-Netherland. I wondered what it was going to take to get past being a sex object. Apparently getting on, of all things, didn't do it. Not even writing a couple of books.

It's called "history," I told myself as I drove up the Parkway. *Your* history. It trails along after you, wherever you go. And always will. So you had a perky ass, and somebody remembers, is that so bad?

The thought made me smile as I watched the sun's last rays flinging themselves across the landscape, glad to be getting back to my own burrow up on the hill once again. Where nobody would be thinking about my former ass, except maybe me . . .

In the end, simple maintenance was the thing that brought about the shift back to the West. No mind-boggling, philosophical enlightenment hitting me squarely between the eyes. No grand decisions on *Life,* or where-would-the-proper-location-be-for-best-pursuing-the-chosen-career-of-my-twilight-years. None of that.

Maybe it was nothing more than the sight of the mammoth oil tanker-truck laboring up the hill that did it, coming to pour gallons of the stuff into the pipe alongside the house, glub-glub-glubbing down into the storage tank that connected with the furnace, gallon after gallon after gallon, month after month after month (and the oil prices going up and up).

And there was the snow to be plowed in winter, the grass to be cut in summer. Yews to be sprayed (with tobacco juice) so the deer wouldn't eat them. And then along came something called Dutch elm disease, which started to ravish every one of those stately and beautiful trees within chomping distance. And if that weren't enough, acid rain was beginning to fall on everything.

The serpent had arrived in paradise in liquid form.

There were some other things, too, giving me little pushes here and there. Fragments of memories or things that had happened, been said, when I was out West. Things I'd suddenly remember on long winter nights, up on the hill.

Like going out to Hollywood Park with J.J., one day . . .

I hadn't been to a racetrack since hooking up with Artie. Had practically forgotten there were such things. J.J. asked if I would come by and pick him up—he couldn't see well enough to drive, himself (probably seeing, as he did tennis balls, two cars instead of one). He asked that I come a little early, if I would be so kind, as he would like, if I didn't mind, to go by way of Little Tokyo. J.J. said there was a bonsai tree exhibition in back of the Buddhist temple that he would like very much to see—that is, if I didn't mind.

Not only did I not mind, I looked *forward* to seeing a bonsai exhibition back of a Buddhist temple. I mean, I didn't know there *was* a Buddhist temple in Little Tokyo, and had never ever seen a bonsai exhibition in my life and probably never would have seen a bonsai exhibition in my life if J. J. Cohn hadn't been there to bring it to my attention.

Which was the kind of a guy J.J. was. Always coming up with suggestions for seeing/doing things you wouldn't have thought of doing yourself in a couple of million years. He'd call up and say there was a showing from Nepal over at the county museum. Or from Egypt. Or Israel, or Outer Mongolia and shouldn't we go. Once we went to see and hear his friend Arthur Rubinstein do *his* stuff, and attended a party for him afterward, at Zubin Mehta, the conductor's, house.

J.J. had interests in every direction. He hadn't just *happened* to go to the bonsai exhibition. He, himself, had more than a hundred of the dwarfed trees, which he tended and trimmed like real sculpture. Nor did he just happen to pop out to the races. He had a permanent table in the Turf Club, and while there, would study the Racing Form with fierce concentration, keep in close touch with the odds, then bet with the precision of a calculator, as if what he did were going to change the universe. He had a place in the Napa Valley, too, raising fields of grapes for a nearby winery, and I wouldn't have been surprised to learn that J.J. stomped on the grapes himself.

What had been so lovely was that I'd learned, seeing J.J. again after so many years, that he was still going about his life with the same enthusiasm, and curiosity—and beans—that he'd always had. And we're not talking about a *boy,* here. Maybe he had *been* a boy when he started his career at Metro-Goldwyn-Mayer back in the twenties. But now J.J. was an elderly gent, no two ways about it. I had no idea how old he actually was. I suppose I could have found out. But whatever for? *He* never talked age. His own or anybody else's. It apparently wasn't a subject that interested him. But with his wizened visage and shiny dome with the snow-white fringe, the wild, scraggly eyebrows over squinting eyes peering out into the world as best they could, J.J. had to be way up there.

But here was the most intriguing thing of all. The same line of thought seemed to keep coming back to me up there on the hill in Connecticut. Kept circulating round and round like clothes in a dryer in there in the back of my head, somewhere.

And that was, that the more I had got around my former stamping ground out there, the more my circle of acquaintances had grown, adding a few new faces as I had gone along, the more I'd begun to discover that, in the land of Eternal Youth, J.J. wasn't the *only* not-so-young-as-he-used-to-be person still passionately involved in something or other. Not the only "senior citizen" who was still turned on by some project or other, *exactly the way he or she had always been.* These sorts of people seemed to be all over the place, out there. These on-in-years people who understood the spirit of living so well.

For instance, there were Amanda and Philip Dunne (he who had scripted *How Green Was My Valley, The Ghost and Mrs. Muir,* plus a host of other things), with their enormous telescope aimed at the heavens, not wanting to miss a single cosmic happening up there if they could possibly help it. And if you went down to visit them at their Malibu place, which was up on a cliff alongside the Pacific Ocean, you had to freeze your buns off going out to look at some obscure star in some far-off galaxy they had just discovered and wanted to share their excitement and wonder of it all with you. They also kept an eye on the diminishing condors, fed humming birds, raised roses, and God knows what else, all with passion.

Danny Kaye had built an entire Chinese kitchen, apart from the main one, to do his Chinese-chefing in. The Wylers skied as if they planned to win the downhill at the next Olympics. Jean Negulesco *(Three Coins in a Fountain)* painted every canvas in sight. Eric Ambler still wrote every day. So did Billy Wilder. And John came to town to see about a movie he was going to do. Huston, that is. And of course I had run into him. There didn't seem to be too many places in the world I could go *without* running into this ex-husband of mine.

All of them. Doing. Working. Reading. Studying something. As if there were some kind of deadlines to meet. (John's emphysema was *much* worse than it had been in London, but of course, he seemed not to pay any too much attention to that.) Even the producer I'd visited in the wheelchair, though his taste might be questionable, I guess I'd have to give him at least one brownie point, since he'd still been in there pitching the only way he knew how.

If I had imagined that getting on would be treated like some dread disease by everybody in the youth-oriented land, how mistaken I'd been. There were even some who seemed to handle it better than in most any place else. And I couldn't help but wonder why. Until, one day, I remembered something J.J. had once said, when we were all sitting around the Club talking. "There never was a day," J.J. had said softly, "that I wasn't eager to get to work. It was always something new, something exciting, every day."

And I thought, aha. That's it. Not only did these people share a mutual work experience, all members of the motion picture industry, *they had loved what they were doing.* Been passionately involved. They had been *exactly* where they'd wanted to be. Doing *exactly* what they'd wanted to do.

Loving what you did meant that you'd look forward to tomorrow, didn't it? Because you would be liable to have a wonderfully good, full, fruitful day. And if you didn't, there was always *another* tomorrow coming up right away.

And so. Before you even *knew* it. The business of looking forward had become a habit. The business of trying to create a good, full, useful day for yourself, working at something you simply adored working at, became a habit. And then became the only way *to* go. Became the only way you knew *how* to go.

And so that was what you did. The way you went. For the rest of your days. The way those friends of mine back there in California were going.

At least, that was how it seemed to be to me, looking back at them from the top of my hill. That having had a clear direction about where you were going in your younger days helped you to make a decent life for yourself in your later years.

It certainly did seem that way to me as I thought things over up there on the mountaintop. Thought my friends out there in the West would be pretty good people to be around . . .

When a buyer came along, I packed up (again) and moved on (again).

Nature, though, gave one last tug, even as I was about to drive away.

Knowing I would never pass this way again, I stopped to take one last lingering look across the valley.

Though spring was near, several feet of snow still blanketed the ground. The trees, not yet having begun their greening, gave the appearance of a spread of dark lace flung across the white cover below.

And there, on one of the bare limbs, sat a lone cardinal, come to call in my final moment, a bright spot of scarlet midst all the gray and white . . .

I could not have asked for a lovelier farewell.

# PART THREE

# *Something Old, Something New*

# *Nineteen*

**W**ell, okay, here I was, once more, in my familiar setting, in the middle of a jumble of un-hung paintings and lampshades and end tables and stacks of book cartons and crates filled with I couldn't even imagine *what* at that point. On the ninth floor, I still had a view, this time of the grass and trees of Beverly Hills that I didn't have to do one damn thing about except enjoy.

The very first carton that I unpacked—after the essentials, that is—was the one filled with a pile of research I had already started gathering in preparation for the next, the number three book I had in mind to do, the news of which had not been greeted with the slightest bit of enthusiasm on the part of my publisher, however. He in fact had told me flat out what a dumb idea he thought it was. "Not for me you don't do any historical novel," he said tartly in his put-down way, "they even write those things by computer these days."

Carefully, and in an orderly fashion, I laid out my material in neat, precise stacks on the work table I had brought along from Connecticut, the same one that had been Artie's and that I had acquired by default. Continuity was entering my life at long last. And if I truly could just learn to *think* before I leapt (as I'd faithfully promised myself I woud), maybe I could keep things on a steady keel from here on in. It was surely worth a try.

The book I had in mind, in spite of my publisher—my *ex*-publisher, obviously—was about a daughter of Queen Isabella of Spain, she who had given the money to Christopher Columbus that enabled him to sail across all that water and discover he had been right all along about there being reachable land over there to the West.

The daughter, Juana by name, had been present through the whole period. Through all the many discussions held at court about the possibilities of such a voyage. Been there through the discovery itself, and the return of Columbus afterward, with what he called "Indians," all bared and feathered, in tow.

And Juana, all the time, had been so young, so beautiful, so brilliant and talented, and the one who should have inherited the Spanish throne when her mother kicked the bucket, and who might have shaped our world so very differently, given the chance.

But her father, Ferdinand, greedy to hold on to all the power for himself, labeled her crazy (his own *daughter,* he did this to!) and managed to lock her up and keep her off her rightful throne.

As a result she has gone down in history as Juana la Loca. "The Crazy One." And it just wasn't *so.* And I'd decided to prove it wasn't. I was quite taken with the idea. Had come to feel at one with Juana. (Well, she *was* a princess, after all!) And since I had lived five splendid years in her country, and knew about the bum rap she had been given, I'd come to feel it was practically my duty to come to her rescue—even if I was almost five hundred years too late. So Juana had become sort of a part of my budding continuity too, by jingo.

Because of her, it was UCLA and its research library that I hied myself to first. And sure enough, it had a Spanish section the size of Rhode Island, a large part of it in Spanish, too. So while I was at it, I enrolled in a Spanish refresher course, to see if I could maybe finally conquer that bloody subjunctive, because now it looked as if I would be reading in yesteryear *español.*

My work schedule in place, my spirits high, I began to get out and about going here, popping over there, rather hoping to meet some present day filmmakers, this time around. Now that Hollywood appeared on the way to becoming truly my hometown again, I was getting curious as to how the system worked these days, without the big studios holding the fort as they had in those days of yore.

The only trouble was that when I did meet them, I didn't even know it half the time. Like what happened during the trip up to J.J.'s spread in the Napa Valley.

My sister Julia, from Atlanta, had come out for a visit that summer. I was delighted when J.J. asked us both to pay him a visit up at his Napa residence. I had never been there before.

Julia and I drove up the coast all the way to San Francisco plus a teeny bit farther. It took seven hours, or thereabouts, but it was worth every minute of it! J.J. had this old Colonial house—or whatever they call that style in California—with a green mountain in back of it, and row upon row of grape-growing vines in front of it, stretching all the way across the floor of the valley until they reached the ring of mountains on the other side.

The first thing we did on arriving was to have lunch. Then he went through the winery that J.J. sold his grapes to, something, believe it or not, I had never done in all my years in France. Dark and cool was what it turned out to be.

After which J.J. told us we had been invited next door for an afternoon libation.

Now, to get to this "next door," we had to walk along a curving dirt road through acres and acres of the grape-laden vines—I mean, everybody around there had endless stretches of grape-growing vines—until we reached a very big, very handsome Victorian house, with porches all around, surrounded by *its* vines.

Although it was only four-thirty or so, the people inside the house were already at dinner. A bunch of them, too, around a mammoth, oblong table, maybe twenty or twenty-five or so enjoying themselves with their food and their drink. Several huge bottles, jeroboams I think they're called, of red wine sat in the middle of the large table, bottles that took a bit of muscle even to pick up to pour.

But somebody managed, and three chairs were pulled up to the table so that sister Julia, J.J., and I could squeeze ourselves in to join the group, for a glass of wine only, as it hadn't been all that long since lunch.

As the family (and maybe friends) laughed and talked and ate and drank, a big man with a dark beard—evidently the host, though I couldn't be sure—kept walking around the table with a movie camera on his shoulder photographing everybody.

The scene that the man was filming around the table brought to mind a movie I had seen recently called *The Godfather*. I whispered as much to a young man I was squeezed in next to. Who proceeded to give me a very strange look, as if I had made a faux pas.

That reaction alone should have given me some hint as to who the big man might have been. But in my day only cameramen had to do with cameras. Nor had the camera, back then, been of a size you could even hoist up on your shoulder the way the big man was doing that afternoon.

We three had our wine, bid the gathering good-by, and went on our way, back down the winding road through the rows of vines. "That's some house," said I to J.J., walking along, "whose is it?"

"Didn't you know?" J.J. responded with some surprise. "It's Francis Ford Coppola's."

I turned to stare at him. "You mean . . . the *director*?"

"I thought I told you where we were going . . ."

"You mean the director who made *The Godfather*?"

"That one, yes," said J.J. quietly, with a touch of amusement at my shocked reaction.

I was mystified that I hadn't caught on with all the clues right there in front of me. Boy, I was going to have to sharpen up my antennae *considerably* if I didn't want the world to pass me by. What with time doing its sneaky little vanishing act with every tiny tick of the clock, I wouldn't want to go around missing any *too* much more, would I.

* * *

And so when Anne and Kirk Douglas invited me to a shindig of theirs, I kept on my toes the whole time I was there, I can tell you. I maybe even overdid it.

What it was was a reception for Kirk's son, Michael, who had gone and got himself married.

It was—it truly was, I have to admit—highly entertaining to go to big Hollywood parties. Everybody always looked so *damned* good. All those faces recognized around the world, in smashing, latest-style clothes, jewels of all shapes and sizes glowing around necks and arms and hands of women *and* men. I mean, it *is* the town's profession to look good, after all.

At the Douglases, as was usually the case, now, there were the faces I had known before and those I was seeing for the first time. Burt Lancaster, Johnny Carson (Artie and I had met Johnny when he was just starting out, with wife number two and a set of drums in his living room in an apartment over on York Avenue in New York City), Jack Nicholson and Anjelica Huston (my distant "relative") among the former.

And then there was another face (among the latter ones) that I was sure I actually *knew* already, it seemed so familiar to me when I happened to glance over and find its owner looking straight in my direction. So sure was I that I did know the person, I started to smile, but then all at once realized who it was, and that I didn't know him at all.

It was Warren Beatty, whom I happened to admire enormously. Most everything about him. His looks. His screen persona. The pictures he had chosen to produce. Even his politics.

But whom I had never met. So he couldn't possibly be looking at me. He had to be looking at somebody behind me.

I edged slightly forward so he could see past me, turned back to the group I was standing with, and went on chatting.

But a few minutes later, when I glanced that way again, there were Warren Beatty's eyes, looking straight at me.

There was no mistaking it, this time.

I gave a little nod, then. But he didn't respond. He just

continued his unwavering gaze. Shutting out everything except the object he was looking at.

Me.

Evelyn Keyes.

It was most disconcerting. Why was Warren Beatty looking at me this way?

It couldn't possibly be because he . . . because . . .

Or could it?

How many times had I played this scene before (off-screen and on)? That my eyes would meet somebody else's across a crowded room. And the excitement would begin to well up, knowing something special was about to happen . . .

Could it be possible that Warren Beatty had taken a look (across *this* crowded room), and decided that I was to become a member of his rather exclusive group of female companions? (Oh yes. I had always admired his choice of women, too.)

*Don't be ridiculous,* I said to myself sharply. Surely Warren Beatty knew that I was of another generation. That I was . . . old enough to be his *mother,* for godsake!

But then. Another thought came scurrying up. Maybe not. After all, I *had* been away for a very long time. Perhaps he didn't even know who I was! And the lighting at these kinds of parties was always awfully good. (Would they have any other kind for a Hollywood party?) So soft, and low and rosy. Very, *very* flattering. So much so, that, who knew, perhaps I actually looked like my former self.

The way I had looked when these things happened with fairly steady frequency.

My heart quickened its pace a bit.

So what if I *were* older than he? Did these things really matter, anymore? In this day and age? Weren't we all free, at last, to do what we wanted, with whom we wanted, when we wanted?

By then, Warren, who had been edging his way forward, was a mere two feet away, his eyes still upon me.

"Why," I whispered (rather huskily, I expect, already into my role), "are you staring at me this way?"

He gazed deeply into my eyes. "It is so strange," he whispered back. "I'm about to film a remake of *Here Comes Mr. Jordan,* so I've been running it for the past three weeks and looking at your face every day, and now here you are."

Ah so . . .

Mr. Beatty *did* know exactly who I was. *Did* know I was old enough to be his mother. Knew very well that *Jordan* had been made back in the early forties, when he had been the tiniest of tots.

At least the encounter afforded me another nice laugh at myself once I got out of there and into the safety of my own quarters.

Damned if I hadn't done it again.

Boy. Set me back on the old stamping ground, present me with a situation I am familiar with, and I instantly respond as if Scotty had beamed me back to yesteryear, and I am once again that "girl" you catch occasionally on the late late movie.

I snapped on my faithful reminder (lacking Artie), the harsh, ever present, overhead light that is found in most bathrooms and placed myself directly under it.

Take a good look, sweetheart, said I to my image, since you certainly do have this tendency to become forgetful. As you can observe, the lines have not miraculously disappeared since the last time you looked. See? Around the eyes? On the forehead? See the look *in* the eyes? *See?*

*That face does not play love interest* anymore, baby-doll, on-screen or *off!* It plays *aunt,* remember? Possibly even great-great-*great* grandmother by now. Wicked-witch-of-the-West. Anything *old.* Got that straight, sweetie-pie, I said to the mirror. And any "little tucks" you might be considering having done wouldn't *change one fucking thing.* Has your little pea brain got *that* straight as well, angel face?

My image sighed, shook her head, and picked up a toothbrush.

I doubt it, I thought, brushing away. Doubted very much if

I had truly got it straight *yet*—the business of getting over the hill. It seemed like one step forward and two backward all the time. I'd think I had it down pat, then a Warren Beatty would come along. The old movies with the young me in them that wouldn't go away didn't help. Nor did the young stills of my former self that people kept bringing around to be signed. People always comparing me to my younger self. *I* kept on comparing me to my younger self, for crissake!

God. Here I had met another contemporary filmmaker, and instead of *mentioning* that I was interested in doing something once in a while, and if anything came along in a picture of his (aunt, witch, grandmother), would he kindly think of me, what had I done? *I had backed away from the man as fast as I could.*

Honest-to-Pete. If I didn't get my act together pretty soon, I wouldn't *have* an act to *get* together.

The encounter with Warren, however, did not go to waste. In fact, it helped me enormously to remember quite clearly, and thoroughly, who and what I was, and just where I stood at the moment in the scheme of things, when a couple of guys I'd known back in those earlier days came around to pay me a visit . . .

# Twenty

The two guys didn't come together, I didn't mean that. As far as I knew, they didn't even know each other. They actually came around, oh, maybe a couple of weeks apart. But what was remarkable about their visits, and why I remember them so well, was that their behavior was identical. *Identical.* Like echos of each other.

I had come across the gentlemen at separate gatherings and had said, hey, why don't you come around and see me one of these days, and let's catch up. I did that when I came across old friends, having been away and out of touch for so many years.

These two were now middle-aged men, my contemporaries, if you will, guys I had known in my youth, who had been youths, too, at the time, and who had been, each in his turn, how shall I describe it, a false start, so to speak. But we had stayed friends (and why not), only at this point I hadn't seen either of them for the twenty-odd years I had been elsewhere, living my other lives.

They looked pretty good (each in turn). Still had their hair. Had kept reasonably flat abdomens. But here was the thing. Immediately after polite exchanges of greetings, they each in their turn took out a packet of cigarette paper, a vial of herb-looking stuff, which was clearly marijuana, and began to roll themselves a joint. *Each of them.*

To my knowledge neither gentleman had smoked grass in his earlier years. But of course since I'd been away, anything could have happened. They, too, could have got caught up in the goings-on of the swinging sixties, thinking pot was ''hip,'' the ''with-it'' thing to do. But even if I hadn't sworn never to take so much as even a puff of any kind of funny (or even *not* funny) cigarette again after the absurd fiasco with the art dealer back in London, I was under the impression that grass-smoking had fallen from grace by now. That health, and filling your body with vitamins and green vegetables and whole grains instead of drugged smoke, was what had become the chic thing to do these days, particularly in California.

My two middle-aged pals, however, appeared to be a couple of beats behind in the chic department, though apparently neither of them realized it. I got the impression they each thought they were hot stuff. First one and then the other (on his day) held out his lit joint to me, assuming that I had to be as ''hip'' as he was.

The shake of my head didn't faze either of them, though.

They went right ahead on their own, sucking smoke deep into their lungs and, as I watched, got their buzz on.

And then each (in his turn) rose and, movements loosened due to their buzz, ambled to where I sat, dropped to his knees beside my chair (identical action on both days—*identical!*), and proceeded to put his arms around me, nuzzle in my hair, slurp a tongue around my ear, wriggle it across my cheek to seek my mouth, and plunge in.

Since I merely watched their actions, response on my part (on a scale of one to ten) at zero, their rhythm soon became unhinged. Because this was where I was expected to join in. Where I *had* joined in back in those earlier time zones. So they knew I *knew* my role in the proceedings, and if I wasn't playing, something had to be amiss.

The realization that they had made a tactical error in judgment did manage to penetrate their drug-fogged brains (each in his turn); I have to give them brownie points for that, at least.

They departed shortly thereafter, managing to scrape enough manners together to each make a fairly graceful exit. They had never been total clods. Before, that is. It had been pretty cloddish to come to see me with their funny cigarettes and sexual machismo—along with their outrageous assumption that my body (such as it was) would still be available for an extracurricular afternoon quickie. (Oh yes. These men both had long-standing marriages and grown-up children at this point.)

So what were they doing, these middle-aged gents? Upholding their old gay-blade reputations (at least in their *own* heads), sneaking around getting laid of an afternoon, being so hip and with-it with their pot-smoking?

But why me? This old broad of an earlier era? I doubted that if I went up to the Sunset Strip where hookers were wont to ply their trade I would even have been able to get myself arrested.

I came up with a guess as to why. Could it have been because I had known them in their prime? When their parts (private ones, that is) were working gorgeously? When they were virile, and *looked* it? And their power to charm anyone they chose, to woo and to win, was still intact? So that now, if something . . . uh . . . mistimed, to put it delicately, they could simply shrug ruefully, grin boyishly, and murmur, "Ah, but we remember when, don't we dear."

For the first time ever I began to have a bit of sympathy for the aging male, particularly the heterosexual one, he who felt called upon to keep "having his way with the 'fairer sex.' Because in order to do so, by nature's design, he had to . . . well, get it up was what he had to do.

Up to then I had been thinking that women, exclusively women, were the ones to suffer the slings and arrows of the getting-older process, what with such a big accent on their youthful good looks and wrinkle-free skins and tight derrières. So that when these lovely attributes began to fade, the jig was up, the winnowing-out not long in coming.

But after the two guys came around, I began to revamp my thinking. Remembering back to the wheelchair Lothario, I began to look at these maturing males in a different light. To understand just what this ability to have a hard-on must mean to them.

Everything, as it turned out.

I looked up "impotent" in Webster's. It told me it meant "weak, helpless, feeble, powerless."

So it seemed that this ability to produce erectile tissue at a moment's notice was all tied up with the works: power, success, the winning of all life's little (and big) dreams—whatever they may be.

Wow. Imagine the panic of the dyed-in-the-wool so-called ladies' man the first time his apparatus functioned somewhat under par. Poor baby. I wouldn't exchange the sighting of a first wrinkle with *that* shock, for all the tea in China.

What made it doubly tough on a male, too, I decided, were the games we boy/girl types had been conned into playing through the years. Those of us, that is, who hadn't been born yesterday. *He* had to play natural-born leader (no matter what), bold, fearless at all times, plus being (at a moment's notice) a good fuck to boot.

*She,* on the other hand, had to play natural-born nurturer (no matter what), soft, pliable. And ecstatically ready to receive said good fuck any time it was presented. And if we didn't fit our particular roles according to gender, we didn't tell a soul (not even ourselves).

But those days were pretty much gone—I mean, weren't they? To the extent that you didn't have to play those dumb games if you didn't want to. They weren't compulsory, the way they had once been. At least we older women thought so, having learned the hard way. Especially someone like me who had made the run several times.

Sometimes even ones who had hung in for a lifetime of living together learned it. Especially widows who had ended up nursing, for years and years, a terminally ill spouse, thinking all the while what were they ever going to do without him, suddenly realizing, one day, how much better off they were now that he had departed.

Like when the old dog you loved finally died, and you discovered, after many bouts of tears and sorrow, how nice it was you didn't have to walk him, anymore. That you were free to do the things you'd always wanted to do. Free to be . . . your very own self, at long last.

Straight *men,* however, more often than not, persisted in hanging on to their old pose in their later years. No doubt it was very hard for them to give up the "big boss" image of themselves. Hard to admit to not being as brave and strong as they used to be. (In fact, never had been.)

So I found a lot of them not all that much fun to be around. Especially those who felt they had to try and prove (mostly to themselves) that their sexuality wasn't waning. Like the ones who had just visited me.

Gay men, on the other hand, were quite pleasant to be around. They had had, it seemed to me, an experience somewhat akin to women's. They always had had to go around pretending to be something they weren't.

But now all of us could stop hiding behind false fronts, and be ourselves. Whatever it was. So women and gays, for the most part, got along splendidly. And what was terribly fortunate was the number of them who enjoyed being around yesteryear movie stars. So whatever the reasons for it—and they were myriad, I dare say—I was discovering how splendidly it all worked out in a world that apparently never intended to abandon the Noah's Ark arrangement for social events.

Worked out . . . *most* of the time, that is to say. Not each and every time, alas . . .

# *Twenty-one*

The invitation sounded really great. "Want to go to a party next week?" one of my gay friends said to me. "Rita Hayworth is going to be there, I understand."

Well, hey, Rita.

We went back such a long way, Rita and I. She had been in the very first picture I ever made at Columbia, playing Glenn Ford's "love interest." (I played his kid sister.) That was it, the only time Rita and I ever worked together. But Columbia was a small lot and our paths crossed constantly—in hairdressing, in makeup, at Harry Cohn's gatherings.

One day, I remember going to Harry's office for something or other, and he was about to run wardrobe tests of Rita when I came in. Some she had made for a picture she was about to do. "Come sit with me while I look at these," Harry said.

So there was Rita up on the screen, doing this boring thing we used to have to do, test the *clothes* for the flick we were about to make, to see that at least they would be doing *their* job properly. Rita Hayworth, up there on the screen in Harry Cohn's darkened private screening room. Probably one of the handsomest people our species has ever produced. That shock of red hair framing a catlike face. (She ought to have been able to purr, and who knows, maybe she could.) The willowy body. She flowed when she moved, all in one piece, graceful as a spill of ribbon touched by the wind.

Rita. Up there, all by herself. Doing nothing but turning this way and that to show off some new clothes Jean Louis had just designed for her. And she did it so stunningly, knowing her camera, knowing exactly what to do in front of it, that she made me remember the moment all these years.

Rita. I had given her a baby shower once upon a time, too. For her first. I can't imagine why. I had never given a baby shower before, nor have I since. All Columbia's female contract players were there, so it must have been something the publicity department arranged. Rita looked the way you are supposed to look when you're having a baby. (Beautiful and slightly ethereal, right?) She wore something black, with long full sleeves, and enormous cuff links, stones of some kind, like topazes. Or maybe even emeralds, for all I know.

Rita. A part of such a big chapter in my life. How terrific it would be to see her, again.

"Ohmyyes!" I cried to my friend, "I would love to see Rita again! It's been such a long time since I have!"

"She might not know you," he then said to me.

"Of *course* she'll know me!" I scoffed. I thought he didn't know of our long acquaintanceship. And I proceeded to explain it.

But he, the idiot, didn't explain to me what *he* meant. He allowed me to find that out for myself. (Which I doubt I will ever forgive him for.)

She looked great. The hair, the figure, all the things that made Rita Rita, were still there. A little older, of course, but then weren't we all.

I hurried to where she stood with some man I didn't know.

"Hey, Rita!" I cried. "It's Evelyn Keyes! How in the world are you?"

Rita looked at me with absolutely blank eyes.

I thought she wasn't absorbing the fact that this person from so many years ago had suddenly reappeared before her.

"Evelyn Keyes!" I repeated, gaily. "My God, it's been forever, hasn't it!"

But Rita simply continued to look at me as if I were some alien creature that had just dropped in from Krypton.

That was when the man next to her spoke up. Slowly, and distinctly, he spoke, separating his syllables. *"E-ve-lyn-Keyes. Of course you remember E-ve-lyn Keyes."* His tone was a scolding one.

Rita had turned to him when he had begun to speak, watching his mouth, his eyes. Hanging on as if to a life raft to his every word.

And then she answered him, like a little girl, learning a lesson, repeating the exact words he had spoken, "Of course I remember E-ve-lyn Keyes."

But it was to the man she spoke, never turning my way again. I believe I was already forgotten.

I saw her twice more, at other gatherings. There was never any sign of recognition. Of me or of anybody else. She never even knew where she was, her friends (if that's what they could be called) leading her about like a docile puppy.

My two pictures of Rita. The two images, in my head, glued together forever and ever. The one of Movie Star perfection. Love Goddess in her prime. The other a befuddled woman who didn't even know anymore that she had once been Rita Hayworth.

It was almost more than I could bear. Reality, something I had managed to skirt fairly well up to then, had come at me all of a sudden with a fierce angry rush. Got me before I could duck. Who would have thought Hollywood would be the place to finally have to confront it, *mano a mano.*

Hollywood. Make-believe heaven. Where I (who had lived a fantasy life since the age of two, inventing daddies, inventing playmates) had come to earn my living, thereby enabling me to continue my fantasy world, and even getting paid for it, each and every day, all the live-long day.

When would the line between make-believe and reality ever have had a chance to sharpen up? And who wanted it to? Better to keep real life sandwiched in between the make-believe one; that way you could always switch off and flip over into another script any time the going got to be not to your liking (in either world). Move on. And on. And on. Until the moving became a kind of buffer between you and the nasty jolts real life insisted on doling out from time to time. I'd never been there when anybody I'd been close to got zapped. I would have already moved on. Would only hear about it from a safe distance. Say, from the other side of the world. Or at least another city.

But now.

Rita. Dear, gentle Rita.

I couldn't get over, when I started putting it all together, to how great an extent she had affected the course of my life. When I hardly knew her at all.

First there was Columbia. Padding my breasts (in the beginning), because Rita's were larger. Adding hairpieces to my head, because her hair was thicker. When I heard her making a political speech (on the radio), I wanted to get into the act, too. Show that I, too, was a caring and solid citizen of these United States of America. (For my pains I was put on some of the Joe McCarthy-type blacklists being kept at the time—a fact I recall with a sense of pride.) Hearing her say, one day in makeup, that she didn't intend to spend the rest of her life on a soundstage, encouraged me to fly the coop, too, to take off for England and other points east, not wanting to be the one to be left out of life's little adventures.

And now, once again, Rita Hayworth had touched me profoundly . . .

If only I could have put my arms around her and told her these things. I might at least have given her a chuckle or two.

Even in her disorientation there was still a gentle sweetness in Rita that was reminiscent of Marilyn Monroe. They had both been so-called love goddesses in their day, Rita maybe even having an edge on Marilyn. But Rita didn't die soon enough. Didn't die young and beautiful. Didn't kill herself.

What is it with us humans? We take medicines, have operations, do aerobics, eat whole grains and steamed broccoli and bananas to hang in there as many years as we can, and yet we worship the ones who don't make it. Does that make sense?

If Marilyn had lived on, since she tended toward plumpness, she would probably be going around in one of those tent-shaped dresses that are supposed to hide the blimp-shaped body underneath, and doesn't, bleaching her hair (what was left of it) to hide the gray, all still with the little-girl voice, and she would be an embarrassing and sad joke to whom no one would pay the slightest attention at all. Instead she has become this symbol of female movie star quintessence, frozen in her peak years forever and ever. And Rita Hayworth, who could as easily have become such a symbol, didn't quite, because she *did* live on. It is in this fashion, alas, that the cookie of cinematic renown has been known to crumble . . .

# Twenty-two

Days seemed to become more and more precious after my encounter with Rita. I realized soon after how acutely aware of my surroundings I had become as I drove along Sunset Boulevard, one morning, on my way to the UCLA research library, to dig up further material for my pending historical novel.

The day was about as close to perfection as a day could get. Not too warm, not too chilly, a soft sun blanketing the landscape, the trees lining the Boulevard miracles of some sort with their ability to grow so tall and stately, the flowers blooming everywhere in all the colors of the rainbow and then some, works of unduplicatable art.

I got this overpowering urge to reach out and gather the whole thing in, right into my heart, so that I could cherish it and keep it with me forever. Or at least for the rest of my days here on earth.

Dear Rita, I thought. Still having her effect on me. Even helping me to understand how lucky I was, not only to still have my health (and wits), but to have found this thing I loved doing in my later years. I even adored these trips to the research library. It comforted me, somehow, being in the middle of this vast labyrinth of books. Row after row of them. Crissing and crossing, floor after floor. I loved the musty smell, the quiet, the coming across another human being here and there, as intent on a search as I was. It was like being on a treasure hunt, on a quest for a nugget of gold, or a pearl of, in this case, information that would bring me one step closer to a clearer understanding of what made Princess Juana, the young and brilliant daughter of Queen Isabella of Spain, Columbus' patroness, and leading character in this next novel, tick.

Although this part of my life had become the binding that held me together these days, I didn't stop trying to weave myself back into the woof and warp of the Hollywood fabric. And it turned out to be an absolutely super period for doing so.

Looking back, my timing for being in the right place at the right time for one of those made-to-order, once-in-a-lifetime acting roles appears to have been rather faulty. But my ability for finding myself on hand when new and interesting eras were in the process of being created seems to have remained impeccable throughout.

As I was settling down in town, this time, the motion picture industry, having discovered that it had a history worth remembering, was busily honoring (before it was too late) the filmmakers who had helped make it so.

And since it happened that my tenure turned out to be at the dead center of those particular years when so many of the films that were now being called classics had been made, I was often invited to attend these occasions.

They were always big, razzle-dazzle black-tie affairs, taking place in the ballrooms of the best hotels, where a thousand or more people dressed to the nines would mill about, looking each other over, then seat themselves at big, round, white-clothed tables with fancy-flowered centerpieces, to be wined and dined before the proceedings began on the raised plat-form before them. All reminiscent of an earlier time when even Academy Awards (before they became a TV spectacle) were presented in this fashion.

What was particularly interesting when an icon of yester-year was being feted was that the stars who had worked with him (once in a while a "her") would turn out, too. And ev-erybody could find out how the years had treated them. Whether they had held up well, kept their figures, or gone to pot. (I imagine I got the once-over here and there as well.)

J.J. and I got all dolled up and proudly went to the American Film Institute's evening for our friend Willie (Wyler, that is), when he was presented with its Life Achievement Award. Au-drey Hepburn was there, I remember, and she looked splen-did, still her reedlike and elegant self. Bette Davis was there, too, and she *didn't* look all that good. (But then Bette had always defiantly held onto her smoking habit with all the in-tensity of a baby with its pacifier, so it was no wonder.)

Actually you never see too much of the guest of honor at these things (or his/her spouse) except from afar. But we made up for that at Talli and Willie's wedding anniversary some time later, where only a few hundred or so of their most "in-timate friends" were gathered, as well as their children, all grown up now—the one Talli had passed up *Gone With the Wind* to pop out, plus about three more.

And whaddaya know. Who else should appear but old John

Huston, ex-husband in person, over from London, no, make that Ireland, I guess. He and Willie had been friends since the Dark Ages. "John!" I cried, "I didn't know you were in town!"

Then John, as was his habit said, "How are you, honey?" He spoke in a tired way. Poor baby. He was a little more stooped, the cheeks a little more sunken. The emphysema was taking its toll.

But then he added something else to his greeting that surprised me. "Still writing?" he asked.

Well, well. It was the first time he had ever acknowledged—to me, anyway—that I had done such a thing. I had sent both my published books to him, but he'd never responded in any way, shape, or form. Not to say thank you, but no thanks. Not to say you're really lousy, I'd forget it if I were you. Or, maybe you'll improve if you keep on trying. Absolutely nothing. Zero response. Zilch. Which rather surprised me since I'd always been under the impression that John had been generous with his time to "young and struggling" talent connected with his profession. (Perhaps the same did not apply to a former little wifey and/or camp follower.)

But now he was coming through, and I answered his inquiry happily, pleased that he had asked. "Oh yes, I *am* still writing! And do you know, John, I think I've finally found a little niche for myself at long last, isn't that something!" I was trying to—I wanted to—share my good feeling with him.

But the only response he gave me was the tiniest of nods, accompanied by a mere suggestion of a smile that never even reached his eyes. And then he moved on. Turned away, and *moved on.*

Anger struck at me as if it were a rattlesnake. *Now look here, John!* I felt like hissing at his departing back, I am not *committing any crime,* or anything! I'm not *harming* anyone—nobody even has to *read* a damn *thing* I put down on paper if they *don't want to!* Nobody has to *publish* it, either! Reviewers can simply toss it into their wastebaskets, for all I care! And so what! I wouldn't give a *fig*—no, that's not true,

Rehearsing my steps on a Columbia sound stage . . .

. . . on stage in *No, No Nanette,* dancing up a storm.

On the road (literally) with
*No, No Nanette.*

Leading cast in big production
number, "I Want to Be Happy."

At the piano with Don Ameche.

With Betty Garrett (l.) and Jan Sterling (r.) in *Breaking Up the Act*.

With producer-pal Tab
Hunter . . .

. . . and "the Kid," Allan
Glaser.

Partying with George Burns . . .

. . . in a more casual mode barbecuing with Allan.

"Old husband, new friend"—Artie, March, 1990.

Me "on up the road" at Talli's tennis court.

I *would* give a fig, a big fig—*but it would not stop me.* I'm not doing it to please *them,* out there, I am doing it for *me, me alone!* For this glorious sense of *accomplishment* it gives me every day! For this exciting focal point I can wrap my life around, that makes me feel so *whole,* so *rich,* so complete and *fulfilled,* every single day of my life! Couldn't you at least say *you are happy for me,* John? *Say it, whether you mean it or not?*

Fortunately I said none of that to him. My passion in the matter would have probably bowled him over, and I had the feeling it was all he could do to move from one place to another. *The man was not well.* A fact that didn't seem to want to sink into my brain. I kept confusing this tall person I kept running into with that vital, interested-in-everything man I had once known.

Another notable event that came along was yet another *GWTW* anniversary. I had had more anniversaries with that flick than I'd ever had with a husband or anything else. I had been to one of them shortly after we'd returned from Europe. It had taken place in Atlanta, again. Melanie (Olivia de Havilland) and Careen (Ann Rutherford) had been on board. The city fathers, maybe mothers, too, had tried hard to re-create the first time out with a parade through town, and a fancy-dress ball. But this one, the fortieth (the *fortieth*!), was being celebrated in the Los Angeles County Museum.

In a museum.

When I hadn't been looking I seemed to have turned into a museum piece. Wasn't that something. Me, the "baby."

All kinds of people from everywhere even started coming around to look me up, too (evidently in my museum-piece capacity), people who were writing books, magazine articles, putting together documentaries on some yesteryear Hollywood personage. They wanted to find out what recollections I might have stored away on the subject of their particular choice. What inside-dope-straight-from-the-horse's-mouth anecdotes I might be able to reveal about the one I shared some back-then time with.

They came to ask me about the columnists of earlier years, about Louella Parsons and Hedda Hopper and Sheilah Graham, and how it was they wielded so much power. Came to ask about Harry Cohn, he who ran Columbia Pictures in its heyday, and how it was he wielded all that power. They came to talk of Cecil B. DeMille (he who had opened the door for me), because it was about to be his hundredth birthday, and evidently *the* definitive book was being written about him for the occasion.

A TV crew showed up at my digs, hauling their camera and lights and sound after them. Their interviewer, the British journalist Michael Freedland, brought up the rear. All the way from London he had come to find out what tasty tidbits might still be lingering from my encounter with Al Jolson, The World's Greatest Entertainer, as he called himself. The Brits were making a documentary on Jolie (as his friends called Jolson), because he, too, was about to have *his* hundredth birthday.

God. Most everybody I had known back in my acting-career days would now be (alive or dead) turning a hundred. Even Harry Cohn wasn't too far behind. Which meant, if I thought about it, that they actually *hadn't* been in the spring-chicken division when I'd been around them. They had been—it was hard to admit, but it was so, it was absolutely *so*—in the neighborhood I was approaching today. Al Jolson had to have been *past* sixty when the success of *The Jolson Story* had snatched him back from the jaws of show-biz oblivion and plopped him down on Stage Center once again.

And here was the thing. Nobody had thought anything about it. Jolson's resurrection from the ashes of obscurity hadn't seemed so much an *age* phenomenon as a question of a style that had gone out of favor somewhere along the way and was being rediscovered again. Because, back then, we were *used* to seeing plenty of sixty- (even seventy-) somethings all over the movie screens. Not playing bit parts, either. Playing *leads*. Often even *starring* in their own movies—something one seldom, if ever, saw anymore. They hadn't played wimps all the time back then, either, or eternally some kind of sad sack or bag lady the way oldies seemed to have to do every time out, nowadays, if they want to keep on working. On-in-years actors used to play people *in charge,* for crissake, I thought, remembering back; like heads of banks or corporations. Ethel and Lionel Barrymore played them. May Robson and Charles Coburn. And they *looked* their ages, too. The way Miriam Hopkins had. They hadn't gone out and had their faces all "tucked up."

It was the Jolson interview, the remembering Jolie and talking about him at length, that had got me started thinking how you seldom even saw actors *around,* anymore, who looked . . . well, frankly *up* there. A Beulah Bondi, for instance. A Jane Darwell. What had ever happened to all those great faces? I wondered. Had they disappeared beneath all those famous "tucks" so prevalent around town?

Yep, I'd bet anything they had. Apparently lived-in faces were out. Ersatz youth was in.

Was *this*, then, the new Hollywood everyone had kept trying to warn me about, knowing that I was getting up there myself?

But when had it happened, I inquired of myself, this discarding in the flicks of everybody over (or those who looked over) thirty? That appeared to be the magical age beyond which you dared not get (or look). "You can't trust anybody over thirty." Wasn't that the phrase being bandied about for a while back there? And the Beatles hadn't helped a hell of a lot with that song of theirs that conjured up some enfeebled, decrepit, toothless fellow who had to be spoon-fed at age sixty-four.

Well, guys, you should have been there, on that soundstage, listening to Al Jolson at that age recording the songs for a movie about his life. I was there. I heard. I saw. There, in the soundbooth even, headphones over his ears, the man was a force of nature. Niagara Falls in Person. The San Francisco Earthquake. And I learned later that he had only one lung at the time.

*Something Old, Something New* ■ 185

Ah, but The Beatles *hadn't* been there. And tastes, along with people, refuse to stay put. And if I was still having any lingering doubts about the way things stood during this, my latest foray into the Hills of Hollywood (and Beverly), the *Los Angeles Times* made it crystal-clear one morning about seven, even as I evaluated the situation.

Right there, in my home-delivered paper I read, in terribly precise print, that for the first time in history, it was the young who were sitting around the campfires (of Hollywood) telling the tales instead of the elders. Since the beginning of time, the elders had been the ones doing that, around all the campfires the world over.

Well. Wasn't it a good thing, I said to myself, that I was into something else besides the acting business. Wouldn't it be simply awful to spend your life *dreading* the inevitable—the sight of yet another wrinkle?

And it would happen. Nothing could stop it. Nothing. Absolutely *nothing*. Time simply kept marching right on, willynilly. Little-tuck-taking or not. So it *had* to be a losing battle, didn't it, the attempt to hold on to eternal youth—which appeared to be necessary though, if acting was what you wanted to do.

There had to be another way. And there was. I had already seen it. My friends were doing it. *Something else* was what they were doing. They must have seen the youth takeover coming and gotten out when the getting was good and into other things besides pictures. Willie, with Talli, kept traveling to places as far as the South Pole. Besides his cosmic gazing, Phil Dunne was writing a political column, and J.J. was doing his million and two things, all of them carrying on with the same gusto with which they had pursued their studio careers.

So that was that. Sensible people went on to other things when they got older. And kept themselves intact. That's all there was to it. It was certainly what I was going to do. Going to *keep* doing.

But then. Wouldn't you know. Didn't it happen to me every single time? Every time I spent hours working my way in and around one of my oh-so-earnest think-throughs, arriving at some oh-so-Big *Important* Decision for myself, along came something that would knock the entire conclusion right out of the box.

I met a superstar. And I mean a fellow who by superstars was a superstar. He had not only won an Academy Award for his movie work, he was a stand-up comedian to boot, doing his thing in the hottest spots in the world. And if that wasn't enough, he had also written a few bestsellers in his spare time.

Not only that. He had been—and done—all these things for one hell of a long time, *without changing any direction at all.* Because this superstar, in the middle of the youth take-over, was a member of the eighty-something gang . . .

# *Twenty-three*

I had never met George Burns before, even though I had been at a party back in the middle fifties where he had been present. But he hadn't been my dinner partner on that occasion; instead I'd been seated next to his great good friend Jack Benny.

I have no idea why that was the seating arrangement. Jack Benny and I had absolutely nothing in common. Not only that, he was not a person who bothered whatsoever with the usual dinner-table small talk, apparently preferring, instead, to save his scintillation for his performing chores.

Jack Benny spent the entire time—ignoring not only me, but the other four people around the table as well—with his ear attuned to the conversation going on at the table nearest us. And when he'd hear something that one of the men over there said that struck his fancy, Jack would, all at once, out of no-where, no matter that someone at our table might be in the middle of recounting something, whoop with raucous laughter, slap the top of the table so that everything on it bounced up and down—plates, silverware, glassware, even the center-piece.

George, of course. George Burns had been the man at the neighboring table, whose every utterance sent Jack Benny into such spasms of laughter. (Clearly George's number one fan, Jack even went so far as to conveniently die at the right time, too, so that George could do the part in *The Sunshine Boys* instead of Benny that gave George the Academy Award and his latter-day stardom.)

Artie had, on occasion, spoken of George, and said he was a witty man. Back in radio's heyday—and Artie's, too—he, his clarinet, and his orchestra had been on one of those big, pop-ular weekly shows with George and Gracie. Even Artie said that George had a way with a story, and unlike Benny, was apt to tell them off-stage as well. Artie still remembered some of them back there in Spain. I remembered one Artie had told me, when I came across George at another dinner party—and *was* seated alongside him, this time—at the Bistro restaurant in Beverly Hills all these years later.

It was a story about a pushy acrobat back in George's vaude-ville days, who always made a point of getting to each new theater first in order to set himself up in the best spot in the best dressing room, so that everybody else had to take pot luck.

Finally George had had it. Had had enough of always being stuck in a corner, or down in some dark closet miles from the stage, and resolved to get to the theater first in the next town, and take the best spot for himself, for a change.

He made it, too, and set up his makeup in front of the good mirror. After which he hung a white shirt on a wall peg nearby, opened a box of graham crackers he had purchased on the way, took out a few of them, dropped them into the corner basin, turned on the water and left it on until the crackers became a soft, khaki-colored mush. He then proceeded to wipe this concoction all over the tail of the white shirt he had hung on the wall peg.

It looked exactly like . . . what you would think it would look like if you saw some brownish-looking goop on the end of a white shirt-tail.

With that George sat down in front of his nice lighted mirror, and began to get ready for the evening show.

Soon the acrobat came rushing in, taken aback at finding someone there ahead of him. Even so, he proceeded to lay out his stuff, spreading it over twice as much space as necessary. All his things were out and in place, though, before he caught sight of the shirt hanging on the peg.

He stopped dead. He stared. "Jee-zus!" he muttered, his face twisting with disgust. *"Whose . . . is . . . that!?"*

George had been waiting. Hoping for that very question.

George reached over to the shirt, scooped up some of the khaki-colored goop on the end of the tail with a finger, brought it to his mouth, and took a taste. "Not mine!" he then told the acrobat cheerily.

Looking at George with utter revulsion, the acrobat began to back away, shoving his things back into their case as fast as he could, and fled the room.

George had no trouble with him the rest of the tour. All George had to do was appear and the acrobat would clear the room, even if he had gotten there first.

Now, at the Bistro, there in Beverly Hills, dining on osso buco alla Milanese and crisp green salad, I told George Burns how Artie Shaw had told me that story on a mountaintop in Spain. "Did you, George?" I asked him, with a smile, "did you really do a thing like that?"

The George that America (and probably Tanganyika, Kamchatka, and Lower Slobovia, too) loved appeared. Behind the thick lenses of the enormous round spectacles that covered half his face, the eyes began to twinkle like lights through trees on a windy night, his mouth pursing as if a smile was being held back as he said something that was practically a trademark. "I lie a lot," murmured George Burns, with obvious good humor.

George had being liked down to a science. When you walked into a restaurant with him you would feel affection emanating from the entire place. The customers, the waiter, the busboys, the bartenders. Their eyes would follow him to his table, the choice one, naturally, having been saved for him.

Then, during the meal, they would creep over, singles and/or in groups. All ages, too. Old ones, to be sure, hoping some of him might rub off. Young females who wanted to kiss him. Young children with awe in their eyes. They thought he was God, having seen the picture in which George played him. You had the feeling George might single-handedly be able to turn around the way people thought about old age. (Maybe even, I thought hopefully, help the young to feel somebody over thirty *can* be trusted, after all!)

Famous for his timing, George had waited at that first meeting until coffee had been served to tell me an Artie Shaw story.

It was such fun, hearing it. Like listening to a parent tell you what the guy you were going with had been like as a little kid. First George told me how handsome Artie was in those days when he was on the *Burns and Allen Show* with them—in his mid-twenties, then, and a head full of curly hair. And overflowing with temperament (which hadn't changed one whit through the years, even if his head of hair had). On that particular afternoon George was telling me about, they had finished rehearsal, and George had repaired to his dressing room to take a rest before the evening show, when an assistant stuck his head in to say Artie was coming to talk to him. That Artie was very upset about something, and didn't know if he could do the show that night or not.

Always emotional, always highly charged, Artie had been, George told me. So he thought to himself, oh dear, oh dear, poor guy. George had just seen the headlines in the afternoon paper stating that Artie and the beauty Lana Turner, whom Artie had married less than three months earlier, had broken up. That Lana had moved out of Artie's place up at the top of Summit Ridge Drive.

The kid has got to be thrown for a loop, thought George, knowing how devastated he himself would have felt if Gracie had left him. And he was wondering if maybe one of the musicians in the band might take over for the evening show so that Artie could go home and have a good cry, when Artie burst into the room.

"I'm really sorry, kid," George began gently, "maybe we can . . ."

*"No,* George, I *cannot* do it!" Artie interrupted, standing stiffly in the middle of the room, a fist clutching a clarinet. *"I cannot take two minutes out of that last number! It will ruin it completely!* You'll have to cut out some of *your* dialogue, George, or shorten a commercial, but you *must not spoil my number!"*

I laughed, as George obviously thought I might. He had certainly described your basic Artie Shaw. The one who puts on blinders and attacks the work at hand with the ferocity of a buzz saw. "Oh yes," I said to George, "that's Artie, all right. The years haven't changed that part of him one little bit."

George then shook his head, as if in wonder. "How could he do it? How could he have just . . . upped and walked away from that great career of his?"

George wasn't asking for an answer. It was his way of saying Artie Shaw was bonkers. Because George, I would find out after spending some evenings around him, had wanted *one* thing, and one thing *only,* ever since he was a little kid singing on street corners for nickels and dimes, and that was to be in show biz. George *went* for what he wanted, and *got* what he wanted, and then hung onto it for dear life ever after, happy as a lark in the nest he had made for himself in this world, the thought of changing course never once crossing his mind.

He had settled down with Gracie in a big, handsomely furnished house on a shady street in Beverly Hills (where else?) more than forty years earlier, and he had no plans to ever leave, except to go do his show-biz things—unless he was "booked," as he would say. (His biggest journey ever, I expect, was moving from his own bed over into Gracie's after she died, so he would feel less lonely.)

Now, how was a guy like George going to be able to understand a guy like Artie, whose mind never *stopped* thinking of changing course. What Artie had wanted since *he* was a little kid was . . . well, more. Yeah, that was it. More. There was nothing for him but to keep on going. Trying. Doing other things. To touch. To feel. To fall in with each new experience, and learn all he could from it. That's what he *had* to do. It couldn't be helped.

Once I tried to explain all this to George about Artie. But George only began to look at me as if *I* were bonkers.

Ah well, maybe he did have a point. Else what was I doing down there with Artie in that out-of-the-way Spanish village, doing a goddamn Siamese twin act. Artie going around in his khaki pants and baseball cap, I in my black leather pants and boots (from the Rue Sainte-Honoré in Paris), my ninety-odd pairs of shoes and designer outfits I had brought along tucked away forever, the chic hair streaks done in a fancy shop in the Place Vendôme rapidly growing out, not a clarinet in sight, nor a movie camera, not even a Brownie. Throwing away everything we had ever known, bent on transforming the two separates that we were into this complete and wonderful *whole.*

Yeah . . . A *coupla* nuts, I guess.

Except I remembered such a glorious day back then, perfection itself that day was, the weather spring-fresh, the leaves newly arrived, birds twittering sweetly, soft fleecy clouds floating in an azure sky. We were in Barcelona that day, Artie and I, having driven down to see about some damn thing. Furniture, maybe, or linen, some household necessity, and we were walking along what was called *Las Ramblas.*

*Las Ramblas* was (probably still is) an interesting street, its opposing lanes of traffic divided by a very wide median of oh, maybe thirty feet, where there were kiosks and stands for most everything—cut flowers, newspapers, food, pottery, tickets for concerts or for *Las Corridas,* the bullfights. Lots of people were always about, buying things, sitting and talking, especially about bullfights, since a café nearby was where the matadors hung out.

Lots of people were just strolling along, taking in the sights, as Artie and I were doing. Arms entwined, enjoying the day, so in love, and happy at last. Just another couple, walking along, no one paying the slightest bit of attention.

Artie squeezed my arm. "Do you realize," he said softly, "we could never have done this before?"

By "before" he meant the places, the days, when we'd been recognizable, and people would have stared, or come to chat.

"I know," I murmured, as on we walked, so peacefully content in our anonymity. In having found "reality" at last. Because that's how Artie had put it. That where we were, and how we were living, was "real." That all the other life we had had before hadn't been. By the "other" life, he'd meant the George-and-Gracie kind, back there in Beverly Hills. My former connection with Columbia Pictures. All that hadn't been real. That's what Artie had said, that day, walking along *Las Ramblas,* in Barcelona, Spain.

I told George (doing some twinkling, myself, as I told him) that the way he lived wasn't really real—I knew because I had got it straight from the horse's mouth, a.k.a. one Artie Shaw.

As I expected, George pursed his lips, and twinkled back. "Then do me a big favor," said he with his sugar-sweet voice, "and don't wake me up."

George's life, however, actually did become a bit unreal at times.

Like the time he invited several of us to go along with him down to Disneyland. George was to be guest speaker for a gathering of cardiologists. Was this real or what, I asked myself, a bunch of heart doctors in Disneyland?

We piled into the chauffeur-driven white stretch limo and took to the freeways—George's manager and his wife, George's heart doctor, and me. George had had a triple bypass when he was a mere boy of seventy-nine, so naturally his doctor wanted to show him off. I mean, George was his doctor's superstar in more ways than one.

On arrival we were guided to one of those enormous banquet rooms hotels have for such affairs, filled with a positive sea of round tables as far as the eye could see, set up for dining with the usual white tablecloths, silverware, little bowls of flowers in the center, and in this case cardiologists and their mates seated around them all.

Our group was taken to one of the tables in the center. And George, as guest of honor, was led to the dais to join a long row of other speechmakers, seated facing the room on their raised platform.

I had never been in the company of that many doctors before, one at a time being the going custom, as far as I knew. And I had never been in a heart specialist's presence at all. There were two at our table, the surgeons who had actually performed the operation on George, so I suppose you could call it Old Home Week—for them, anyway.

The difference between this group and any other I had ever encountered before was immediately discernible.

There was not a salt shaker in sight. On ours or any other table. Nor was there an ashtray. None. Goose-egg time for containers of ash. These heart people clearly took their doctoring seriously.

The menu, too, was exemplary for heart care (indeed, for the care of every other part of the anatomy as well). It was roasted chicken, green beans, and a salad. Fruit for dessert. And then decaf. And that was it.

And lemme tell you about the air. Like heaven. As fresh and clean as a baby's breath. Because nobody smoked. A couple of hundred people together in one room, and not one of them smoked. Not before the meal, not during the meal, not after the meal. Even if there was somebody there who was absolutely dying for a drag of something, who would have had the nerve to venture even a puff in so rarified an atmosphere?

Nobody, that's who.

Well, *almost* nobody . . .

Upon the dais, the smallish, pixie-faced, triple bypassed going-on-ninety guest of honor was lighting up, as was his custom his habitual cigar. Great billowing clouds of dark smoke rose from him like Mount Vesuvius going berserk into otherwise pristine air.

And did anybody at all ask him to refrain? A man twice their age, a famous stand-up comedian, still standing up and doing it around the world, and getting paid more for it than they earned in spite of their exorbitant fees, about to stand up for them, alive and well, a happy example of what their surgery could do, a monumental draw on screen and stage and television, who wrote bestsellers, was a sex symbol to boot, and who also from time to time played God?

Not only was his smoking not referred to. Someone got him an ashtray.

Later on that night, when it was all over and I was back in my little yellow Honda (the Subaru replacement) and driving myself home, I picked up the conversation I'd been having that day on *Las Ramblas* back there in Barcelona so very long ago.

Listen, Artie, I said to him, maybe you were right about show-biz reality after all. You sure would have thought so if you had been in Disneyland tonight.

Except . . . on the other hand, it's all perfectly real for George, isn't it? I mean, what else does he know?

And come to think of it, what was real about two Americans going to live on the Iberian peninsula and thinking they had found reality there?

Isn't, I asked Artie, reality only relative, after all? In the eye of the beholder, as it were?

The great thing about these conversations I was prone to have with Artie *in absentia* every so often, was that I got to do all the talking.

A message was waiting on my machine—a handy mechanism I had acquired recently—from a friend who said Ross Hunter was trying to get in touch with me. And in case I was interested in finding out why, she had left a number where I could call him . . .

## *Twenty-four*

***R**oss Hunter!* What in the world did Ross Hunter want with me?

If my memory served me right, Ross had been under contract to Columbia as an actor back in the forties when I had been there. It was after I left town that he became this hotshot producer over at Universal, doing the Doris Day/Rock Hudson comedies, the smash hit *Airport,* and God knows what else. I couldn't imagine why he would be looking for me. But I most assuredly intended to find out.

I dialed immediately.

To do a play was why. He and his partner, Jacques Mapes, Ross told me, were going to produce one. And though this play would have plenty of singing, and some dancing, too, it was not a musical. It was a *play,* about a singing trio, à la the Andrew Sisters, who had entertained the troops during World War Two down in the South Pacific and were now being invited to Washington by President Jimmy Carter, who had conveniently been there during the war. And who, according to Ross's play, had seen this trio perform. Now Carter wanted them to entertain at a benefit that was about to be thrown for American vets in Washington, D.C. But that part, Ross said, the benefit part, would all happen off-stage. The action of the play would take place in the trio's guest suite at the well-known Watergate Hotel.

Would I, Ross wanted to know, be interested in playing one of the girls?

That was what Ross said. The word he used. *Girls.*

It was the word George Burns used, too, for all females up to and even beyond his own age. Once I tried to explain to him (just for fun) that I wasn't a "girl" anymore. "I am a *woman,* George," I told him gaily, "all grown-up and quite mature, I'll have you know! I can tie my own shoes, plait my own pigtails, and everything!"

George only scrunched up his face as if he had bitten into a lemon. "Wo-man," he repeated, with some disgust. And informed me that Gracie *wanted* to be called "girl," and would probably have kicked him out of the house if he'd ever called her—he scrunched up his face again—*wo-man.* Once at a party at Swifty Lazar's house, I went so far as to ask Connie Chung to explain to George why "woman" was the appropriate term for us over-eighteen females.

There Connie was, on the national news all the time, telling us things of importance. I thought *her* telling George would give the explanation a weight that I hadn't been able to achieve.

Ms. Chung didn't get anywhere, either.

So I thought it might be wise to keep my own counsel with Ross Hunter, who was talking to me about doing a play. "Hey, that sounds exciting," was all I said to him. "You bet I'd be interested. Do you have anything I can read?"

Ross said he would send a script right over.

When we'd hung up, I jumped to my feet. I began to pace. Up. Down. All around. My heart having speeded up to a lively tempo.

Out of the blue again. From the very place my best things had always come.

I paced some more. I had never done a play from scratch. Movies, of course, were *all* from scratch. In fact, the rehearsal of a movie was the only thing that ever got *on* a screen, I thought. But for the stage? I'd never done anything that hadn't been done before. What a fantastic *learning* experience this would have to be!

*Something Old, Something New* ▪ 197

I stopped dead in the middle of the room. Was I doing it again?

I whirled around and went over to the mirror. Are you doing it again? I asked my image. Are you about to make some snap judgment again to go hop, skip, and jumping off into another direction, the way you've been doing *all your life*?

No no, I said to me, not a-tall, not a-tall, I had taken my typewriter along on tour before, hadn't I? I would do it this time, too.

I whirled around again and went to my desk, where a very small pile of pages lay. They were the beginnings of the novel, the one about my beloved Spanish Princess, *Juana La Loca*.

I touched them tenderly. If I did this play, I wouldn't have to leave Juana behind. I would take her along. Pack her up, along with the research I'd gathered from my darling library, and I'd *find* time, in and around rehearsals, to keep her pages going. T.S. Eliot had worked in a bank, hadn't he, Maugham in a hospital? Surely acting on the side wasn't all that bad. And Ross had said we would only do a couple of dinner theaters to sharpen up the play, tighten and fix, before going into New York.

Into New York.

I had never been on Broadway. Or even off. Hadn't particularly had any desire to. Not, I thought, pleased it could now happen, that I'd *mind* being there! And there were loads of libraries all over New York, probably chockfull of delicious tidbits about Juana that I hadn't dreamed of.

Of course, I reminded myself, I'd better read the play before getting carried away, it might very well not be anything at all.

It was, though. Its premise was very good: three middle-aged "girls" meeting for the first time after thirty or so years, playing catch-up in their suite while they rehearsed and re-learned their musical numbers of long ago.

Where it *wasn't* so very good was in some of the dialogue. The three women seemed to be stuck in a kind of time warp in their phraseology, in their attitudes. As if the author (who was in his late thirties, or thereabouts) had looked at some old forties movies (when the three women *would* have been girls), and fashioned his characters after the earlier period.

Except this wasn't a period piece. This play was taking place in the capital of the United States in the seventies. For instance, one of the roles was an alcoholic, and the whole thing was treated like comedy relief—complete with old-fashioned supposed-to-be-comic, falling-down pratfalls—the way drunkenness used to be looked on in the forties, before we learned the stuff was a drug, the condition a sickness, and not very funny at all.

Ah, but surely, I quickly concluded, anything jarring or inappropriate would soon be gotten rid of in rehearsals—that was what going-on-the-road was all about, was it not? We'd all known *that* since we were born, those of us who'd ever listened to old show-biz stories, or seen old movies.

So off we went—Betty Garret and Jan Sterling playing the other two parts—to the first stop, down in New Orleans, and soon were totally absorbed in the work at hand.

The theater was the smallest I had ever played in. The audience would be sitting right under our noses. So what Ross did was stage the action as intimately as a movie's. (He was filling the director's chair on this venture of his.)

It seemed dead right. Comfortable as could be. What fun it was, too, doing the musical numbers, thoroughly enjoying ourselves in every way. And so it was that in no time at all we fell plop into that slightly dangerous "we can't miss—success is ours!" frame of mind, convincing ourselves we were absolutely on the right track, whoopee! So that I (and the others, I assume) merely dutifully learned the dialogue handed me, preoccupied as I was with all the business it was necessary to remember, all the dance steps, the songs, the props, the entrances and exits and cues, all else forgotten, any trouble-in-paradise thoughts gone right out of my head.

Rock Hudson, a great and good friend of Ross's, came opening night, and got top billing in the reviews the next day, simply by being in the audience. Below him we cast members were finally remembered (called "women," too, by jingo), our performances praised, our standing ovation noted.

But naturally the reviewer couldn't stop *there*. It had to be observed (I think it's in the sacred rule book of show biz to do so) that we were "names from memories of Hollywood past." After which our gray hairs were dutifully recorded, even though I wore a wig without so much as a single strand of gray anywhere in it, and Jan's hair was bleached to within an inch of its life. (I have to admit, Betty *did* have a smidgen of the gray stuff, but hardly enough to be worth reviewing.)

Nor, alas, did the reviews end *there*.

For those of us who continued on to read the not-so-small print, we learned that "dramatically the play was thin," and that "ultimately not much happens."

There was some talk of rewriting to be done. But nothing came of it. Little bits here and there that made no improvement whatsoever. I said something to the two other "girls" over lunch one day about how the dialogue seemed dated to me. But they both said it was the way people talked.

Another day I was chatting with a friend back in Los Angeles, having called to check in, find out how she was, what she was up to. And I got this brainstorm when she said she was about to leave for New York. Why, I asked her, didn't she swing by New Orleans and catch our play?

I didn't remember, anymore, where I had met Cynthia Lasker. At the Wylers, maybe, or the Philip Dunnes. All I knew was that it seemed as if we had known each other forever instantly.

Cynthia was a theater buff. She had seen everything that had ever appeared on the Great White Way I would swear, so I thought I would probably get a pretty good reading from her on how we were doing, what our expectations might be.

I didn't have to do any too much persuading. Cynthia rather liked the idea of seeing a show before it got to the Big Town up north.

She was rather small of stature, Cynthia was, but nobody knew it (including her), because she thought big and wore ridiculously high heels. But at five foot two, who could blame her. She usually traveled in terribly elegant circles of high finance and posh salons and haute couture, but you could give her a hot dog and a backlot baseball game, and it would be all the same. Cynthia Lasker was equally at home wherever she went.

Which probably explained how she was able to manage so deftly, the way she did, not to have to tell me (or Betty, or Jan) how she had reacted to our play. How she prevented the subject from even being brought up.

Cynthia (the non-pro) became the entertainer of the pros (Jan Sterling, Betty Garrett, and Evelyn Keyes), that was how.

It was immediately after the show, when we had all gathered in the damp, cramped Green Room backstage to recoup from our on-stage workout, and wait until our audience had gotten into their cars and taken off before we, too, went on our way.

I had told Cynthia to join me there. Which she did. I had scarcely finished introducing her all around when she said, apropos of nothing it seemed to me, "I heard a joke on the way here."

She surely must have known what she was doing, because we all turned to her, and almost in unison, cried, "Oh, tell, tell!" I suppose we didn't want to hear what she had to say about our play any more than she wanted to tell us.

I even remembered the joke later, something I very seldom can do, for some reason.

A man (Cynthia told us) is walking down the street with a three-legged pig on a leash, and he meets an acquaintance. "What are you doing with a three-legged pig on a leash?" says the acquaintance to the man.

"Lemme tell you about this pig," says the man, *"this pig* is the greatest friend anybody ever had. Do you know that when my house caught on fire and it was all ablaze and filled with smoke and I was asleep and would have died, that this pig came in and woke me up and led me out to safety?"

"My my," says the acquaintance, "that was really something, all right. But tell me, how come he only has three legs?"

"This pig," says the man, *"this pig* is unbelievable, do you know what else he did? Do you know that my tractor fell over right on top of me, and there I was, deep in the mud, my head stuck right down in the muck and the mire, I could not breathe in and I could not breathe out. I would have died for sure. But this pig, *this pig* came along and pulled me out of that muck and mire and he saved my life, that's what this pig did."

"Wow-ee," says the acquaintance, "that sure is one good pig, but you still haven't explained why he only has three legs."

"Well for cryin' out loud!" cries the man, disgusted with the other's denseness. "With a friend like *this,* you don't want to eat him *all at once,* do you?"

It was only after Cynthia had left town that I caught on to what she had been up to. And loved her for it. She had simply been following an old show-biz tradition, was my guess, called "always leave 'em laughing." Better than delivering the honest truth to somebody, any day, wasn't it? Hadn't Artie once said, "Can't you *lie* a little once in a while. Kesi—(that was the nickname he'd given me back in Spain)—say something *good* about me for a change?"

Maybe, I decided, we should hire stand-up comics for funerals, for divorces, for telling a friend her play wasn't going to make it to the Big Time.

Well, listen, I already knew it. We all did. It was just that nobody wanted to admit it out loud. What for, if you didn't have to? (Tell a pig joke, instead.) Isn't a marriage always over ages before anybody ever faces it? And speaking of "ages," don't we all get considerably farther over the hill before we acknowledge *that* little fact? And who ever dies, for crissake? Not us. Those people over *there,* they do dumb things like that. Never us, right?

We were already committed for another engagement in San Antonio, so we went on over to do that one, too, before we folded. And I was awfully glad we had. Because that's where the early morning show *Good Morning, America* found me.

It's amazing what those people can accomplish when they set their minds to it. I don't see how drug czars get away with anything. People seem to be able to locate me anywhere. There was yet another observance for yet another *Gone With the Wind* milestone, damned if I remember what this one was (probably when it crossed its trillionth-dollar mark). What I do remember is what fun it was getting up at four in the morning (honest!) and stepping outside into a still dark-of-night world and climbing into a long shiny-black limo to be driven through the empty streets of that Tex-Mex town to a television station, where I sat down in front of a camera, somebody pinning a microphone to my sweater for me to talk into, stuck another in my ear so I could hear the voices of David Hartman (the then host of *GMA*) talking to me from New York, Olivia de Havilland, too, with a *GWTW* celebration she would naturally be there. Evidently all this hookup, thanks to the miracle of TV, was gathered together and sent out to wherever *GMA* goes, and that includes L.A., because the next thing I knew, the *Love Boat* company was in touch, wanting me to play somebody's mother on their show. (Not "aunt," this time, but you can't win them all.)

*Et voilà,* I was right back where I'd started from.

# PART FOUR

# "Old Husband, New Friend"

# Twenty-five

There were still moments when I would again wonder if I had made the right move, coming back and settling down in Tinsel Town, for what appeared to be my last hurrah. I well knew it was getting far too late—it *was* too late—to go popping here and there, anymore, in my accustomed manner. I *knew* that. And yet. Some quick flash of memory would show up on the screen in my head. Some little thing. Like the sweet fragrance of grass being mowed wafting in through a window. A cat waiting quietly on top of a fence post for an unsuspecting mouse to scamper by. The brilliance of a sky on a crystal-clear night that can never happen, anymore, not in a big city. (Certainly not in L.A.) And then . . . I dunno . . . a sort of disquiet would permeate my being for a while. The *permanence* of it all would begin to weigh heavily (As it had up on the hill in Connecticut, too, but more so, now, with time so persistently shrink, shrinking, the way it was.) It sometimes felt as if all the doors, the exits, were being plastered over, and if I didn't make some kind of move soon, I would get closed off for the rest of my days. So that living here loomed up as an Important Decision.

This familiar unrest persisted until I returned from San Antonio, to go to work on a Hollywood soundstage for the first time in, oh, more than twenty-five years.

And discovered how good it felt to be working on a movie-TV set again. To be in the lights, acting in front of a camera, again.

It was like coming home (even if I was playing somebody's

mother!). Like maybe a little chick feels, nestling down under its mother's wing, among all those soft, downy feathers, so cozy, so comfortable and . . . safe.

That's what it was like. And there were all those incredible connections, too. *Love Boat,* for instance, was being shot on the old Sam Goldwyn lot. Where I had made the movie *Enchantment* for Sam Goldwyn himself. And the director was a man who had once been a gangling kid whom Charles Vidor, then my husband, had first cast in a picture and started on a show business career, and here he still was, a director himself now. The camera operator had been on many a picture of mine in the Columbia days, and here he still was, going strong. The dialogue director had been on John's *Red Badge of Courage,* shot on the place both John and I had owned out in Calabasas, called Keyston Ranch, a combination of both our names.

It was pretty much like that all over town, wherever I went. A perfect setup, I told myself, for the loner I was. And I was that. I didn't even pretend to myself that I was anything else, anymore. But it *was* very nice to run into friends and acquaintances from time to time, especially when I didn't have to *live* with them! (You know how it goes, a great place to visit . . .)

There was another something that I became aware of, too, about the entertainment business as I went along, something that I found to be very winning. In what other pursuit, for instance, did you see so many different ages all working together? You never saw kids working in banks, did you? Or restaurants? They don't drive taxicabs, either. Are never clerks in stores, not even grocery ones (though they used to, I believe, my brother told me he had worked in one as a kid—it was where he learned to deal in figures so well, adding up the items being sold to a customer on the brown paper bag holding them, precalculator time—knowledge he put to good use later in the real estate racket).

But you saw kids on Hollywood sets. From brand-new-borns on up through the teens, right alongside grownups. And I mean working for money. Getting paid. All these various ages working together. And I rather liked that. I mean, I liked that a lot.

And so since I wasn't going anywhere else, anyhow, I decided maybe I just ought to get myself an agent for acting. Maybe I could continue to do one of those TV things (like *Love Boat*) once in a while as long as I was here. Become truly an integral part of the community (again). These shows had short shooting schedules for the guest performers, so it wouldn't interfere too much with my book-in-progress and the continued visits to the research library.

Boy. If I could manage to arrange my life in such a fashion as *that,* I told myself, all would be beautiful, indeed.

Except the next time I was in front of a camera, it wasn't for a TV show at all. It was for yet another documentary.

About the Life And Times of one Artie Shaw.

Well, well, and well.

*Artie* they were going to do! And he nowhere *near* a hundred!

Artie. My God. I hadn't seen Artie, hadn't heard from him— hadn't heard anything *about* him—for a very long time. Years. Seven, eight, or nine of them. I'd lost track of how many.

All of a sudden, damned if I didn't miss him. All of a sudden the good times came swooshing back in as if they were a helicopter dropping down for a landing.

It had been ever thus with me. When I haven't seen someone for a very long time, someone I had been close to (I mean, close, *indeed*), I dunno, for some reason only the things I liked about the person seem to be the memories that linger on. As if all the not-so-good things had been weeded out of my head and tossed away with the passage of time.

So when the letter from Toronto arrived, stating that a Brigitte Berman, who had already made an extensive documentary about one jazz great, Bix Beiderbeck, was about to make one about *another* jazz great named Artie Shaw, and was hoping that I would consent to being interviewed on camera for it, talking about my particular years with Mr. Shaw, I instantly wrote back to tell her you bet I would.

Ms. Berman had written that she planned to visit Bagur, our village in Spain, to see if she could photograph the house we had built there. Planned on going to Connecticut, as well, to trace the swath Artie had cut through that state.

A thorough job of Artie's life was what she had in mind. The music man. The thinking man. The driven man. Hoping to find out what made the gentleman tick, if that were possible.

Boy. I would like to see that documentary myself, I thought. And so when Brigitte came along with her crew and lights and camera, I gave her my best shot. I had a splendid time, too, making a sentimental journey with Artie, sitting there on my own couch, in my own living room in Los Angeles, going back to those days overlooking the Mediterranean, where it swept up to the shores of Cataluña. To when we hunkered down alongside Lake Wononscopomuc, up there in the foothills of the Berkshires. All now about to be recorded for posterity.

I did so look forward to seeing the finished film. Brigitte promised to let me know when a local showing would be held. She added that it wouldn't be any time soon, since the documentary was to be of feature length.

Ah, well, one could hardly do the life of Artie Shaw in a much shorter space, now could one. After all, it had taken him quite a while to live it, had it not.

Meanwhile I began looking around for an agent. Somebody to find me those occasional acting jobs I now thought would be delicious to have. And who, when I found him, told me a few basic truths. Like the first thing I would have to do was to go around and meet producers of the shows, and the people who cast them. I had been away a long time, he said, and they all had to get to know me again.

"See what I look like now, you mean," I said to him a bit sullenly.

"That, too," he murmured gently.

I got it. "You mean . . . they won't know me at all."

He gave me a tiny little rueful smile.

First I bristled. But almost immediately got off my high horse. Because what he said was so clearly the way things were bound to be.

He set up some appointments for me, and there it was again, the way it used to be, me all caught up once more with the way I looked, what to do about my hair, my makeup, what to put on. Better be something a little dressier than jeans this time, I decided. Though not anything that might make somebody think I was still trying to be young or anything—I wouldn't want that. On the other hand, I didn't have to look frumpy, did I, just because I wasn't as young as I used to be.

Jesus, I thought, what an extra-stupid concern to have. Because I was *older,* I had to be careful not to look *younger.*

First I got dressed up. Sort of. I put on a beige suit, high heels, the wig I'd used for the play. I even got out some jewelry.

Then I took a look at myself, took it all off, and got back into my jogging clothes and Reeboks. It wasn't going to matter diddledy-do *what* I had on. Everybody was going to be doing the same bloody thing the reviewers had done. Observing the lines on my face. Giving me gray hairs whether I had them or not. Classifying me as a decidedly non-Charlie's-Angel type. At least I could be comfortable on the drives around town.

There were some here and there who knew me. Others who hadn't the remotest notion who this un-young person in their office might be. Some breathed, "Oh my, you're . . . you're a *legend*!" Others said, "Uh, how do you spell your name, please?"

I was thoroughly getting to know the "changed" Hollywood, though. That was at least one thing for sure I was accomplishing. I mean, knowing the Big Studio System was kaput, and actually *seeing* where the shattered pieces had plunked themselves down, were two different things.

Everywhere was where.

I visited offices in big thoroughfares, visited them stashed away in tiny side streets. From Culver City to glorious downtown Hollywood. From Santa Monica to the San Fernando Valley, and stops in between.

There were no Harry Cohns anywhere. No Cecil B. De-Milles, no one-person-who-made-decisions, as far was I could see, the way it used to be. Anywhere. They all seemed to come in groups. And were all quite young. Younger than I, anyway.

Yes, the youthful campfire tale-tellers certainly did appear to be the ones who had taken over. Straight from cinema school, they had come. (Or maybe the accounting department.) There had been no such school in the days of yore. I don't think you had to go even there, though, to be a casting director. One young man asked me if I knew how to act in front of a camera. I guessed *he* was learning as he went along. Well, that *had* been the method in those earlier days, so no reason it wouldn't work again for him. It was just that he'd obviously better hurry and learn it all before he was thirty, or else he'd never reach pay dirt.

I kept learning a few things, too, as I went around town, one of them not being all that thrilling to know. And that was that after the American Indian—who actually couldn't even get himself arrested since the demise of the Western—women over forty were the least-hired group in the Screen Actors' Guild. Over *forty*.

Yeah. Well. The news was hardly a surprise. My expectations hadn't been all that high anyway. I had been away far too long.

Ah, but something might come along, said I to myself, who knew. Or it wouldn't. That gave me a fifty-fifty chance, did it not, which wasn't all that bad. And either way was fine. Anyway, nothing was going to top the days I spent wending my way through the still-fresh mornings to my bibliothecal heaven, when I entered the campus grounds, parked my car and followed the path past a few studying students, and into my particular section.

I had come to absolutely adore my travels with Isabella and hubby Ferdinand and the children. Not to mention the ladies-

and gentlemen-in-waiting, the hundreds of serving people, the cabinet members, the clergy, the advisers, in fact the entire court of the so-called Catholic Kings. Theirs was the only monarchy—in Europe, anyway—that never had a palace of its own, I had learned. They'd spent their entire reign riding around over their domains, setting up camp wherever night fell.

But what a camp. Woven tapestries to create walls. Silver chamber pots to empty their bodily wastes into. And servants to empty the pots, of course. Entire kitchens, and sleeping quarters, and throne rooms (including the thrones) went along with them. Their wardrobes, furniture, animals to ride, to milk, to eat. And children's tutors, I mustn't forget those. The children, my Juana, had the most brilliant educations imaginable; languages, literature, art, mathematics, the likes of which are unheard of these days, all the while traveling continually. And since Christopher Columbus hung out with the court for a while, too, for about ten years, with *his* children, I wouldn't be surprised if astronomy and navigational matters were studied as well. It made me think what a crying shame it was that the Spaniards didn't introduce this kind of educational system into the New World when they came to conquer.

I would become so engrossed in these doings at times that all else would be forgotten. I seemed, somehow, to relate to the nomadish life (having moved around so much, myself), to actually relate to Juana herself, in a way I didn't quite understand as yet. And I was looking forward to seeing if I could discover why, as I wrote along, having fun filling in, with my own imagination, the spaces between the facts I gleaned from the library, creating encounters between my characters, between Juana and her queen mother, for instance, between Juana and Christopher, that very well *could* have taken place. It was an absolute ball.

I was so caught up in my fifteenth-century family that when Cynthia, one day, said come to lunch with her and Talli to a new restaurant she knew, I told her that I couldn't, I just couldn't.

"What," she demanded to know, "is it that is taking up so much of your time, now?"

She shouldn't have asked. Because I told her, I'm afraid, and rather earnestly at that—I do have a tendency to get earnest, sometimes, when I'm enthusiastic about something, as I was about Juana. "I'm going to rescue this Spanish princess!" I cried passionately. "She's gone down in history as *La Loca,* The Crazy One, and she wasn't, she *wasn't,* I don't believe she was crazy at all!"

Cynthia's expression clearly implied that if Isabella's daughter, Juana, wasn't off her rocker, she, Cynthia, knew who *was.* "Rescue an obscure Spanish princess?" she answered with a touch of disbelief. "Whatever *for*? Who in the world *cares*?"

Nobody but me, it would seem.

The tiny pang of guilt I felt about not going to lunch with my friends and being so satisfied with my solitary endeavor didn't last any too long. And they certainly didn't mind in the *least,* for crissake, whether I went to lunch with them or not. And I—I dunno—I just didn't want to interrupt, at the moment, the routine I was into, the long drives back and forth from home to campus, sitting in my corner of the library, searching through dusty, often yellowed-from-age books and pamphlets, sometimes sinking down on a bench outside, under a tree, watching the students as they passed by. I couldn't remember ever being more content, more at peace in my entire life.

In my browsings I'd once come across something George Bernard Shaw had said. And since he'd lived to be ninety-three, I figured the guy must have known what he was talking about. "Be so busy," said G.B., "at something you like doing you won't have time to ask yourself, am I happy?"

I'd written it down and tacked it up on my bookshelf where I could see it every day.

I found another saying, too, that turned me on. So I wrote *it* down, and tacked it along side G.B.'s. "To be thrown upon one's own resources," I'd read, "is to be cast into the very lap of fortune; for our faculties then undergo a development

214 ■ *I'll Think About That Tomorrow*

and display an energy of which they were previously unsusceptible."

That was Ben saying that one. Franklin, that is. And he'd lived to eighty-four, without any antibiotics or fancy surgery to help *him* hang in there. And we all know what a wise old bird he was, what a full life he managed to lead.

It made me feel good to look up and see my quotes up there. Especially Ben's. Had I, ever before, I wondered? Been thrown on my own resources?

I wasn't at all sure I ever really had been. I mean, completely, without backup. I'd always *thought* I had. But hadn't I, maybe, been fooling myself? Hadn't I always had someone, some *man* or other to fall back on? A man somewhere I could pick up a phone and call if I ever got desperate, and say "Help!?" I'd even had youth and good looks to fall back on if I needed *them*.

But now. They were gone. All of them. The men, the youth, the looks. All of them, gone. Gone, and, my God, good riddance, I thought. I had now, according to Ben, been "cast into the very lap of fortune."

I didn't know why it made me so contented. Only that it did. And if it were so, that I was in the lap of fortune at long last, better, thought I, late than never.

Why was it, I often asked myself, that everybody was so fearful of growing older? And they were, they most certainly were. I had surely found *that* out! Most people seemed to spend their entire youths *fretting* about it. And why, *why,* hadn't any older person ever told me of this marvelous sense of *freedom* one has being older? Why wasn't I told, so that I could have been looking forward to it all these years? Looking forward to being rid of all those miserable twistings and turnings, all those anxieties and gyrations and should-I's and shouldn't-I's we are prey to through our younger days!

Ah, but then. Maybe some older person *did* tell me how it was going to be—maybe they *all* did, the on-in-years folk I used to be surrounded by as I wafted along my earlier pathways. Or maybe the way they all conducted their lives spoke

*"Old Husband, New Friend"* ■ 215

*for* them. Maybe it actually had rubbed off, willy-nilly, and that was what was guiding me now through this present portion of human existence that the press, the community, the IRS insists on calling senior citizen.

Boy. What a weird thing it seemed for Evelyn Keyes (baby of her family, baby of the DeMille office, baby forever in her own head) to be called. But there it was. Along with the big surprise of how very comfortable it felt being there . . .

I was so wrapped up in campus life, in my fifteenth-century royal-family life, up to and including how and what kind of horses were ridden, especially by the womenfolk (especially by Juana), along with various ponderings on the state of my own hop-skip-and-jumping psyche, that I almost missed the magazine article about Artie . . .

# *Twenty-six*

I could not believe my eyes. The magazine said that Artie Shaw had a new band.

But he had always said never. That's what he had always said. Wasn't that what he had always said?

So much—again—for "never."

The headline read "Swinging without his clarinet." And there was a picture of him. He looked pretty much the same. Less hair. But he had grown a sizable mustache, to make up, I guess, for the loss on top. The quotes certainly sounded like the same old Artie. "When asked why he didn't play the clarinet, anymore, Mr. Shaw said, 'My standards got so bloody high it was torture. People always ask me why I don't play for my own amusement. I say, "what's amusing about it?"

That was the Artie I had known, all right. But the fellow with the band was not—even if somebody else was playing his instrument.

So the music man had been there all the while, hadn't he? Oh, I had known it. All you had to do was watch the way he listened to music. Nobody listened to music the way Artie listened to music. *Nobody.* With every ounce of his being he did it.

Ah, but then. Hadn't Artie done everything with his whole being? So without a doubt the energy he used for finding just the right tiles for the fireplaces, the perfect light fixture for the front entrance, the *forme juste* of door, of window, of walkway, was the same that cared about and watched every phrase he and his band played, that nursed the tone, the texture, the nuance of every single note, down to the last tootle.

I certainly hoped, with all my heart, that this was the stuff Brigitte Berman of Canada was getting for her documentary. It would be great fun to see what Artie was up to—without having to be there. I did so admire Artie—his drive, his concentration—from a distance. Another case of a great place to visit, but I didn't know if I ever wanted to be in his company again. I even admired his anger—and the things it caused him to do—from a distance.

Like the time he made a citizen's arrest. I personally don't know many people who have done a thing like that. Artie actually used to call himself The Last Angry Man. He felt, furthermore, that it was his *duty* to be one, too. That, as a good citizen, one should not just sit and take things without a squawk. That if we just sat and took things that turned out rotten, then it was our own bloody fault that it was so. Artie took the part of the Constitution that says "Government *by* the people" in dead earnest.

And so, one day, when he was driving along the main drag of the small Connecticut town in which we lived, he came upon a line of maybe ten or twelve cars, all trailing along behind a huge tractor pulling one of those wide things called,

I believe, a furrower. Sitting astride the tractor was a New England farmer, one of a breed that can be quite cranky if they have a mind to, and I guess this one had decided to show the city folk arriving for the weekend a thing or two about rights-of-way in the country. He and his rig were dead center in his lane of the highway.

Artie joined the long line behind the tractor (thank *God* I wasn't with him!), then several more cars pulled in behind him, because the farmer hadn't edged over one inch, and there was a double yellow line so no passing was allowed anyway. There were any number of places along the side of the road where the farmer could have moved over to let the cars pass, not to mention that he shouldn't have been on this main thoroughfare with his farm vehicle in the first place. *There was a law against it.* And Artie knew it. He had had a dairy farm himself once, up in that part of the country.

By the time there were more than twenty-five cars in the relunctant caravan, The Last Angry Man suddenly had had it. Fortunately he was in his Porsche, the kind of car that, as we know, instantly responds if you choose to speak its language.

Artie revved up its motor and went sailing past the line of cars ahead of him, past the tractor and its trailing furrower—on the wrong side of the yellow line, mind you—zoomed down the road to Town Hall where the procession would have to pass, pulled to a stop, leaped out of his sporty car, and dashed into the office of the First Selectperson (as the mayor was called in that burg), shouting to everybody in sight—clerks, secretaries, passersby—"I want to make a citizen's arrest! Come outside and be my witnesses!"

Artie insisted that each and every person either gather outside on the street, or stick their heads out of the windows to watch the approach of the farmer and the long line of cars forced to trail along behind him. And when the motorcade finally arrived, he demanded that the First Selectperson stop everyone in it and hold them all until the sheriff got there.

It took nigh onto an hour before the deed was accomplished. Meanwhile the twenty-five (or so) cars and their irate drivers, all the people at and around Town Hall, not to mention the farmer and his clumsy tractor (and furrower) who was to be arrested, all had to wait. And wait. And wait.

Artie, without a doubt, was the least-loved person in the town that night. I know I wouldn't have done much loving if I had been present. And yet, at a distance . . .

As I sat looking at his picture in the magazine and reading the article about him and his new band, I wondered if the passing years had changed the man who'd done what he did that day. And doubted it. I didn't imagine mere years could have wrought much change in such a man's spirit. Probably only death could manage anything like that . . .

It was truly strange how my feelings about Artie never seemed to change. I didn't understand it, myself. All this time, not having seen him, not having heard from him, and it was still the same. As if we were related. The blood-kin kind. The unchangeable fact-of-life kind. He had been my husband. Really and *truly* my husband. My mate. A part of me. As an arm is. None of the other marriages had been remotely that way. I had known all the while, somehow, none of them was going to last. They had never felt the least bit permanent.

But with Artie. I hadn't known, never even suspected, it *wouldn't* last. And so I still seemed to feel—and supposed I always would—attached to him, somehow. Whether I ever saw him again or not. No matter how he might feel about it all. That was his concern, not mine.

But it certainly was going to be interesting to see from a safe distance—on film, that is—this, uh, relative of mine.

I cut out the article on him, tucked it into the carton where those things went, and continued my involvement with Juana, her Mom, and their nomadic court.

Every morning, before I got down to *Juana,* though, I would always play around on my machine for an hour or so—it could be a letter to somebody, a little essay or story, even a lecture that I never intended to give, but wanted to get off my chest for my own amusement. They were like warm-up writing exercises, a way of honing this latter-day craft I had chosen for myself.

One day, a friend came by when I happened to have left one of these pieces on the living room coffee table, intending to do some further work on it when I had the time. "What is this?" my friend wanted to know, picking the pages up.

Hilda Marton was her name. She and husband George, were a connection to those great Paris days of mine that I loved so much. They'd been living there then, and had moved back to California about the time I had. I'd had some good times with the Martons. The end-of-year holidays spent skiing (well, I tried) at their place in Kitzbühel, Austria. Attending a glorious Moroccan bash in the exotic city of Marrekech, sitting on cushions around low, round tables, picking and eating with our fingers, Berber-style, from a whole, deliciously cooked lamb sprinkled with powered sugar set in the center of the table.

And if those exciting times weren't enough to win a person's heart, George was also a literary agent, and an international one at that. And Hilda had been a reader at Twentieth Century Fox, as well as a writer of movie scripts, so she could poke around in my written pages any time she felt like it.

"Oh," I told her, "that's just something I'm fooling around with."

"Do you mind if I read it?"

"Not in the least!" I was pleased that she wanted to.

I couldn't believe what she said to me a few minutes later, looking up from my piece that she had just read. "This," she told me, smiling from ear to ear, "ought to be in *Sunday Calendar*!"

*Calendar* was the entertainment section of the *Los Angeles Times*. My piece was about the motion picture business. The "then" and "now," from the point of view of an old hand (myself).

I gulped. I blinked. Never in my wildest dreams had I ever fancied writing for a newspaper.

But if Hilda Marton said that was where my little piece belongs, well then, *that was where it belonged!* Hilda Marton ought to know what she was talking about! And for heaven's sake, here the thing was, already written (just about), and wouldn't it be nice—bloody marvelous, in fact—if it were actually *used*, if it got into print, the way written things were supposed to do?

But how did I go about getting to the *Sunday Calendar*, in that big newspaper place, over there in the middle of glorious downtown Los Angeles?

Well, I had noticed in the *Sunday Calendar* a separate little box on the second page that had "Irv Letofsky, *Sunday Calendar* editor" printed inside it.

So that's who I called. I dialed the *Los Angeles Times* number, asked for Mr. Letofsky, and the next thing I knew, I was talking to the man himself. Nobody had said, "Evelyn who?" Or even "How do you spell that?"

I told Mr. Letofsky I had written this piece. And Mr. Letofsky said send it along.

I hurriedly fixed the odds and ends that needed fixing and sent the piece out in the evening mail.

A few days later Mr. Letofsky was on the phone again. This time *he* was calling *me.* "We'll use it," he said.

Which was how I became a columnist.

That first time I saw my name in lights on the marquee of the Radio City Music Hall, even seeing *I Am A Billboard* in the window at Doubleday's, were nothing compared to opening up the *Los Angeles Times* that Sunday morning and seeing my first byline in there.

Mr. Letofsky gave my pieces a name, too. He called them "KEYES TO THE TOWN," and he began to run them about once a month. That meant, of course, that I had to change my reclusive ways, again. It meant I was going to have to get out more, get around more, in order to have material for my column.

And *that* meant, alas, that I couldn't spend as much time with my *Juana* as I had been. But, I told myself sternly, it didn't mean I had to *lose* her, either. It just meant that her project would be slowed down a bit, *that was all.*

Fortunately I had recently met the absolutely perfect person to do the getting around with.

How to describe Marvin Paige. Casting director didn't quite do it, though he was that, and evidently a superb one. *He* certainly knew everything that had ever been done, and who had done it, living or dead. (And that included writers, directors, technicians, up and through the twenty-fifth electrician on the farthest corner of the catwalk.)

Marvin was the head caster for the afternoon soap *General Hospital,* and it had been among the leaders of the pack for any number of years. So he must have been doing something right.

However, that wasn't my connection with Marvin. I had never done his soap (or any other soap, for that matter). No, my connection with Marvin Paige was my Star-from-the-Golden-Era status. Marvin was seldom seen out anywhere without a Golden-Era-caliber female at his side (ah yes, we were all still sticking faithfully to the old Ark arrangement). And Marvin was seen everywhere. Everywhere, that is, that had to do with show biz—and most particularly the show biz of yesteryear. Because, besides his casting chores, Marvin was a devoted historian and passionate archivist of the entertainment business, and therefore always on the lookout for more material for his own research library-in-progress. You went anywhere with Marvin, and he immediately glommed on to everything he could in the way of programs, tickets, place cards, anything that would help him remember the occasion, what it was for, who was there.

Me, I began to string along with him, on the lookout for material I might use for a column. I did have to get done up to go, unfortunately. Do something about my hair, concern myself with clothes and shoes and such. I couldn't just crawl into my sweats and Reeboks, more's the pity. Otherwise, though, these big "do's" became far more interesting to me than before. It was a whole new ballgame, observing them through my brand-new columnist eyes.

Once in a great while Talli and I would decide to drop the

Ark nonsense and go to one of these functions together. We were hardly helpless flowers who needed men to "escort" us anywhere. We had been all over the world without any help, why not a Hollywood shindig or two?

At one such affair I ran into John again. How was it in other towns? Did people keep running into their exes like this? Actually I had recently caught John on the TV show *Sixty Minutes*. (I doubted there were too many people catching their exes on that program, either.) The interviewer had asked John, if he could live his life all over again, would he live it the same way? And John, to my surprise, answered, "God, no."

Well, said the interviewer, some people say they would live their lives the same way. To which John replied that such people were assholes. To be sure, the word was bleeped, but not enough that we listeners couldn't hear the true word loud and clear.

Seeing John in the flesh, I wanted to ask him what he would have changed. I had always thought he'd had one hell of a life, and believed John had thought so, too.

I imagine smoking was one thing he would have changed, having learned the hard way how destructive it could be. But it wasn't the right time to ask him anything. He had a white patch over one eye. A cataract operation was my guess. He looked really shot.

I told him who I was, in case he couldn't see too well with the eye he had left.

"How are you, honey," he murmured, as was his wont. He even got to his feet. But then he had to sit right down again. The strength to remain standing wasn't there. I quickly patted his shoulder, kissed him on the cheek, and moved away, not to tax him further. Poor, poor baby.

It was along about then that Marvin came up with, of all things, an acting part in his soap. The part of a grandmother (yep, it had come to that). But would I, he asked, audition for the producer the way everybody else who worked on the show did?

Although I had vowed never to audition again even for God himself, when I read the description of this grandmother, it gave me such a good laugh that I succumbed. "A woman," the script informed me, "of lasting beauty with class, earthiness, descended from Maximilian (Hapsburg Emperor of Mexico) and an Aztec Princess—aristocratic, down-to-earth, practical, with inner strength, spunk, inventiveness, humor, compassion, and a large capacity to love and care for others." (A role clearly written for me, right?)

The challenge of showing all *that* in a couple of pages of dialogue was too big a temptation to resist!

Besides, since I'd never been on a soap, never even watched one, actually, though I knew all America did—even college kids had got hung up on them—it seemed time to get in on the action. Even Elizabeth Taylor had been on one, and if Elizabeth did something, you *knew* it was the "in" thing to do!

Things got even better when I walked into the producer's office and found two spotlights hanging from the ceiling. Two spotlights aimed at the very spot I was to stand and read the scene I'd been given.

I had never seen spotlights in anybody's office before. *Anybody's.* Not in Harry's, not in David's, not even in Cecil B. DeMille's, and *he* made Spectaculars.

The producer, then, proceeded to take a chair directly below me. So that the view she had was of the under part of my chin.

Now. If there was anything I had learned from my years in front of a camera, it was what a good angle was, and what a good angle was *not.*

The under-chin angle was most definitely one of the *nots.* Particularly for demonstrating "aristocratic" qualities, "beauty and class," or even a "capacity to love and care for others."

The jig was up, then and there, and I knew it. You always do. Naturally I didn't get the part, when had I ever from an audition? But this time it was quite okay. Better than okay, actually, it was terrific. Because what I did get was something far better.

I had got myself some *column* material!

It looked as if I couldn't lose, anymore, no matter which way things turned out.

At least that's what I kept telling myself . . .

## *Twenty-seven*

At long last the documentary on Artie was done, wrapped, in the can (having taken at least a couple of years or more). Brigitte Berman, its maker, called from Toronto to say she was coming to town with it. That the world premiere was to be held at Mann's Westwood Theater (near my beloved UCLA research library) and would I please attend.

You bet. I'd been looking forward to seeing what Artie was up to, what he looked and sounded like after close to ten years, especially since running into John as I had, who had faded so. Though Artie, of course, was not only younger than John, he was—as far as I knew—in better health, having had the good sense to stop smoking when he was still ahead.

I wasn't disappointed. I was, in fact, moved.

Mann's was a big theater, and it was packed, and it was like visiting an old friend, sitting there in the dark, watching Artie.

Brigitte had done a splendid job. She had taken Artie all the way from birth to the new orchestra of his I had been reading about. And if it's true that after forty we are responsible for our own faces, then Artie Shaw could give himself a pat on the back.

As a youth, the fellow had had those matinee idol good looks. As a young band leader, he had been no slouch in that department, either (as George Burns had informed me). But this ripened, on-in-years fellow up there, I found to be the most interesting of all. A thoughtful, erudite, articulate "senior citizen," overflowing with knowledge accumulated through a lifetime of searching, reading, studying, trying a bit of everything. Going here to find whatever he was looking for. Going there, too, in case it was over *there*.

And yes, Brigitte had gone, as she said she would, to our little Spanish town of Bagur, Provincia de Gerona, and photographed the house Artie and Evelyn had built up on the side of that Catalan mountain, photographed the breathtaking view below, the reddish earth jutting into the dark-blue of the sea, the rugged beauty that was the tree-sprinkled coastline, winding its way along the restless waters until it disappeared into the horizon.

The sight of it all fairly took my breath away.

To Connecticut, too, Brigitte had gone. There, in the dark theater in Westwood, was the big white Colonial house we had first settled into on our return to America, the glacier lake stretched out before it down there among the trees. Truly handsome.

Yes, I had been dead right when I said in the film that Artie Shaw had been one of the better things that had happened to me.

Artie, most naturally, had been shown this story-of-his-life on film someplace or other before the Grand Opening. Had heard what I had to say about him in it. Even so, it took him a month to get around to giving me a call.

But before he did, something else came along that made more sense than most any other thing I had been up to for a very long time. (Maybe *ever*.) Something that, by the very nature of it, could gather up all the little pieces of my various endeavors and put them together into one workable form. And it wasn't anything that I had ever thought of myself, oddly enough. Though after it was suggested, I couldn't imagine why I never had.

It began at a gala dinner dance that the *Love Boat* folk threw for their thousandth guest star, inviting the 999 others who had gone on before (thereby giving me further column material!) to celebrate the occasion. So there we were, all 1,000 of us, in the big ballroom of the Beverly Hilton Hotel, saying Hello! Hello! Long time no see! Kiss-kissing, hug-hugging, dressed in fancy duds, everybody in their usual good shape. (*Love Boat* wouldn't have anybody who wasn't on their show!) We ate and drank and were merry as could be as we were given a floor show and a screening of various clips from some of the previous episodes.

It was almost time to leave when Tab Hunter came over to say hello, hello.

Not that I'd ever met Tab. His career had blossomed in the fifties, about the time I was getting ready to cross the sea for foreign shores. Though, of course, I knew very well who Tab Hunter was.

Handsome was what he was, the good looks enhanced by the dark suit and black tie he wore. What a marvelous invention men's evening clothes are. They perk up even the most average of men, and help deal a knock-out blow for the Apollos, like Tab. (If you ask me, women would be wise to find a similar such uniform presentation for themselves, instead of the absurd and expensive rigamarole they go through.)

"Hello," said Tab, "I'm Tab Hunter." He had great teeth, too, I saw.

"You certainly are!" I told him emphatically.

"I read a book of yours, a novel," he then said.

"Oh! Did you!" I was always so pleased when someone had read my novel. It was the one Kirk Douglas always said would make a good movie most every time I ran into him, and that he was going to talk to one of his sons about it, but never did.

"I wonder if my partner and I could come over, one day, and talk to you about it," Tab then asked me.

"With pleasure," I told him.

I'd heard that Tab had become a film producer, these days. Wouldn't it be something if he, too, thought he could make a movie out of my book! Boy. Then I could thumb my nose at Kirk. I would rather enjoy that, I thought.

*"Old Husband, New Friend"* ■ 227

I gave Tab my phone number, and said any time. Talking never hurt anybody, did it.

Three guys came over, Tab and two others in tow. One was Perry Bullington, who had read my book first, some time ago, actually, and had thought that it would make a good movie. But in the press of daily hassle (he was casting director for Cannon Films) it had slipped his mind, he said. But recently he had been packing his books to move, or maybe dusting them, doing something that caused my book to fall off the shelf and land at his feet. As if it were speaking to him. Destiny, this Perry Bullington said, had stepped into the breach.

Destiny, schmestiny, I liked what he said. (I've never minded people perking up a story in the telling. Better than boring everybody to death, no?) He had taken the book to Tab and his partner, who also agreed it would translate well to the screen.

It was the partner who then spoke up. "We hope you will be interested in doing the script for us, yourself," is what he said.

Allan was the partner's name. Allan Glaser. A child. A goddamn *baby*. A slim, schoolboy body, a shock of thick, dark hair over a perfectly smooth, unlined face. Probably all of nineteen, I thought. (I would learn he was actually just going on twenty-five.) The new Hollywood I had heard so much about, those youths that had taken over the campfire, was right there, sitting in my living room.

"But," I told him, "I've never written a script."

"We know that," Tab said, his blue eyes dancing, "but we think you could."

"Your book is so visual," Allan said, "and the dialogue is already there." His brown eyes danced.

"If you'd be willing to try," Tab said, "we'd be willing to gamble."

"Because we don't think," Allan added, "it would be a gamble at all. We know you can do it."

My heart began to pick up its pace. Me? Write a script? Writing a movie script had never so much as even crossed my mind. It was what other people did. The Billy Wilders. The Dalton Trumbos. The John Hustons.

But Ev, sweetie, the little voice tucked away inside my head whispered to me, these people hadn't been *born* knowing how to write scripts, had they? All *men,* too, I suddenly realized I'd been thinking about . . .

Was *that* what was somewhere in my mind,? That only men wrote scripts? With a shock I realized that I never even acted in a movie written by a woman. And what was worse, that fact had never even occurred to me until that moment. Then the next revelation fairly boggled my mind. Only men had been called upon to write (rewrite and re-rewrite) the movie script of *Gone With the Wind.* A book written by a woman. About a woman.

I told Perry and Allan and Tab I would be delighted to turn my novel into a movie script for them, and thanked them for asking me.

Actually I had decided, then and there, it was my *duty* to do so, or at least make a run at it, not only for myself, but for my gender as well.

I couldn't go so very wrong, could I? Hadn't I spent all those years reading, memorizing, acting in *scripts*? Surely I'd learned in the process what worked and what didn't. Hadn't I been around some pretty good filmmakers? Hearing what they had to say, listening to their comments on this movie and that? Watching them in action? My God, once, I'll never forget it, we were having script trouble on a film of mine called *Mrs. Mike.* Dick Powell was the producer (as well as the leading man), and I asked him if he would like John's help. (John was the fair-haired boy among directors/writers in the Hollywood community at the time.)

Dick, of course, was thrilled. Such a talent available and for *nothing,* too! We all met on Sunday—John had read the script the night before—and I remember to this day what John told Dick and the writer of the script. A book is one thing, John said (*Mrs. Mike* was based on a book), and, as a rule, read over a number of days. So that whatever tragedies might occur in the book will be stretched out over those days. But when you put the same number of tragedies into a screenplay, and they are seen in the length of time a movie runs, say an hour and a half, they will be too close together. And it won't work. They will overwhelm the audience. There is not enough recovery time between them. So that the first tragedy will be sad. The second very heartbreaking. By the third, the audience won't be able to take it, anymore, and they will begin to laugh in self-defense, and there will go your movie. (It was exactly what the screenwriter had done; squeezed the whole book into the movie script, and as a result, poor Mrs. Mike [me] was losing a baby, nursing the sick, losing a baby, being lonely, going through a diphtheria epidemic that ravaged the settlement in which she lived, losing another baby in practically every scene.) Nobody, said John, would finally give a damn, and he doubted if anybody would even hang around to see the picture through to the end.

Fortunately Dick and his writer listened, and *Mrs. Mike* didn't turn out too badly. (Only one baby was lost on the screen.) Pacing in a screenplay, I had learned, was everything. A little item I would try and remember when I went to work on my own.

By then I had cartons upon cartons full of my *Princess Juana* research stacked under my working table, in all the closets, under the beds, even taking up space in the kitchen cabinets. The several chapters I had written by now were stacked on top of the desk. There was no room for one single other thing.

So. There was nothing for it but to gather it all up, package it neatly so I'd be able to find it again one day, cart it off to my storage place, and put it alongside the other unpublished novel, the endless notebooks filled with enough ideas to last me into the twenty-first century, and forget it for a while.

Never mind, I told myself. After I had all those piles of money from the screenplay and the huge success of the movie that followed, I would *then* go back and finish my historical novel for my very own pleasure—and publish it myself, too, if I had to!

But first things first. I was back in the picture business, I was. On the other side of the camera, this time. And who's to say. Maybe where I'd belonged all along.

Since the story to be told was in book form at the moment, the number-one thing that had to be done, it seemed to me, was to change it over into screenplay form, and then go from there.

But before I could so much as begin, who in the world should call but Artie. A voice from another life. Another place I'd once thought I'd belonged . . .

"So you don't hate me," was how he began after all those years of our not having spoken to each other.

"Oh course I don't hate you!" I said back.

And that was that. All that was said of that aspect of the interim. Over. Done with. Finished.

And we were off. As if there had been no time lapse whatsoever. Two hours' worth. Not starting over, simply continuing as before, as we had done every day in Spain and the years afterward everywhere else. It's a mystery to me the thing I keep hearing lately—that families don't talk to each other more than seven minutes a day. "What's for dinner?" "Do your homework." "Mother called." "How is she?" "Okay." "What's on TV?" Over and out. Artie and I had never *stopped* talking since we had known each other.

We went from a discussion of the documentary to what I was up to, what he was doing with his new band (which he doubted would be commercial, since nobody was dressed in flashy clothing and dancing around strumming guitars). He said he thought jazz orchestras ought to be subsidized, the way symphony orchestras were. After all, he said, jazz was American culture, and symphonies belonged to the European one.

We also covered politics, the state of the world. We even reminisced about Spain, Artie particularly remembering a fishing trip we made to Andorra, the tiny country up in the Pyrenees Mountains above Spain and below France. Up, up we went, to a fresh, tumbling stream so pure that trout lived in it, and how the inn where we stayed cooked his catch for us every evening.

We made a date for dinner the following night.

In my life again? I couldn't exactly say that; he had hardly been out. No matter he hadn't been around, somehow he had popped up every so often, willy-nilly, something he had done, remembered, a place we had gone. On occasion I would find myself quoting something he had once said. Or someone would ask about him. Or his music would suddenly be there, in a store, in an elevator, in somebody's house. Yes, he had been around most all the while, one way or the other.

He was to drive down from wherever he lived up north, and since he had never been to my place, before, as soon as he was announced downstairs, I stepped out into the hall to wait for him. At least he wouldn't have to search for which door my apartment was.

There wasn't going to be any surprise in store for either of us as to what change in appearance ten years might have wrought. I had just seen him in his film, all up to date. And he had seen me in his film, all up to date.

The elevator door opened and closed, footsteps could be heard approaching along the hall—and then there he was, Artie Shaw in person.

I was truly glad to see him again. "Hey, Artie!" I called out happily. "Welcome!" Twenty-nine years earlier, he had approached my Paris apartment-on-the-Seine in just this way.

He was still ten or fifteen feet away when he greeted me this time. "Hey," Artie called out to me. "A little old lady!"

That was Artie's greeting after not seeing me (in the flesh) for these ten years.

If I had been flattered by the reviews of me in his documentary (still striking, still beautiful as ever), if I had been thinking that my daily four-mile jog, eating whole grains, steamed vegetables, and fruits with their peels, were going to help me hang onto my youthful looks into perpetuity, Artie was here to set me straight. As he had been doing ever since I had met him. And on the same subject, too. Was there any point in telling him I was still five feet five—as I had alway been? Older, sure. I'd have to concede that. But who wasn't? We were getting older even as he strode down the hall toward me. That actually anybody who had been being born at the time we *met* would now be twenty-nine years old—and if a "she," already probably *too old for him!*

Oh listen, I hadn't just been spinning my wheels as I had got older, I'd figured a lot of things out I hadn't even suspected in the earlier days. (How could I have? It *takes* getting older to figure *some* things out!)

Poor Artie. Imagine. I had been a threat to him from the very beginning of our relationship. Because, you see, *I kept getting older* . . . and older . . . and older, with every single day that passed. I simply would not stay as young as I had been when we met. And worse. I wasn't as young as he would have preferred me to be even then. Only recently did I come to realize what Artie had been doing all the while, even back there on our mountain top. Even during the throes of first passions.

He had even then been comparing me to *a younger me.*

He had told me back then (although it had taken all this while to put two and two together) that he had met me before. At some big gathering or other. Alas, I didn't remember the occasion at all. He told me he had been most interested, but that I hadn't given him the time of day. I had been with John, at the time, and obviously looking neither left nor right. I had also at the time—how shall I say it—been in my prime. The young, the gorgeous movie star, and wearing something quite smashing, too, I wager. But it would appear that I had had the audacity not to stay that way.

I decided that night over dinner, though, that maybe Artie had got used to the way I looked now. He'd arrived at eight, we went to a restaurant in the neighborhood, and talked-talked-talked again, this time until one in the morning. Another five hours. We really did have an awful lot in common. We were still thinking alike, believed in the same things, were still voting for the same people (which, in the end, is everything, no?). If he could become my best friend, and I his, wouldn't it be just about perfect?

We thought we might be able to manage it if we didn't get too close. We had, uh, bifurcated (doesn't it sound like the dirtiest world you ever heard?) the marriage contract. Which means, I believe, you delegalize the signed agreement. (I had let him do it. Once again, I had avoided responsibility. And for him I think it took the threat away. You can be friends with an older woman, you just can't be married to her.) We still had binding agreements between us. (You know, property things.) So we were glued together, like it or not.

We parted that night, in good spirits, believing we had accomplished something, arrived at some understanding.

# PART FIVE

# *Trying a New Point of View*

## Twenty-eight

It turned out to be no-end satisfying, the business of translating my very own book into my very own movie script. And it again crossed my mind as I worked along that this might very well be the best time I'd ever had in my entire life.

Oh sure, sure, I said to me, and how many times have you thought *that* before?

Yeah, yeah, I instantly agreed, I'd thought it before. More than once before. Often before. And meant it, too. Each and every time, too. With all my being. And I was no Pollyanna, either. Anything but. I'd been cutting out articles for years about the hole in the ozone layer up there, the over-population, the disappearing rain forests, the nuclear leakage. But what was wrong with treating your life span, anyhow, the way kids make their ice cream cones last as long as they can by licking them slowly, even if they know they won't last forever? Didn't we all learn to do that at a very early age? So why throw away a valuable lesson you'd learned as a kid just because you were all grown up and everything, answer me that, I said to me, and kept my good thoughts firmly in place.

Every couple of weeks or so, Tab, Allan, and I would get together for what is known as a "story conference."

Unlike the solitariness of book writing, a screenplay is group effort. Everybody connected with it wants to get into the act, from producer to director to actors to money-people. (Which might explain why movies so often go astray. Too many cooks, and all that.) John used to have these get-togethers regularly when he was working on a script. Somebody or other was always showing up out at the Tarzana spread, and then much talk and scribbling would ensue in the study, sometimes out on the long terrace in back. John almost never worked alone. And as soon as I began to have these story conferences with my partners (as I liked to call them), I understood why.

It was plain fun, not going it alone, that was why. Hard to think of as work (after all, I had already laid the foundation), this shared responsibility of fixing and changing and cutting. True, the cutting would leave holes in the script (a story about a sixteen-year-old girl whose dazzling looks draw people to her, each of them believing she's the answer to their particular fantasy), then I would have to go home and on my own tie it together again. But mostly the process had the same feeling as a good rehearsal of a play or a movie. When everybody's pulling together, feeling pleased about what they are creating, looking forward to accomplishing great things.

I began to learn the latest Hollywood vernacular, too, as I went along (when in Rome, right?). I found out you don't "have" things, anymore, the way you used to. You "do" or "take" them, it would seem. Like you *do* lunch, and you *take* meetings. Although the same things still go on at both of these gatherings that used to go on. I mean, you still talk at meetings, and you still eat and drink at lunch (and talk plenty there, too).

Mostly I learned this latest with-it stuff from Allan, who was the youngest of the group, and into these things. Actually Tab, Allan (Perry had gone back to his casting couch), and I were, I thought, not a bad combination. Tab, under contract to Warner Brothers for a number of years, having made a flock of pictures—one for John, too, along the way—had evidently not been just another pretty face. He was very script-wise, understanding what would work and what would not. And Allan, the kid (damn, I was going to have to stop thinking of him as a kid, he *was* over twenty-one, after all!) was the wheeler-dealer. And one smart cookie. He seemed to have known what he wanted at the ripe age of one. And gone for it, too. And that was to be a producer of films.

From Virginia, Allan had chosen (he'd been in a position to choose, having had top grades in his graduating class) the University of Southern California for its cinema school. That's how these latter-day hopefuls have to go about it, these days, if they want to knock on Hollywood's doors, go to cinema school.

But when Allan learned how many students went through the School Of Cinema and out the other side and into a dead end, he switched majors. He went for business, instead, as well as political science, with some cinema and theater arts classes thrown in. He had the good sense, that young man, to pay heed to the *second* word in that phrase bandied about all over the place, "the entertainment *business.*" A little item too may of us often ignored (myself included).

We had a common passion, the kid (whoops, there I go again) and I. And that was research libraries. Allan could take up residence in them the way I could. Had obviously been running around to them all his short life, looking up information, finding out things, from the price of tea in Beijing during the Manchu Dynasty to the color of the horse Alan Ladd rode off on in *Shane*. And though I had Artie back to use as my walking-around encyclopedia once more (it was one of the reasons I was glad to be on speaking terms with him again), now I had Allan, too, for walking-around-encyclopedia duty, and he was handier. He would even go with me when we were on the prowl for something. (Our picture was going to be period, the year 1937, so we had to find out what clothes looked like then, and hairstyles and houses and cars and such.)

When Artie and his orchestra came to perform at the Hollywood Bowl that summer, I took my partners with me to hear—and see—them do their stuff.

We had stayed in touch, Artie and I. Mostly by phone-talking marathons. Plus a meal here and there. It was fascinating to listen to this man who had been my soulmate once upon a time, without being involved. See and hear things that used to drive me bananas with a touch of amusement (and sometimes amazement) now. It hadn't taken too long to find out he was still the same roller-coaster-restless fellow I had known before. The years hadn't appeared to change that aspect of him, or slow him down; he still often sounded like a man trying to throw off some remaining shackles. Even with his orchestra going full swing, one day he'd said on the phone, in what seemed to be a kind of funk, that he was thinking of moving to New Zealand. (It was Australia he'd spoken of going to next when we were living in Spain.) But not long after that he told me he was having an alarm system put in his house, so I assumed he wouldn't be going to New Zealand, after all. One thing *had* changed, though, since my day, if I could believe him. He said, one night, that he had to hang up and go fix dinner. Fix his *own dinner*! *Artie*?

"Y-you're . . . going to . . . f-fix your *own* . . . *dinner*?" I had gasped, believing my ears were playing some kind of trick.

"It's Swanson's Chicken Kiev, three minutes in the microwave, that's all there is to it," said Artie Shaw, as if he had been doing things like that all his life. "The market down there," he went on, "has a salad bar, too, anything you want, all chopped up and ready to go."

Hardly a big deal, one might think, a full-grown man slipping a prepared package into a microwave oven, picking up an already-chopped salad at the market, himself. But this was the guy who had said tending to the kitchen and the meals was the little woman's concern, even if she had been a movie star. My God, to my knowledge the man had never even been inside a grocery store before. Maybe he had come a long way, baby, after all!

This fixer, then, of his very-own-dinner, was the man five thousand strong greeted with unbridled gusto when he stepped onto the stage of the Hollywood Bowl that July night to take his place in front of his already-assembled orchestra.

I hadn't been to the Bowl since, oh, probably since the Ice Age. An outdoor theater, vast, a shell-shape cupping the stage area making excellent acoustics, it was the perfect place to witness, and listen, to Artie Shaw and his orchestra for the first time in my life.

I had never before seen or heard him doing his thing in person. On radio, yes, on records. Even in the movies he had made with Lana Turner and Paulette Goddard once upon a time. Even as recently as in San Antonio while I was doing the play down there, while I was in my dressing room getting ready to go on, Artie's clarinet would come wafting into me over the house speaker. The stage manager put on a cassette of his every night before showtime, knowing my connection.

I tried to stop breathing for a while, in case the in-and-out taking would interfere with any single sound that might be coming from the stage up there.

It was not the old Artie sound. It was a brand-new Artie sound. It was now-jazz. Today-jazz. It was so absolutely thrilling, so beautiful. Artie only led, of course, but his hands did the most extraordinary things. As if they were shaping the sounds that issued forth, moving them, pushing them, curling them all around this way and that. It was as if the music came from his fingertips, themselves.

The entire place rose to its feet in a standing ovation when it was over. So did Allan. So did Tab. And so did I.

This, then, was Artie Shaw. Who, and what, Artie was, it would seem. All that talking, all the attempts at making other lives on faraway mountaintops apparently hadn't changed it a whit. Had only hidden it for a while, nothing more.

No wonder we had had such *tsimmes* all the time, the two of us. We had both been pretending to be something we weren't. And to make matters worse, hadn't even known it.

But cut! Print that scene, and prepare for the next—that of bifurcated wife weaving her way (with friends) across the Hollywood Bowl to The Star's dressing room, who happens to be her (are you ready) husband of yesteryear.

Zoom in for a dramatic entrance.

Oh well. We were scarcely noticed, surrounded as Artie was by a throng of admirers. He had on his Star Hat, too. I could tell by the half-glazed look in his eye. (You do go into another gear when you're performing. You kind of have to.) So our congrats were quick, and so was our exit. It was no time to intrude with memories of other times, other places.

Besides. I had to get home and get a good night's sleep. I had a million things to do on the morrow. I had to finish the scene I was working on for our script before I went off to do some acting again.

Yeah, that's right. Acting . . .

## Twenty-nine

**M**y producing pair didn't mind if I took a little time out to do a bit of acting on the side. Tab did the same, himself, once in a while. It was only for a week, after all. A smallish role in Angela Lansbury's successful series, *Murder, She Wrote.* Imagine. An hour's story shot in one week. They do that, now. The four hours of *Gone With the Wind* took six months to accomplish. (Of course, costs were different, there were places you could buy a house for two hundred dollars back then. I saw that was so on the back of an ancient newspaper clipping about *GWTW* someone sent to me.)

It was a pleasant enough break, the few days up north in Mendocino, California, along a beautiful stretch of coast, where the company was shooting. I wouldn't have wanted to be away from my budding screenplay much longer than that.

By then it had become my main focus, the screenplay, my *raison d'être* of the moment. Damned if it hadn't begun to look as if my grasshopper days had truly come to an end at last. I didn't seem to want to go anywhere except to my typewriter. (I didn't even envy my friends when they took off for exotic places. Like Talli to Budapest, Cynthia to Bejing, Hilda to Vermont for the foliage season, J.J. to Japan for God knows what reason. I rather pitied them, actually, for spattering themselves around like that!)

Yes, my times, they certainly kept right on a-changing.

Back again, Talli did get me out on Wilshire Boulevard, one day, along with a string of other well-meaning folk, to stand on the curb (there were blocks and blocks of us) holding up posters announcing in large letters that we were for a nuclear freeze. At noon, too. Some cars honked in sympathy, but a few of the big city buses seemed bent on running us down. They came whizzing by a few inches from the curb, so close they knocked our signs all about. (Evidently the drivers felt that a nuclear death was preferable to driving those buses for a living every day in Los Angeles.)

More people kept coming around to talk to me. To glean what information they could from the "museum piece." About this one. Or that. Somebody wanted to know about the director Joe Losey, who had become something of a cult figure. About the black-listing days. Even about Pauline Potter, Hattie Carnegie's head designer of yore, who had made an entire wardrobe for me once upon a time, thanks to John (they were friends) and was dead now. (Actually everybody I was being asked about was.) Not to mention *GWTW.* The people who wanted to hear some damn thing about *it,* and the people in it, were never ending. Never never *never* ending.

And through it all, there was my old husband and new friend, Artie, often on the phone for one of our long raps. He, too, had gone off somewhere. He and his orchestra. To New York, to perform. One of the calls was on his return.

"Guess who showed up," he said in a strangely hushed voice.

"I can't imagine . . ." This wasn't like Artie.

"Jonathan, on opening night."

Number two son. I was aware that Artie hadn't seen or heard from Jonathan for quite a number of years. I knew Jonathan. He had come to visit us, once, at the Connecticut establishment. A gangly, charming, into-everything nine-year-old, who had fallen in love with our place and wanted to come live there. Which appeared to have irritated his mother, Doris Dowling, no end. So it never happened.

"Little Jonathan," I murmured, still remembering the young boy, "my my. How in the world is he?"

"It was very emotional." Artie's voice was husky. "We both cried."

"Cried . . ." I murmured. I was touched. Artie didn't often cry. "It's, it's understandable, after all this time . . ."

"You know," Artie then said, "how hard it is for me to express love."

I was taken aback. Artie was wrong. I hadn't known that, at all. How could I not have known *such a thing as that*? Had I done it all? Had I interpreted all the talking, the insistence on the double bed for us wherever we went, and a million such other things, as *love*?

We would have to have a talk about *that* sometime. But not then. Because he was saying, "You know what Jonathan told me?"

"What? What?"

"I'm a grandfather."

"You're . . . *what!*" Little Jonathan? Come to think of it, he had to have got past nine. Like around thirty, I decided, doing a quick addition on my fingers. Quite old enough for making babies. "You mean, he's all grown up and married and everything? Little Jonathan?"

"No, not married, not even together. I guess they met here, but she's Brazilian and she went back down there to have the baby."

"I see." I might have known it wouldn't be your run-of-the-mill arrangement. It never had a chance to be, did it. "How do you feel about this turn of events, Artie?"

"Strange. There are my genes, going on without me, somewhere in Brazil, of all places."

Artie also told me that Jonathan had become a tattoo artist. That's what he said. Tattoo artist. That was a puzzlement to us both. Neither of us had ever known a tattoo artist. Never even met one. We both wondered how it had come about that Jonathan had taken *that* up. But backstage at the Blue Note in the Big Apple right after a concert-that-was-a-happening wasn't exactly the place or time to find out. Jonathan would be coming to California one of these days, Artie told me, and if I liked, we could see him.

I tell you. It wasn't necessary to leave my typewriter or travel to exotic lands for a bit of drama to come into my life.

The script pages kept gradually increasing. Slowly, slowly. A screenplay wasn't something you simply popped out overnight. I couldn't, anyway. Not my first. I was feeling my way. (And I was the world's lousiest typist, I might add; half the time was spent fixing something so even *I* would know what it was.) Nor would I allow the guys to read one page of it, either. Not until it was done. I wanted a critique on the whole product, not on bits and pieces that might be changed, anyway, before I was done.

They both went along with it, said absolutely, do what you feel you have to do. Oh, we were in such splendid accord, it was really nice. Hug-hug, kiss-kiss. I loved them both and hoped they would love me (after they had read my script!).

Even so I went off to act again. It was only one more of these week things, right in town, this time, and how could I *not* do it. Steven Spielberg was the producer, with Joe Dante of *Gremlins* directing and if *that* wasn't up-to-date Hollywood, what in the world *was*.

We shot at Universal, on a very old soundstage that still had the ancient Lon Chaney *Phantom of the Opera* set on it in the background. Such a marvelous blending of the old and the new (in a town that has destroyed the greater part of its history). It was a lovely experience. Eddie Bracken *(The Miracle of Morgan's Creek)* played opposite me, a pro if there ever was one. We were a couple of ghosts, living in the attic of a house we used to own. When a vulgar, raucous couple moved in down below in the house proper, we decided to scare them off. But being the most inept of ghosts, we had to look at a couple of modern movies to learn how to scare properly. (A moral, maybe, somewhere in there?)

It was fun. Was it possible there might be a few parts around, after all, that could be enjoyable to do as you got on up there, besides baglady?

Not only weeks, but months, too, flowed by (they do, don't they, when you're having fun?) and sure enough, one day, Artie called to say Jonathan had come to town. Would I like to have dinner with them?

"What about on my birthday?" I said.

"Oh," said Artie, "is that coming up?"

Sentimental he was not, Artie. But then, neither was I. Birthday dates and big holidays had all got lost in the moving around. So I had learned long ago that if I wanted to be remembered, feted, on any special day (like my own birthday) the best thing to do was to speak up and say so to the person (or persons) I wanted to do the remembering. That way I'd never be disappointed.

We were meeting at my place, and Jonathan arrived first. And my God, how he had grown. The former little boy was taller than I, now, by a lot, too. Still long-legged, with a cowboy build now, wearing some kind of cowboyish hat to match, as well as boots. There was a lot of Artie in his face, one could see that instantly, especially around the eyes. How about that. I'm afraid I was grinning all over the place.

"Jonathan! My God, how great to see you!" I cried.

"Good to see you, too," he also said, minding his manners.

"Do you remember me at all?" I asked him. "You were such a little kid, then."

"Oh sure. You and Machito and Garbo."

I laughed. Those were the dogs he was talking about. Machito, a German shepherd we had brought back with us from Spain. Garbo, a toy schnauzer I had picked up locally for one of Artie's birthdays. It had been Jonathan and I and the dogs who had mostly run around together. Into the lake. Into the woods. To the bowling alley. To the petting zoo. Out in the little boat we had that we kept hitched up to the dock down at the edge of the lake.

Jonathan had brought a present for my birthday, a lovely, off-white egg of, I don't rightly know what, marble perhaps, some kind of sleek, heavy stone. I was touched.

"It's from Brazil," he said.

"Oh? Have you been there?" I hadn't realized that.

I learned that, not only had he *been* there, he had *lived* there. That he spoke fluent Portuguese. And that he was going back there, too.

Artie arrived and off we went. Over dinner I then learned that tattooing was a great way to travel and earn your living as you went. You could go anywhere, set up shop when you got there, and do quite well. How about *that*. Maybe I had chosen the wrong profession, said I.

I enjoyed my birthday party enormously, dining with father and son like that. It was the perfect way to have a family, I decided. Just the way it was. No more. No less.

I assumed, that night, that Jonathan was returning to Brazil to join the mother of his child.

However. I would find out, on up the road, how wrong my assumption had been.

"And by the way," Artie said, as he dropped me off, "I wonder if you *could* do something for me . . ."

"Anything!" I exclaimed enthusiastically. We were all glowing from the champagne we had imbibed celebrating the birthday person, me.

"You *said* we were family again," Artie continued, evidently needing to reassure himself, "that you'd be there if I needed you."

"Yes I did—and I *meant* it, too!" I told him emphatically.

"Then could you take care of my dog when I go away?"

"Your *dog*!"

"I go out with the band every so often, and I don't like to leave Chaucer with strangers . . ."

*"Chau-cer?"* Wasn't that an early English poet?

"He's a great dog," Artie said, "no trouble at all."

"What kind of dog is he?"

"An English sheepdog."

It figured, didn't it, with Chaucer for a name. Weren't they those elephant-size animals with the long, shaggy hair covering the eyes that looked like animated rugs? "But Artie," I said worriedly, "my place isn't all *that* big."

"He's thirteen years old."

"Thirteen! Wow!" Machito and Garbo had both died at nine. I had never known a thirteen-year-old dog.

"He's an old man, gentle as can be," Artie told me, "and well-behaved. I don't even have to use a leash when I take Chester anywhere."

*"Chester?"*

"That's his nickname. I know you. You'll be crazy about him."

So. In a matter of months, by way of my old/new friend, I had got a stepson, a step-grandchild. And a stepdog named Chaucer whose nickname was Chester.

Fortunately it was only the dog who would be coming for a visit of any length . . .

# *Thirty*

Four days later. That was all the time that passed before there Artie was, dog Chester in tow. This time when I waited at the door it was this big gray creature loping along on all fours that turned the corner first. Except it didn't look like any sheepdog that I had ever seen. Instead of the long shaggy stuff, this one had a stubble of maybe two inches all over his frame. The legs were like beanpoles and the head simply enormous compared to the sheared-down body.

"W-what happened to his coat?" I cried out, thinking the poor dog must be suffering from a skin disease or something.

"I cut it off," said Artie, "all it does is get snarled up, it's a nuisance, and anyway, this is California, he doesn't need such a heavy coat."

Who would get a sheepdog and then cut off the thing that made him a sheep dog? Wouldn't that be *why* you got a sheep-dog? Because you liked the *look* of all that shaggy hair? Artie Shaw, I thought, is not like other people. He just isn't, and that's all there is to that.

He had brought Chester's food, his vitamins, his two bowls (for food, for water), his bed, and his leash. I mean, this dog wasn't going to do without anything he was used to, except Artie, and now he had me, and that didn't take him any too long to find out. He waited at the front door after Artie departed through it, looking puzzled. Then he hurried out onto the balcony when he heard the car start up below, even though my apartment was nine stories up. But when it had gone, he turned around, looked at me for a second, and then came over.

Somehow that dog knew. Chester *knew* I was the one, now, in charge. I fed him immediately, always a winning thing to do (to people, too, right?). I told him about Machito and Garbo, and how I missed them sometimes. He leaned against me then, and put his big head on my lap, as if he knew what I was talking about. (And who's to say he didn't.)

It soon became routine, Chester's being dropped off for visits, some of them lasting for weeks at a time. Soon he was trotting down the hall and through the front door as if he were coming home. Maybe Artie took advantage—I never said no, Chester couldn't come—I was, in truth, quite glad that he did, since you really can't run around too many places with a dog nearly as big as you are in tow, even one that's thirteen years old with good manners. And so I got a lot of work done, so much, in fact, that before the year was out, I finished the first draft of my screenplay.

I didn't even read it over, I simply called my producers to tell them so, I was that excited.

It was Allan who answered the phone.

"Eureka! I've done it!" I breathlessly informed him without so much as a hello first.

"Done what?" said Allan. "Brought Harry back from the dead?"

If I had said it once, I had said it, oh, a good hundred times—when the guys were sitting around plotting what and how and where they would take the script (once it was ready) to get it on the road—I would invariably say, "Oh *God,* I wish Harry Cohn was still around, he would do my script in a *minute,* I just *know* he would!"

They made me nervous with their talk of this fragmented unbeknownst-to-me Hollywood filled with Joe Blows here, Jack Thingumbobs there, people who couldn't make decisions on their own, and furthermore didn't stay put for too long, anyhow, replaced by another set of Joes and Jacks (and sometimes, glory be, even Jills!) who couldn't make decisions on *their* own, either. No wonder I longed for Harry Cohn, a head of a studio who *stayed* head until he died. (And made *all* the decisions.)

"You behave yourself," I said to Allan (well, he *was* a kid, damn it!), "or I'll tear it up and start all over."

"Don't tell me! You . . . ?"

"Yes, I've done it, a *whole entire draft.* Chester and me."

I don't think he used his car. I think he flew over. He was being announced, and at my door, out of breath, in less than a minute. (Well, that's the way it seemed.)

I handed the manuscript to him with as much pomp and circumstance as you can muster up for a plain brown manila envelope. Chester had awakened and come over to stand in attendance, like a major domo, watching the action.

"He-e-ey," said Allan, taking the thick package in both hands. "You didn't have to make copies for us, I could have . . ."

"Oh, I didn't, I didn't make copies." The envelope was quite fat.

Allan blinked a couple of times. "You mean . . . all of this is . . . is just *one* script?"

I laughed. "It's only a first draft, Allan, just a changeover, really from book to script *form,* so we can read it like that and see . . ."

"I can't wait—"

". . . what needs trimming, maybe you'll have suggestions . . ."

"I'm going straight home and start reading . . ." He was already backing out the door.

"And Tab, too!" I called out after him.

". . . and Tab, too . . ." His voice trailed back as he ran down the hall and into the elevator.

I looked at Chester, and he looked at me. "What if they don't like it?" I said to him worriedly.

Big soulful eyes gazed up into mine. His back end wriggled ever so slightly. Don't worry, they'll like it, I swear this was what he told me. He was such a dear dog. Always saying just the right thing. I gave him the Purina tidbit he was hoping for, and satisfied, he returned to his snoozing.

Artie called shortly after to say he was in town and could swing by to pick up Chester if that was all right. It was the good Artie that showed up, too, the one who made it all worthwhile to stay his friend, the one in an upbeat mood who bounced and skipped from one exhilarating subject to another. We took Chester out for an emptying session, and then drove all the way to Malibu for a late lunch by the sea, of pasta and salad and a big plate of steamed broccoli (yeah, Artie had gotten into health, too) while he told me what he had been doing at the recording studio; editing a tape he had made with his new orchestra, sometimes demonstrating with doodle-de-bopping a few bars, or thumping some beat on the table with fingers.

It reminded me of times back in Spain when Artie would want to describe some musical passage, and he would use himself, or any instrument at hand—except the clarinet—a recorder, a piccolo, a tin whistle, even a piano or guitar, any old thing at all (except that clarinet).

I loved those times. He also said he had been reading some knockout book that he would pass on to me when he finished it. I loved that, too, reading books that Artie had read and written notes and little observations in—they were usually as interesting as the book.

My interval with him had certainly kept my mind off my being-read movie script all afternoon.

The sun was going down by the time we got back to my place, but it was after Artie had departed, taking Chester with him, that I listened to the messages on my answering machine. One of them said to call Allan as soon as I came in.

My apartment faced west, and sometimes the setting sun put on quite a show. This was one of those times. Sprays of orange stretching across the horizon, reaching up to touch puffs of clouds floating by, looking for all the world like swirls of cotton candy fresh off the vendor's machine out at the State Fair.

Allan answered. "It is the best first draft of a screenplay I have ever *read*!" His voice cried out exuberantly into my ear.

Tab got on the extension. "It is absolutely great!" *he* cried, slightly more reserved, though not much.

"It has Academy Award possibilities, I just know it!" one of them stated. "This is very, very *exciting*!" exclaimed the other.

"Of course it's too long." I think Tab was the one who said that.

"Oh yes," I said, "I know."

"I've started reading it again"—it *was* Tab who said that—"I'm making notes."

"Oh good!"

"A few little suggestions here and there, if that's all right?"

"You bet that's all right!" I yelped. "I want all the help I can get!"

They said a few more extraordinarily delicious things, and

before we hung up made a date for the next day to begin the trimming.

Then I just sat there for the longest time, watching the magnificent show in the sky, glowing along with it. Happiness, I thought, smiling to myself, isn't the grandiose event they've led us to believe it is. No cataclysmic, soul-stirring, everlasting happening that will rattle your life and put you on the road to heaven-right-here-on-earth. It's only little bits of things. Minute droplets, here and there. A few words on the phone. A setting sun doing its thing. It mattered not in the slightest that the words I'd just heard might be of an exaggerated nature. That the guys might very well be turning themselves on, as well as me, since they had made an investment in me and needed to feel they weren't fools for having done so. Buoying one's self up, spurring one's self on, has always been a rock-bottom necessity of show biz, has it not. If you didn't believe in your own project, who the hell else would?

There was a lot of work up ahead, I was aware of that. Two hundred and fifty-three pages was at least a hundred pages too long if not more. Then money had to be found for the making of the movie. The proper cast, too; a distribution deal. We had a long way to go, I knew all that. But the knowledge took absolutely nothing away from the moment. I had learned long ago, maybe when I was not more than two or three or four, back when my imaginary playmate and I were dreaming big dreams together, that nursing the thought that something might *not* come to pass wasn't the least bit of fun at all. So I sat there as the last rays slid down behind the far edge of our planet and the city lights came twinkling on, imagining it was already Oscar night, and there was my name being called out, not for acting, but for screenplay. I even gave myself a standing ovation as I tripped down the aisle up onto the stage.

It was very nice . . .

Off I went the next morning to my partners' house, where we had held most of our story conferences, since they had more space than I did. They usually fed me, too. And I liked that. I never planned on picking up one damned pot or pan again if I could help it. There had been a time when I enjoyed having people over and messing about in the kitchen. But that was when I had a big, roomy country one that everybody could loll around in and keep me company—and lots of help, too, for all that chopping. But these days I preferred being taken care of. Which, no doubt, is a sure indication of approaching childhood number two.

I especially liked going over to Tab and Allan's house. It was up in the hills, you looked down through trees with a glimpse beyond of tall city buildings out there in the distance. You could have been anywhere—the south of France, Australia, Sicily. Maybe even Istanbul, for all I knew. Tab collected antique furniture of rich, old woods, and whippet dogs. And if that weren't enough, he liked to cook. I mean, the man enjoyed it. You couldn't go about it the way he went about it, unless you did. With gusto, with flair. With downright panache.

This day he was flipping an omelette as I walked in, big enough for us all, done to just the right consistency and brownness, filled with little bits of things, minced onions, I think, chopped black olives, some other odds and ends. he switched it onto a platter and to the table, talking all the while, his blue eyes and great teeth sparkling, good-looking face shining with pleasure. "Do you know something," he said, exuding high spirits, "this script is going to be a little jewel, I just know it!"

"Ah, you think so?" I murmured uncertainly, taking the large serving fork and spoon he was handing me.

"I *know* so!" Tab told me gleefully, whirling around to grab up a basket of rolls, along with a crock of butter.

"Well . . ." I said a bit uneasily, "I like the 'jewel' part, all right. But . . . that *little* part, that's not so good, is it?"

Allan joined us, and while we ate the two of them proceeded to teach me some cold, hard facts about the present-day motion picture business.

Tab, it seemed, hadn't been making a value judgment with the word "little," but rather explaining what size budget this particular kind of script would warrant. Not too big a one was clearly what. And the reason he and Allan gave me was utterly depressing.

The script wasn't about a big subject. Wasn't about war in the jungles, with killings and shootings and bombs exploding and ripping people apart. It didn't have fleets of helicopters and chases on ski slopes or anywhere else. Didn't have spaceships the size of Mount Everest landing on the planet Krypton, it didn't even have a shark that hankered after flailing legs, and got them, too. My script wasn't about anything like that. It was simply a story about, well, people. Human beings. Members of my own species. Caught in a moment of change, and stress, at a particularly trying time in their lives. An ongoing, as it were, human condition.

To my astonishment I learned that these sorts of movies, ones that dealt with human emotions, with the trials and tribulations and hangups and flounderings and confusions caused by ass-backward values that our species wallow in throughout our lives, had been given a particular classification all their own. They were called "classic" films. Can you beat that? Such a fancy name that, when translated, simply meant low-budget. I supposed the posh appellation referred to earlier times, when "people" stories were *de rigueur,* adored by moviegoers, and made big bucks at the box office, too. (Things like *The Old Maid* with Bette Davis, *The Lost Weekend* with Ray Milland, *Kitty Foyle* with Ginger Rogers.)

Well, I couldn't have written about jungle warfare or a killer shark if my life depended on it. So I would have to continue as I was, willy-nilly, and see what happened. One thing I knew. *Nothing* at all would happen if I didn't try *some*thing, would it?

Meanwhile, between work sessions with my producers, getting a column out here and there, I tried to keep my social life from dwindling to zero. There were more tributes. One for Olivia de Havilland that took place in Palm Springs, in the desert, and became an overnight stay. But I couldn't *not* go. Olivia was practically like a relative. There was one for Billy

Wilder, too. How could I miss that? Hadn't I known Billy all of my grown-up life? Besides, I liked him. Cannon films gave a bash for their new building, and showed us all how to throw a party for a few thousand or so people. You use a three-story garage, with food and drink on every level, and an orchestra on top, that's how. There is plenty of room, that way, and it matters not at all if anything is spilled. Even the limos have plenty of space in which to pick up their illustrious passengers.

I also took the time (some five hours of it, to be exact) to give an interview to a writer who was doing a book on John. I couldn't not do that, either. First, because it was John, and second because I am most sympathetic to people who write books!

And in doing so, I came up with the most sensational idea . . .

## Thirty-one

Why didn't I just (when the script was finished—when the last dead wood was weeded out) pick up the phone and call John Huston? I mean, I *knew* the man, for crissake. Tell him I had written this thing, tell him I'd like him to read it?

I wouldn't say anything about what I really had in mind. I'd first better find out what he thought of my effort, hadn't I? Of course, if he didn't think *any*thing of my effort, there would be nothing to talk about, would there? But if he did, I would then ask him if he would find it, perhaps *amusing,* to direct an ex-wife's screenplay!

Looking back at my Huston days, I realized I'd never worked

with John. It never even occurred to me, to tell you the truth. In retrospect I simply did *not* understand myself at *all*. How, living with the man under the same roof for four-plus years, as well as being on reasonably friendly terms the many years following, all taking place during my salad days, and he the hottest director in town, how was it that it never crossed my mind even once during the entire time to do anything professionally with or for him? *Not once*. That only now, at this considerably later date, had I gotten around to even *realizing* it.

How was that *possible*? I was utterly baffled.

But of course if I knew the answer to that burning question, it could very well explain the overabundance of near-misses of almost every sort that I had had in my long life, I would bet anything.

Well, I wasn't going to make the same mistake again, by George. Even though anything coming from calling John now would be about the longest shot a person could make. His health had become shaky indeed. Emphysema never got better. Only worse. I had heard that he clanked around attached to an oxygen tank most of the time, these days. I had even seen a picture of him in the paper with those little tubes in his nostrils that are part of the breathing paraphernalia.

But, he was still doing things, still directing things. And you mostly *sat* while you were directing, anyhow, even if you were perfectly well, didn't you. And John's system of directing, in any event, was to give the actors free rein to do their own thing, let them find their own way. Not so very taxing, I told myself. (I even believed it.)

Of course I was pretty certain that he would have projects lined up even far past the time he might have left. But I was going to call him, anyway. At least that was a step in the right direction for me, even if he said no. Sure, it was up to my producers to do the wheeling and dealing, that's what producers were *for*. But if I could help out, get an old master (whom I just happened to know!) lined up to direct this ''little jewel'' of a film of ours, wouldn't that be a nice surprise for them?

So when I felt that the script was in reasonably decent reading condition, I began scouting around to find out where exactly John might be at the moment, and as luck would have it, learned he was, of all things, right in town. More or less. Not actually in Los Angeles proper, but over there alongside the Pacific Ocean in Malibu, which was near enough. Certainly nearer than the place where he had last taken up residence down Mexico way, in a small fishing village somewhere south of Puerto Vallarta, so isolated it took a trip by boat to get there. My guess was that his lung condition had put a damper on continuing to reside in such a difficult-to-get-to place.

I called the number I had been given, and sure enough, the rich, mellow voice that I knew so well was soon on the other end of the phone line. Lung troubles hadn't changed that aspect of the man.

I explained why I was calling. That I'd written this screenplay, suddenly feeling slightly uncomfortable as I said it. As if I were entering John's territory without being invited. Hadn't *he* been the screenwriter? Winning awards left and right for them? Surely proof he was one of the best?

"Written a screenplay, have you, honey?" murmured John into my ear, in inimitable Hustonese. Polite enough. Though without a great deal of enthusiasm that I could detect.

I plunged ahead, anyway. I couldn't let a thing like that stop me, now.

"Yes I have, and I'm hoping, John, that you'll be interested in reading it. That you'll have the time . . ."

"Why, of course. I'm dying to read your script, dear," he told me, this time, as if he *were* interested. "Tell you what. Why don't you leave it at Paul's, and I'll have someone pick it up."

"Oh, right away, John!" I cried joyously. "I'll take it there right away!" He meant Paul Kohner, who had been his agent since before The Flood, and who still had an office on the

Sunset Strip, not too much more than a stone's throw from me.

I hung up, positively elated. So *pleased* with myself! What great fun this was going to be! If I could get John to direct maybe I could get together a whole company of people I had known in my earlier days to help make this script into an honest-to-God motion picture. Wouldn't that be something? To turn this thing into a marvelous sort of homecoming project? Maybe, I thought merrily, I could even get Artie to write the musical score! And *all* of us win the Big Award the following year! (Dream *big* I always say, what have you got to lose!)

I thought of Kirk, then. He who'd said so many times how he thought my book had picture possibilities. *He* had a production company! *It* had been making films through the years! His sons made films. Kirk would know about getting this show on the road! He could executive-produce, and Allan and Tab do the line producing.

All a-flutter, I got on the phone again, and called Kirk's office.

And he was *there.* He could have been in Timbuktu, or Tierra del Fuego; you could never depend on filmmakers to stay in one spot. My luck was holding. Oh, wasn't that a good sign! When things worked, they worked, didn't they!

"Hey, Kirk," I said, with a certain pleasure, when he came on the wire, "you know that book of mine, the one you've often said would make a good movie?"

"Oh yeah!" he responded instantly, the book-button pushed, "that's a really good little book." ("Little" again!) "I've often thought it would make a damned good picture."

"I know! That's why I'm . . ."

"I meant to speak to Peter about it. He's very good at . . ."

*"Kirk!"* I interrupted. "Why I'm *calling* is, I've put the little book into script form."

"Well, I've always thought," Kirk went right on, "a wonderful screenplay could come out of your book."

*"Kirk, listen!* I've done it! I've *written* a screenplay."

"You are certainly a good writer, I've always thought so."

"Would you like to read it?"

"Peter is such an excellent judge of . . ." Suddenly his voice was muffled, as if he had put his hand over the mouthpiece, another faint voice coming in from somewhere. A secretary? I had gone through two of them to get to him. I expected he had a lot of business going. After all, Kirk was this big superstar.

He was back on the line. "Sorry," he said, "an overseas call just came through I have to take. Can I call you back?"

"Of course!" I told him, and hung up quickly.

Oh my oh my, wouldn't it be something if Kirk were to be connected with the making of the film, too, oh it all seemed to be shaping up in a positively gorgeous fashion, didn't it!

Though, I thought, I'd better wait until Kirk called back before I said anything to my "boys," Tab and Allan, about it. About what I was up to.

And so I did just that. I waited. And waited. When Kirk didn't call back all that day, I didn't think anything about it. Obviously there had been an emergency.

But when I didn't hear the second day, nor, in fact, the third—didn't, in fact, hear for the rest of the week—there was nothing for it but to come down off my high.

For some reason, I concluded, Kirk was apparently avoiding even reading my screenplay. *Even so much as reading it.* For what possible reason I couldn't imagine . . .

Well, yes I could. I *could* imagine. Actually imagine more reasons than one, none of which I cared much for. Especially the one that suggested that, in this terribly youth-oriented place, everyone, including Kirk, was afraid even to have anything to do with something an older person (me) might come up with. (Kirk's repeated references—he'd done it before—to his son's talents at judging scripts gave me that idea.)

Was it possible the entire town was engaged in throwing out the baby with the bathwater, including Kirk Douglas, no spring chicken, himself? (George Burns had made a movie about three old men, and had bragged all the while about the very young director/writer who was guiding them through their paces, as if this were a plus. I remember wondering how the hell a twenty-one-year-old could know anything about eighty-something-year-old men. And the fact was, he didn't. I saw the movie and it wasn't anything but a bunch of clichés that the young believe getting older is all about.)

So I told Allan (*my* young one!) what I had been up to. About my surprise that didn't come off. And why he had better keep me a secret. "I'm over thirty, Allan—wa-a-ay over—and nobody's supposed to be."

Allan winked. "I won't tell," he grinned, "if you won't tell. But you could be ten and I doubt that the Kirk thing would go anywhere. As far as I know, his company only does things with him in them." He smiled teasingly. "But a nice try."

"Even John," I said sadly, "hasn't called back."

"Well, look . . ." Allan was hesitant, seemingly searching for the right words. "John's a great idea. And maybe he could do it. But I tell you the truth. I don't know if we could get insurance on John, anymore. And that's awfully risky."

I had forgotten about insurance. That everybody who was indispensable to a flick, who could cause a delay, and therefore cost money if anything happened to them, had to be insured for the length of the shooting schedule. It was, indeed, doubtful that John could pass muster.

Well, that was that, wasn't it. The best-laid plans of mice and Evelyn. You can't go home again; everybody knows that. Now I knew it. And why. Everybody's dead or got emphysema. As Gertie once said about some place or other, "There is no there, there."

I knew, too, how well I knew it, when your dream goes spla-a-at!, get a new one, but fast.

My best bet, then (and probably my *only* bet, screenplay-wise, what did I know about putting a flick together?), was to pay attention to what Allan was doing, and help *him* out in any way I could.

But I didn't even know any of the names of the places he said he was planning on taking the script to. Except one.

"Hey!" I told Allan, "I know Sam Goldwyn!"

"This is Junior," Allan said, straight-faced.

"Whaddaya think, I don't know *that?*" I said, rather crossly. "But he lives in the same house his father did."

"No kidding!"

Hah. I knew something about present-day Hollywood the whiz kid didn't, how about that. That was because I had recently been there with Talli. Since hubby, Willy, had directed most of his pictures for Goldwyn Senior, the two families had been friends, and had remained that way through the years. Talli and I had gone to the same big house I had visited of yore, dined at the same table, seen a movie in the same projection room. It was true continuity, the likes of which I had seldom, perhaps never, seen before. Not in Hollywood, anyway.

"I've even been there," I told Allan.

"Lately?"

I tweaked his nose. "Yes, lately, *child.* Do you want me to call him for you, or anything?"

"Mmm," murmured Allan, "that might help. Though, actually, he's only a rather distant possibility, since his company mostly sticks to negative pickups."

"What the hell is a negative pickup?"

"Films that are completed, already. Goldwyn rarely puts financing into production."

"I see . . ."

So this was the kind of stuff producers talked about. "Then what's the point of taking the script to him? Isn't it financing we need?"

"To get a distribution deal," Allan said. Then he grinned his impish grin. "I'm hoping the script will turn him on and he'll give us half the production money, too. Then getting the rest ought to be a cinch."

Why, I thought, this was like a big game, like a chess game, with the players themselves acting as the pieces, so you had to be careful or you could fall—or get pushed—right off the board, couldn't you.

My spirits went spinning into high gear, again, the juices

churning at full speed. I *liked* playing games! It was just a matter of learning the rules of this one, wasn't it?

"Yeah, go ahead and call Goldwyn." Allan decided. "A personal connection is always helpful. It just might work . . ."

How would it be this time when I phoned, I wondered. How do you spell that, or not *the* Evelyn Keyes, I've always been such a fan of yours!

At the Goldwyn establishment it was the former. "Pease?" the secretary said, sounding a bit bored.

"No, *Keyes.* K-e-y-e-s."

"And what is it you want to talk to Mr. Goldwyn about?"

"I will tell *him* that when I speak to him, if you don't mind, please tell him who is calling!" I said rather imperiously. I can do it, if I have to, although I always feel slightly ashamed afterward.

Sam came on at once.

I had always liked Sam the few times I had occasion to be in his company. Had found him warm and quite nice. (Had liked his father, too. How not, since he'd always greeted me by calling out, no matter where it was, "Ah, my favorite actress!") Sam kept up his merited good impression by asking me to have a script sent over to him that very day. (He, in fact, won my heart forever because of that no matter which direction the outcome took.)

Even though I knew by then not to let hopes get up too high, I did, anyway. So did Allan. We kept turning each other on, saying he'll love it, I just know he will. It's down his alley, I'll bet you anything, and on and on. And when Sam only took two days to get back to me, I knew this was it. Nobody is ever in a hurry when the answer is "no," I told myself.

His secretary was the one who called to say that Mr. Goldwyn wished to talk to me, and then proceeded to give me the telephone number of his car.

That's right. His car. He was on the way to his office and would I be so kind as to ring him there. That he was expecting my call.

Wow. Was this the now Hollywood, or what. Not even

Harry Cohn had ever called me—nor had me call him—from a *car*. (Once I had been *given* a car with a telephone in it, my initials on the door and the pink slip along with it, but the guy had inherited his riches and as we know, that was never the kinda fella I ever went for. So I gave the car back, along with the attached strings.)

I imagined the grand movie mogul sitting there in his chauffeur-driven stretch limo (make that double-stretch, if there is such a thing) shiny black—no, something more stylish, royal-blue, perhaps, the grille work in gold, a shade that could only come from the eighteen-karat stuff itself, the inside terribly plush, thoroughly equipped, not just with telephone, television, but with fax machine, computer, probably hot tub, breakfast tray, with hanging plants, too . . .

He answered instantly, and the moment I said, "This is Evelyn," began to speak.

He did twenty-two minutes on my script. I know because a little clock happened to be at my elbow. Sam Goldwyn, Junior, absolutely raved. Simply *raved*. About my script. He said it was one of the best he had ever read. He said the construction was perfect, the characters beautifully drawn, that the pace, the tempo, couldn't be better. He said everything good that could possibly be said about a screenplay.

And then he said no.

After twenty-two minutes of nonstop praise for my movie script, the movie-mogul turned it down. He said he was sorry (he did say that), but that his company already had an exploitation picture with a black and white couple in it in the works.

"Ex-ploi-tation" picture? Mine? I didn't even know there was such a classification. My script was about a love story. That happened to be between a white girl and a black boy. Exploitation?

If I was confused about the explanation, I wasn't about the final result. Junior was turning my screenplay down for whatever reason he could muster up. It reminded me once again of Mike Todd's loaded query in those earlier days. "Do you want the short no or the long one?"

At least Sam was doing me the courtesy of giving me a long one.

I couldn't knock that. A few manners never hurt anybody. I would continue to think kindly of him in spite of his turndown. (Though it might not stop me, you understand, from hissing in his ear the night the picture won every award in the book, *"See, Sam! See . . . what a mistake . . . you made?"*)

The offer of a movie—to *act* in, not write—didn't come along a minute too soon. It was going to be shot back East, too, so it would get me out of town and away from all this fancy wheeling-dealing I'd been attempting to do and making such a bust of. It wasn't my job, anyway, was it. It was my producers' province, these apparently necessary machinations, so I damned well ought to get out of the way and leave them to it (especially Allan, the one in the currently popular age-group of the under-thirties.)

Before it was time to depart, though, I finally did hear from John.

He called from a Cedars-Sinai Hospital bed.

Now. John could have waited until he got out of the place. Rung me, say, from wherever he was staying in town. (After all, he had already let two months go by before calling as it was.)

But wasn't a hospital a more arresting place to call from? "I'm just coming out of intensive care," he added, as well, to give the occasion an extra dollop of drama.

John had ever had a certain stylish flair for presenting himself. In the way he dressed. In his entrances and exits. Even the way he sat in a chair and talked. Stuff from which drama is created.

It turned out he had called to explain why he had *not* yet read my screenplay.

It was in no way an apology, mind you, but simply an explanation, no more, no less. And he proceeded to list the reasons, there from a hospital bed in the Cedars-Sinai Hospital, quite matter-of-factly, as if he were reading a laundry list, or the offerings on a menu of a second-rate restaurant.

He said he had had cataract operations in both eyes, followed by a torn retina in one. He mentioned a back problem, difficulty with a tooth, then the sniffles that had landed him there in Cedars because of his ailing lungs. *"It's been coming at me from all sides!"* John pronounced in his golden voice. Without a trace of pity. Making it all sound rather absurd, actually.

In fact, the way he cataloged it all made me chuckle even as I felt tears fill my eyes. "Oh John," I managed to murmur, "I'm so sorry, please don't concern yourself with my silly script, don't you even *think* of it again."

He was tying up loose ends, wasn't he? In this case Evelyn's screenplay she had sent him to read and he hadn't been able to. But now that he had spoken to me, it was taken care of, and he never *would* think of it again.

What I didn't know, didn't sense, was that John had just bid me farewell . . .

# *Thirty-two*

The city of New York hadn't changed all that much since the last time I saw her. A delivery fellow on his bicycle leaped from the street up and over the curb heading straight for my person as I walked along West Fifty-eighth Street. Fortunately his brakes were in order and he managed to pull up three inches from my kneecaps. Farther on a darling teenage kid, black, was doing a nice, loose step on the edge of the sidewalk that I was enjoying watching as I passed by—until he looked over at me and snarled, *"What you smilin' at, honky bitch?"*

At the corner of Lexington, a young woman, also black, not much more than twenty if that, held up a sign. It read, "Please help me. The police locked up my boyfriend and then raped me seven times in front of him." Bloomies' hadn't changed, either. They still sold everything anybody could possibly want—all you needed was lots of money.

The movie, happily enough, was being shot considerably to the North, up in Washington Heights, in and around a big, handsome mansion built back in Revolutionary times, where George Washington had actually slept, and Aaron Burr had actually lived. That, by some miracle, hadn't been torn down, but instead preserved, furniture and all, and turned into a museum one could visit (for a price), and now being rented by a movie company for a couple of weeks' shooting (for a price). It was serving as the house where my screen character, along with my screen husband, resided. We were playing a couple of vampires. Rich ones, at that, to be living in such splendid circumstances. As my character explained in one of the scenes, the way to get rich is to buy up all the real estate in sight and then live on for three hundred years—the way we vampires had.

It was a far cry from all the screenplay business I had got caught up in back in Hollywood, and if respite from all that constant plotting and planning was what I needed, it was certainly what I was getting, and in spades.

One Larry Cohen was the writer of this new cinematic adventure. He was also the director of it, as well as the producer, evidently a latter-day whiz kid, though I confess I had never heard of him before. Clearly my loss, though, because he already had a kind of cult following, and at the time we were shooting, a retrospective of eleven of his films was being presented at Joseph Papp's Public Theater in downtown New York.

Larry dealt in the horror-fantasy genre, always with a jaundiced eye turned on the mores of our species. As in the scene in which we vampires are found by the "outsider" leaning over a prostrate cow, drinking (supposedly) its blood. (Well, we all know how vampires are.) When I observe the disgust on the outsider's face, I say to him, this is better than what you "normal" people do. You *kill* your animals, take their lives away altogether. After we are finished, this animal will live to get up and walk away!

Since there weren't too many cows wandering the streets of New York, we had had to travel up to a farm in New Hampshire for the proper ambiance. Which was how I found myself, one rainy night, in the middle of a grassy pasture bent over the neck of a zonked-out Holstein, with a camera aimed my way.

An odd place, maybe, to think of yourself as fortunate. But I did, sitting there between takes, on the damp grass, the falling rain soaking through the cotton dress I was wearing, my nose practically buried into the hide of a cow, which was giving forth a rather strong odor of milk and dust and manure, thinking how lucky I was to have a profession I could turn to once in a while that was seldom a bore. Sure, sometimes tough, sometimes difficult, but very rarely dull. Not even playing kissie-kissie with a hulking beast out in the middle of a field in the rain.

Besides, none of it lasted any too long, anymore. Not for me, anyway. In no time at all I was in a car being driven down a turnpike, then, bingo, sitting in a plane that was crossing this rather large continent of ours, and zap, there I was right back where I had started from.

I checked in with my producers immediately upon arriving home. I so liked the whole idea of, ah-hem, "checking in with *my* producers."

Allan's enthusiastic voice went into high gear at once. "Welcome back!" he whooped through the wire. "Do you know everybody I've spoken to has gotten excited when I've told them I have a script by you?"

"Oh, really?" I murmured, wondering how that could be, and having a feeling all the exuberance was some kind of a smoke screen being thrown up, to hide . . . exactly what, I wondered.

Allan was chuckling away on the phone. "Some say, 'Oh, you mean the columnist.' They've read you in *Calendar,* and they all say what a good writer you are!"

I was getting more alarmed by the minute.

"Uh-huh." These compliments were so profuse that I had to believe the results of Allan's (and Tab's) latest forays had met with the same result as that with Sam Goldwyn. I'd been in show biz too long not to recognize the sounds of bravado, of camouflage covering up the empty spaces where things had been left unsaid.

"This picture is *going to be made!"* yelped Allan. "I just *know* it is! You wait and see!"

Which was how I found out we were still at square one. That the kid, was, indeed, playing cheerleader to keep the team spirit vibrant and strong. Maybe one person had said something decent, and Allan (in good show-biz tradition) was turning it into an entire town. "I'm waiting, I'm waiting," I smiled, "and I'll have to, won't I, since, tell me the truth, they aren't exactly lined up out there, panting for the chance to make our little movie, are they?"

Allan gave a sigh that was reminiscent of steam engine days, and then began to let go with what was obviously a backlog of pent-up frustration. The trouble with this town, he growled, is that nobody wants anything original anymore! They only want whatever they've already *done,* and made a bundle with! Is it Action, they ask. Comedy? Horror? If it isn't one of those, they won't even *read* it! Allan groaned.

Well, no, I hadn't written *any* of those types—unless one classifies a man calling his wife by a name other than her own at the moment of orgasm as horror.

"Never you mind, sweetheart," I told Allan, feeling it was probably my turn to play cheerleader, "someone's out there with pots of money just dying to finance our little picture. You just haven't found him—maybe it's even a 'her'—yet!"

Playing this cheery game does have a tendency to make one

feel more upbeat. So when Allan and I hung up, I thought it might be the ideal time to check in with Artie. With one of us up, we would stand a better chance of not running into trouble.

Alas, my upbeatness didn't last two seconds.

Chester was dead. Big, gray, gentle Chester-Chaucer. Dead.

I suppose Chester's demise should have been expected. A big dog, at thirteen, is . . . what, in his nineties? A ripe old age.

But ends always come as shocks, somehow. I understood Artie's being very upset. But why was I? I guess I had become attached to the dear creature, more than I realized. Well, you do, don't you?

But his death had happened so suddenly, even so. He had been off his food, Artie told me, the night before. And then he sat down, and simply would not go for their evening stroll, which was totally unlike him. So Artie took him to the vet the next morning.

Chester managed to get into the car, then out of it when they reached their destination, just fine. He even stopped to touch noses and exchange tailwags with a little girl dog on its way out.

Then he walked into the vet's examination room, lay down, and died. Just like that.

A perfect gent to the very end. If we could all exit as gracefully as that, Artie and I both said.

Artie came to town often for quite a while after that. For dinner, for movies, I believe he was also doing some recording in some studio in downtown L.A., and he would swing by for a while afterward. The house, he said, felt empty without Chester, and he kept wondering if he should get himself another dog. When he asked, one day, if I would do something for him, I expected him to ask me to come with him to a pet shop.

That wasn't it, at all. It was that he had to have a cataract lens implant, and would I keep him company while it was done, and drive him home afterward?

How about that? Two of my men, John and Artie, getting their cataract operations the same damn year. They had both read furiously all their lives. But that wasn't why they needed cataract operations. I had learned why people did a number of years earlier. From my ophthalmologist, who was peering into my eyes through that big, complex machine of his at the time, doing his every-couple-of-years' examination.

"Mmmhuh . . . mmmhuh . . ." he sort of muttered as he went along, half to himself, half to me. "No sign of cataracts yet."

"Of course not," I told him as he peered along.

"What do you mean, 'Of course not'?" He said, rather sharply.

"My family doesn't get cataracts," I told him, rather smugly.

"If you live long enough," he then said to me in a very firm way, "you'll get cataracts."

"My family all live a *very* long time," I informed him in my superior way.

Doc stopped what he was doing. He pushed his big machine out of the way. He fixed his own eyes straight into mine without benefit of machinery. *"If you live long enough,"* this ophthalmologist said to me in no uncertain terms, *"you will get cataracts!"*

That was it, then. The two gentlemen of my acquaintance had hung in until cataract time caught up with them. If John could get through it, Artie ought to come through with colors flying. And I would be more than happy to see him through the process. What are bifurcated wives for, after all!

Besides, since it was to be done up near where he lived, I would have to go up there, wouldn't I? And I rather looked forward to that. Terribly curious to see where Artie lived, and how. Without me, I mean. The only places I had ever seen him living before were the ones I'd had a hand in, too. And we had had discussions (and arguments) ad infinitum over every piece of furniture (and where it went to the last quarter-inch), over every color, drapery, rug, bookshelf, lamp, picture, down to the bed linen, the towels, the pots and pans, the last teacup. (Artie had never considered the furnishing and decorating of a house the little woman's work; only the cleaning of it, the running of it, particularly the kitchen part of it.) It was going to be interesting to see what he had done without interference.

I should have known what to expect, since Artie had never been able to discard a single thing. Not even a rubber band. Even in that twenty-five-room house we had for a while, all twenty-five rooms managed to have stuff in each of them before we took leave of the place.

The first hint came when I espied his garage. Made for two cars with room for only one, since most of the second space was filled with pile after pile of only God-and-Artie knew what.

But that was merely the beginning. Inside, the house resembled one of those flea market places, the kind that is crowded to the rafters with everything imaginable. From big to little to tacky to snazzy to stylish to trashy art to junk, with no differentiation among any of it. The fun being, of course, to wander through and see if you could locate the pearls somewhere in the chaotic conglomeration.

Artie's dwelling place was like that.

Everything seemed to have come to rest wherever it happened to have landed. (Knowing Artie, though, it all probably had an order that was not discernible at an uninitiated glance.) A miserable bunch of plastic flowers, for instance, hung alongside a Mondrian. Stacks of mail-order catalogues, coffee jars of pencils, a clipboard with a cartoon on it, a bowl of paper clips, were set down alongside an old, hand-carved ivory chess set, antique paperweights and kaleidoscopes, delicate porcelain statues of birds and flowers.

And stacks of books everywhere. *Everywhere.* On tables, on the floor, on chairs. In fact, *everything* was on chairs. Paintings, too. Manuscripts and stacks of sheet music on the piano bench, bunches of things you had to remove if you wanted to sit down and doodle. And clocks. From intricate ship bells to Mickey Mouse. You couldn't have found a place to put down a teacup if you had wanted to.

Well, it was Artie's nest and he was welcome to it. Mainly I had to remember not to make any suggestions. Remember that I was long out of it. Even the Spanish things that had wound up in his possession didn't move me, oddly enough.

The long, hand-carved table, the big chests he was using for end tables, the two-foot-high statue of the patron saint of Spain, Santiago, on a horse, carved out of wood. All of them had been such a part of me, I had once thought. Only it all seemed so very long ago, now.

I did feel rather sad that I didn't feel much of anything. But even that didn't last too very long . . .

# Thirty-three

The eye operation turned out to be not much of anything. We drove to the eye clinic, and while he was inside I waited around, read, took a turn about the grounds, read some more, walked some more, until he came back with a patch over one eye. Then I drove him back to the flea market house.

After a snooze, he was all gung-ho about going out for dinner. He chose a place he knew not too far away, a small Japanese restaurant, and there he told everybody who asked (and some who didn't) how come there was a patch over his eye.

Since I didn't have much to do, except order, I sat back and watched the action. Watched the two of us. This, yes, middle-aged (plus) couple, older than anybody else in the restaurant, senior citizens, if you will, the man with a patch over his eye, having just had the operation so many senior citizens are heir to, these days, the young hostess, the young waitress clucking politely but not terribly interested. What does a cataract operation mean to the young?

My mind wandered back to our Paris meeting, Artie's and mine, there on the Île St. Louis, the River Seine flowing past on both sides, and I thought how little I would have been interested at that time, too, no doubt simply thinking (if I thought at all) the word "cataract(e)" to be a French word meaning "waterfall," nothing more.

I visualized the young woman, with her good skin, her silky hair, often described as beautiful, though she didn't particularly think so and didn't much care one way or the other. She simply accepted her good fortune in that department and took it from there. There were so many, many more women who were more beautiful in the world in which she moved; everybody there had good looks so that looks didn't count for much, you had to have more, much more, to make your mark; intelligence, the ability to work your ass off, the ability to pinpoint what it was you wanted. And that included a mate from time to time.

Up the stairs he had bounded, his energy electric, the bandleader of renown, the clarinetist whose sound was known the world over (a sound so cherished that recordings of it had been buried deep in the ground in case of nuclear holocaust), his vibrant good looks palpable, his intense eyes alive with expectation as they took the woman in.

They seemed made for each other.

But then time—a lot of it—went by . . .

Above the eye patch, on Artie's head, a billed cap was perched at a jaunty angle, covering where the dark, curly hair didn't grow anymore. What was left was streaked with gray, and curled nicely around his ears, as did a hearing aid around one of them. His shirt was a rough weave of nubby, natural-colored cotton with a faint orange stripe, over it a sleeveless vest of the same nicely faded orange, with lots of pockets and zippers all around. Designer jeans (also properly faded) were held up with a belt sporting a sizable buckle of turquoise which I remember was designed for him by an Apache Indian artist once-upon-a-time, when we'd stopped for a spell in Scottsdale, Arizona. Nike sports shoes adorned his feet.

It was a good, up-to-date look.

And there I was, sitting across the table, in a blue jogging suit, a blue-and-white scarf around my neck, white Reeboks encasing my feet. Spectacles hung from a chain around my neck. I, too, was beginning to have a few gray hairs if anybody insisted on looking very closely. A woman who looked like the one this man with a patch over one eye would naturally be with. A couple, getting on. Who had known each other for a very long time.

So this, I thought suddenly, as I looked us over, is what became of Cindy and her Prince. This, right here, is the "ever after" part of the story in living, breathing color.

And not too bad, either, I finally decided, not too bad at all. I, in fact, rather *liked* the way we looked—lines, gray hairs, and all—maybe even better than before.

"What are you smiling at?" Artie wanted to know from across the table. "Can I have this?"

Without waiting for an answer to either of the questions he'd asked, he reached over to my plate and took a piece of my tempura (things fried in batter so you can't tell what's underneath), brought it to his mouth, and bit into it.

"Ugh!" he promptly said, with great disgust. "It's a carrot!"

"Eat it," I told him, "it's good for your eyes."

"A little late for that," said the man with the patch, and dropped the carrot with a bite out of it back on to my plate, picked up one of my shrimps, and began munching away on that, instead.

So *I* ate the carrot. I had been eating Artie's carrots whenever he was served them in restaurants ever since I had known him. I *liked* carrots.

Still feeling in fine fettle on the way back to the house, Artie asked if I would like to hear some new stuff he had just put together with his new orchestra.

A warm rush went through me. Some magical thing always happened when Artie and his music got together in the same room. Something I didn't really understand, and was rather awed by. Artie seemed to go to another place that I knew nothing about. I didn't know music on his level; my few years at the piano hardly qualified me for the big time. I knew he was grateful that I could at least sing in key, though. He had had a wife who couldn't, he told me, and who insisted on singing around the house all the time. Needless to say it was one of his shorter-lived marriages.

These musical moments, strangely enough, hadn't occurred all that often, since I had come across Artie after he had abandoned not only his orchestra but his clarinet, too, "forever." He was articulate enough about the reasons why (that the life would have killed him had he kept on), but those times I'd observed him listening to music had always made me wonder. It had been as if he stepped inside the music, or it into him. They, he and the sound, became one, off in a land of their own.

"Oh my yes," I told him delightedly, "I would love to hear whatever you've been up to."

And so I found out what the man had done to the entire top floor of his on-his-own house.

He had removed all dividing walls and turned the entire space into one big studio-library. The ten thousand (or so) books that he dragged everywhere with him the way a snail does its shell covered the walls, with more rows of shelves zigzagging here and there through the center, holding the sound equipment, things for recording and playing and such. Of course he had made some similar arrangement in all the three houses we had shared together, but this was the first time he had used an entire *floor*.

He put on something, and off he went to his private place, eye patch and all, while I listened, too, and watched, and enjoyed being part of a special moment once more.

Finally, around midnight, Artie remembered that he had had an operation that day, and that he was due to see the doctor again the very next morning. So we went back down the stairs, and I learned some more basic truths about the flea market house.

There were four rooms in one wing of the first floor that could have been, were obviously meant to be, bedrooms. Places to sleep. But only one of them had been so arranged. The other three were an office for a secretary who came several times a week, another a utility room, the third a downstairs office for Artie (although there was a monstrous-sized desk upstairs in the studio, one that had followed us around everywhere we went, too). There was no guest room. Visitors evidently were not expected, not encouraged to come.

The trouble was, what did you do with a bifurcated wife whose presence you had called upon to help you get through your eye lens transplant?

The living room couch was what. Fortunately it was good and wide—and long, too. And the master of the house did show me where the sheets were. He did do that. I had to make the couch up, natch, because after such an eye operation, the doctor had told him not to bend over.

It was just like old times. I was the one to make the beds (on help's days off), even *before* any doctor told Artie not to bend over. He watched me, though, and directed the proceedings. (Tuck here, pull there, he would say, as if he knew how.) He also remembered to ask me how my script was doing. I told him Tab and/or Allan were taking it here and there. Well, let them, Artie advised, and forget it. You've done all you can. Get on with your life.

Yeah, well, that was reasonable enough advice, wasn't it? I could hardly disagree.

Then he told me Jonathan was back from Brazil with a wife.

"No kidding!" (I wasn't sure I had known he had *gone* to Brazil.) "Did they bring the baby back, too—your grandchild?" Wouldn't it be fun to see a grandchild of Artie's! See if things kept getting passed on. Like so much about Artie showing up in Jonathan.

"Oh, he didn't marry the baby's mother," Artie said, heading for the kitchen.

I had to laugh. Of course not, what was I thinking? "Who, then, did he?" I called out after him.

He couldn't hear me, he seemed to be banging around in the fridge, or something. So I stopped what I was doing and went to the door. "Who *did* Jonathan marry?"

"Another Brazilian, he speaks the language, you know . . ."

"I know."

"She's a pretty little thing"—he pulled out a bottle of cranberry juice—"can't speak much English, though, we'll have dinner with them next week, if you like. Want some juice?"

It wasn't exactly the steadiest continuity one might be able to conjure up, but it was a reasonable, and amusing, facsimile. And I was beginning to think continuity wasn't too bad a thing, after all.

"Why not," I said to Artie, "on both counts."

Having poured a glass of juice for himself, he shoved the bottle toward me, and pointed. "Glasses are up there." He was that kind of host.

Although I went along, he drove himself to the doctor the next morning, who pronounced him fine, and I went on my way. He didn't need me to play nursie, anymore. And I had work to do. Ever since I had first begun to put things on paper, the uneasiness would creep in when I wasn't able to sit down at my machine for at least a little while every day.

Artie and I had dinner with Jonathan and his bride the following week. And Artie was right. Vera was her name, and she was very, *very* pretty. Little, too. Delicate and slim, with soft, dark hair to the shoulders. She and Jonathan made a handsome pair. Young pair. Above all, young, this latest Cindy-and-her-Prince combination. In the flower of those first, delicious months. When the promised dream (that you still believe in) has come your way. You've found each other, and now the world, the future, is yours, all yours, for the taking, its road strewn with love and happiness for the rest of your lives.

Ah well, I thought, watching them across the table whispering happily together in Portuguese, what they don't know won't hurt them. Besides. Who's to say how it will be for them, there are as many ways as there are people, after all. And so what if it doesn't last any too long? They probably didn't even expect it to. Surely the young aren't as naive, anymore, as we used to be. Though I wouldn't bet *two cents* on *that* little fact, either, I thought. Just thank your lucky stars, I said to me, that *you* don't have to go through any of that *mishegas* ever, ever again . . . "What?"

"Want these?" Artie was saying.

It was his carrots he was talking about.

Some weeks later Artie, evidently bent on continuing his role as paterfamilias, came up with a splendid idea. Why didn't the four of us, he and I and the newlyweds, go down to, say, Ensenada for the Christmas holidays?

Well, hey, how about that! A regular family outing. Just like any other folk—the parents, the offspring, together at Yuletide. (Of course, Artie, being Jewish, had had miserable Christmases as a kid, what with the whole neighborhood having trees and Santa coming with presents and he'd never had a single damn thing except envy and jealousy, and had been running from those particular holidays ever since. But that was neither here nor there, anymore, and maybe this trip could fix those old feelings once and for all. And if we believe in the tooth fairy, we can believe that, too.)

I was really pleased to be included for several reasons. First I enjoyed being with Jonathan and Vera. Besides being good to look at, they were bright and lively and enthusiastic about things. And I hadn't been south of the border for at least a couple of eons. And I had had some very fine times down there in earlier days. Had I, perchance, I all at once wondered, been asked along because a, uh, bifurcated stepmother added a bit of *stability* to the occasion!?

It was a lovely thought, was it not, and it didn't harm a soul, did it, for me to think it in the privacy of my own head. (Besides it gave me a nice giggle.)

Before the holiday season came around, though (before it was time for me to put on my family hat), I did a few things with some friends I hadn't seen for a while, so wrapped up in script doings had I been. J.J. and I, for instance, went off to the races a couple of times. I even won fifteen dollars on one such outing, using my "scientific" method (that is to say, betting solely on gray horses!). Talli and I went to the opening

*Trying a New Point of View* ■ 279

of a new museum for contemporary art. She'd always been very good about seeing to my cultural needs. There were more tributes with Marvin, the casting director/archivist. Hollywood never ceased loving Hollywoodians, nor did Marvin. Allan had that disease, too. It wasn't enough to have two former movie stars in his grasp—me, the scriptwriter, Tab, his producer partner—he insisted that I take him along to some book-to-be-published party I'd been invited to, so he could see (among others) Mae Clark, who had had a grapefruit shoved into her face by Jimmy Cagney in 1931. (1931!) So I went. If it was gonna keep Allan's spirits high, his enthusiasm keen to keep trying to get my script on the road, I'd do (well, almost) *any*thing. How was I going to win that Academy Award if my screenplay never even got made into a movie?

But that night Allan told me he was talking to a network, and that they were thinking of turning it into a miniseries. So I might have to start thinking about an Emmy, instead.

He had waited, mind you, until *after* the book party to impart this new bit of information to me. Actually while we were driving along Sunset Boulevard in that fire-engine red sports car of his on the way home.

I turned to stare at the kid, there in the dark, the street lights flashing on and off across his perky face and shock of black hair.

*"Miniseries?"* I yelped. "But . . . but . . . but . . ."

"We could make a mint of money!" he cried. He sounded exactly like Mephistopheles, in person.

"Ah . . ." That certainly *was* a winning thing to hear. I mean, who couldn't use a mint of money? I mean, you can always think of *something* to do with it, can't you? "But television's never been what we've had in mind."

"Television," cried Allan, all hyped up over this direction now, "is *everything,* these days! Fifty-five million more people would see it even if it were the lowest-rated show on the Nielsens that week! No telling where it could lead, you know!"

"Yeah . . . I guess so . . ." It was just that I'd never much thought of an Emmy one way or the other. I had never even watched their presentation show. It had always sounded like the name of an elderly aunt I'd met once down there in the piney woods of Georgia who'd kept her lips pressed so tightly together in disapproval of *everything* it looked as if she hadn't had any.

"Of course," Allan was saying, "you'll have to make the script a lot longer."

"But you just had me cutting stuff out all over the place, for crissake!"

Allan thought that was funny. "You can put it back now. Wouldn't it be easier to make it longer than shorter?"

"Maybe," I conceded.

"You've got your book to work from—God knows you've got the material."

"It's true, it's true . . ." I began to get excited. "By jingo, I could use things I didn't even get to—when will you know?"

"Not until after the first of the year," he said, "everything comes to a halt in this town around the holidays . . ."

It was just as well I was leaving the place. So I wouldn't be sitting around in a pother about some miniseries and whether it was the right way to go, or not. What did I know, anyway?

Hah. As if I even *had* a choice. God. I was in no position to be choosy. And listen, I told myself, that's all right, too. People with multiple choices, they can as easily make the wrong choice as the person with only one choice. And anyway, why are you thinking of it at all? You are stewing over nothing, absolutely *nothing.* Just because Allan mentioned a deal doesn't mean there *is* a deal. It's a nervous tick with him, dreaming up these deals, I reminded myself. This isn't the first time he's done it, it won't be the last. Forget it. You've got things to do. Trips to make. The goddamn Jolly Season is nigh, get the hell out of town and forget it.

It was with relief that I finally greeted the day of departure . . .

# Thirty-four

For the journey Artie had chosen his gray Bronco II with the orange stripe and big, fat tires, a car I happened to be crazy about. I adored sitting up high the way you do in it, up above the rest of the traffic. It's such a safe and comfortable feeling, and you can see everything for miles around.

After picking up "the children," who settled themselves onto the back seat, off we went, heading south.

It didn't take long for the passing scene to strike a familiar note. To become reminiscent of other Artie-Christmas seasons before it, this driving along past festively lit and decorated front yards and twinkling windows, all dressed up but going nowhere, while we, on the other hand, were headed, well, someplace *else.* Oh, we had had, on occasion, stay-at-home Christmases just like other folk back in Connecticut, with the snow piled high outside, ten-foot highly decorated trees in, with dogs and cats milling around and colorful skaters out on the frozen lake and people invited in to share. But through them all, Artie was always—I don't know—uneasy, somehow. Behaving as if he were a guest in the house, and couldn't wait to go home.

I had never been to Ensenada before, but it turned out not to look all that different from any other Mexican town designed for the tourist trade. Plenty of hotels. Restaurants everywhere, and the main drag filled with shops, *tiendas,* one after the other, each of them filled with merchandise begging to be bought.

Our reservations were at a hotel called La Pinta, as in one

of Christopher's discovery boats. I shared a huge room with brother (sister, mother, papa) Artie. There were two double beds, and a discreet bath/dressing room around a corner. A large enough space so that we wouldn't run over each other.

After we'd checked in, off we went to dinner, where everybody (but me) ordered lobster *(langosta)*, fresh from the waters of the Pacific Ocean lapping at the shores of the town. (I ordered *fajitas con queso*. Damn it all, when in Rome.)

While we ate, I learned that Vera's father had been a college professor, was political, too, and during a change of guard had had to flee Brazil for France, where Vera had been educated. Since I knew that French schools didn't fool around, that they thoroughly educated their *élèves,* I wondered how this background matched up with that of an American tattoo artist raised in Beverly Hills who had fled school at a very early age. What would happen, I began to wonder, after the physical attraction wore off?

But of course I didn't have to know, did I? *They* did.

After dinner we went shopping. What else?

I've never known why the shopping craze has been pinned on women. Every man I've ever known has been a shopping nut, with Artie leading the pack. In and out of every store we went. In and out, in and out, looking at this, feeling that, trying on the other. Belts, Artie bought, more belts, as if he didn't already have two hundred million, another vest, another sweater. He bought a wooden turtle, too, evidently the one thing he *didn't* have to make the clutter complete in that flea market house of his.

And that was about it. How we spent our time there. Going for meals. In and out of stores. The young pair would take off on their own once in a while, and who could blame them? We did take a turn around the harbor one day, in an ancient, rickety fishing boat. We passed a seal sitting on a buoy looking like an old man taking in the sun. We saw an anchored Soviet freighter that was badly in need of paint. We didn't know if that was a sign of what was coming, or not.

I didn't know if any of it helped to bring Artie and Jonathan closer together. After all, that *was* sort of what the trip was all about (besides being escape time for Artie). Maybe just being around each other was a beginning. It was hard to tell if either of them even had the need, anymore. I assumed that they once upon a time had. But God knows what resentments had accumulated somewhere deep inside their psyches by now. It wasn't easy, being human, I knew that. I even thought I knew why.

I had read, somewhere, that ever since we had crawled out of the sea and up into the trees and back down again, we had kept our original brain structure. We had added on to it, to be sure. But the feelings we'd had from the beginning, the sensory messages, the nonthinking reflexes of fear, hunger, sex, anger, want, what-have-you, had remained the same. Exactly the same as when we had first crawled up onto land. Those things, the nonthinking reflexes, *had remained as primitive as ever.*

So it would seem that we *Homo sapiens* (as we so fondly call ourselves), we who can split an atom, fly to the moon, invent computers, who pride ourselves on our superduper brain capacities, are in reality being constantly manipulated all over the place, being pushed and pulled and shoved and downright *manhandled* by a bunch of the most *primordial* reactions and emotions imaginable, which we haven't been able to rid ourselves of even after wrestling with them for billions of years.

Not that lack of success in the matter had stopped too many of us from keeping on trying, I thought cheerily, listening to the four of us chatting animatedly in our various languages as we walked along. And sometimes we even won, here and there. Jonathan and Artie looked as if they might have a chance to do so as they strode on ahead together, looking good together, like father and son, to be exact, down the main drag of Ensenada in Baja California.

Though I couldn't help but wonder about the way the minute we'd arrived Jonathan had rushed out of the car, evidently to go find a drink machine, because while Artie was still at the desk checking us in, Jonathan had reappeared with a beer can in his hand. The whole scene seemed to be making him just a wee bit nervous. And one could easily understand why, actually. A new wife he didn't know any too well as yet? Along with an old father he didn't know too well, either, both at the same time? A combination like that was liable to make most anybody the slightest bit uneasy.

For my part there'd been a little something else that had caught my attention. You do start noticing the damndest things when you begin to live in such close proximity. And that was the number of times Artie was going to the john.

I finally poked my nose into the matter just after we'd returned to our room from dinner on the night before we were to depart. Because Artie had hurried, pell-mell, straight to the bathroom. Which reminded me that he had left the table twice during dinner for the very same purpose. "You seem to be going to the john an awful lot, Artie," I said to him when he came back into the room.

"*Get-ting older sucks!*" muttered Artie Shaw grumpily through a sweater he was pulling up and over his head.

"Yeah, well . . ." I said patiently. That wasn't the first time he had ever said *that*. "But is there a reason why you . . . ?"

"My goddamn prostate is acting up," he growled then, having plopped down to begin untying his Nikes.

I had heard of the word, before. But . . . "What, exactly *is* a prostate, Artie?"

"Something," he said, rather angrily, "you better be glad you haven't *got!*" And off he went back to the bathroom. This time to brush his teeth, as the sounds told me.

Well, I thought, that was good news. I mean, the fact that I didn't have one, since it was evidently something that "acted up." My friend Hilda went to the john a lot, too. Maybe *she* had one, I thought, amusing myself.

Next morning we all got back into Artie's trusty Bronco, heading north, this time, and in nothing flat, that particular sojourn was history. But we all knew where the others would be. How to keep in touch. And that was something, I guessed.

What with the phone, the car, the plane, no one would have to be too far apart from the other. That is, if we didn't want to be.

Once home, it was again my producers that I called first. I'd tried not to think of them, or what might be happening, while I'd been away. But once back on the road and headed in their direction, I had begun to have visions of those great heaps of money, as (more or less) promised by Allan.

"Have we got a lot to tell you!" he promptly exclaimed into my ear, as I'd hoped he would. "Come on over—come for dinner, we'll feed you!"

My spirits rose. It did sound like good news. Better than not having a prostate, even. "You mean, tonight?"

"Can you?"

"Well," I told him, "naturally I'm booked solid for the next five years, but I'll manage to squeeze you in, somehow—and I'll begin, please, with gold caviar on paper-thin toast followed by a soufflé de volaille à la reine . . ."

"How about peanut butter and jelly, with Tootsie Rolls for dessert?" said the kid.

We gathered in the kitchen while they brought me up to date, Allan and I and the whippets weaving in and around Tab as he shifted here, went there, stirring something on the top of the stove with a big wooden spoon, rubbing another herb over the chicken in the oven, chopping up more tomatoes for the large bowl of salad on the butcher's block in the center of the room.

"It's going to work, this time," Allan said excitedly, "I just know it!"

"They called *us* back, you know," Tab flung over his shoulder, the blue eyes dancing.

"I didn't know," I whispered. That was very *very* good!

"They *wanted* something like *Georgia Peach* . . ."

"The same exact period and everything," Allan added.

"No kidding . . ." I could feel my heart thumping. "Wow . . . Well, what's next, when do we sign?"

"The script is in New York, right now."

"New York!" I frowned. "What for?"

"Everybody and his brother," Allan sighed, "has to pass on a project in television."

"It's not," Tab twinkled teasingly, "like your Harry Cohn days. Have a glass of wine, it's good for you." And he poured some Cabernet Sauvignon from the Napa Valley into two glasses, and handed me one, keeping the other for himself. Allan, smart kid that he was, never touched the stuff.

I took a sip. "Like who?" I asked. "Who passes on things? I don't know the first thing about the workings of television."

"Well, first," began Allan, a crunch of corn chip he was chewing punctuating his progress, "there's the director of acquisitions, that's where you go first."

"Then if they're interested, it gets sent to the director of divisions . . ." Tab waved the big spoon to make his points, "drama, sit-coms, mini-series, etcetera, to see where it might fit, where it belongs."

"Don't forget advertising," Allan said to Tab, "they have to like it, too."

"And the various vice-presidents," Tab said to Allan.

"And assistant to the president."

"Not to mention the president, himself."

"Not to mention the chairman of the board."

"You're putting me on," I laughed.

"I wish we were," Allan sighed, "and you should have seen the stack of scripts on that desk!"

"I don't think I want to hear any more," I told them, and took a *big* slug of wine, this time.

"They liked it," offered Tab, "that's the main thing, it lets us know what a great property we have"—his knife whacked into a tomato as he beamed at me with his charm in full force—"thanks to you." With a flourish the tomato pieces landed in the salad, which was swished around a couple of times; then the food began to get switched to the table, with Allan and me actually helping to do it. (Well, I brought along the rolls.)

I ought to have been more elated than I was. I had producers with such an upbeat outlook. Who really *cared*. And said such nice things. But if this deal went through, and my story got made at a network, wouldn't all those people Allan and Tab just mentioned have a say in what was to be done to my script? Every last one of them? And whatever I had started with, whatever I had had in mind, could very well disappear off the face of the earth, never to be seen or heard from again after that many people had their go at it. Hadn't I already learned what happened, just with my *two* partners, who'd insisted that I reduce the script to 125 pages, not because it would *improve the story,* but because "that's what people read"?

I went home in a rather depressed state. But not until after I'd been fed. Roast chicken (basted with something utterly delicious), rice (with the little bits of things in it), sliced zucchini, done something tasty to by Tab. There were ice cream and cookies for those who wanted them. (Not me. Why jog if you're going to louse it up later with all that sugar.)

I talked it over with Artie one evening when he came to town, telling him of my dilemma over dinner.

His thick eyebrows came together in a frown. "You mean somebody's *interested?* Jesus! What's your problem? Take the money and run! That's what you wrote it for, didn't you?"

I started to tell him of the game I was playing with myself about winning an Oscar for screenplay. But then thought better of it. Artie didn't play games like that. Those eyebrows would go wild.

"Writers don't make movies," Artie went on. "Banks do. You don't want anybody monkeying around with your words, get back to your book."

I laughed. I could always depend on Artie to make things crystal-clear. He was right, of course. Dead right. And that's what I could always do—would do—when this was over. I would go back to *Juana*.

But.

*This* was what I was doing *now,* this *screenplay.* What I was dead in the middle of, and I certainly did not intend to abandon ship in mid-cruise, not see it all the way through. I'd hate myself too much in the morning if I did such a thing as that.

So if another rewrite was in order, this time to *lengthen* the work-in-progress, so be it. You gotta swim with the current if you don't want to drown. Look at it this way, I told myself, you will now learn how writing-for-TV works. And that couldn't hurt, could it? The medium was, after all, here to stay . . .

I'd been told a story once, of this very old Irish woman, who had worked hard all her life, cooking, sewing, digging the potatoes, tending the chickens, raising the children, nursing them all through sickness and health, her own fine until in her ninety-third year she came down with a very severe case of the flu.

At her age she wasn't expected to last the night. And so a priest was called to give her the last rites. From her bed, the old woman looked up, saw the priest above her, heard what he was mumbling, and realized why he was there. She, herself, had called him in many a time for just this same purpose. She knew that her own time had come.

"Oh . . ." murmured the old woman weakly, a breath on the evening air, "but . . . but . . . I haven't even lived, yet . . ."

At least, I thought, that's a statement it doesn't look as if I'll be able to make.

# PART SIX

# *On up the Road*

# *Thirty-five*

**W**hile my producers carried on with their Big Business Negotiations, having—pardon me, *taking*—meetings, discussions, making back-and-forth calls with all those network bigwigs, I busied myself looking over the material at hand, figuring out what I thought might work well on the little screen and such. And, as long as I had the time, I also wrote one of my columns. I went off to the post office early one morning to mail it in to my newspaper, the *Times,* arriving when the place opened because there's seldom an overabundance of would-be mailers lined up to send off large masses of parcels as early as that.

And it was there, of all places, that I picked up a quite startling and unexpected piece of news.

As I came back out through the swinging doors, after dropping my envelope off inside, a guy climbing onto his motorcycle spoke to me as I passed him by. "Hello there," said he to me, "aren't you Evelyn Keyes?"

When I confessed that I was, he introduced himself and told me he was on the committee for selecting the Oscar nominations of the feature-length documentaries. "We just ran the Artie Shaw one," the man on the motorcycle said, "and I probably shouldn't be telling you this, but from the reaction, I think it has a good chance of a nomination."

"No *kidding!*" That possibility had never even occurred to me! "Wouldn't that be wonderful! Thank you for telling me!" I cried, and restrained myself from giving a perfect stranger a big hug right there in the parking lot of the West Hollywood branch of the United States Post Office.

The second I got home I dashed to the phone to call and tell Artie the glad tidings, forgetting it wasn't much past eight, and that he wasn't as early a riser as I was (I had been up since five, jogged for an hour, cooked and eaten my bowl of rolled oats, plus a banana), and on top of that that he was undoubtedly the world's worst waker-upper.

*"Artie!"* I yipped into his ear. *"Guess what I just heard!"*

"Whaaas . . . at?" It sounded somewhat like the moo of a cow in labor.

"There-was-this-guy-I-ran-into-at-the-post-office-" I rattled on, quite in a dither, "and-he-said-he-was-that-they-were-the-Academy-was-"

"I can't . . . you . . . don't . . . later . . . call . . . ?"

I had to give up. It was as if I were talking to mush. Something must have gotten through, though, because he was back on the phone within the hour, with a normal voice. "Now, what was that all about?" he inquired quite clearly. "You know, before I've had coffee, I can't . . ."

"Yes yes, I know, I forgot, but it isn't every day . . ." And I told him what the man on the motorcycle said.

Artie always quieted down when he was pleased in any way. He would not make a good TV game-show candidate. (It was when things went wrong that he got plenty noisy, the theory being the squeaky wheel gets the oil and all that.) And he underplayed the news I gave him to the hilt.

"Well, that's nice to hear," he said, mildly, "but I can't imagine it has a chance. Why would the Academy be interested in a jazz musician?"

"They'd be interested in a well-made documentary," I volunteered.

"Brigitte did a good job," he conceded. But he wasn't going to allow himself to become too interested. I understood. Didn't I go around cushioning myself all the time? It's your showbiz training, something that must be learned early on in the game, if you plan on surviving it. It's a pretty good thing to know for life's little surprises as well, if you ask me. The difficulty, though, is creating just the *right* thickness of cushioning around you. Generating just enough so it helps soothe the hurt, but not so thick it will cut you off from ever trying again when something doesn't work out, or prevent you from ever feeling again with all your heart and soul. It's tricky, all right.

As it turned out, Artie's reserve could have been for more than one reason, subconsciously or not. Because by the time the nominations were announced, he was in the hospital.

Both Artie and I had been blessed with these remarkable genes. So remarkable we hardly knew they *were* remarkable. So I was taken aback when he had informed me that he was going into the hospital the following day.

"I changed doctors," he told me on the phone, "and the new one says it's got to be taken care of tomorrow."

"Good God, Artie," I whispered, in shock. "What? *What's* got to be taken care of?"

"The thing I told you about in Mexico," he snapped irritably, obviously thinking he'd been telling me about it all along. "Could you possibly come up and help me out?"

"When? When do you have to be . . ."

"The doctor's calling back to tell me the time. If you could come up now, today, if it's early, you'll be here."

"Sure, Artie," I said quietly, "I'll put some things in a bag and be along . . ."

He was very perturbed, that was easy to see. And with reason. I didn't believe he had thought it was anything to go to a hospital about. And what *was* that thing he had told me about in Mexico. Pros-trate—no, pros-*tate,* wasn't that it?

Before I left I looked it up in the dictionary. "A gland," I read, "situated just before the neck of the bladder in males, and surrounding the first portion of the uretha: (Gr. *prostates,* standing before; before, and stem, *sta,* to stand.)"

A gland, then. But why the hospital? A little farther on the page I found another word which might explain it. *Prostati-*

*tis.* The dictionary told me that meant an "inflammation of the prostate gland."

Ah so. Artie had something, then, that was like the inflamed ankle tendon I had, one time. Only not in as convenient a spot. But why the hospital? Mine went away by itself in a matter of days. Perhaps something inside you was a different matter?

I paid scant heed when, as I was gathering up my things to leave, Allan called to tell me that the network was passing, after all. That after all this *mishegas,* these carryings-on, the bastards had decided that my story "didn't quite fit into their season's programming."

Whatever the hell that meant. And who cared, anymore? I had other concerns to attend to right now, and the truth was, I hadn't *really* wanted to go that way, anyhow. An old Mel Brooks saying came to mind as I snapped my bag shut and went out the door. I think it was on a record of his called *The Two Thousand Year Old Man.* "Let 'em all go to hell," says the ancient chap, "except Cave Seventeen."

By the time I got up there, Artie was back to his normal, semi-keyed-up self again, any sign of undue agitation gone—probably forgotten, too. After telling me we had to be at the hospital at eight the next morning, the reason for going there wasn't mentioned again. Instead he went back to trying to decide whether to order an electronic chess set he had come across in a mail-order catalogue.

Artie did a big business with mail-order catalogues. Stacks of them had always come every month (and apparently still did), from which he'd order everything in the world, from gadgetry to clothes, to kitchen ware, tools and furniture. Once he had sent for a four-foot-high thermometer to put on an outside wall of our last house, where the temperature could easily drop to a below-zero reading overnight, so it was good to know that before you ventured out, and this enormous thermometer could be seen from practically every front window of the house.

Life with Artie had been lively, I could certainly say that for it.

I'd never seen a hospital before like the one we went to. To be sure I wasn't exactly an authority on hospitals, but here and there, sure, one has had reason to go to one, to visit a friend, if nothing else. And God knows we've seen them on the big screen and the little, and because of friend Marvin, casting as he did for *General Hospital,* I'd forced myself to watch a couple of episodes. So all of them, the hospitals I'd seen, off screen and on, have been colossal in size, with lots of halls and endless rooms, and people in white (and sometimes green) scurrying hither and yon, sometimes pushing sallow-looking people in bathrobes along in wheelchairs or on rolling stretchers, everybody looking slightly harassed, ready for the worst.

And inside the one Artie went to was pretty much the same as the others. But *outside.* Well. You wouldn't have known it was a hospital if it hadn't said so at the entrance. There were trees and shrubbery planted all around, the places for parking among them in various locations, so you didn't see that mass of metal in front of the building the way you usually do. The building, itself, was a one-story (imagine, one story!) structure done in a kind of adobe, early-California-style-you-wouldn't-find-anywhere-else-in-the-world architecture. It seemed to me that if one did have to go to a hospital to have something done, this was the ideal place to have it done in.

I went in with him, to learn the lay of the land, see where I might locate him later, and find out what time I should come back for him. A nurse behind a desk checked a chart and told me I'd best call in in the late afternoon, as she didn't think Mr. Shaw would be awake before then. If then.

"Oh," I said, surprised, "it's not a local, then."

She looked at me as if I didn't have good sense. "No," she said, "it is not a local."

She gave me the phone number of the desk, and I took my leave. There was no use asking what, exactly, was going to be done to Mr. Shaw. She probably wouldn't have told me, anyway. I didn't think I wanted to know, anyhow. My friend Cynthia always seemed fascinated with health details for some reason. One of those who, when she asked how you were, really wanted to know the particulars. She would even tell you, chapter and verse, about the condition of the health of some friend of hers whom you had never met. She probably should have been a doctor. My dentist always insists on showing me the tooth before he fills it with gold, shows me the neat hole he has *drilled into my tooth* with that noisy, whirring thing. I understand that he is proud of his work and wants to show it off. I am happy he takes pride in his work (especially if he's doing it in my mouth), so I dutifully hold the mirror and look. But I *don't want to see the ugly, jagged goddamn hole in my tooth without the filling in it*! My hope was that Artie would tell me later that operations "suck," and that would be that.

We had driven over in the Bronco again, and so I had the pleasure of driving the darling car through the rolling hills and back to the flea market house all by myself. It was a crisp February day, the air clear for a change, and Artie's view of mountains topped with snow was quite spectacular. I had brought some work along, but it was too tempting to step outdoors and breathe in (what seemed to be) clean air, and watch a red-tailed hawk making lazy circles against the blue, blue of the sky. You seldom saw that sort of thing down there in the big city where I had taken up residence.

A cat came around the corner, and froze in its tracks when it saw me.

I had sighted the same cat when I'd been here before, skittering by in great haste, and Artie had said it was a wild one. It was quite a handsome cat, with a longish pale, silvery coat, snow-white chest and paws, and enormous eyes of lime-green.

I froze, too, the way the cat had.

Once, back up on the Connecticut mountaintop, on one of those wintry days at the end of a long cold season, when the trees are still bare, the snow half-melted and the ground all soggy, as I stepped out the door to bring in some firewood, a creature came scurrying by headed for the woods, looking like no animal I had ever seen before, until I realized it was a cat, so pitifully undernourished it was mostly bones, and when I said, "Kitty . . ." it quickly turned around, as if it hadn't heard a human voice for a very long time, and hurried over crying "me-eow" in the most pitiful way. And when I fed it, it was ours from then on. (I suspected that some summer people had dumped it at the end of their stay; they did that around there, those monstrous humans.)

I tried the same approach with the silver-coated cat in Artie's patio.

And by jingo, it worked! The cat turned out to have the loudest purr I had ever heard in my *life*! Moving like a snail in order not to alarm my new friend, I slid back the door into the house, made my way to the kitchen, found some milk in the fridge, found a saucer to pour it in. And found, too, that the cat had followed me in, though keeping a safe distance.

When I leaned down slowly and placed the milk-filled saucer on the floor, and the kitty-cat approached—with caution, to be sure—and began to lap away, it was a lovely, warm feeling, indeed.

Artie now had a new pet to take Chester-Chaucer's place, if he wanted it. It even had the same coloring as Chester, too, that was the nice part.

When I called the hospital in the late afternoon, I got the first hint that what Artie was going through might not be exactly a picnic. They said he couldn't talk because he was in intensive care.

Now, I might have been more alarmed had I not recently received John's call from intensive care. And he had survived and gone on his way, even with those lousy lungs of his. I concluded that was probably what they did with everybody who came to a hospital, these days, afraid to be sued if anything went wrong. Everybody and his uncle certainly seemed to be sue-happy lately, according to the newspapers I'd been reading.

I watched the sun go down, watched the evening news,

then picked up one of Artie's many books lying around, this one with the title "Qi," curious as to what it meant.

Of all things it turned out to be about Eastern medicine, written by an American who had graduated from Harvard Med, and gone to Beijing to intern. What he said, in essence, was that Western medicine had discarded Eastern medicine with the advent of the pharmaceutical companies and all those billions of dollars that were to be made by selling us at stiff prices antibiotics and tranquilizers and pep pills and sleeping pills and vitamins made with chemicals in a factory instead of herbs that could be found for nothing out in the fields, herbs that would do the same things for us as the expensive pills did, and that Chinese doctors still used to cure/help their patients.

Why in the world was Artie Shaw reading about Chinese medicine? I asked myself. Was he planning to go *there* next? I remembered that talk about New Zealand a year or so ago. And on the way back from Mexico, he'd noticed some houses along the Baja coastline for sale, and insisted we stop and look them over.

A restless, restless fellow. Or maybe he was thinking of taking up the study of Chinese medicine. Nothing whatsoever would surprise me about Artie. Nothing.

Or, was it just his mayfly approach again, touching here, there, everywhere. Where had I read—Albert Einstein had said it, I think—it is better to have imagination than knowledge? Artie simply had the curiosity of a, well, of a cat. They would make good companions, then, he and the kitty cat.

I thought I might miss him if he went off to China. I might not want to be around him all the time, but I rather liked to know he was *there,* somewhere. He was my continuity, for crissake.

I laughed out loud, all by myself, there in the flea market house. Couldn't I have picked a more solid ground than Artie to look to for my continuity?

No. It seemed that I couldn't, was the simple answer to that question. If I had *wanted* a way of life on more solid ground, I would have *chosen* it years ago, wouldn't I have?

I would like to know, though, why he was reading a book on Chinese medicine. I would have to ask him when I saw him next.

But as it turned out, I wouldn't be asking him much of anything when I saw him next . . .

# Thirty-six

The next morning they said I could come and see him, though obviously not take him home, since he was still in intensive care.

I didn't know what to expect. I had never been anywhere near an intensive care ward before, not even as a passerby. The nurse at the desk told me to go pick up a phone on the wall outside a big door down at the end of the hall, which was what I did. And when a voice answered, I said, "This is Mrs. Shaw. Is it all right if I come in to see Artie, now?"

I had already figured on the way there that it would be better to use the old appellation. That a legal spouse would be expected to come around, but God knew how they would treat a bifurcated one.

"Yes," the answering voice told me, "come right in."

When I stepped through the big, swinging door, a most extraordinary sight greeted my eyes. It was a big room, longer than it was wide, and up and down each wall the long way were rows of beds with bodies on them, none of them moving, their eyes either closed or staring into space; things, gadgets, hospital paraphernalia attached to them.

A nurse in starched white stepped forward. "Mrs. Shaw?" she whispered. I must have nodded, because she beckoned and moved toward the end of the room.

And there was Artie, in a cubicle, all by himself, apart from the other bodies.

Jesus Christ, it was scary. Tubes were in his arms and going somewhere under the sheet that covered him, and instruments were all around winking and blinking and zip-zapping crazily, instruments that were attached to *him.*

He was totally out of it. He didn't know I was there, didn't know *anything,* actually. He was breathing, though. I could see he was doing that. So I knew that he was at least alive.

The nurse was straightening the sheet, checking one of the instruments. I didn't know what to do with myself. There wasn't any chair, they didn't want you hanging around there, obviously. I sure as hell wasn't going to sit on the bed.

"Uh . . . how is he?" I finally whispered, asking about as dumb a question as anybody could under the circumstances. He looked ghastly. Kind of yellow and lopsided, somehow.

"He'll be fine," the nurse said softly, "just fine."

I had the craziest thought. Was Artie in here separated, apart from all the other bodies lying around with *their* tubes and buzzing instruments because he was in direr straits than they, or was he getting some kind of intensive care ward star-type treatment?

"Uh, why don't I . . ." Artie hadn't moved. ". . . just come back when he wakes up?"

The nurse fiddled with a machine. "That will be fine," she said to me over her shoulder. Her standard reply to all questions, I guessed.

"In the afternoon? Shall I come back in the afternoon?"

"That will be fine," she said again. She was pretty, with dark hair and blue eyes, and that would be nice to wake up to. Imagine having to do this all day, every day, I thought.

I tiptoed out, and, at the desk, asked for the telephone number of Artie's doctor. Fortunately they wrote his name on the slip of paper, too, because I suddenly realized I hadn't even known that.

I waited until I got back to the house to call him, though.

"This is Mrs. Shaw," I said to the doctor, too. "I just went over to see Artie, but he wasn't even awake . . ."

"I almost lost him," the doctor said back, "he'd waited much too long, his condition was nearly out of . . ."

*Almost lost him?* The doctor went on talking, but my ears had clogged up as a chill wind of about forty-below went sweeping through my arteries. But it was supposed to have been nothing at all!

". . . we had to give him two transfusions he lost so much blood . . . surprised not to have found any cancer . . ."

I was stunned. Absolutely stunned. Who'd said anything about cancer, who had even *thought* it? The doctor was who. But he hadn't found it. I did hear that. *I had heard that.*

I managed to thank him and hang up the phone. But then I just sat there in mild shock, unable to move for the longest time. It was such a reminder of what a precarious hold we living creatures had on staying that way. A roach skitters along; zap! comes a foot. A deer munches a leaf, zing! flies the bullet. A buzz saw of a logger fells the thousand-year-old redwood in the wink of an eye. We humans construct our buildings on top of faults, drive cars, fly planes, defying the odds. And live all the while in these incredible bodies of ours, made of a network of cardiovascular systems and livers and hearts and bladders and *glands,* all chugging along to support this thing called life. And even if the fault doesn't shake, the car misses all the others, the plane stays in the air, no matter how many whole grains are eaten, how many miles are jogged, something in the system of this assemblage of ours goes phtt!, one day, and that is that. Over and out.

How could one squander one single precious, irreplaceable moment of it? And yet we did. We all did, didn't we? All the time . . .

The mountains in the distance caught my eye. A violet with shadows of deeper purple in the recesses. Beautiful. The pale pink of the clouds floating behind them touched me, some-how, as if the act of being able to see this view was life, itself. I stepped outside to somehow become a part of it. While I was still able. Before something zonked *me.*

As I stood there, enjoying, the kitty cat appeared. And when I spoke to it, came over, purring like a running motor. It even did me the honor of permitting me to reach down and stroke its silvery fur. I was positive I knew exactly how it felt to be knighted by the Queen. (Or was it a King? It would have been presumptuous of me to investigate *that* aspect of kitty on such short acquaintance.)

In the afternoon I went back to the hospital without calling ahead again. If I couldn't see Artie right away, I would just hang around until I could. I was too uneasy not being there. I needed reassurance, after speaking with the doctor, that Artie, indeed, would be all right. Maybe see him open his eyes. Hear him at least groan. Something besides that inert body lying there.

For him not to be anywhere *at all,* not even in Beijing, was more than I cared to contemplate. How would it affect *him,* I wondered as I drove along, this close-call business, if it had touched me the way it had, a mere bystander?

I now knew exactly where the intensive care ward tele-phone was, and went straight to it. "It's Mrs. Shaw again," I told the answering voice, "is this an okay time for me to come in and see Artie?"

"Uh . . ." There was a pause. "Just one moment, please . . ."

I waited.

It was a different voice that came back on. One with a slightly foreign inflection. "Please to wait where you are," this one said to me, "I wish to come out and speak to you."

My heart flung itself wildly against its rib cage. Ohmygod. Was Artie . . . ? Had he had a relapse after I left? Was he . . . *dead? Dying?* He had looked so . . . so really *pitiful* earlier.

I waited, frozen to the spot. Too terrified to move.

The nurse who stepped through the big door was dainty of build, with a round, childlike face and big brown eyes that were filled with worry. Filipino, I guessed. "I just thought you ought to know," she whispered urgently, "before you go in, that Mr. Shaw . . ."

"Yes?" I stopped breathing.

". . . is very, very upset . . ."

*"Upset?* Oh!" I stared at her. "Then he's not . . . not . . ." I started to breathe again. "What's he upset about?"

"He is unable to find something that he says he must have . . ."

"Ahh." I almost burst out laughing. Yes, well, that would upset Artie, all right, not to be able to *find* something. It was the story of his life, being upset when he couldn't find something. I doubted, though, that it was the time or the place to explain that to his nurse. Or explain the reasons for it. "What is it," I asked her instead, "that he can't find?"

"I don't know what," the nurse said, shaking her head, "I can't seem to understand what he is saying."

"Perhaps I'll know what he's talking about."

She seemed relieved. "Yes, thank you. Please to come in . . ."

It was a sight no one would believe, I expect, except me (and maybe Artie's other wives or members of his band). There he was, surrounded by those still-attached bubbling instruments and tubes, on a hospital bed, having one of his discombobulated outbursts, the ones he has when threatened with disorder, he who had been two transfusions away from death only the day before, flailing about as best he could under the circumstances, glaring first in one direction and then the other. *"Look at this mess they've made!"* he roared in full and unweakened voice. *"They've just dumped everything, every which way, I can't find a goddamn thing!"*

It was a mess, I had to admit. Somebody had unceremoniously flung his things into hospital containers, all jumbled together; his bottles, brushes, pencils, his books. In the same situation I might have had a fit, too—if I could have gotten together the energy he was displaying. A couple of other nurses circled discreetly at a distance, expecting the worst, I imagined—a ripped stitch, a heart attack, something any decent, properly behaving patient in intensive care should have, something they would know how to handle, as they obviously didn't this display of noisy exasperation.

"What is it you're looking for, Artie?" I said quietly, trying to give him an example to emulate.

He didn't emulate. *"My Equal!"* he yelled. "What in God's name have they *done with it?"*

His . . . *equal?* What the hell was he talking about? "Uh, what does it look like?" (I needed a clue.)

"A *bottle* for crissake! It's a *sweetener,* I can't drink tea without it!"

On that table that swings over the bed they have in hospitals was a pot of something. Tea, obviously.

I started rummaging through the jumbles in the trays as the fray continued behind me, Artie giving his candid opinion of the nurses and of hospitals in general. Knowing, at least, that what I was looking for was a bottle, helped. And I found it, too. Underneath most everything else, turned face down. But when I turned it over, there the label was, in sizable letters for all the world to see: EQUAL.

"This it?" I brought the bottle up for Artie to see.

"Thas' it . . ." he murmured, suddenly quiet, like a baby that's been given its pacifier. He had finally run out of steam, Artie had, and not a minute too soon for somebody who was running on empty to begin with.

The next day they took him out of his cubicle and into a private room, and kept him there until the end of the week. And I can tell you, since I was in and out during the day, it wasn't a lot of laughs for anybody, Artie or the nurses. Not to have control over his own person was most trying (to say the least!) for Artie, not to mention for the nurses who were supposed to be in charge of him, and who no doubt were most happy to see the last of this cranky, demanding patient, even if he was the great band leader their parents told them he was!

Meanwhile I had stayed on at his house, scribbling when I could, keeping the cat relationship going until Artie could come along and take it over. *Schlepping* more things to the hospital he felt he couldn't do without, bringing messages that came in. Like the one about a tour for the orchestra to the Scandinavian countries come summer. Like the news that Brigitte Berman's documentary on him had actually gotten an Oscar nomination. She had called all the way from Toronto to tell him what had happened in California.

I think Artie was pleased. Though he'd actually made more fuss about his missing Equal.

But then I made a big mistake. I mean, a B-I-I-IG mistake.

I cleaned his refrigerator.

I don't know what possessed me to do it. I am not a fridge-cleaning freak or anything. Clearing out a closet, something only I can do, is about my limit in the cleaning-up department. And I usually postpone *that* until I'm forced into it by moving from one place to another.

But as I was going to fetch Artie the next day and return him to his own digs, I decided it would be a good idea to pick up some staples, some basics, to replace the ones that had come to no good in his absence.

So I stopped at a market, gathered up some eggs, some milk, butter, fruit, even a few veggies (though no carrots, heaven forbid), plus a few other odds and ends.

Except when I got back to the house there wasn't any place to put anything. Artie's fridge was stuffed to the gills. He used to say his boyhood dream of the perfect home was one that had a refrigerator full of everything you could possibly want to eat at all times.

He was obviously making a run at his old dream. Only, the way he was trying to achieve it, the having-it-all-all-the-time, was to never throw anything away. *Anything.* No matter its age. His fridge clearly hadn't been cleaned out since Methuselah was around. Everything in there was stale, moldy, or shriveled, and sometimes all three. So I decided to do something about it, as a nice, homecoming surprise, even if it was nine o'clock at night.

Well. I tell you. I got myself into a bit more than I reckoned for. It was going on ten-thirty by the time I sniffed and peeked into every single jar, bottle, plastic container, and half-ass-wrapped package, wanting to be sure not to throw out some exotic herb, or gourmet treat that Artie might be saving for a rainy day.

By then I'd discovered the appalling state of the shelves. Wretchedly sticky with spilled God-knew-whats. So there was nothing for it but to take them, one by one, over to the sink to scrape and scrub and tidy them up. And while I was at it, I cleaned the two bins below them, too, sloshing soapy water around in them and rinsing, sloshing and rinsing, over at the sink.

By then I had had it. I mean, I was *tired*. It had been a long day. And so. Although the floor *underneath* the bins was an appalling, icky, slurpy *mess,* I decided to do that part on the morrow. You couldn't see the mess with the bins in place, so nobody would know about it but me, anyway.

That was my first mistake.

But then I made a second mistake, as well.

There was a metal strip that fit between the two bins. That had fallen out and onto the floor when I slid them out to wash them. But now that the bins were back in place, I couldn't make the metal strip go back in to the place I thought it went.

Screw it, I thought. I was far too tired to figure it out. Tomorrow, I thought. I'll think about that tomorrow, I said to me, in good sister Scarlett style.

And with that I laid the metal strip on top of the shelf that served as the lid for the bins, and retired to my couch for the night.

Shortly before noon the next day, I went over to pick Artie up. He had lost weight, I decided. I could see a difference now that he was back in his gray-with-the-blue-trim jump suit. He had a sort of punctured look, too, the way people do after a siege in the hospital.

But he seemed to pick up energy the closer he got to his house. And when we arrived he walked right in without a single wobble. Almost as if nothing had happened at all in the way of physical trauma.

Later, when I got around to looking back at that day, I couldn't imagine why I hadn't realized ahead of time that, what happened next, would be *exactly* what was *bound* to happen next, if I cleaned up the man's messy refrigerator. It was *his* mess, wasn't it. In *his* fridge. And therefore, *his order.* Had I not recently witnessed another vivid reaction (in a long line of such reactions) to his order being tampered with even as he lay on an intensive-care bed? I, who had resolved to be careful not to move one single thing in his flea market house while I was staying there by so much as an eighth of an inch from where I found it. And I hadn't, either.

Not until I had got to the fridge, that is.

Had I reverted, without thinking twice, to former times, when the kitchen, and things pertaining to food, had been the little woman's domain?

Artie's face, when he opened the fridge door, informed me of the error of my ways. A mystified look filled his eyes as his heavy brows clashed head-on in a deep frown.

"I cleaned it up, Artie," I hastened to tell him. "It was in a bit of a . . ."

"Where is the cranberry juice?" He sounded alarmed.

"There it is, behind the milk . . ."

*"It belongs over there!"* He grabbed the bottle and shoved it vigorously across to the opposite side. "I had . . ." He began rummaging, sliding things around, ". . . a piece of apple strudel in here, somewhere . . ."

"Oh, Artie!" I laughed, "You must have had it in there for a couple of *years,* that thing was dry and hard as a rock."

"What . . . is . . . this?" He had spied the metal strip I had laid down on the bottom shelf.

"That's just something that goes between the two bins, I couldn't get it back, but I'm going to fix it later . . ."

He picked the strip up and started trying to push the thing back in between the bins.

"Look, Artie, I'll do it later, why don't you just . . ."

With considerable irritation he yanked on a bin, which, most naturally, jumped all the way out of its slot. Thereby revealing the soupy, black goop below it. Wouldn't you know.

"I thought you said you cleaned this!" He snapped angrily, as if I had promised to do so, and had not done it.

*"I am going to do that part, later,* Artie, now why don't you just go . . ."

"Always *later, later,"* he muttered. And with that began to dart around the kitchen, grabbing up paper towels, cloth towels, and sponges. Then, before my eyes, the man got down on his knees and began to clean up the goop, himself.

I watched with utter fascination. To my knowledge Artie had never cleaned anything in his life, before, except maybe the barrels of his guns. I had seen him do those. Probably his clarinet. He had probably cleaned that. And his telescopes and microscopes, or any other precision instruments he might have had around for toys. But never, ever, the bottom of a fridge. Nor the top part, either, for that matter. Or any other thing in a household.

He paused briefly to look up at me with blazing eyes. "You're just standing there! *Aren't you going to help me?"*

I didn't bother to answer. I was too busy thinking what a good imitation of an ungrateful *boor* he was giving.

"I'd better get somebody else in here, then," he growled most irascibly. "I'm going to need *someone* to help me!"

As a way of answering *that,* I departed the kitchen to go and begin gathering up my things. It was time to get out. After sinking into one of those dudgeons of his, it took Artie forever to get back out again, poor chap. How so very nice it was to be able to simply pack up and leave, take a walk, get the hell out of hearing distance.

As I exited, I heard him on the phone, making arrangements, talking hours and what had to be done. It sounded as if he were talking to a nurse. For his sake, I hoped it was.

Driving along 101 South, I couldn't help but wonder if he could have hurt himself in some way back there. And found that, at least for the moment, I really didn't much care one way or the other. Maybe if he had, it would be some kind of lesson for him, and he would learn to control that temper of his a little better. Though if he killed himself, a lesson wouldn't help very much.

Though, if his blowup the day after (the very *day* after!) his encounter with the grim reaper had done him no harm, it wasn't likely that this one would, either. Actually, it was almost as if this latest outburst had given him a fresh spurt of energy.

And then I had a new thought . . .

Could that be *it*? The reason for all those unreasonable temper tantrums of Artie's? A *renewal of energies*!

I had often wondered why a person of Artie's brilliance—even genius, it's been said—with his capacity for learning, and absorbing what he'd learned, bisecting it, sorting it, and putting two-and-two together, didn't have control over his own temper.

Did I have the answer now, I asked myself gaily, having fun, driving along in my little yellow Honda? Could it be that Artie *needed* to have these periodic eruptions in order to generate new surges of his life force—the way Popeye needed spinach? Maybe Artie had learned to take a highly destructive emotion and make it work *for* him, learned to *use* it to recharge his own inner turbines when they appeared about to falter!

Or, I smiled, had I read one sci-fi book, seen one *Star Trek,* too many?

At least, I thought with amusement, taking the Coldwater exit and sailing down the ramp, Artie and his shenanigans had served to give me a quick and entertaining trip home . . .

# *Thirty-seven*

It was good to be back in my own digs. The lovely hush of unoccupied rooms reached over and encircled me like a comforting blanket after the racket I had just been through. Even back in my school days I had loved coming home to an empty-of-humans house.

I dunno. It has always given me a sense of freedom, being by myself. Able to let my thoughts dance and prance in any direction they liked. To read what I liked, listen to what I wanted to, do nothing at all if I felt like that. I don't remember ever reading in any young people's book how delicious solitude can be. And that's a pity. Because wouldn't it help the young never to be lonely, never to be bored, if they knew they had something that would always be right there for them no matter what? That is to say, their very own companionship?

I got myself a piece of string cheese and a stalk of celery out of my fridge, opened the doors to the terrace wide to let in some genuine Los Angeles smog, and was starting to munch when things began to rumble and shake.

My first thought was that Artie had picked up his refrigerator and tossed it, disgustedly, down the hill. (Easier, by far, than cleaning up all that goop.) My second was ohmygod, an earthquake is upon me.

Quickly I stepped under a doorframe, the way they tell you to, and watched my paintings flap against the walls, little things on the coffee table jiggling up and down. In a matter of seconds it was all over, though the building continued to sway a bit afterward. I could tell because the highrises in Century City over on the horizon appeared to be moving back and forth beyond the glass doors. I hadn't even had time to get scared.

From an Artie cyclone to a quaking earth. It was quite enough for one day. And though it had crossed my mind earlier that maybe I ought to call and tell Artie about my progress with the cat up there, that if he played his cards right, he could have a furry friend to help step into Chester's place if he wanted it, I now thought to hell with it. Those two were just going to have to find each other on their own, without me. I was through. (Maybe.) I decided to wait until morning to call Allan, too. What I needed most at the moment was a little peace and quiet. And a good book.

I waited until 7:30 (A.M.) to call Allan. As I'd already done my crack-of-dawn routine it seemed like noon to me. I think I woke him, as I did most everybody I called. But Allan (the kid) managed to rally rather well—and even pretend that he actually had been wide awake. "Thank goodness you're back!" he yipped (if a little hoarse). "Have I got things to tell you!"

"The miniseries is back on track, after all?" I chirruped.

"You never know!" cried the cockeyed optimist. "Maybe it'll get on next year—but I'm not waiting."

"I *hope* not!"

"I need to talk to you!" Allan almost whooped with urgency—he was coming to, fast. "What are you doing today?"

"Well, number-one thing, I've got to write a column, and I was thinking of going to the Academy library to look up dates." I was always doing that. I never knew dates, including things I myself had done. They were all suspended there in midair, everything that had ever happened, forever circling, like astronauts in their spaceships, round and round, round and round.

"Why don't you come to the USC library with me, instead?" Allan wanted to know. "You could find anything you need there, they've got a great file on you."

"They *do*?" But how could I go to USC instead of UCLA? Wouldn't that be unfaithful, somehow?

But if they had a great file on me . . .

Vanity won. I overcame my reservation without too much struggle. "What a *splendid* idea!" I exclaimed to Allan.

"We can do lunch there, too, and talk."

Over salads in a sort of pub-looking place, Allan told me he had met someone he was thinking of giving the script to to read. A long shot, he said.

He went on talking, but I was only half-listening, my mind echoing "long shot." God. Wasn't *everything*? Life itself, for crissake. Yesterday I had been up north picking up Artie at a hospital, where he had almost kicked the bucket but hadn't, had a fracas about a refrigerator, experienced an earthquake, and today was on the University of Southern California campus talking about a script I had written that might, just *might,* be made into a movie. I sometimes had the image that my existence was like a rack of billiard balls being shot around by a cue stick, racing here, rolling there, zip, zap, whoosh, all around a table lined with green felt. "What? What's that you said?"

"I said that she liked the idea."

*"She?"*

". . . and she's with a small company, and that's *very* good . . ."

A small company for a little picture, is that what he meant, I wondered?

". . . and they are looking for Academy Award material, too," Allan was saying.

"Of course they are!" I cried. "Who *isn't,* for Pete's sake!"

"A lot of producers aren't," Allan told me earnestly, "A lot of them would rather make a buck on a sure thing than try to . . ."

"What's a surer thing than winning an Oscar!"

"Oscar winners don't always make the big money," the whiz kid told me, "far from it. You stand a much better chance with something really sensationalistic that spatters blood and guts all over the screen than aiming for an Oscar with a touching little humanistic drama, these days.''

"I see . . ." I didn't have a single murder in my script. Not one intergalactic laser battle. "Allan, my sweet . . ." I reached over, and took his hand. "Why," I asked quietly, "are you bothering with my foolish little script, when it has all these odds against it, for heaven's sake?"

Allan's smooth young face melted into a delicious, gentle, half-smile. "Because," he said softly, "I would like to win an Oscar, too, when you win yours."

I had to smile, too. Of course that's what he wanted. I should have known. There the kid was, back in Virginia, growing up on yearly Oscar broadcasts, saying to himself, one day . . . one day, I, too . . .

You do have to learn it young, the "having-a-dream" game. I am convinced if you don't catch on to it right there on somebody's knee, you'll never know how to play it. (Won't have it in your repertoir for your later days, when you might need it most.)

Allan, the darling boy, knew how to play the game to the hilt. Was I going to get in his way? Not on your life, I wasn't! I was going to join in!

We laughed happily, and Allan said, "How would you like to visit a nice, big library?"

We paid the check, grabbed hands and made a dash through the traffic of Jefferson Boulevard like a couple of kids (one, legit, the other a pretender).

It was an honest-to-God-no-kidding library, all right. The wide marble stairs flanked with columns made the Twelve Oaks plantation in *Gone With the Wind* look downright puny. Huge paintings adorned the walls, chandeliers hung from the ceilings. Not only that, somewhere in the endless rooms and floors off the stairs were all the books, newspapers, magazines, periodicals, and anything else that had ever been printed.

And that included a file on me, as promised.

Allan behaved as if he owned the joint, showing me every

nook and cranny. And I knew I had found a new and valuable place for future treasure hunts.

We had covered the place from top to bottom and were walking back down the stairs when Allan said suddenly, seemingly out of nowhere, "I think I'll call her, now."

"Call who?" My mind was miles from the earlier conversation.

"The woman I was telling you about at lunch."

"Ah." The one who was looking for Academy Award material. I hoped I had it for her. Was Allan looking to me to tell him to go do it, to call her? His face had the expression of a poker player who either has a full house or wants you to *think* he has a full house. "Well, why don't you?" I ventured to suggest.

"Will you wait while I do it?"

We were making our way back across campus to where the car was parked, walking along a curved pathway through the parklike atmosphere of blooming things and trees and manicured lawns. Students, too, were everywhere. In groups, in pairs, or alone, strolling along, studying here and there like they were supposed to. "You couldn't have picked a better place for me to do it," I told Allan light-heartedly.

"I'll be right back," he called over his shoulder as he hurried off.

We had stopped alongside a gurgling fountain encircled by a low wall. So I took a seat on that to watch the sights.

A fancy new convertible, a Cadillac, was parked nearby. It looked as if it were being readied for a raffle or something. On the other side of me, a little way down, a couple were posing for a photographer. They did it in a professional way, as if they were models and knew what they were doing. Except their faces were painted half yellow and half purple. Punk rockers, or some such, I wondered? Was this what they meant by generation gap, I asked myself?

I was about to go over and ask the couple what they were up to (I mean, you've got to try to bridge that gap a little bit, don't you, we can't be total strangers to each other, the young and the old, like separate species), when Allan bounded back. "She wants to see the script," he said, quite out of breath, "so I'm going to take it over there right now while she's hot."

"Now?"

"Now," he informed me. "Let's get going."

I looked at my watch. Three o'clock. He could make it, assuming it wasn't San Diego or some such. I grinned at him. "I'm with you, kid." I did like his spirit. (And his dream.)

We hurried to the car, hurried along the freeway west as fast as the law allowed. Allan dropped me off at my place and went on his way, to conquer the world (or at least one small movie company). I wished him luck. Hopefully he knew what he was doing. Mike Todd always dashed around in this fashion, I knew that, made these quick decisions. And he had won *his* Academy Award.

A great invitation was waiting in my mail box. It was from the Canadian embassy. They were having a reception the Sunday afternoon before Academy Award night for the Canadian nominees, which, of course, included Brigitte Berman, she who had made Artie's documentary. I must have been on her list. Oh wasn't that splendid! There was even a note from her saying she would be in town for the big event and to please come to the reception.

You bet I would. I wouldn't have missed it for anything in the world. It was like old times. I hadn't been around Oscar nominees and winners and such for donkeys' years. And, I all at once realized, I used to take that sort of thing for granted. Some picture or other I had been in, or the pictures of people I worked (or played) with, were almost regularly being nominated for something or other, and very often winning, too, beginning with *GWTW* with its thirteen nominations and eight wins.

For fun I got out the big book the Academy had sent me called *50 Golden Years of Oscar* to see just how many Oscar connections I'd actually had. And it wasn't too bad a collection at all.

After *GWTW* came *Here Comes Mr. Jordan* with seven

nominations and two wins. Another picture I made the same year, *Ladies in Retirement,* had two nominations. Then the pictures Charles Vidor directed while I was with him, *Cover Girl* and *A Song to Remember,* got nominations. A picture I made at the same time, *A Thousand and One Nights,* got one. Then *The Jolson Story* came along with its six nominations, and two wins.

By then, John was in my life, and winning his two Oscars— one for direction, the other for screenplay—for *Treasure of the Sierra Madre,* with his father winning yet another for supporting actor. And Claire Trevor, in *Key Largo,* another picture that John directed that same year, won an Oscar as well. And John's nominations came along as steadily as clockwork for a number of years after that: for *Asphalt Jungle, African Queen, Moulin Rouge,* among others.

And then there was Mike Todd, running around the way Allan was now, getting his *Around the World in Eighty Days* on the road, all the time I was around him. So it seemed only fitting that a documentary about Artie had been nominated. That Allan, too, would make his mark. That I, too, just *might* . . .

My my my. I *was* getting carried away, wasn't I?

I snapped the book shut and put it back in its place on the shelf, and sat myself down at my desk. On the other hand, said I to myself cheerfully, why not? When in Rome. It *was,* rather, the town preoccupation at this pre-Oscar time of year, everybody getting caught up in the coming hoopla, busily speculating as to who would win the coveted trophy, this time around. And wondering how it would feel to be up there, yourself . . .

A perfect time, I decided, to write a column on the subject, using that night John had flung his first Oscar into my lap and made a dash to the stage to pick up his second one of the evening.

Which was what I was doing when the phone rang. And there was Allan's voice filling my ear again. "She's going to read it!'' He practically yelled, ''This is it! I know it is! I *just know it is!*''

Well, maybe it was, and maybe it wasn't. But one thing I did know for certain and that was how much I dug the dear boy's *style*. That kid really knew the way to go, damned if he didn't . . .

# *Thirty-eight*

**B**ut then a while passed without a single word from Allan, not even a peep. So I began to think that here went one more of the kid's brainstorms down the tube. That maybe it *was* getting time for me to get off this particular merry-go-round, maybe it was time to follow Artie's advice; to leave the deal-making to Allan and Tab, and get on with what I wanted to do, what I *could* do without waiting for other people to make decisions.

But of course, the second I decided to zip off to storage and retrieve *Juana* again, that was the moment the kid checked in.

''Please come over right away!'' he cried, positively breathless. ''That way I can fill you and Tab in at the same time!''

''Oh, Tab's back?'' Tab had been off someplace doing an acting chore.

''Yes, and we've got to talk, got to make plans, Angela wants to take a meeting with all of us—''

''Who's Angela?''

''The one who's been reading our script and she wants to see us tomorrow!''

''No kidding,'' I breathed, my heart taking flight.

"So you've absolutely got to come over here this very minute!"

"Will you feed me if I do?" I demanded to know.

"Well, let's see, there's some popcorn here, and . . . oh yeah, here's some Alpo . . ."

"I'll be right there." Smartass kid.

What, I wondered, driving along, did people do before the phone and the automobile. It seemed to be the way I spent my life, somebody saying something into my ear, after which I proceeded to go get into my car (or be picked up by one) and go someplace else. When we'd left Texas and gone to my grandmother's house in Atlanta, where the road going past her front door wasn't paved until the day some black men, wearing thick chains around their ankles with heavy metal balls attached, and guarded by white men holding rifles (or maybe shotguns), came along and paved it. After that cars began to pass by more frequently, and I would sit and watch by the hour, a little girl, maybe five or six, trying to imagine where the people in them might be going, and what they would do when they got there.

Now I knew. It was to talk about turning a screenplay into a movie.

Tab was browner than ever. It was no use telling him it wasn't a good idea to get a lot of sun. Everything Tab loved to do was done out in it. Taking the horse he owned (and loved) out for exercise. Or schussing down some snowy slope on skis, come winter. I trusted all that energy would stand us in good stead if we ever got down to business.

Tab said he had run into John, of all people, in the airport. That John was being pushed along in a wheelchair, with a bottle of oxygen hanging on it, those little breathing tubes up his nostrils. Tab said the sight made him feel like weeping. He said John asked what he was up to these days, and Tab told him he was producing my screenplay. "Are you now!" John had said, between breaths. "Then you'll do fine! Evelyn's a very talented woman!"

Imagine that. John might not get around to *reading* my

script (or anything else of mine that I knew of), but that evidently wouldn't prevent him from speaking well of me. To somebody else. Whether he meant it or not. Well, I was never going to understand, was I. A little late, wasn't it.

Impatiently Allan had us gather around the dining table, anxious to give us the lay of the land. "Angela read the script over the weekend—and she liked it!"

"Angela who?" Tab wanted to know. It turned out Tab had gone to military school as a lad, and he liked *order*. (Like another chap I knew.) Like knowing an *entire* name.

Angela *Schapiro,"* Allan told us. She had asked him, do you really think your script can win the Academy Award? And when Allan answered that yes, he did think so, she had said that she thought so, too, and to talk her into a deal. And that was why we were all going over to her office, tomorrow. To do just that.

*"Oi ve ish vermeer!"* I yelped, making an utter botch of the little Yiddish I *did* know. "I don't know how to talk business! It is absolutely Greek to me!"

"You won't have to," Allan said, "we'll do that part."

"Then why do I have to go, at all? Haven't I done my part?"

Angela wanted to meet all three of us, Allan told me.

Yeah, well, I understood that, and who could blame her. I would, too. Would like to meet the people I might be turning over a few million dollars to. Would she think us worth it, was the big question at hand. Allan, the up-to-date generation. Tab, from the fifties-and-sixties, me bringing up the rear with my "Golden Years" experience. What more could anybody ask for, if you asked *me*. Did we not possess the wisdom of the ages among the three of us? (Motion Picture-wise, that is to say. I wouldn't know how much further than that into the sagacity department I would venture to go with the likes of us!)

It was another of those companies scattered about the Los Angeles Basin; no great gate at the entrance, no gateperson to check your credentials. Nevertheless, you couldn't just walk right in. There was a receptionist. There was a secretary. And finally there was Angela Schapiro, in person.

She was a Brit, first of all, Allan hadn't told us that, with the posh accent that went with it. She had an envious mass of tightly curled blond hair, watchful blue eyes, and she was living proof that the woman who had become a duchess by marrying one of her country's former kings had been bloody-well *wrong* when she'd said you can't be too thin. You damn well *can* if you're past thirty. (I know I'd let my own weight go up ten pounds in recent years.) Angela Schapiro was *not* too thin. She was exactly the weight that was right for her. (It is known as *zaftig* in some circles, I believe.)

You knew at once here was Somebody. Here was the new woman. No Marilyn, she. This one was in charge. Of herself, of her office. I liked her on sight. Liked her sound (it was all I could do not to start imitating her speech). I liked what she said, too. I even liked the suggestions she made for the script. It even crossed my mind I just might have found my latter-day Harry Cohn!

We came away from there, elated, on a high, all three of us. "This is the right move," said Allan with relish, "I know it is!"

"She's got a good feeling for the script," added Tab, "that's for sure."

"And it's a small company," Allan said, "the script won't get lost . . ."

Ah, the before-time (often called foreplay). When it looks as if what you've been dreaming about is actually on the verge of coming true. These are the delectable moments all right, these interludes of anticipation, who can deny it. And a good thing they are, too, since we humans seem to spend the major part of our lives looking forward to something that isn't there at all, with only the hope that it *might* be there, some day.

And damned if I wasn't right there again. Caught up in yet another of those better-than-your-run-of-the-mill times, thinking maybe the world really, truly, *was* going to be my oyster, after all, the Sunday afternoon that I, taking Allan with me, was to go to the Canadian embassy's shindig for their country's Academy Award nominees. Artie, I was sure, would be there, too. After all, he was the star, was he not, of nominee Brigitte's documentary?

I hadn't seen or heard from Artie since the fridge episode. This would be an easy way of learning if he'd fully recovered from his hospital experience, as well as finding out what had happened to the kitty cat. Find out if the two of them were on a purring basis, as yet.

My usual sweats and Reeboks didn't seem quite the thing to wear to another country's embassy, even if it was located in cool L.A. And there *was* stuff hanging in my closets for getting done up when I felt I really ought to get done up. Things I'd picked up, oh God, all over the place. Skirts and sweaters from Milano or London; boots, bags, scarves from New York, Rome, Barcelona. Vests, jackets, pants, what have you from Atlanta, from Paris, Miami, Acapulco. Enough to last me the rest of my days, and they'd certainly better because I had no intention of ever collecting them together again. All those fashion tips they blather on about on TV and in magazines; how this is the "latest," or that is "in" or "out" this season, have come and gone several times too often during my lifetime, and now sound to me somewhat like advice the head of the insane asylum gives to the inmates. It is hard for me to believe that I, too, once tottered about on those perfectly absurd high heels. Chinese girl-babies used to have their feet bound *for* them at birth. But we modern women make this decision to cripple ourselves, *ourselves.*

I fished out a bright red sheath, a black jacket to wear over it, found some red shoes, a long, narrow red-and-black-and-white scarf to swirl around my neck a couple of times, a chunky gold ring with red stones in it (from Palm Beach). Allan had on a dark jacket and tie when he arrived to fetch me in his snappy red sports job, and off we went.

I must have donned the right combination of things (Allan had, to be sure, how can you go wrong with the standard male attire of jacket and tie?), because, yes, sure enough, Artie was there.

And upon first sight, upon very first *glimpse* of his bifurcated wife, he made a judicious critique of her appearance.

And not just for her—for my—ears alone, mind you. All kinds of people were standing around in the gardens, sipping, nibbling, chatting, including Brigitte and her Canadian partner, as well as other nominees and their retinues. "Hey," Artie called out in anything but a stage whisper, "you look pretty good for an old lady!"

Heads snapped around in our direction. And then some of the people kind of edged away. I guess they had never heard a "gentleman" give a "lady" such a winning compliment, before. But then, they didn't know Artie Shaw, did they.

I guess I must have shaken my head, or something. In amazement over his consistency, probably, since it was the same, identical greeting he had met me with every time I had seen him since—well, since I had gotten older.

But Artie must have taken my shake for a denial. (Hadn't he always said assumption was the mother of a fuck-up?) Because he then added, "You *are* an old lady, you know."

"No shit," was what I then said. Probably repeating the same exact thing *I* had said on previous occasions.

At which point those people who hadn't as yet moved on proceeded to do so.

Now it was Artie's turn to shake *his* head. "Difficult as ever," he stated, and *he* moved on.

Thereby missing what I could have told him about *his* appearance.

The man had never looked so good since I had known him. The week's hospital stay had caused him to lose just the right amount of weight, so that the slight bulge beginning to show around his abdomen had disappeared, the jawline had tightened, his skin had a healthy glow to it, and his eyes fairly sparkled. Apparently his near-collision with the Stygian Ferry, and endless flares of temper over sugar substitutes and cleaned-up refrigerators to who-knew-what-elses, all had agreed with him. Maybe, I smiled, amused at the thought, I was on to something, after all, with my theory about the way

Artie recharged his inner turbines! It might pay to keep a sharp eye turned on the fellow, might it not!

Brigitte drifted over again, and (unlike Artie) she *whispered* in my ear, "Will you have lunch with me, Tuesday, if we win Monday night?"

I smiled and whispered back. "Couldn't we have lunch, anyway, whether you win or not?"

She laughed and squeezed my arm. "I'll call you the first thing Tuesday morning." Allan and I took a swing around the embassy grounds, looking everything over, and then took our leave. I gave Brigitte a quick hug on the way out, telling her I was keeping every possible thing crossed for her. I didn't think she had a chance, though. Weren't documentaries that won usually about cancer? Or conquering space? Or climbing Mount Everest, things like that?

I watched the proceedings Monday night, anyway. At least I would hear Brigitte's name called out as one of the nominees. And Artie's too, for that matter, his was in the title, itself; *Artie Shaw: Time Is All You've Got.* It would be the conversation at lunch, the evening's happenings, and I wouldn't want to say I hadn't even watched.

What a good thing I had. Not only was Brigitte's name (and Artie's) called out, it was called as winner.

Brigitte Berman from Toronto, Canada's documentary on the life of Artie Shaw had actually won an Academy Award! There she was, in my own living room, being handed one of the shiny golden statuettes!

And she still had it with her when she came around to pick me up to go to lunch the next day.

Still in a state of high excitement when she'd called earlier, I had fully expected her to say, so sorry, could we have lunch another time, and I would have understood, my God, how many of these special moments come along in a lifetime.

But no, that wasn't it, she'd only called to tell me what time she was picking me up.

Off we went, Brigitte and her partner, and Oscar, to join several other Canadians—I do believe I was the only "foreigner'' present—at this terribly chic restaurant on the Sunset Strip, where we all gathered at a large round table, with golden, shining Oscar standing in the center in all his glory, and enjoyed a celebration.

The rest of the room shared it, too. There were nods, and smiles all around, and people stopping by, whether they knew Brigitte or not, to offer her their congratulations.

Single-handedly, Brigitte from Canada had managed to make the occasion into a hometown gathering, personal and cozy, the way Academy Award events were when I first arrived. *GWTW,* winning its umpteen Awards, did it in the Coconut Grove, a night club filled with the palm trees and make-believe monkeys hanging from their branches. People sat around at tables, got fed, and watched the proceedings that took place on the dance floor, the presenters, the winners, right there within touching distance, if you were ringside (as I had been).

As I turned to tell Brigitte what was going through my head, she turned to me and leaned forward. And this was what she said to me right there in the moment of her glory. "I'm preparing something you would be just right for. Would you be interested in doing it?''

For heaven's sake. How about that. The woman was already plotting ahead. The celebrating of winning the top prize wasn't over, even before her name was engraved on the base of the Oscar, the woman had her eye on some other spot up there on the distant horizon.

Well she was absolutely right, wasn't she! This particular dream was over, wasn't it. Finished. She had set out to do something, and she had done it. There was the proof, sitting right there in the middle of the table. And so it was time to move on, move on to, well, to the next thing.

But would she meet with the same success again? And did it matter whether she did or she didn't? Wasn't the planning, the plotting, the looking ahead to where that bright spot shone so alluringly up there ahead, beckoning to you in its oh so enticing way, wasn't that what life *was,* the very living-of-life, *itself,* this journey to the bright spot ahead? And it didn't matter all that much whether you ever got to the shining spot or not. Because if you did, then it was over. Though, of course, it was quite all right if you *did* make it. Sure Brigitte might make it there, again. One never knew. That the possibility of making it was always there, made it very nice. And joyous, too. Wasn't the celebrating lunch, today, a lovely way to go? It was just that when you did make it, you'd soon have to find another bright spot to focus on.

Artie once told me a story about a man in the construction business who had been forced to retire. He hadn't wanted to, but he had reached that age when his company kicked people out. He felt terribly lost, from then on, without anything to occupy his days. So, one day he decided he would do some traveling, he had never had time for anything like that, before.

Off he went, over to Europe, going wherever the travel agent suggested he go. He went to London, he went to Paris, he went to Rome. And it was all right, it was something to do. But then, one day, he arrived in Florence. The buildings there impressed him enormously. And he got an idea. He decided it might be kind of interesting to know more about them. Like when they had been built, who had designed them, what kind of materials had been used in the construction.

And so he lingered on in Florence, tramping around all over the city, looking at this building and that, caught up in the beauty of what he was seeing. So much so, that he began to wonder, if he stayed on, would it be possible, even at his age, to actually enroll in a class on architecture, perhaps at the university he often passed.

He was on his way there, one morning, overflowing with great anticipation—when he had a heart seizure, fell down, and died.

Artie had said that this was a story with a very happy ending.

I threw my arms around Brigitte and gave her a very big hug, indeed. "All in the world you have to do when you want me," I told her, merrily, "is whistle!"

And that was the truth . . .

## Thirty-nine

I added Brigitte's maybe-one-day item to my list of who-knew-just-what-might-happens, knowing from experience how prudent it was to have as many bright spots as possible up there ahead (eggs not in one basket, and all that). After *Juana* (always and forever *numero uno),* there was the screenplay to be (I hoped) turned into a flick. There were columns to be written, occasional acting jobs to come along here and there.

It not only looked—it even began to *feel*—as if I were really back in Hollywood for good. I mean, the really-truly-for-keeps kind of back. And it was okay. It was quite comfortable. Like the Screen Actors' Guild had held on to my original membership number all these years (they do that, it seems), and that surely did make me feel connected. As if I were actually in the spot I was *supposed* to be in, for a change.

It even seemed like an okay thing to do—since Angela and her company were going off to shoot another film before they got around to ours—to accept an invitation to go down to Birmingham, Alabama, and do *No No Nanette,* again. Allan and Tab could hold the fort, it was their turn, anyway. I had done my work (until rewrite time), and anyway it was only for a couple of weeks.

I thought I'd better call Artie and tell him I was going away. I dunno. Just in case. I didn't know in case *what* exactly, but there the feeling was.

Besides, I wanted to know what if anything was going on

with the kitty cat up there. "Listen, Artie," I said right away when he answered, "I've been meaning to tell you. That time I was up there in your house by myself, that pretty kitty cat came around and so what I did was . . ."

"You mean 'The Colonel'?" Artie interrupted, "Oh, he's a great cat. He's around here all the time, now, friendly as can be!"

Ah ha. So it was a "he," and he'd been given a name. Artie did that when he had affection for something. (Or someone. As I had been nicknamed "Kesi" during the blissful times.)

Well. I didn't have to concern myself about Mr. Kitty, anymore.

But what I did have to concern myself about at this point was getting back into dancing shape. I had kept up the tap right after coming off the big tour of *Nanette,* when I was still in the house on the hill, where I had a rather spacious—as well as tiled—laundry room. I used to put on my tap shoes and go in there almost daily, to dance and dance and *dance* to my heart's content all around the washing machine, the dryer, the ironing board. Tap was such good aerobic exercise, and could be done in rain, sunshine, or snow. But since I'd left the house behind, that part of me had got misplaced, somehow.

I simply refused to entertain the thought that maybe I wouldn't be *able* to get it together again. If I could jog for an hour, I told myself, I ought to be able to tap for five *minutes,* for crissake.

But what I needed to get the tippy-toes into tapping condition was plenty of space and a good, hard surface, like my old laundry room floor.

Who, I wondered, among my friends had such a thing? Talli's laundry, I knew, had only space for machines. But what she *did* have that was spacious enough was a tennis court! It was ideally placed, too, away from the house. The land in the back of her house sloped down, and the court had been built at the bottom of it, sort of in a hollow. You had to go down-stairs to get to it, so that it couldn't even be *seen* from the house. You hardly knew when anybody was even playing ten-nis down there. So you surely wouldn't know if one lone person, in tap shoes with a cassette player discreetly murmur-ing her dance tunes, was fooling around down there. Espe-cially if it was at the crack of dawn, before even tennis players were about, say around five or five-thirty.

"Why not, indeed," said Talli when I asked if I could use her court, "it's just sitting there all alone at that hour, you can keep it company."

I laughed. "I'll bet you didn't think you were creating a dance floor when you built that court, Talli."

Talli's smile did the Cheshire cat one better. "We didn't build that court," she told me softly. "Fred Astaire did . . ."

Well. It didn't hurt a bit to keep in mind that Fred As-taire's very own twinkling toes had once moved around the exact same surface on which I now went through my own paces. Fred and I, down there on his former court in the fresh, new air, with the deep-pink bougainvillaea spilling over one of the walls, a magnolia bursting with ivory flow-ers leaning over another. Pines, planted years and years ago, zooming straight up to the pale lavender sky, and, glory be, a member of the elusive red-tailed hawk family often perched on the top of one of them, scanning the neighbor-hood for its breakfast.

Not at all a bad place to get ready to go do a musical show.

The engagement, itself, was pleasant enough, too. Boys and girls from the University of Alabama made up the chorus, for which they got some kind of credit. Local actors played the other roles, all in all an extremely competent company. For me, doing *No No Nanette* again was rather like finding an old pair of shoes you'd forgotten about in the back of the closet, shoes that held fond memories, and that you now had the pleasure of walking around in, once more.

But in no time at all, it was over and done with, and there I was, headed west again, seated next to a business-type fellow in a suit, tie, proper shoes, the Florsheim kind with the little holes in the toes. In his mid-thirties was my guess. He gave me a glance and a curt nod without even the tiniest warmth or interest in his eyes, his thoughts as clear as if he had said them out loud; Why do I always get the old broads next to me, why can't I for once get some gorgeous chick next to me on one of these long, boring trips?

Would it make him feel better, I wondered, if I told him I had been young once upon a time? And that it had been said I wasn't so bad-looking in those days, either?

Nah. He had me pegged. "Live in Birmingham, do you?" he said indifferently. It was a statement, not a question. I didn't know why he was making the effort. Nothing else to do, I supposed.

"No," I told him, "I live in L.A." I could have simply said "yes." I didn't know why *I* didn't. Nothing else to do, I supposed.

"Been visiting your family, I expect," he said next, in a throwaway fashion. Of course, what else would an elderly female be doing flying around in planes if it weren't to go visit her family. Grandchildren, most likely. Grown ones, at that.

I couldn't resist. "No," I told him. "Actually I came to Birmingham to dance and sing in a musical there."

"Wha' . . . ?" The look was quick, this time, with a couple of blinks. Then a frown.

I smiled sweetly at him. In a grandmotherly way.

After a hesitation he grunted, and forced out, "Heh, heh, heh," showing he knew a joke when he heard one (even one that was pretty stupid).

With that he'd had enough. Turning away, he called for a bourbon and water, and plugged in his earphones for the coming movie, over and out, he'd done his bit to observe plane etiquette.

*On up the Road* ■ 331

*  *  *

Back on my own stamping grounds, I went almost immediately into another *Murder She Wrote* episode, remembered
principally because of a particular conversation around the
makeup table, one day, as we actresses were getting our noses
dusted (even though we were playing nuns) for the coming
scene.

The makeup artist, a woman, started it by telling us she had
been to the Bolshoi Ballet the night before, and that, no doubt
about it, she was into men's thighs, especially when they were
dancers'.

Jane Powell, who was playing the head nun, said mmm, she
didn't think she looked at thighs. It was hands that caught her
eye, and the face.

I joined in. What about sound, I said. Didn't they think the
*sound* of a person was important as well?

Ah yes, said Jane (who sings), yes, yes, the sound, too. I
told them that John Huston's *thighs* were like matchsticks.
That he looked like one of those Alberto Giacometti sculptures, but that he had a great sound which had served him
rather well when it came to members of his opposite sex.

We found ourselves amusing, dressed as nuns, the way we
were, discussing men, as we were, in such blatantly sexist
terms.

I had no way of knowing, of course, that the sound of which
I spoke, John's rich-as-melted-caramel speaking voice, was
about to be stilled forever. Perhaps even as we were conversing.

Dressing for work early the next morning, I chanced to flip
on the TV news. A young woman I had never seen before in
my life, sitting behind a desk, with a little microphone pinned
to her lapel, was the one who notified me.

Newscasters have a special someone's-just-died manner they
adopt for terminal announcements. So when I heard John's
name, and the tone of the voice the young lady had fallen
into, I knew. I *knew*.

I was suddenly chilled. And stopped what I was doing to

sit down. In Rhode Island, she said. Had John ever been *there,* before, he who had been almost everywhere? He should have been in Ireland, for this last event, should he not? But there you are. When you're dead, "where" doesn't really matter for anything, anymore, does it?

The newscaster went on to tell who John was, what he had done. But I didn't much listen. I knew who he was. What he had done. I did notice it was August, I did do that, the same month in which he'd been born. So that meant he must have just got past his . . . what, this being 1987 it had to be, my God, his *eighty-first* birthday? That number seemed as unreal as his dying, since in my head the man was still the forty-year-old he'd been that first night I'd come across him . . .

It was hard to understand it was all over. Finished. Completely. Over and out. Just like that.

Death. Are we ever ready for it? I wasn't surprised at John's, not really, how could I have been. It was truly remarkable he had lived as long as he had.

It was just that . . . he had been a part of *my* life, once upon a time. An important part. I had been a Huston, myself, once upon a time. I was listed as a "Huston" in the index of the autobiography he wrote. I had shared his bed for a number of years, his house, his journeys, his billiard games, his art gallery prowlings. The man had read James Joyce's *Finnegan's Wake* to me, for God's sake, propped up in our double bed, me sitting cross-legged at the foot, the dogs lying all around, in that warm-honey voice of his. I even believed I understood it. At least while he was reading it to me.

It was that same voice that whispered to me, the first night I met him, "How . . . would . . . you like . . . an adventure?" And caused me to be instantly prepared to go anywhere with him. And I did . . . for a while.

Over the next few days, people would call here and there, almost as if I were the widow, to say they were sorry. Even Artie. "So he's gone," said Artie gently.

"Yes . . ."

"Maybe it's best. These last months couldn't have been much fun."

"No. It's terrible not to be able to breathe." I knew. I had once not been able to breathe, myself.

"How do *you* feel?"

"Well . . . you know . . ."

"Yeah . . . but he had a pretty good life."

"But do you know what he said on *Sixty Minutes*?" I told Artie. "That if he had his life to live over, he wouldn't do it the same, again."

"But he would," said Artie wisely, "he would do it exactly the same."

"Yeah. I suppose. Oh Artie," I sighed. "Please take care of yourself. You're the only living husband I have, anymore."

"I'll do my best," Artie chuckled, "for both of us."

People kept calling, some even came around, including Jeffrey Selznick, one of David O.'s offspring. He came to tell me that he and brother Danny were going to make a documentary about the making of *Gone With the Wind* in honor of its fiftieth anniversary which would be coming along soon, and they hoped that I would participate.

Jeffrey and Danny had been little tykes back in those earlier days. But Jeffrey said he remembered me, even so, because I had always treated them like equals. I had never talked down to them, he said, or anything like that. And for that reason they had always liked me.

I was so very pleased to hear I had behaved decently. Of course what Jeffrey didn't know was that I'd talked to them as if they were equals because I'd thought of myself as a kid then, too, even if I had been taller.

Then I got a letter from some people who were going to make a documentary about John. The "official" one, they wrote. "Family-approved." That they had actually met John before he died, and that he had given them his approval, too. They wanted to know if I would participate in the making of this documentary.

There seemed to be an almost steady stream to my door, that fall, of those seeking information from me, not only for their documentaries, but for their books, their future excitingly revealing tomes and perspicacious essays on those talented folk of Hollywood's famous Golden Years, of whom I seem to have known a goodly number.

I seldom turned anybody down. As a fairly recent arrival to "museum piece" status, I took the position that it was the least I could do, to pass on to posterity what little knowledge, or thoughts, I might have on motion picture colony lore to those who were interested in such matters. My turn, as it were, to become a "walking encyclopedia." Wasn't that what "getting on" was all about?

The two young people making the documentary on John, a man and a woman, thirty-somethings, came around to pick me up and drive me out to the San Fernando Valley where they had hired themselves a studio to do their interviewing in. I spent three hours with them, talking about John in front of a camera, of life at Tarzana with the horses, of the visit to his place in County Galway.

And it was strange. Almost overnight one speaks differently of someone who has died. I had so often talked about John, before. Written about him at great length. But that afternoon . . . all at once it wasn't the same, anymore. He was gone. Finished. Forever. Perhaps it's like reading a book. The story is in a state of suspension as long as you are reading along. Anything can still happen. Can take a turn in this direction or that, the possibilities endless. Until you turn the last page . . . and know the whole story . . .

And then, somehow, it was Christmas again, what with time still tearing by (these days faster than the speed of a rocket blast-off from Cape Canaveral), and somehow it was Artie I wound up having Christmas Eve dinner with. I don't really know how it came about, it wasn't planned, it was just that, there we were, at dinnertime, and it happened to be the twenty-fourth of December.

We had stayed in touch all the while. By phone if not in person. Actually we had a splendid relationship on the phone, talking of everything under the sun, for hours and hours at a time, two suspended voices without bodies. And it seemed quite the best way. We got along fine if we kept our distance.

We wound up at an Italian restaurant in Hollywood, Artie's choice. He ordered, too, and a splendid meal it was, of pasta carbonara, a veal cutlet, with broccoli (again), this time shaped on the serving platter like a flower in bloom. And then the spirited talk began, swerving and swooping around like laser beams at a rock concert, from the Chinese doctor who was giving him herbs, to something of Aldous Huxley's he was rereading, to a comic he'd seen on the telly, to the paintings of Mondrian whose technique he was studying, to clothes, to plain gossip, which he did well, too. (Also contrary to the popular belief, I've always found men not only the biggest shoppers among us, but the better gossips, too.) He even—would wonders never cease—gave me a recipe for fixing broccoli (sauté chopped garlic in virgin olive oil, add chopped broccoli already steamed, chopped ham, and sprinkle it all with parmesan cheese). I never thought I would live to see the day that Artie Shaw knew a recipe. That was a Christmas present all by itself. And if that weren't enough, we managed to finish the evening without a single altercation.

Tab and Allan had me over for dinner, too, before the year was out. Allan surprised me by putting on an apron and placing the chicken on the outside barbecue, himself. I don't mean to imply it was a monumental accomplishment or anything, forking up pieces of raw chicken and placing them on a grill over burning coals, it was just that I hadn't realized he could do anything but put a production of a future motion picture into place. (The male animal was beginning to make himself useful around the kitchen, it would seem.)

A scenic designer was there. A costume designer. Somebody who was a production-sheet maker-upper. Also someone who did publicity. All raring to go to work. All that was needed was for Angela Schapiro and her company to cough up six or seven million bucks so we could all begin our "little" movie.

Tab swished around the green things in the big wooden salad bowl now sitting on the buffet table, pulled the cork out of a bottle of wine, filled some glasses, and held his own up. "Here's to next year," he said, with a positively radiant smile.

Allan grabbed up a glass of water. "It's ours!" he cried. "Next year is *ours!*"

We all drank to that . . .

New Year's Day morning, I went down to Talli's (and Fred's) tennis court for a tap workout, that being the best possible way I could think of to start off another year. Ever since I had returned from Alabama I had been doing just that, a couple of times a week, figuring if I didn't keep the dancing going, this time, I probably would never be able to get it together again. (No doubt about it, it was time for me to start thinking of things like that.)

I also had another splendid excuse for going over to Talli's. Among the ways she was trying to save this planet of ours was not to throw her old newspapers away, but instead gather them all up and cart them off to a recycling place. So I, with guilt firmly pushing, had gotten into the act, too, and begun not throwing *my* old newspapers away as well. Which meant that, most of the time, I was driving around with these stacks of old newspapers in the back end of my little yellow car, until I could leave them off at Talli's garage.

Was *this* any way, I asked myself one day, for a movie star to wind up? *Schlepping* tons of old newspapers around and tap dancing all by herself down on somebody else's tennis court at the crack of dawn?

You bet! I answered myself, quite happily, and damned lucky she is that everything's worked out just the way it has!

It *was* wonderful, wasn't it. On this first day of January, as I arrived at the court, the sun was just sending its very first rays over the distant trees, and for one split second, catching the wings of a tiny hummingbird in flight. Caught the beak of that watchful hawk up there in its pine tree. Turned a sliver of a cloud behind him into gold.

And the grass. The grass had been freshly cut! There is no perfume in the wide, wide world that can come near the fragrance of freshly cut grass, I swear.

And life. Life, itself, in its purest, most unadulterated form, seemed to surround me. Insects flitting and buzzing and bobbing hither and yon. The birds flapping from tree to bush to dew-washed grass, making a perfect landing every time. Even a small plane that came out of nowhere to wend its way across the expanse of blue sky seemed to be a perfectly natural phenomenon as well.

Feeling positively heady, I flung both arms upward and waved vigorously in its direction. Unbelievably, the wings up there waggled back and forth in reply!

"And Happy New Year to you, too," I said, and chuckled, suddenly wanting to move, move, *move,* but immediately!

I turned on the music cassette I had brought along with me, and began to tap my way around Talli's (and Fred's) tennis court, the bright new sun acting as my personal spotlight!

What better way could there possibly be, I thought with glee as I turned, as I whirled, to get a brand-new year going than to be giving the ol' cardiovascular system a vigorous workout.

Health. You had to have it, it was something you simply had to hang on to, didn't you, if you wanted those years to *keep* coming along on schedule every twelve months. And I did want them to come. Oh, I did. I needed flocks more to come along, in order to get everything done that I had to do. First there would be the rewrites on the screenplay once the shooting got underway. Then I'd have to get back to *Juana*. The book about my Spanish princess and her *mishpochen* had to be finished, that was an absolutely necessity, the same as breathing in and out.

And then there was another little something that had been brewing as of late, sort of simmering and churning around back there in a corner of my head; and that was an idea for another screenplay. Oh, *such* a good idea, too, it was, and I couldn't *wait* until I had the time to sit down and think it through.

And as I went on tapping, yet another little thought sneaked quietly into being . . .

That if these years did continue to roll in for as long as I planned for them to, maybe, in such a youth-oriented town as this one in which I had set up shop, wouldn't it be positively foolish not to begin giving serious consideration to the business of having a few of those . . . uh . . . "little tucks" done? Well, it *was* food for thought, anyway, was it not? When in Rome and all that . . . ?

On the other hand it wouldn't be such a bad idea, either, to keep in mind just what it was that happened, in the end, to the Roman Empire!

Taking one more turn, doing one last shuffle, I clicked off the cassette, slung it over my shoulder, and prepared to leave the premises. I had a lunch to go to over at Cynthia's house (she who knew when to tell a good pig joke back in New Orleans). Who was awfully good, too, about feeding me every so often.

Driving back along Sunset, merrily humming an accompaniment to the music that continued to spin round and round in my head, the questions I'd just been asking myself kept trying to sneak back into my consciousness. But I wasn't having it. Enough already. Why in the world on such an exquisite day was I thinking about such nonsense.

What I'll do, said I to me as I headed on down the boulevard, I'll think about all that tomorrow.

After all.

Tomorrow *is* another day. . . .